Gary Haynes studied law at university before becoming a commercial litigator. He is interested in history, philosophy and international relations. When he's not writing or reading, he enjoys watching European films, travelling, hillwalking and spending time with his family. He is a member of the International Thriller Writers Organization. You can contact Gary via his website and social media sites.

Also By Gary Haynes

Tom Dupree series:
State of Honour
State of Attack

The
Blameless
Dead

Gary Haynes

LUME BOOKS

LUME BOOKS

First published in 2019 by Lume Books
85-87 Borough High Street,
London, SE1 1NH

ISBN 978-1-83901-165-8

www.lumebooks.co.uk

'Only the dead have seen the end of war.'
George Santayana
Soliloquies in England and Later Soliloquies (1922)

'At this hour
Lie at my mercy all mine enemies.'
William Shakespeare
The Tempest

PART ONE

GENESIS

CHAPTER ONE

Berlin, late April, 1945.

Pavel Romasko crouched down beside a scorched wall, the floor covered with charred beams and shattered concrete. He gritted his teeth and inched towards a shell hole by his head. The stench was almost overpowering. He'd first smelled it a minute ago, even before he'd entered the abandoned building. He winced, feeling queasy. He guessed it was coming from the adjacent street.

Craning forward, he listened for a familiar sound: the whining gears and diesel engine of a Tiger tank, the *click-click* of the iron-heeled boots worn by the Waffen-SS. The sound of potential death. But the immediate area was quiet. There was only the faint discharge of Soviet howitzers, and a muffled burst of machine-gun fire from somewhere to the north. Pursing his lips, he whistled — just loud enough for his assault squad to hear from what was left of the adjoining room.

He forced himself to stand up and edged past a jagged girder, dangling from the half caved-in ceiling. He shuffled towards the open doorway. Warily, he stepped out. The stink enveloped him and he almost gagged. He knew now that the sewers had collapsed, that scores of corpses lay rotting among the debris.

But he'd smelled a hint of something else too, despite the carnage. Just briefly. It had had a fragrant element, reminding him of a regular childhood experience, a memory that reverberated like the chimes of a prayer bell inside his head. For a few moments, he pictured the old Orthodox church that had dominated his remote Russian village. The bearded priest was swinging the elaborate incense-burner, suspended from gold-plated chains. It had been the same odour. Hadn't it? He blinked, shook his head. He couldn't make sense of that.

He decided, with an odd lack of enthusiasm, that he'd imagined it. The effects of the war played tricks of the mind, of the senses. Looking over his shoulder, he counted all seven of his men as they emerged from the remnants of the four-storey civic office building.

A few muddied documents were scattered on the ground, stamped with the official Nazi Party eagle, its head turned to the left, and an emblem he failed to recognize, but which looked to him like a decorative wheel, with a geometrical design of squares at its centre. Even a blackened flag had survived the bomb damage. Hanging beneath a crumbling windowsill, the swastika flapped against the bullet-ridden façade, the movement both panicky and defiant, Pavel thought.

His men were conscripts. A few still wore their padded khaki jackets and mustard-yellow blouses. Most, their green field tunics and forage caps. All the clothing was lice-ridden and smeared with soft ash. Months of exposure to frozen winds had darkened their skins and narrowed their eyes. They'd been engaged in hazardous reconnaissance missions. They'd slept rough and had existed on a diet of raw husks and dried horsemeat. Haggard and weary now, he reckoned they'd aged well beyond their years.

And me, he thought.

He was twenty-three but looked a decade older. His yellow teeth ached, and when it was damp, he limped, an old calf wound from the

Battle of Stalingrad. He'd been fighting in the Great Patriotic War since the beginning, almost four years before. Pavel was a regular Red Army man, a full sergeant, despite his youth. One of the few Soviet soldiers that had survived the initial German onslaught. He told himself he was lucky, but he was plagued by fretful nightmares. The savage conflict had destroyed his secret faith in God.

He pulled off his favoured ushanka, a fur cap, and scratched his shaven head. Sinking to his knees, he lit a cigarette made from rolled newspaper and discarded butts. He watched the others pull down their earflaps or blow on their hands. The cold was sharp and brutal, like flint. He inhaled and passed the improvised cigarette up to the next man, shielding it from the wind with his cupped hand.

'It doesn't help,' he said. He knew nothing could curb the smell.

Fetching a map from inside his jacket, he began calculating their position as best he could. The street was broad and crater-filled and stretched for a hundred yards or more to the north and south before bending out of sight.

Must have been a main thoroughfare once, he thought, doing his best to locate it.

The battle had left it a wasteland, with smouldering tyres and pools of burning oil. They'd come upon it by chance, following a rout of their infantry platoon, a sustained counter-offensive by at least a hundred men of the Berlin garrison. Pavel had led the squad under a baroque archway and down a cobbled side street. When he'd been sure it was safe, they'd veered off into the office building. At least ten comrades had fallen. He could still hear their pitiable screams in his head. But he knew the slaughter was almost at an end.

It began to rain. Big grainy drops that exploded on the bare skin of his hands and forehead. Putting on his steel, dome-shaped helmet, he glanced up. Clumps of black smoke hung low in the slate-grey sky, almost shrouding it. He grasped his PPSh-41, a Shpagin submachine gun; he reckoned he had about half of its seventy-one cartridges left. It was the most reliable small-arms weapon of the war. Even the Wehrmacht Heer, the German Army, coveted them. It never jammed. Not even at minus fifty degrees Fahrenheit in the winter of 1942–43. A winter that at the time had never seemed to end.

Straining to get up, he held his back. He was exhausted. 'Put your helmets on. Ukrainian, on point.'

The Ukrainian was a sinewy man with outsized ears. He half stumbled forward, using his bolt-action rifle as a crutch. He spat, wiped his mouth, and mumbled something to himself. He had a miserable look on his drawn, mud-streaked face.

He hates being on point, Pavel thought. They all hate being on point.

Moving with short, cautious steps, they kept close to an ancient wall that was stone-built and encrusted with dead lichen. It afforded some cover, but they were about three feet above the true level of the street. Tons of rubble had built up where the pavements had been; broken chunks of flagstones, twisted iron bars and heaps of crumbled bricks. The buildings that remained were hollow and smirched, teetering in this dismal place.

A shot rang out and a bullet skimmed the wall with a sharp *crack*, creating a billow of dust and careering fragments. He heard a comrade groan in pain. His men sank down, aiming their weapons in an awkward, random fashion. No one had pointed out the direction of the muzzle flash.

'Fucking ricochet,' another said.

Pavel scrambled forward. The injured man was twenty-seven, a hog farmer from a small town near Minsk, with five children. He was slumped against the wall, panting. He'd dropped his Mosin-Nagant carbine and was grasping his arm. Blood poured out in rivulets between his fingers. The round had penetrated his bicep. Picking up the carbine, Pavel led him down the short slope of rubble. At the bottom, there was a tangle of metal, covered with serrated stone slabs from a broken lintel.

His men followed close behind. They'd hunkered down, fearful of a further shot. Reaching the make-do shelter, they flung themselves prostrate behind it. Pavel pulled out a field bandage and used it as a tourniquet to stem the blood flow. The farmer bared his teeth like an excited chimpanzee. His men were nervous. He knew what they were thinking: If the shot had come from a sniper, they were in a precarious position.

Pavel scanned the handful of vantage points with his army-issue binoculars, looking for the unknown shooter. But he could only make out smashed eaves and protruding joists, caressed by grey smoke. There was little chance of spotting the passage of a shadow, or a sudden glint of metal, the usual giveaways. He shivered. Blasts from unseen German flak guns, firing, he guessed, at Soviet tanks, had erupted close by. The sound was jarring. He felt uneasy. He thought about moving back down the street, towards the burned-out Wehrmacht half-track, but no further shots had been fired.

It's no sniper, he thought. Not a squad either. Just a lone infantryman. He'll keep his head down and wait for a better opportunity, he decided. That, or he'd already fled.

He checked at street level with his binoculars. Nothing moved, except the huge rats, scampering over the dead he'd smelled. Many of the corpses were bloated, others black-green like serpentine stone, a sign of putrefaction. Some still looked almost fresh. Old men. Mothers. Children. He knew they'd been killed by shrapnel and dislodged masonry, as well as indiscriminate fire from both sides.

'Go on now,' he said.

A couple of minutes later, they came to the end of the wall. He glanced at his wristwatch, decided there were several hours of daylight left. The street still looked deserted. He knew the civilians were huddled in their cellars, or in one of the cramped, underground shelters, where even the adults had to urinate where they stood. He didn't blame them. The city was an earthly Hell, full of chaotic fires and toxic fumes. He'd been told that the British and Americans had carpet-bombed it for months. Then, on the twentieth of April, the ongoing Soviet artillery and rocket barrage had started. Hitler's birthday, his captain had said. Pavel had gotten red-eyed drunk that night.

A filthy hand patted him on the shoulder before pointing south in front of his head. He held up his binoculars. A platoon of Waffen-SS was approaching from less than seventy yards down the street. About thirty men, he estimated, with a smattering of heavy machine guns and mortars. They moved in single file, parts of their grey-green uniforms whitened by dust. Weaving in and out of the mounds, they resembled a colossal and hoary snake.

He reckoned they hadn't seen them, but he needed to make a snap judgment. He wasn't afraid of the Waffen-SS. He'd killed scores of their ilk in the conflict, sometimes with nothing more than his short-handled shovel, his entrenching tool. But he knew a firefight would be suicidal. He looked around. There was only one option.

He pushed the Kid towards an open doorway some thirty yards to the right. 'Go,' he said.

Pavel called him 'the Kid' because he was nineteen. He'd fought alongside him since Stalingrad, just over two years before. He watched him as he ran, the German greatcoat he allowed him to wear looking massive on his wasted frame. It had fitted the Kid when he'd first worn it, but he'd lost a stone and a half in two months. Dysentery. Many suffered from it. Mercifully, his infection hadn't been virulent and he'd all but recovered.

The doorway was the access point to a bunker. It was set back from the street in what was left of a concrete island amid a grassed square. The grass was black and pitted by firebombs. The iron railings that had surrounded it were piled on the ground, mangled and covered in severed bricks and clumps of mud. It looked as if the perimeter had been evacuated some time ago.

'We going in, sergeant?' the farmer said.

Pavel heard him wince in pain, although he tried to disguise the sound with an exaggerated grunt.

The bunker seemed to be empty. It offered sanctuary — for a time at least.

'Yes,' he said.

But knowing the bunker could be a nest of fascists, he felt a spasm in his stomach.

CHAPTER TWO

Pavel used his binoculars to watch the Kid sprint over the collapsed entry gates. He nodded to himself when he registered the young eyes scouring the chosen route for a trip wire, or signs of a landmine, as he'd taught him to do. The Kid stumbled. But after manoeuvring around hillocks of mud and fetid pools of unknowable depth, he reached the bunker's opening. It had taken him nine seconds.

The others waited for the all-clear: arms held sideways at shoulder level and flapped. Seeing it, they followed the Kid's path towards the ruptured steel doors, felled by mortar shells, at the front of the bunker. They couldn't be seen by the Waffen-SS platoon now, and Pavel felt sure they'd make it.

There was a Volkswagen Kübelwagen, a bucket-seat car, on the remains of the driveway that linked the bunker to the street. The tyres were flayed, the bodywork peppered with holes such that it resembled a giant slab of Swiss cheese. Pavel guessed it had been strafed earlier in the day, probably by an Ilyushin Il-2, a Soviet ground-attack aircraft known as the flying tank. Running past the vehicle, he noticed that the occupants, a couple of Luftwaffe officers, had been hit by hundreds of rounds. They had no faces left.

His men kneeled, or bent over, catching their breath after reaching the bunker's reinforced doorway. Pavel untied the sodden tourniquet from the farmer's injured arm. He took a fresh field bandage from his canvas backpack and secured it tightly around the bloodied upper limb. The farmer nodded in appreciation.

The doorway was about twenty feet square. The floor was wet in parts, with a mixture of blood and rainwater. The walls, as thick as the armour on their T-34 tanks, had had large chunks blown out of them. At the rear, a concrete stairwell dropped into blackness.

It smelled of paraffin, an underlying rankness, and what Pavel considered was a whiff of incense too. He did his best to ignore it.

'Move down now,' he said. He watched his men turn around and face the stairwell. They began to shuffle forward. 'Wait for me at the bottom.'

'We should hang them when it's over,' the Muscovite said, as he descended the first couple of steps. 'Every fucking one. Or let the NKVD loose on them,' he went on, referring to the brutal Soviet secret police.

He was a squat man, with a broad face. Eyes like black diamonds.

'Even the young ones?' said Doc. He had a fragile-looking frame and shrew-like features. His hair was always a little too long and he scrubbed his fingernails vigorously every morning. 'They're victims too.'

The Muscovite snorted, spat on the ground. 'They'll just grow.'

'You're a cretin.' Doc shook his head.

'What you think, sergeant?' the Kid said.

'Get your arse down those steps.'

Doc was an educated man, Pavel knew, a teacher of classical music. He thought the war must have been even worse for a man like him. What he'd said was right too.

He squatted down just inside the sheltered doorway, covering the retreat of his men to a safe distance down the dark staircase. He'd check the bunker was clear. If it was, they'd rest for the night. He rubbed the stubble on his face with his thumb and forefinger, adjusted the strap of his steel helmet, and surveyed the skeleton of a Gothic church to his right. The blown-out windows looked to him like empty eye sockets. He'd seen too many of those. He was seeing them now, even when they weren't there, he thought.

Below it, a middle-aged man in a crumpled brown suit had been strung up from a lamppost, a wooden sign attached to string around his neck. A fate that seemed common for Berliners. He'd seen their grotesque bodies hanging from grey-coloured trees, from protruding iron bars. Even from the roofs of crashed trucks. Traitors. Deserters. The innocent. Murdered by the Feldgendarmerie, the German military police, and packs of their own people. The fanatical, even now, Pavel thought. The man reminded him of an effigy.

He'd not heard any commotion after his men had started down the concrete steps. The nearby flak guns and tank fire seemed to have ceased too. There was still just the faint rumble of Soviet artillery, the odd crackle of small-arms fire in the distance.

Now he saw them, about forty yards away, as they came around the old wall. He raised his binoculars. But the platoon of Waffen-SS crossed the street and disappeared into one of the many alleyways that led into it. Putting his binoculars into their pouch, he decided to wait for another five minutes. Just to be sure.

He craved sleep. His body ached in every joint. He let himself relax, his head bowing. His eyelids fluttered. He tried his best to stop them from closing, but it was a futile exertion.

Pavel's eyelids flicked open, startled by sudden movement, something he'd thought had sounded like the scrambling of heavy-duty boots over shale. Intuitively, he swivelled around. He saw a grey shape running towards him. The right arm was pulled back. He knew that meant a stick grenade. In the confined space of the bunker's entrance and stairwell, the consequences would be devastating. Briefly, he pictured the blood and flesh of his comrades, his charges, splattered up the bare walls. Something he'd avoid at any cost.

Still squatting, he let off a burst from his Shpagin. He held the drum magazine with his left hand, as he pushed it up in an arc. The muzzle smoke spread out and the brass casings somersaulted vertically before clattering onto the concrete about him. The discordant music of war. Of death. The rounds hit the shape in a crescent from waist to shoulder. It was flung back onto the rim of a bomb crater, filled with rancid water. It didn't move again. Pavel knew he must have looked like an easy target.

The grenade, with its long wooden handle, exploded with nothing more than what he regarded as an exaggerated *phut*, something he put down to his familiarity with the near deafening discharge of close by artillery and tank fire. But it threw up chunks of aggregate in a white-grey smokeball, the shockwave making the body lift off the ground. It blew off what looked like an arm, or a thigh.

Hearing his men running up the steps behind him, he said, 'Get back. I'm alright.'

He took out his binoculars. He saw the tattered field grey uniform. The dead German girl was about fifteen years old, her lower thigh looking as if it had been gorged upon by one of the packs of now wild dogs that roamed about the city. But he remained unmoved. Besides, he thought she might be better off dead.

The Red Army liked to rape at night, after they got drunk on pilfered schnapps, or antifreeze from jeeps when alcohol wasn't on hand. Girls as young as eight. Stooped crones. It didn't seem to matter. The hopeful took to smearing soot onto their faces and teeth and cutting their hair or tying grimy rags into it. The hopeless jumped off buildings or into swirling rivers. They took their young with them too, wrapped like bundles of bread against their empty breasts. It sickened him. But he guessed all wars sent people spiralling into madness.

Deciding the street wasn't a good place to be for either side, he took point after re-joining his men. He told himself it was only right he took his turn, although he hated point duty as much as they did. He knew he shouldn't. It was perilous, and they deserved a sound leader, but he did it anyway.

The passageway took a sharp left at the foot of the concrete steps. It proceeded in the form of a long corridor, which he reckoned passed under the street and on towards the half demolished civic office building. All but a very few lights, affixed to the walls in wire cradles, were broken. The way ahead appeared narrow and ominous. The floor was cracked, damp and slippery. Water leaked from exposed overhead pipes and spilled patches of oil were prevalent.

He knew explosions had happened further on. The air stank of stale smoke and acrid sulphur. He told his men to be careful, to watch out for the sand buckets, fallen plaster and wooden benches. There were scattered documents too. He stooped and picked one up and held it a few inches from his squinting eyes. He risked igniting a match against the wall. He just about made out the outline of the same unknown design on the paper as had been on those few pieces he'd seen in the street. These looked as if they'd been dropped in a chaotic retreat. He blew out the match.

With almost no visibility, it was impossible to tell how far the corridor receded. And there were other corridors now, branching off the main one. It appeared to be a complex underground facility. But he decided not to allow his men to use their torches. Not until he was sure they were alone.

Turning to them, he said, 'We'll make sure it's clear. Share what food we have and what we can find. Then rest for the night.'

A few nodded. The rest just looked bleak.

If it's clear, we'll get up at dawn, he thought. Make our way back to company HQ. Get fresh orders.

He got about thirty feet before seeing a steel door, a couple of yards away. Black liquid that looked like stale blood or oil had oozed out from underneath it. He halted his men with a raised arm. He pointed to the Kid, circled his hand over his head and thrust it down: To me. The Kid came forward, his sunken face full of belief. The Kid nodded to him.

Squatting to one side of the door, Pavel pulled down on the metal handle, checking to see if it was locked. He couldn't risk lobbing in a grenade. The bunker's damaged ceilings appeared too fragile. The door was unfettered. He kicked it open, rushed in, followed by the Kid.

Inside, he grimaced, moved his Shpagin around in a semicircle, although the dark was almost impenetrable. The stench was even more revolting than in the street. Rank and overwhelming. He held his throat, choking on it. The Kid almost vomited too. There were bundles on the floor, but he couldn't make them out, and there was something smouldering at the room's centre.

'It's clear,' Pavel said. He coughed, spat.

He watched the others shuffle into the large, square room, which was devoid of furniture, of any means of artificial light. They covered their noses and mouths with the sleeves of their jackets or blouses, before hastily replacing them with dirty handkerchiefs and strips of bandages snatched out from their pockets.

'It stinks like a fucking slaughterhouse,' the Muscovite said.

It does, Pavel thought. But what the hell's been slaughtered?

CHAPTER THREE

'Turn your torches on,' Pavel said.

He was still unsure whether all the bunker had been abandoned, but he felt he had a duty to investigate what was in the room. Besides, his curiosity was getting the better of him.

The three that had them, did so. The others lit matches or flicked open cartridge-shaped storm lighters, taken from captured German soldiers. The Heer were flagrant looters, irrespective of their rank. They stole everything, even those items they had no use for. Pavel and his men hadn't redressed the balance, but they still took what they could use. He'd leave the real work to the Soviet trophy brigades.

The torch beams played over the floor and Pavel saw that naked corpses lay face up there. They were positioned in organized lines, like cadavers in a mortuary. They'd been tortured. At least three had had the tops of their skulls hacked off. The craniums had been cleaned and were dotted about the room, used as bowls to hold small piles of smooth stones. A pile of bloodied Red Army uniforms was in one corner.

Pavel grimaced, shaking his head. All their noses and ears had been severed, the legs and arms and hands and feet. But most of the removed body parts looked as if they had been put back in place against the heads and torsos, such that from a distance they could be taken for whole. Pavel wondered why they'd been put back together, like sickening jigsaw puzzles.

He smelled incense. The scent of it clawed at his nostrils, even above the sweet and suffocating stench of decomposing human flesh. He walked towards the source. There, in the centre of the room, was a huge, rusted iron vat, like a witch's cauldron. Beneath the orange embers was a foot or more of ashes.

It was an irreconcilable sight in a German bunker, and it made his head ache simply to consider what its presence might mean. It was something truly out of the ordinary in a world where violent death had become as ordinary as day passing into night.

Pavel walked back to the dead bodies and crouched down. 'Over here,' he said, pointing to the head closest to him.

Illuminated and upon closer examination, it was evident that the man had been shot in the back of his neck. Pavel motioned with his hand and the torch beams highlighted each head and body in turn. He duckwalked down the line, seeing that all were the same, the backs of their necks smeared with sticky brown, coagulated blood, the torsos tied with woven rope. He just hoped they'd been executed before the butchery, but something told him that hadn't been the way it had panned out. He stood up. Spat on the floor.

'Highlight all of their faces,' he said.

The beams scanned across all twelve. He recognized them as Soviets. Uzbeks or Kazakhs, he guessed, even given the sliced human tissue. Mongolian volunteers or northern Asians from Siberia, perhaps. He didn't know for sure. Not one looked older than his mid-twenties. He knew the Germans murdered Red Army prisoners at will, but this was something different. Something unholy, whatever that means now, he thought.

The Kid lit a cigarette. Pavel noticed that the boy couldn't stop his hand from shaking.

There was the sound of erratic footsteps and a heavy fall. They all turned, ready to kill, even the injured farmer. A slim man was sprawled on his back in the doorway. He was bareheaded, but still retained his round, steel-rimmed glasses. His field grey service uniform was all but covered in plaster dust.

After a pause, one of the beams picked up the three pips on his left collar, the hated insignia on the right. A Waffen-SS Hauptsturmführer, a captain, Pavel knew. It was obvious the German was close to unconsciousness. His face was ashen, his brown hair matted with sweat. A small line of dark-red blood popped in and out of his cracked mouth in unison with his laboured breath. His eyes were the colour of aubergines.

Looking at the Kid, Pavel said, 'Check him out.' Although the German was in a bad way, he knew he could be hiding a pistol or grenade.

The Kid walked over to him, tossed away his cigarette, and slung his Shpagin over his shoulder. Kneeling, he pushed the captain onto his side. Patted him down. Nothing dangerous had been concealed. With one knee on the German's chest, he rifled through his pockets. He took out a packet of cigarettes, a half-eaten chocolate bar and a tanned-leather wallet. The officer mumbled, his head rolling from side to side.

Standing over him, the Kid raised his Shpagin, about to use the stamped-steel muzzle to cave-in the German's face, which was turning sallow. The others flicked open their lighters and lit matches again to further brighten the room.

'Wait,' Pavel said. He nodded to Doc, knowing he could speak almost fluent German.

Doc handed his carbine to a comrade. He moved over to the badly injured officer, waving the Kid out of the way. Reluctantly, the Kid shuffled a few steps to his left.

The Muscovite positioned himself at the doorway. Squatting, he kept watch on the corridor. 'I want his boots,' he said.

Crouching by the officer's side, Doc cradled his head. He tipped water into his parched mouth from a battered water bottle. The officer coughed and spluttered, dislodging much of the liquid. To Pavel, he looked beyond saving.

'Ask him if there are more SS here?' Pavel said.

Doc spoke to him in German. But the officer just moaned before emitting a guttural snarl like a nervous dog.

'Ask him if he wants to die here?' Pavel said.

Doc translated, and the German raised his right hand about six inches above the polluted floor. He tried to spread his fingers.

'Five,' Pavel said in German.

The officer blinked.

'Ask him why these men died here. Like this,' Pavel said to Doc.

He heard the officer strain to get a few words out. 'What did he say?'

'Not me,' Doc said.

'They always say that,' the Muscovite said. 'They think it'll save them, the stupid bastards.'

'Ask him again,' Pavel said.

Doc did, and the officer struggled to raise his head and breathed a few rasping breaths like an asthmatic. Doc leaned forward, and held him up at the neck, enabling his enemy to speak into his dirt-stained ear. He whispered two words. A split second later, Doc stood up. He'd let the officer's upper body fall to the concrete, as if the German had told him he was contaminated by some contagious disease. One with no cure.

'Tell me?' Pavel said.

Doc didn't respond for a few seconds. Then he said, 'Doctor Doll.'

Pavel shook his head. 'He's delirious.'

The Muscovite, still squatting by the entrance to the room, sniggered. 'Just kill him.'

Pavel thought he was a stupid ape. He'd never liked him. He knew he would have displayed extreme brutality if he hadn't kept him in check. But part of him knew the Muscovite was right. He had no means, let alone the inclination, to deal with a dying SS officer. Besides, the man was all but dead as it was. But he wasn't a murderer, even after all that had happened. Why start now?

But in his mind, he watched the Kid hit the officer in the head with the sturdy muzzle of his Shpagin. Short powerful strikes, creating deep gashes in the yellowing skin. The sound, he knew, would be like splintering wood. Retribution for what had happened here, if only of an imaginary nature.

The officer made one brief, ragged gasp and died, as if Pavel had willed it.

Nodding, the Kid lit another cigarette. But after his second inhalation, his hand stopped midway between his hip and mouth. His emerald-blue eyes seemed to glaze over.

'I want to go home now, sergeant.'

It'll end soon, Pavel thought.

'I know,' he said. 'Just be patient. It'll be over soon.'

He knew too that he would have to remain vigilant. His ultimate responsibility was the protection of his squad, every one of them. Even more so in what he knew to be the last days. The war was an infernal vortex that had sucked life from the world. He swore that his men would not be the ones to finally leave it sated.

Deciding the bunker was either too bizarre a place to spend the night, or too unpredictable, he took a firm grip on his Shpagin. 'We're leaving.'

Half a dozen explosions erupted from beyond the room. White light steaked through the corridor like flash lightning bolts. The ground vibrated, as if a platoon of Tiger tanks was rumbling by. The shockwaves travelled down the walls and the Muscovite was thrown back against the doorframe. It erupted into flying splinters, as lethal as blow darts. For the first time since he'd met him, the Muscovite looked serene.

Pavel knew the blast had killed him.

Some of his men had sunk or been propelled to their knees. Others stared wide-eyed and trembling. Plaster and brick dust fell from the ceiling. There was a deafening, creaking sound: the hull of a ship hitting an iceberg.

They all rushed for the door, just as an iron girder swung down from out of the dimness, like a huge and lethal pendulum.

CHAPTER FOUR

At night, before Pavel fell asleep, he always prayed to a God he no longer believed in. He didn't know why, except that he didn't know what else to do. He prayed that his Russian village hadn't been burned to the ground. So many had been, both during the initial advance of the fascist beasts, and in retreat, as reprisals. On his way to the defence of Stalingrad after the German offensive against southern Russia, Operation Braunschweig, he'd heard that millions had been forced into a murderous slavery, and millions more Europeans had already died. He hadn't been able to conceive of such things and hadn't believed them at first, even though he'd been fighting since 1941 without rest.

But he'd seen all a man had to see to continue to risk his life willingly as he'd gotten closer to the city. Children had hung from trees in deserted and wrecked parks, like mahogany marionettes. Old men had had their eyes burned out. Women's bodies had lain in the frosted earth, with babies still in their arms. The German invasion had caused famine and disease too, the air for miles about replete with the smell of the dead and the carcasses of donkeys and horses. Barns had been burned to the ground, the smouldering ruins unable to hide the charred bones, so many had there been.

Asphyxiated corpses had been recovered from shallow graves without a mark on them.

But Stalingrad hadn't fallen, even though the Soviets had suffered over one million casualties. He'd survived the hellish battle. He knew now he could survive this.

'Stalingrad,' he said, creating an impression of it in his mind.

It had been the flagship of the Soviet Union. Before the war, he'd once walked between its towering, blond-stone blocks of flats, and had marvelled at its modern factories and ornamental gardens. It had stood elegantly for twenty miles on the banks of the Volga River. But after seven months of ruthless fighting, he'd seen the city ravaged and reduced to a flaming skeleton.

He'd fought the German Sixth Army. There were other armies there. Other Axis nationalities. His enemies had come from Hungary, Croatia, Italy and Romania. Many had died from the cold or typhus, it had to be said. But the Sixth Army had included 30,000 Russians, a fact that had been kept secret from the ordinary Soviet people. Pavel and his men had called them Hilfswillige, volunteer helpers. Some had been the remnants of the pro-Tsarist White Army, old men in Pavel's eyes, that had seen a chance to exact what had been a festering revenge against the Bolsheviks. Some had seen it as a way of escaping the horrendous conditions of captivity. Others, however, had simply been traitors. They were all dead now, he guessed, their last moments spent tied blindfolded to a wooden stake, their shattered and bloody bodies the result of unimaginable torture by SMERSH, the main directorate of military counter-intelligence. He saw them often in his imagination.

But Pavel hadn't speculated about the fate of his wife and two children, because he knew his mind wouldn't be able to cope with it. He just told himself that they were alive. Safe. Even though he'd heard no word from them.

Now, close to unconsciousness, he knew that the previous explosions that had taken place in the bunker had weakened the ceiling even beyond what he'd thought before, and the explosions that had just occurred had caused it to all but cave in. Bulky debris covered some of his men and the mutilated corpses. Concrete slabs. Strips of metal. Mounds of plaster and powdery dust. Legs had been crushed by iron girders. One comrade puked a foul-smelling mixture of blood and a bile-like fluid, his life force draining away, Pavel knew.

They've done their duty, he thought. But he felt responsible for their deaths. He mourned them in silence, although he was on the verge of weeping.

Squinting, he spat a little onto his curled fingers, did his best to rub the dust from his lashes and the corners of his eyes. Through his still blurred vision, he could just about make out that others had survived the collapse. The Kid and Doc were among them. But Doc was writhing on the decimated floor, blood leaching from a gaping wound to the side of his head.

Pavel felt his eyelids closing. The Kid scrambled over to him and he sensed him cradling his head. He fought the dark with what strength he had left.

Vaguely, he heard the Kid speaking. 'Don't die. Not after all we've been through. Not now, at the end. Don't die, sergeant.'

The smell came to him once more. Fragrant and smoky.

Incense.

He saw himself watching the bearded priest as he was escorted to an NKVD wagon. He was going to the Gulag, his mother said. He heard himself asking what that was. He watched his mother's tears in reply. The church was razed to the ground soon afterwards. Five massive explosions that made him jolt even now. The precious, centuries-old folk-art icons were thrown onto the resultant fires as if they were mere wooden trinkets.

The world was mad then too, he thought.

I must live.

Shuddering, he focused on vivid images of his village, fifty miles north of Rostov-on-Don. It was still standing. Still populated. Animals rummaged around for scraps of food in their primitive pens. Pigs, sheep and chickens. His wife and children were standing outside the little whitewashed, thatched house. They were waving to him. His blonde daughter and his curly-haired son. They were calling out.

Papa. Papa. Papa.

CHAPTER FIVE

Manhattan, September 2015.

Jed Watson had a rare addiction. It wasn't something he talked about, not even in vague terms after a few drinks. He doubted anyone he considered a friend had the imagination to understand his need. In truth, he knew they'd never forgive him for it.

He arrived home from the office early, as he always did on a Tuesday, calling out to check he was alone. His wife played bridge at a weekly card club in the neighbourhood, and their housekeeper left before 6.30 pm on alternate days. Satisfied, he dropped his briefcase inside the teak double doors and walked past the elaborate granddaughter clock in the entrance hall, his hands trembling.

The spacious apartment was made from Indiana sandstone, with high ceilings and wide cornices, a Spanish-style terrace. It was part of a secure complex, the driveway gates electronic, the lift activated by a palm print in the underground parking lot. He felt safe here.

He loosened his silk tie and flipped down the wall switch in the living room. Moving to the windows, he closed the brocade curtains, even though it was still light outside. There were other times when he could satisfy his craving, opportunities he welcomed, but he relied upon Tuesday evenings.

He fixed himself three fingers of neat vodka and gulped half of it down, flinging his head back. The alcohol caressed his throat and steadied him. Sinking down into the nearest couch, its gold tassels rippling like bar chimes, he picked up a remote off the walnut coffee table and turned on the surround sound system. He had three hours.

He'd loved Dvořák's *Requiem* since childhood, the voices of the massed choir still haunting to him. His father had been a Baptist minister, his mother a conceited adulteress. He guessed his father had listened to it to mourn the passing of their marriage, to wallow in his misfortune.

The requiem rose to the first crescendo and Watson's own mind was deluged with images. Lurid and fragmentary. The slender arm. The curvature of the instep. The now florid cheek. The same images every time.

He drained the vodka and strolled to the kitchen, with its herringbone tiles. He washed the heavy crystal and left it on the polished granite island. He appeared to drift through a dark corridor to his study. The sensor-activated lighting came on and he shut the blinds. Three of the walls were decorated with his collection of wooden African face masks. On the fourth was a portrait in pale watercolours, an aged samurai lady from the Meiji Period, ethereal in its simplicity. He took off his tailored suit jacket and hung it on a coat hook. Slapping his middle-aged paunch, he walked over to his desk, inlaid with bottle-green leather. Bending over, he powered up his laptop, feeling lightheaded, as if he'd just inhaled his first cigarette.

He kept his DVD in a titanium wall safe, secured via free-speech recognition technology. Speech was impossible to replicate, he knew, even for twins, due to the uniqueness of both the voice tract and accent. He couldn't risk anyone watching it. He knew it was a reckless habit. But he deserved to partake of it at least once a week, he believed. He'd made so many sacrifices. Hadn't he? He'd put a heap of money into other people's pockets, for sure. Besides, he wasn't hurting anyone. That had been done already. He just watched.

He lifted the watercolour off the wall, his hands clammy now. He rested it against one of the desk's trumpet-turned legs.

Facing the safe's microphone, he said, 'My special moments.'

The safe door opened silently, magically, as if it was an occult portal, and Watson began humming along to the muted strains of the requiem, a mass for the dead.

He placed the DVD into the drive, the contents so extreme that he'd convinced himself he'd seen it vibrate on occasion. But his wife never came into his study. The housekeeper didn't clean in here either. He cleaned it himself. No one came in here. He was superstitious that way. He'd said he didn't want anyone touching his work papers.

He spun around, thinking he'd heard something above the music. A distant cabinet dragged along? A wardrobe door slammed somewhere? He couldn't be sure. The apartment was susceptible to the odd vibration and unobtrusive noise from time to time. It was inevitable, he supposed, given the number of occupants who lived in the block. But couples had rows they'd never heard, his wife had said. Screaming matches even. He decided to put the DVD back into the safe and investigate. Best to be cautious.

The door burst open with such force that the brass handle rebounded off the wall, dislodging a piece of plaster the size of a child's fist. Watson gasped, his body shaking. He'd registered the two white hazmat suits, the red motorcycle helmets. The noose dangling from one hand, a coarse sack from another.

He began to say something, but it sounded like gibberish. Vomit rose in his throat and beads of sweat sprouted at his temples. A searing pain had erupted in his chest and had streaked over his shoulders to his biceps. He panted and wheezed, his stomach tightening.

He was dragged to his knees, his limp arms yanked behind him. The last thing he saw was one of the African masks, the hollow eyes, the downturned mouth, as the sack was thrust over his head. The darkness swamped him, and his eyelids blinked frantically like the wings of a trapped bird. When the noose tore into his neck, his rational mind degenerated into a kind of madness, and he made a faint yelping sound.

He died less than a minute later, his mouth agape in a silent scream.

*

Doug, the red-faced concierge, his young body swollen by an almost constant diet of pizza, became curious, nothing more, when Mr Watson hadn't left the building before 7:30 am as he always did on a weekday. He became a little concerned when Mrs Watson didn't leave for her daily gym class at around 10 am. He'd seen her return early yesterday evening, her face pale, her manner flustered. He'd smelled a hint of vomit.

They didn't answer their internal landline, so he followed standard procedure and called the nightshift guy, who, after bitching about being woken up, said they hadn't left. He called the duty manager then, who told him they hadn't said they'd be leaving the apartment, although the housekeeper had called in this morning and had said she was too ill to come into work at noon. The manager advised Doug to use his master key to open their front door without entering and enquire if they needed assistance. He did so. Again, there was no reply.

He knew they couldn't get out of the building without stopping first at ground level. The lift doors opened so he could check who was leaving and, more importantly, who was arriving from the secure parking lot. There was a sturdy fire escape at the rear, but he struggled to think of a single reason why they'd use it. Concluding that something had to be wrong, he got the OK to ring 911. But the duty manager had reminded him that their employer would face a hike in its insurance premium if he so much as stuck his big head over the threshold before the police arrived.

*

NYPD Sergeant Cliff Erickson, a leathery-skinned veteran, put on a pair of blue latex gloves, deciding he didn't need to draw his Smith & Wesson 5946 sidearm, his weapon of choice. He thought the assignment as inappropriate as asking him to search a storm drain for a dropped smartphone, but he was a month off retirement, so he guessed everyone was just trying to keep him safe until then.

The apartment's entrance hall was unlit, the immediate room dark. He unhooked a torch from his leather belt, the beam flooding a gilded mirror, the biggest he'd seen. He located the light switch within seconds.

He found Mrs Watson fully clothed on a king-sized bed in the master bedroom, with her throat slit. A vicious gash that resembled an exposed gill. The congealed blood was like a macabre halo encircling her head, the peach-coloured chiffon blouse streaked with it. Her skin was in the last stages of the post-mortem stain, the purple-red discolouration brought about by the blood draining back into the dependant parts of the body. Rigor mortis had set in, the tightening of the muscles, strangely accentuating her elegant features. Her stiff arm was doglegged on the silver inlay bedside table, and lumps of crispy vomit dotted her black shoulder-length hair and the lavender-coloured duvet.

The corpse of Mr Watson was in the study, or at least that's where the body had been dumped, Erickson thought. The flabby neck had a uniform band around it, the colour of unwashed blueberries, the whites of his dark eyes translucent, like those of a stranded catfish. It was obvious the man had asphyxiated through strangulation. Bloating hadn't set in yet, neither had the rotting of flesh, which meant that both victims had died within the last twenty-four hours. It fitted with what he already knew, but the stench of the soiled, unyielding body on the floor made him wince.

He felt the urge to smoke. He lifted his peaked cap off his slick forehead, took out a stick of gum from his navy-blue trousers, peeled off the foil wrapper, and tossed the gum into his mouth. He noticed that the empty tray of a DVD player had been left protruding from the side of a laptop, a disc recently ejected. He clutched his radio, about to report the murders, and began retracing his steps, happy to leave the dirty work to the crime scene unit, although he wondered if the empty tray was significant.

CHAPTER SIX

Yale University, New Haven, Connecticut, five days later.

It was the beginning of the autumn term and Gabriel Hall was standing in front of a pine lectern that had blackened with age at the base. He wore squid-ink jeans and a matching polo shirt. The windowless room was part of an unattractive box-like structure, a modern building by Yale's standards, housing a registrar's office and two floors of classrooms. Several of the law school's classrooms in the Sterling Law Building were undergoing redecoration, and he'd taken what had been offered. A semi-circle of banked half-desks was illuminated by energy-saving strips that gave off insipid yellow glows, the air was stale, due to the room's previous lack of use, and dust motes hung there. About twenty young people were sitting on small, padded seats, with a smattering of foreign and mature students.

Gabriel had all but finished his lecture when he saw a female student, head down, skimming through what he was sure were social media posts on her smartphone, like a bank clerk counting notes. He knew that keeping the attention of all of them for the duration of his lecture was a high bar, but it disappointed him. He was forty years old, his hair a rich chestnut colour, his ash-grey eyes flecked with mauve. He'd taught criminal justice at the university on a part-time basis for the past three years, and was still in private practice, specializing in white-collar crime in New York City. The teaching didn't pay well, but the prestige it generated was good for business, despite the recent controversy over some of the students' denunciations of resident professors.

He decided to change tack. 'Franz Kafka's novel, *The Trial*, is about an accused man who is never told what his crime is. Neither is the reader.' He grinned and saw a few of the students grinning back at him. 'Why? Because the novel's theme is powerlessness. The powelessness that people feel when they're faced with a remote and tickbox bureaucracy. That's not unlike how some of your clients will feel one day. What they are looking for is not sympathy, but something akin to empathy.'

He saw that the student, Summer Cox, the gifted but haughty daughter of a well-connected Philadelphia senator, was still flicking through her smartphone.

'Miss Cox,' he said.

She looked up, clearly a little ruffled.

'Kafka's definition of a lawyer is a person who writes a ten-thou-sand-word document and calls it a brief. If your attention span doesn't extend to the relatively short time I've been speaking, you've likely chosen the wrong profession to pursue.'

He watched her make a face and mouth: *Yeah, yeah, yeah*.

A couple of days ago, he'd volunteered at the local federal public defender's office to act pro bono for an alleged murderer, a young man named Johnny Hockey. A man, elements of the press were calling an anti-Semite, with offensive tattoos. His friends had shaken their heads, saying that the level of publicity it was generating wouldn't do his career any good. What was he thinking? Hockey was accused of the murders of Jed and Esfir Watson.

Gabriel had heard of Jed Watson and had seen the recent photos of him on TV, a mottled-skinned man with hair like blanched wheat. He'd risen to own a respected commodity brokerage in the Financial District after an unremarkable beginning as a photocopier salesman in Bowling Green, Kentucky. He'd been a philanthropist of the arts and a benefactor of numerous children's charities, a friend of the mayor, no less. Esfir Watson had been a Russian beauty fifteen years her husband's junior, a former ballerina at the Mikhaylovsky Theatre, with eyes the colour of a blue iceberg. She'd been known for her lavish fundraisers and aversion to scandal. The suspected racial motive was due to her religion. She'd been a Jew.

Gabriel had done a short interview for CNN already, dismissing that allegation as unfounded. But he'd read the arrest report and knew that if the real reason he was representing Hockey was uncovered, it would both finish his career and threaten his personal safety.

*

Johnny Hockey and his misfit girlfriend, May, had been arrested in their rundown Bronx flat above a greengrocer's shop, two days after the Watsons had been murdered. They'd lain together in the dark underneath a single white bedsheet, both dozing after their feverish lovemaking.

Hockey was twenty-two, with a shaven head, his body heavily muscled. May was raw-boned, with short, spiky blonde hair. She was from Mississippi and he loved her accent. They'd drunk a crate of strong beer between them and had watched videos on YouTube, including one of historical footage of Waffen-SS troops in action, accompanied by the aggressive guitar riffs and violent lyrics of death metal.

The FBI SWAT team had arrived at 5.03 am, dressed in black battle-dress uniforms, blast-resistant goggles, Kevlar helmets and ballistic body armour. A metal battering ram had been used to gain entry, the locked door flying off its rusted hinges. The beams from their torches had scanned every inch of the room, picking out discarded clothes and empty bottles, a standing plywood wardrobe. Following the mundane, there'd been the extreme: a Third Reich war ensign, a bronze bust of Hitler, an array of Wehrmacht replica weaponry.

May had yelled obscenities at them and had been jerked to the floor for her outburst. She'd screwed up her face in an unsuccessful attempt to stop the bloated tears in her eyes from flowing. Her struggle had appeared obstinate rather than vicious, and she'd been subdued within a few seconds, wincing when the plastic flex-cuffs had bitten into her skin.

Hockey had stayed silent, with his hands raised, a dull, alcohol-induced nausea in his upper abdomen and the back of his throat, a skull-cracking headache. He'd seen the tell-tale red dots skittering about the walls and intermingling with the torch beams. He'd known they'd flowed from lasers fixed onto Heckler & Koch MP5 submachine guns. There'd been no point in resisting.

He'd been screamed at to lie face down on the floor. A rubber-soled boot had landed on the back of his knees, his arms pulled behind him and secured there with the disposable restraints. A female SWAT agent had crouched down, holding the barrel of a semi-automatic pistol next to his temple, so that he'd caught sight of it in his peripheral vison.

She'd whispered: 'You move an inch, I'll put a round in your ear.'

He'd seen May frogmarched from the room, her half naked body writhing with a mixture of distress and indignation. That had pushed him to the limits of his compliant mindset. He'd figured that he'd been betrayed by someone close to him. His own body had tensed then, barely able to contain the hate that coursed through his veins like acid.

Later, at a local PD cell — a temporary measure, he'd been told

— he'd consoled himself with the knowledge that the snitch would die screaming.

*

Summer Cox flicked back her strawberry blonde hair and straightened her yellow T-shirt, which was adorned with the head of a cartoon giraffe, its extravagant eyelashes halfway through a flutter, its generous mouth in a pout.

She said, 'Professor Hall, your point about empathizing with clients. What if they're a racist? How does a lawyer empathize with someone like that, unless they have a bit of racism in them, too?'

Several of the students' jaws slackened. Wide-eyed, others half-laughed. A few nodded in agreement. Gabriel felt sure they'd seen his interview on CNN, or had been told about it.

She must have been listening, he thought, unless someone had passed her a note. He didn't know or care. But he could tell she was already regretting her rudeness. Her head was bowed and she looked sheepish as she shuffled her papers.

He felt like exploding into a rant, but held it together and said, 'That's all for today.'

The students closed their electronic notebooks and coloured files and began to leave.

'Miss Cox, do you have a moment?' he said.

She looked around at the young women with her and whispered something to them. He saw them smirk.

'Sure.'

She walked over to him. When her near anorexic body was about two feet away, Gabriel rubbed his left shoulder.

'I'll let that pass on this occasion,' he said.

She bit the side of her plump lower lip and wouldn't make eye contact.

'If it happens again, we'll see what the dean has to say. Do we understand each other?'

She looked up at him now, her green-blue eyes fiery.

She said, 'The dean is friends with my father.'

She left, her gait betraying the nature of an inherited ego. He didn't have the time or the inclination to respond, so he let it go.

He switched off his laptop, gathered up his books, his thoughts returning to the Watson case. He knew that after Hockey's arrest by the FBI, he'd been taken before a magistrate judge for his initial appearance and detention hearing. He'd been refused bail on an unsurprising ground: a danger to the community. This was due both to his suspected involvement in the Watson murders and his previous criminal convictions.

But he hadn't been incarcerated at a usual pre-trial detainee facility, such as the Metropolitan Correctional Center on Park Row, lower Manhattan, known as MCC. He was being held at a federal prison in Upstate New York. The federal public defender had told Gabriel that after some debate between the FBI and the Mayor's office, it had been agreed that Hockey would be sent to a high-security correctional facility. Like the late Mrs Watson, the mayor was Jewish, and he'd encouraged the allegation of a hate crime.

Gabriel had read about Hockey's tattoos. There was the expected swastika and the animal symbol of Nazi Germany, the official party eagle, the Parteradler. There was even an inked profile of the Führer on his bicep. Above his right wrist were the twin sig runes of the Waffen-SS, and a death's head in the same position on the left one. Gabriel had guessed it was worn as a homage to both the cap badge and collar insignia worn by the SS-Totenkopfverbände, the concentration camp guards. He'd done hours of research already.

Gabriel hadn't met Hockey yet, and he was unsure how he should act when he did. But what he did know for sure was that in a federal prison, the Nazi tattoos could save Hockey's life, rather than put him at risk. In that fractious realm, he would be protected by the white supremacists.

Walking across the dusty podium towards the bank of desks, his newfound duplicity began to burden him again. His breath quickened, but there was nothing that could deter him.

CHAPTER SEVEN

FBI Headquarters, Washington DC, the next day.

Special Agent Carla Romero specialized in investigating instances of female kidnappings, often perpetrated with a violent sexual motive. She worked closely with county sheriffs' departments and state-wide law enforcement agencies, with a zealot's enthusiasm. She helped enrol the terrified victims into counselling programmes when she wasn't faced with the tragedy of recovering the resultant corpses. She'd joined the FBI three years ago, after completing a master's degree in international law and spending a further four years working for NATO in Brussels.

The FBI building at 935 Pennsylvania Avenue was a precast structure built in the Brutalist style, with bronze-coloured windows and netting covering the façade of the tower section, due to the crumbing concrete. She entered the main concourse at 9.02 am. Passing the blue and gold flag and the FBI seal on a plaque on the wall— *Fidelity, Bravery, Integrity* — she turned right.

She often wore her ebony hair in a French plait, as was the case this morning. She was five eleven in her flat shoes. 'Junoesque', she'd heard some of her colleagues say, and she hid her curves under loose-fitting trouser suits. She bought a coffee from a vending machine and entered a secure lift, heading for a section chief's third-floor office. He'd called her encrypted smartphone an hour before and had told her to meet him there, although he hadn't informed her why.

She stepped out and took a few sips of the bland liquid. She left the disposable cup on a stone bench and straightened her charcoal-grey jacket, reminding herself that the chief had a reputation for being a hard-ass.

*

Carla and Section Chief George Hester were sitting on chrome chairs at a rosewood conference table. The grey floor tiles looked freshly spray-buffed, the pools of natural light there phosphorescent. They'd been talking about the Watson case for a few minutes. She'd taken notes, which by the look on Hester's face now, he considered a little amateurish rather than diligent, and she stopped, leaving her thick fountain pen on the open legal pad.

What Hester had called 'an abhorrent DVD' had been recovered by the Bureau after they'd searched Johnny Hockey's flat, following his arrest. He'd described it in some detail and she'd been conscious of him studying her face as he'd done so. He'd said that one of Jed Watson's prints was on it. Near the centre, probably left there when he'd pressed it into the tray. The contents had been such that Watson's laptop had been hurriedly scrutinized by specialist FBI cryptographers. Extensive amounts of vicious pornography had been stored on the hard drive, albeit of the legal variety.

'So, you're saying the DVD recovered from Hockey's place had to be the male vic's?' Carla said.

Hester nodded and picked up a mug of coffee, sipping at it. 'Are you sure I can't get you one?'

'I'm fine, thank you, sir.'

Hester was an olive-skinned 45-year-old, with thick black hair and a waistline wider than his shoulders. He wore a dark-blue pinstriped suit and a red tie, held in place by a gold tiepin. He looked Mediterranean, but Carla had heard that his family originated from Donegal, in Ireland.

He said, 'Given what we now know about Watson, I'd say the DVD was his for sure. But that doesn't mean Hockey will be convicted of a double murder. Don't get overly concerned with that. I need you to find out who the female victim in the DVD was, assuming it's not a fake, and where Watson got it from.'

His lower lip curled back over his bottom teeth, as if he found it difficult to speak now. She thought about asking him if he suspected there were more of the same, a perverse trend, but left it. She guessed he believed the DVD was real, that the victim had been kidnapped, possibly trafficked, before her murder on camera. She knew for sure that he didn't want it replicated. Why else would she be here?

'You think Mrs Watson knew about it?' she said.

'I doubt it.'

He rubbed his forehead with his palm, a gesture that said: what does it matter now?

'Read up on Hockey. He has a past. It's all in the file.' He tapped the file in front of him with a gnarled index finger. 'I want you to go down to the New York field office. Speak with the agents on the ground. Then pay Hockey a visit in prison. Get a feel for things first off.'

'I will, sir.' She put her pen into her suit jacket pocket, flipped the pad closed.

He slid the file over to her. 'Apart from Hockey's previous pre-sentence reports and record, there are photos taken from the DVD. You'll report to me on this one and I'll report to the floor above,' he said.

'And my team?'

'There isn't one. This is special investigation authorized by Deputy Director Johnson. You'll work alone.'

'I'm not sure I understand, sir.'

'There's no dead body. No remains of one. We need to know if there's a trail. Your other duties have been reallocated. You have three months to come up with answers. If you don't find any, you'll resume your normal duties.'

She pinched her brow with her thumb and forefinger, unsure how she felt about that.

He looked towards the windows, frowning, and when he turned back, he looked sorry for her. 'Just to warn you, Agent Romero, the photos are tough viewing.'

'Don't worry, sir.'

'I mean… the toughest.' He breathed out and scratched his forehead. 'I told a rookie once that although older agents sometimes appeared cynical to the bone, no one got used to seeing dead bodies, despite the black humour. And if they did, it was probably time to do something different, like become a plumber.' He nodded, as if to himself. 'This one's *weird*. That's all I'm trying to say.'

Carla thought that he didn't deserve his tough reputation.

*

In the HQ's subterranean parking lot, Carla peeled a banana, a late breakfast, as she sat in her dark blue SUV. She owned the vehicle, although she was compensated for mileage and wear and tear. It had been fitted with standard Bureau accessories: an electronic siren, a secure radio and emergency lights. It was a 150 mile drive to the field office, one that would take her the best part of four hours. She set the sat nav for 26 Federal Plaza, NYC, between Broadway and Lafayette Street, before looking down at the file in her lap. The name *Jonathan Lincoln Hockey* was typed on a white sticker in the right-hand corner. Thinking the sixteenth president's immortal soul wouldn't care for that, she opened the file.

A minute later, having viewed all the photographs taken from the DVD, she bent over, almost gagging, her hand grasping the open door. She sat upright, composed herself as best she could, and wiped the traces of salvia from her mouth with a scented tissue. The photographs were unlike anything she'd seen, and she'd seen plenty. Following the images of relative calm, there'd been a heart-rending close-up of the victim's tears. The female had been attacked then, the level of violence both sadistic and controlled; it was as if she'd been sacrificed. But sacrificed to what, or why, she had no clue. She'd figured the Asian-looking girl had been no more than eighteen years old.

'Sweet Jesus,' she said.

She knew now why Hester had been kind to her.

CHAPTER EIGHT

Manhattan, the next day.

Gabriel walked across the pink paving slabs of the little plaza. The confluence of the Hudson and East rivers in New York Harbor added a brackishness to the warm air that was otherwise dominated by the scent of Russian sage in concrete planters. His office was on the eighth floor of a pristine office building and the morning sunlight glinted off the burnished copper cladding and emerald plate glass. It was near City Hall Park, which marked the outskirts of the financial district on the southern tip of the island.

He entered the mirrored lift and scrutinized his near-gaunt face, knowing he wouldn't be able to concentrate on anything but the Watson case. Usually, his clients were accused of embezzlement, money laundering, insurance fraud, insider trading, trademark infringement. The list got longer as technology got smarter. But none of them was a violent criminal like Johnny Hockey.

Connie O'Brien was sitting behind a semi-circular aspen desk, with the translucent glass front of Gabriel's office about three yards to her rear. She'd been with him since he qualified. A well-groomed woman in her late fifties, she always wore fashionably large glasses, her dyed blonde hair held up in what Gabriel viewed as a permanent bun. She dressed well and was attractive, with ample lips and a toned physique that made for a feline quality in movement.

'Hi, Gabriel,' she said. 'You've got five messages.'

'Just the five?' he said.

He'd walked into the reception area from the lift. He picked up a copy of the *New York Times* from the circular table, scanned the front page, feigning interest for a reason he failed to comprehend.

'Only telling you,' she said.

'I need coffee. My mouth tastes like cat litter.'

He glimpsed her pouting, without a smidgeon of sexuality. Something she did as a precursor to scolding him for not calling a client back quickly enough, or when she caught him pacing his office, berating himself.

'If you ask nicely,' she said.

'I need coffee, please,' he said, cracking a false smile.

She shook her head. 'And he teaches at Yale.'

He pushed open the glass door and walked into the sparingly-furnished office, which offered a view of other, larger office buildings. The only indication that this was a lawyer's office was a copy of the state statute book on his cherry wood desk. He looked fondly at the one item that wasn't functional, a piece of abstract art on the wall, a limited-edition print of Robert Delaunay's *Windows Open Simultaneously*. The original hung in the Tate Modern, London. He recalled that Connie had called it 'pretty and inoffensive'. He'd hated that, but had kept it to himself.

He took off his pigeon-grey suit jacket, placed it over the back of a swivel chair, and sat down. He removed his tie and picked up the pile of papers that Connie had printed off from an email attachment. It had been sent by the court-appointed federal public defender.

There was no circumstantial forensic evidence against Hockey, such as a hair or a strand of clothing. The DVD wasn't anywhere near direct evidence of guilt, although a half-decent federal prosecutor wouldn't find it hard to convince a jury that it was somehow credible. There was some flimsy hearsay, based on a statement by the Watson family, that claimed an associate of Hockey had said he'd done it for sure. But the case was in its infancy and with the mayor's involvement, he guessed it was still receiving special attention from the Civil Rights Division at the Department of Justice.

The public defender had written that Hockey was still denying all knowledge of the DVD, adding that its contents had been described as *disturbing*. Hockey was still maintaining his innocence in terms of the murders, too. Gabriel hadn't seen the DVD yet but knew he must. He'd already decided that Jed Watson wasn't the perpetrator of the crimes he imagined he'd find there. His kind didn't go in for the expression of their perversion in real life, or even via the all-but-inaccessible depths of the Internet. Email and credit card payments could be traced. The type of person who bought DVDs like the one obliquely described, didn't risk anything coming back on them. They were strictly voyeurs, although without their patronage, there would be much less of such trade — virtually none. But there were always exceptions. Weren't there?

Besides the DVD, an insurance assessor had reported that several expensive antiques and ten pieces of high-end jewellery were missing from the Watsons' apartment, presumed stolen. Each item was small enough to be concealed in a pocket. The words *red herrings* came to Gabriel's mind, but he couldn't dismiss the possibility that the items represented the primary motive, at least at this stage of the investigation.

Hockey's previous convictions, and the summary of his juvenile pre-sentence and psychological reports, were depressing reading. Hockey's father had been a chronic alcoholic and died when his client was just twelve years old. His mother had taken to crystal meth, which she financed by street prostitution.

As a footnote, the public defender stated that Hockey's girlfriend, May, had been released from FBI custody without charge — for now, at least. She had a record, but it consisted of misdemeanours. There was nothing to indicate the level of violence used in the Watson murders. Besides, she had an incontestable alibi for the evening of the killings, which had already been verified by CCTV footage.

Pushing out the chair, he stood up, turned and peered out of the window. The sky was the colour of wet clay. A heavy shower had started, and the rain ran down the pane like a grieving mother's tears. He felt a sudden ambivalence about Jed Watson's death. But it failed to shock him, although he was determined not to allow the emotion to remain, not even in the most secret cavern of his heart.

He heard the office door open and Connie's footsteps on the carpet.

'Just put it on the desk, Connie. And thank you.'

'You OK, Gabriel?'

'I'm fine,' he said, lying.

He'd learned that the day which haunted a person the longest, began like any other. There was no harbinger, no sensory forewarning or physical omen of what was to come. Nothing out of the ordinary occurred in the minutes or seconds leading up to it. The ruinous event just happened.

CHAPTER NINE

FBI New York field office, the same day.

The female special agent-in-charge, or SAC, one of six at the field office who answered to the resident assistant director, was rangy, with a pasty complexion. The senior special agent with her was Hank Dawson. He was running the FBI investigation into the federal felonies thought to have been perpetrated by Johnny Hockey, and was the man Carla had driven nearly four hours to speak with.

'Take a seat, Agent Romero,' he said.

Hank was bull-shouldered, with short, corn-coloured hair and ruddy cheeks. His eyes were almost turquoise, and sepia at the corners, as if he hadn't slept much of late. She rejected the notion that he overindulged in alcohol. There was a rawness about him, an integrity.

'I'll leave you two to it,' the SAC said. 'Got a telecom in five. Good to meet you, Agent Romero.'

'You too, ma'am.'

The woman left.

The room was on the small side, but neat. They sat at a blow-moulded plastic desk. Carla thought she could smell a hint of disinfectant and wondered briefly if Hank's reaction to the photos from the DVD had been the same as her own. But now she thought that improbable, given his years of service. She noticed a framed photograph of him, and what she took for his smiling family outside a lakeside cabin, on the right-hand side of the desk. She saw him glancing at it, too.

'I have a four-year-old daughter, Monize,' she said.

He rubbed his right eye with a thick forefinger. 'That's nice.'

Thinking Hank wasn't the most sociable person she'd met, Carla said, 'So what do you think?'

'I think the chicken killed Mrs Watson.'

He told her that the autopsy report stated that she'd eaten chicken, probably before she went out. Carla knew that the stomach emptied its contents between four and six hours after a meal. Hank said the chicken had traces of salmonella. Mrs Watson always stayed out to about twenty-one hundred hours of a Tuesday night. But she came home early. Their housekeeper called in sick the morning after. She'd been interviewed, he added, and had run to the bathroom three times.

'So, the housekeeper and Mrs Watson ate the same meal?' Carla said.

Hank nodded. 'The chicken killed Mrs Watson because Mr Watson died around eighteen hundred hours. The killer would likely have been long gone three hours later. If she hadn't eaten it, I guess she'd be eating something else today.'

'You think she disturbed the murderer?'

'I do.'

Carla wondered if the murderer would've waited for her to come home anyway. But no one would know that unless the killer made a fulsome confession.

'Do you have anything else on Hockey?' she said.

'Apart from the DVD, just the tip-off that he was involved in the murders. But the DVD and a tip-off don't equal a conviction.'

'Still no forensics?' Carla asked.

'Not a thing.'

They discussed the case for twenty minutes or so. Hank filled her in on all the details of the arrest and search. He was present at Hockey's initial interview and told her what to expect. He said that the disappearance of the valuables from the Watsons' apartment meant they were either dealing with a targeted home invasion robbery that went too far, or a targeted double murder with benefits. He confirmed that none of the missing items had been recovered yet.

'We're working on the name of the informant,' he said, referring to the individual that had been instrumental in Hockey's arrest, the person who said he'd done it for sure. 'I'm hopeful that'll be a breakthrough.'

'Any clues as to who he is?' Carla asked.

'He is a she. A short brunette, with an eagle tattoo covering half her back.'

He handed Carla some photos, taken outside an upmarket Manhattan hotel. One she guessed the brunette couldn't afford to stay in. She was wearing a washed-out Guns n' Roses vest and part of the tattoo was visible across her upper back.

'We took it yesterday. Claims she's a girlfriend of a Hockey associate. A man that's prone to pillow talk. He told her Hockey killed the Watsons, and she figured it was payday.'

Carla leaned back, finding Hank a little dour. 'The reward?'

Hank nodded, biting his lower lip.

Carla knew the Watson family had put up a half million dollar reward for information leading to a conviction. It'd been publicised on the TV news. She now knew that because of the brunette's information, the Watson family had informed the FBI of Hockey's probable involvement and told them where he lived.

'But how's she getting paid, if the Watson family don't know her name?'

'I guess they *do* know her name. We reckon she had a meeting with them at the hotel to discuss terms. Not revealing her name until they're forced to, was clearly part of that deal.'

'Can't we demand it now?'

'We will, but we have to tread light.' He sucked in air. 'Politics. It may come down to a subpoena. The mayor's, well — ' He clenched his jaw, as if he was stopping himself from saying something inappropriate.

'And her boyfriend, the one who told her Hockey killed the Watsons?' she said.

'We don't know his name either yet. But we will.'

'Where's the brunette now?'

'We've put out a nationwide law enforcement blitz. But as we speak…' He held up his hands.

Hank said that after the meeting at the hotel, they'd apply to make the woman a material witness — once they had her name. That meant she could be arrested and detained on the grounds of securing her testimony, due to the importance of her evidence in respect of the criminal proceedings against Hockey.

Assuming a grand jury indicts him, Carla thought.

She screwed up her face. 'This is great.'

'You should know there were very likely two murderers.'

'How's that?'

'The gloved hand impressions on Mr Watson's neck were of a different size to ones we found on his wrists. But before you ask, there were no glove prints. They knew what they were doing.'

Carla knew that hands were rarely of a dissimilar size, but she was puzzled. 'I thought he was strangled with rope.'

'Guess one of the murderers wanted to make sure, or maybe they got a kick out of it. The autopsy also stated that he had a heart attack, but the rope killed him.'

'Could the brunette's boyfriend be the other killer?'

'Could be,' Hank said, coughing into his substantial fist.

'Thought she would get the reward without dropping him in it?'

'One thing is certain: she hasn't got it yet.'

'Because we're a long way from a conviction, right?' Carla said.

'That's right.'

Hank linked his fingers behind his head. He breathed out audibly through his nose, and Carla noticed a few dark hairs protruding from his nostrils.

'Remember, don't be fooled by Hockey. He looks like a moron, but he's smart.'

'Thank you for your time,' Carla said, getting up.

Remaining seated, Hank said, 'Here's the thing. Let's say Hockey *did* kill the Watsons. But what if it wasn't anything to do with anti-Semitism? What if he killed them just to get the DVD?'

Carla had first thought that was unlikely, given its content and the fact that Hockey didn't have a history of violent offences against women — as opposed to men — let alone murder. But the death of Mrs Watson had to be considered, and Hank had just added to her scepticism. In truth, she didn't have a clue what Hockey's motive was, other than payment for his abhorrent services if he was in fact responsible for the Watsons' deaths. She felt a dull ache behind her left eye as she processed the conflicting information.

The SAC opened the door and poked her small, immaculately groomed head in. 'Hank, I need you for a second.'

'We're done here, ma'am,' Carla said.

She walked down the short corridor to the secure lift. Hockey killed the Watsons to get the DVD. OK, I'll consider that a real possibility, she thought. But why, and did he know what was on it?

CHAPTER TEN

Brooklyn Heights, the same day.

Gabriel lived alone in a house he'd once shared with his former partner, Roxana Habeed. She was from Iran, which she called 'Persia'. Her family were Christians, former members of the Armenian Apostolic Church of Iran, and had escaped after the excesses of the 1979 revolution and the subsequent ruthless dogmatism of the Islamic jurists.

The Heights was a quiet neighbourhood of Brooklyn, the streets lined with sturdy rowhouses and ivy-clothed mansions, with million-dollar views across the East River to Lower Manhattan. Although he lectured at Yale, it was only twice a week, only an eighty-mile drive. Roxana had worked as a marketing executive for a medium-sized firm in Upper Manhattan, near Riverside Park. It had been a joint decision to be based in the borough and, given the location of his law practice, a short walk and subway ride away, it was still a good location.

The terraced property, constructed from Connecticut brownstone, had been built in 1892. The original floorboards had since been sanded down and were now pooled with hand-knotted rugs. Roxana had collected Iranian art and antiques. Powder-blue murals, engraved brass coffee pots, calligraphic panels and Islamic silver vases, which were displayed in glass cabinets. She'd said that what her family had gone through didn't detract from the beauty that the main religion of her country had created. The artworks and antiquity had been a reminder of her homeland, too. Gabriel had known that.

She'd written him a note, stating that everything was now his. When he'd felt able to check the contents of the house, he'd discovered that all she'd taken with her was a selection of clothes and her collection of French films on Blu-ray. It was as if she saw it as a temporary split, but it had happened more than a year ago.

Now he made himself black coffee in the pastel blue kitchen. Taking a sip of it, he looked out of the darkened windows. A moth fluttered about a streetlight below, its body incandescent. His thoughts began to torment him, as they often had of late. He put the mug down on the barn wood table and picked up a hardback book that lay there. A book of paintings by the post-impressionist, Paul Gaugin. He flicked through it. *The Market Gardens of Vaugirard*, 1879. *Four Breton Women*, 1886. *Te aa no areois (The Seed of the Areoi)*, 1892.

They gave him no solace tonight. His thoughts had rested on what was undoubtedly the cause of their split, the mystery of it — and the tragedy.

*

Eighteen months ago, Gabriel and his niece had held gloved hands in Central Park, and she'd swung her new bag, a pink one with a cartoon image of an emperor penguin on it.

The park was quiet, the pools of black ice a deterrent for all but the most fervent joggers and cyclists. The cold air smelled of roasting chestnuts, the few clouds were sinuous and milk-coloured. They walked along the mall, with its bronze statues of literary figures and snow-flecked elms, the leafless branches intermingling like frigid fingers.

He'd worn a pair of hiking boots and a scarlet rain jacket, she a padded ski jacket and knitted scarf. He heard her giggling as she blew with all her might, her breath forming thousands of tiny crystals. Dodging a reckless rollerblade enthusiast, they headed for the Bethesda Terrace, a split-level Romanesque folly made from New Brunswick sandstone. He was childless and took her out once every couple of months. They went to the movies, the zoo, a themed restaurant. He made her breakfast when she stayed over and drove her to school. They hummed along to the popular songs on the radio.

They stopped halfway down one of the terrace's two flights of granite steps and he pointed out the intricate carvings of birds and dogwood blossoms, told her they represented the four seasons. She let go of his hand and fingered the ears of a tawny owl, and he smiled down at her. Birds were her favourite animals, he knew. She was fifteen now. She'd been adopted by his sister and her husband when she was three, but remained a child in all but her body. Her vulnerability, a symptom of a development disorder, filled him with a deep sadness that he'd never been able to express. But his love for her was the closest he'd come to a sense of purity in his life.

Heading across the frosted grass next to the lake, she broke free again to pat a dog, a soot-coloured Yorkshire terrier. He sat down on a wooden bench and took out his smartphone to make a call. He checked his contacts and thumbed the client's number. He heard her laugh behind him, the dog yapping in a playful manner. The call became more involved than he'd intended and although he looked around a couple of times to check on her, he became engrossed for a few minutes.

He pressed the phone's red dot and allowed himself a smirk. The conversation had been productive, and he'd been promised another case from a city brokerage under investigation by the Securities and Exchange Commission. Repeat business was all-important.

Gabriel grabbed the front of his short hair when he realized she wasn't in sight. No dog, either. He called her name again and again, running about like a man avoiding bullets. Feeling nauseous, he rang 911, his breathy sentences high-pitched, his sense of guilt overpowering him.

She had gone.

CHAPTER ELEVEN

Berlin, 2015, ten hours later.

The sky was without a fleck of cloud, the wind light and sporadic. It was 7.12 am Berlin time, and the black kites had left their nests. The old man watched them circling above his terracotta-roofed villa in the district of Kladow, southern Spandau, one of Berlin's twelve boroughs. The villa was situated on the western edge of the city and was surrounded by a high, red-brick wall in a near-deserted position next to a lake. He knew the raptors liked to be close to water, and the little forest of poplar and birch trees on the southern bank made it a near perfect habitat for them.

The villa had an elaborate security system. The doors and windows were fitted with magnetized sensors and vibration detectors, the floors covered with portable pressure mats. Outside and inside the wall were invisible microwave beams that activated cellular warning receptors. He'd always felt protected here.

He stood still in the grassed back garden, a floppy suit with a mandarin collar on his insect-like frame. His bald head was half covered with liver spots, which gave it the appearance of tortoiseshell. He always wore thick, gold-rimmed glasses that enlarged his eyes. He spoke with no discernible accent and lacked any form of national trait. He liked to be an enigma.

Hearing faint footsteps behind him, he turned and saw César Vezzani walking towards him from the French windows. Vezzani, a phlegmatic Corsican, was about the same height as him, but had the kind of robust physique that made for a broad neck. His nose was misshapen, his hair shaved tight to his skull, and his eyes dark and penetrating like a shark's. He was wearing a brown suit and a pewter-coloured, open-necked shirt. Vezzani was the old man's cook, chauffeur, and sometime bodyguard. His companion in life, too.

Vezzani had served in the French Foreign Legion. The old man was rather proud of that. He knew Vezzani had had to change his nationality to that of another French-speaking country to comply with the declared identity rule. He'd never regretted it, he'd said, and had left a Sergent Chef, a senior sergeant. He still wore the Legion's exploding grenade emblem as a gold signet ring. Twelve years in the 2e Rep, the elite parachute regiment, changed a man, moulded him. Vezzani had both done and seen many things, including choosing to keep his mouth shut when a young officer had shot a suspected terrorist undergoing interrogation. The old man knew that Vezzani desired only to serve in an environment that lent itself to occasional bursts of controlled violence. He suspected that he always would.

Vezzani had informed him of the unfortunate events in the US: Hockey's incarceration, the seizure of the DVD by the FBI, and the betrayal of Hockey by his accomplice's girlfriend for a reward put up by the Watson family. It had troubled him. It still did.

He sensed Vezzani behind his shoulder now. 'What news?' he said, without turning around.

'Hockey's accomplice is called Billy Joe Anderson. The girlfriend's name is Charlene Rimes.'

The old man allowed himself a grin. 'They sound like country and western singers.'

'They do.'

'Walk with me,' he said, shuffling off.

They stopped at the far end of the well-tended lawn. The old man looked about, as if he'd suddenly forgotten where he was, or why. He mumbled something, as if he couldn't remember what he wanted to say. But he was lucid, and his memory was excellent. He was fond of play-acting when the mood took him. It was one of the ways he'd stayed alive so long, given the danger he'd faced in his past. Facing a potentially precarious future, why change now?

'Hockey could have picked better,' he said. 'He's a smart, able young man after all. You told me that, didn't you?'

Vezzani was silent.

The old man took a cotton handkerchief from his jacket pocket and dabbed the spittle that had dribbled from the side of his mouth. He knew that if the FBI apprehended the country and western singers first, Hockey would likely be sentenced to two consecutive life sentences. Besides, he didn't know what they knew. He had to find out.

'Can they be found?'

'It's possible,' Vezzani said.

'Find them for me. You know what they need to say. You know what needs to be done. Use the Russian woman.'

She reminded the old man of nineteenth century Comanche women. Their warriors had been fearless and cruel, but it had been the womenfolk who tortured their hostages, burning off the noses and other bodily extremities with red-hot pieces of wood and iron.

'What about Hockey?' Vezzani said.

The old man bit a sliver of skin from the cuticle of his thumb. He bent down and picked some grass from the edge of the lawn.

'He knows very little,' he said.

He tossed the grass into the air, as if he was checking the direction of the breeze, or lack of it.

'And we owe him,' he added.

The old man knew Vezzani had been incarnated in a Spanish prison in Andalucía for eight years. It was how he'd heard of the Russian woman. But he'd never asked him why he'd been imprisoned — and Vezzani hadn't told him. He knew too that the Corsican would have found it impossible to obtain a legitimate position to his liking. It was part of their bond, he liked to think. He was anxious not to give up on Hockey too easily. It could be interpreted as disloyalty.

Vezzani said, 'Hockey will find out about the contents of the DVD sooner or later.'

The old man cupped his hand to his ear and moved it back and forth, as if he was oscillating a seashell there.

'So, make up a story. He'll believe anything you tell him. Can we get him out of prison?'

Vezzani rocked on his heels. 'No. But when he's being transported, it might be possible.'

'You think of a way. You and the Russian woman.'

The old man scratched the back of his bald head.

'Sure,' Vezzani said.

'Meet up with her in the US in a week or two. Better to have him out of there. Better to be sure,' he said, wishing to ease Vezzani's obvious concerns.

Vezzani nodded.

The old man rubbed his hands together. 'Do you feel chilly?' he said.

Vezzani hesitated.

He said, 'No.'

'When you get to my age it's always chilly, I suppose.'

He decided he should go to what he called the ghost house, which from outside looked like a half-derelict structure amid a collection of shambolic outbuildings. He had to satisfy himself that his anonymity was assured, at least for the present.

He began examining his hands, as men do when they've attained a certain age. His were spidery and had protruding veins and deep wrinkles, reminiscent of fish scales.

How will it all end? he thought.

There was not a hint of fear. Fear was an emotion he'd learned to control and scoff at, years before. What he did know was that of the few activities he still enjoyed, killing with his hands would be the last to lose its allure, although he wore gloves for that now.

'I think we should plant some herbs here,' he said. 'Rosemary. The symbol of remembrance.'

Vezzani nodded again. This time soberly.

The old man was remembering the war, the ubiquity of violence let loose on the world. How *had* he survived it all? He didn't know, although at first he'd thrived amid the destruction and chaos, like a weed. Later, it had devastated him. He would gladly have died back then if it had meant those he loved had lived. He'd never questioned that.

CHAPTER TWELVE

Berlin, 1945, the same day.

The Waffen-SS man was a thick-necked section leader, with greased-down black hair. He worked out with boulders and hewn tree trunks, as he'd done since his youth on a Bavarian cattle farm. He unbolted one of the bunker's outer steel doors and stepped out onto the flagstone, his hands on the magazine and trigger handle of his standard-issue MP40 submachine gun, the brown leather strap slung over his right shoulder.

Lutz Richter followed close behind him, the Standartenführer single oak leaf collar patches and the twin pips on his Oberst shoulder straps marking him out. He shielded his pig-like eyes, unaccustomed as they were now to natural light.

They walked up the concrete steps at the opposite end of the bunker to where Pavel Romasko and his Red Army squad had entered, Richter's tiny eyelids blinking.

Three other SS men now exited, all wearing spring-design combat camouflage on their helmets and tunics, together with grey-green trousers. They carried bundles of documents in slatted boxes that contained written reports, detailing certain events which had occurred in the

occupied territories. Richter had been told to document everything —
a Nazi trait. But as dear to him as they were, he'd decided to burn the
papers if there was a chance of them getting into Soviet hands. He'd
never allow the secrets to be revealed to the Jewish Bolsheviks. Lives
were at stake. Precious lives.

Unlike Richter, the men were originally extermination camp guards
before they'd been drafted into a fighting unit, the Third SS Panzer
Division Totenkopf. Heading for what was left of the driveway, they
trudged through shallow puddles of blood and gas, bubbling like the
bowls of macabre hookah pipes in the heavy downfall.

The outside world shocked Richter. The constant if distant shellfire.
The tracer rounds like miniature meteorites falling from the sky. A
sky that was blackened now by the belching smoke, which had all but
hidden the jagged tops of what few buildings remained standing. A
city in ruins. A life in ruins.

He'd been ensconced in the bunker for the past three days. With
the fall of Berlin imminent, the second round of controlled explosions
that had taken place were meant to destroy at least half of it. The first,
smaller rigged ones had supposed to block off the corridors leading
from the front entrance. That hadn't worked either, and eight of his men
had died, some voluntarily, it had to be said. An SS captain had even
been cut off from what was now an escape route by falling masonry.
He sighed, guessing this hadn't been the only retreat to have taken
place throughout the Reich in the last days that had resulted in partial
demolitions and unintended loss of life.

But he was relieved that he'd ordered some of the bunker's contents
to be burned as well as buried. Just to be sure. And he'd been assured
that the most sensitive room had been reduced to rubble, that the
potentially damning evidence had been destroyed by flames. If it had

remained intact, it was sure to have been misunderstood, so outwardly gross were the items he'd reluctantly left there. They would have ensured his immediate arrest. His death by hanging, he believed. But it was all gone. Why worry?

Richter looked too old to be in uniform, let alone the SS, with an obvious pot belly. His grey hair was clipped close to his head, his ears fist-like. A wispy moustache exaggerated rather than detracted from his sagging mouth. He glanced down now at the tailored, earth-grey service tunic of the Allgemeine-SS, an essentially administrative branch that ran the main SS departments, including the concentration camps. Himmler, the Reichsführer-SS, had ordered black uniforms to be worn only by the panzer crews and the so-called Germanic-SS, Nordic collaborators employed to organize the rounding up of Jews in their own countries. But he missed the black. Himmler had said people felt sick when they saw it.

The tunic had been covered with a layer of fine dust like talcum powder, and was now becoming sodden. He wiped the huge rain-drops from his eyes. He squinted as their vinegar-like quality stung his eyeballs and the fine grains they contained became lodged under his eyelids. He took off his visor cap, brushed off the heavy wool and bullion cockade, and stared for a few moments at the imperial eagle, the Reichsadler, perched atop the swastika, the death's head beneath it. Militaristic emblems that he'd embraced with enthusiasm.

The fusty air in the bunker had been replaced by something pungent and disconcerting, a mixture of cordite fumes and countless immola-tions. The stench of both the destruction of the city and the people that had inhabited it, he knew. He watched the orange-tipped ashes rise above the glowing cinders beyond the bunker's crater-ridden garden. As they reached the mass of low-slung smoke, hovering like an airborne leviathan, they vanished forever. The symbolism was not lost on him.

They walked to the front of the bunker and Richter saw a German in uniform, lying beside a bomb crater some distance away. He took out his field binoculars. It was a dead teenage girl, with tendons and ligaments hanging like crimson tentacles from a stump where her leg had been. He sighed.

Taking heavy breaths, the SS men lowered the boxes onto either side of the driveway that now looked like a battered sluiceway, with a channel of muddy water running down it. Richter watched them occasionally scan the wide and wasted street for any signs of the enemy.

He scowled. They were on their own. No more men could be spared. He'd been told that few combatants survived. Only remnants of the Volkssturm, the Berlin militia, together with pockets of Hitler Youth, and two thousand Waffen-SS that were stationed around the Reich Chancellery. The last line of defence against hundreds of thousands of battle-hardened Red Army infantrymen. He feared the worst.

He turned to the section leader. 'The truck's late.'

'It will be here, colonel.'

A rifleman looked petrified, despite the words that had been spoken. He was puny in comparison to the well-built NCO, Richter too, with eyes like coals and the cruel mouth of a reptile.

A few minutes later, Richter heard a vehicle approaching. His men raised their Karabiner 98 kurz rifles and MP40s, straining to see if it was theirs.

'It's ours, colonel,' the section leader said, evidently relieved.

Richter saw the Waffen-SS Opel Blitz truck manoeuvre around the bend. It inched over the twisted gates and proceed up the pitted driveway towards them. A regulation camouflage design, it had a huge frontal engine grille, and two prominent headlamps atop the bulky wheel arches. The roofless truck was graceless, but Richter couldn't remember seeing anything more appealing. Red crosses had been painted over the SS insignia, and a hammer and sickle flag had been draped over the bonnet. They would proceed as far as possible, masquerading as a Red Army ambulance crew. If they were caught, they'd likely be shot on the spot, even though they still wore their own uniforms.

Richter watched his men shoulder their weapons. Two climbed up to the truck's bed as the engine revved. The other pair lifted the first box above the lowered tailgate. They edged it towards the outstretched arms, gasping. The box was secured with thick rope.

'Faster,' Richter said, rubbing his right hand up and down his thigh.

When all the boxes were on board, they were covered with a mouldy tarpaulin, and the SS men positioned themselves underneath it, in each of the four corners of the bed.

Richter had told them it would be a perilous journey, but he'd heard talk of a corridor that still existed to the west of the city. Maybe it was just a story. Maybe it was meant to foster hope among the would-be escapees. Who knew for sure?

He got in beside the driver, another SS section leader, with a thin nose and a severed earlobe, whose regulation goggles were fastened around his steel helmet. He wore a stinking greatcoat.

'Can we go, colonel?' the driver said.

'Yes, quick as you can.'

Richter had told them they would take their chances with the favoured British and Americans, like thousands of other soldiers and civilians that were escaping the capital, and that they should swap their uniforms for those of the Heer as soon as the opportunity presented itself.

He would use the papers in the boxes to prove those named only fought against armed partisans and military units, that they should be given safe passage to the west. He desired only to save them from the wrath of Stalin and his NKVD henchmen. But even if he managed to outmanoeuvre the enemy troops within Berlin's city limits, he knew that still left the Red Army's outer encirclement forces. The Soviets were everywhere, like flies in summer.

CHAPTER THIRTEEN

In a makeshift observation post in the remnants of a three storey, eighteenth century mansion across the brick-littered street from the bunker, Joseph Kazapov had watched the comings and goings with rising frustration and a supressed anger. But there was not a hint of panic. What use was panic? He knew panic could do nothing to ease the predicament someone found themselves in. The collective memories of a hundred old men could not match the sights he had seen in the last four years. A man was not meant to experience so much, and yet he believed he'd remained sane. But nothing surprised him. Nothing shocked him. Nothing brought about the hysteria of the hapless. The myriad hapless. The doomed.

The young NKVD lieutenant, along with three snipers and a signalman, all of whom were dressed in dark-green combat camouflage, had placed the bunker under surveillance three hours earlier. Until the arrival of the Red Army assault squad, nothing of significance had happened, apart from muffled explosions. But then the subterranean facility had erupted in a series of much larger explosions, and seconds later, a handful of SS had emerged.

Kazapov had decided not to act when he'd seen his fellow Soviets heading for the bunker's entrance. No one had thought to tell him what to do if Red Army soldiers had attempted to enter it. Besides, he'd had no way of communicating with them, despite the signalman. He'd seen that the squad had been without radio communication. It had been a good decision.

He'd been told to sit tight, to follow his previous strategy and avoid giving away their position, after his signalman had reported it. He'd already let many roaming Waffen-SS units filter by. Men from France, units of the fanatical Charlemagne Division, together with SS combat platoons from Belgium, the Netherlands and Norway, as well as native Germans. The dregs of a once massive and diverse army.

He'd been told too that if another hour had elapsed, a sufficient Soviet force would've been in place to storm the bunker. He was relieved that hadn't happened. The bunker would've been even more damaged in a full-on assault. As it was, he reckoned that detailed excavations could unravel almost anything, and he'd been promised that he would be the first to investigate its contents. Such a thing was a sign of trust, and he relished the task of searching it. Rumours were already circulating around the NKVD junior officers about its purpose.

A Waffen-SS NCO had been taken prisoner eleven hours before. He'd had certain papers on him that related to the bunker. They were signed by someone that Kazapov had heard of, and after checking his personal records, had been able to pinpoint. As a result, he'd requested the assignment, although he'd done so with a degree of enthusiasm that hadn't betrayed this fact. The chance of speaking to the man, an SS officer, had been enough to spur him on.

At his short briefing, he'd been informed by the NKVD officer who'd interrogated the SS NCO that the bunker was partly a field hospital, and a group of Soviet male soldiers had been taken there, although that hadn't been to administer morphine or liniments to their various non-life-threatening wounds. They'd been butchered. But it appeared that the SS officer who had signed the papers had just left the bunker, together with his subordinates. Kazapov knew he couldn't leave his post to pursue them. In Stalin's world, that could only end one way: face-down in a lime pit, with a bullet to the back of the neck.

He had to live, he told himself. Even more so now, perhaps.

Two years previously, after fighting in the Red Army, he'd volunteered to join a small, NKVD department that had been charged with overseeing the investigations into Nazi war crimes. His foreign language skills were tested — and his allegiance. He'd passed admirably. The department was seconded to the Soviet extraordinary state commission for ascertaining and investigating crimes perpetrated by the German–Fascist invaders and their accomplices. The commission had been established on the second of November 1942, with the Russian acronym ChGK. His decision to volunteer then had not been made randomly, either.

During his first assignment, the ChGK had gathered evidence — interviewing eye witnesses, collating documents, exhuming and identifying victims, interrogating prisoners — in respect of atrocities that had taken place in the Krasnodar Territory in southern Russia after the Germans had left in February 1943. The trials took place in the summer of that year. Seven thousand civilians, including Jews, members of the local communist party and suspected Russian partisans, had been murdered. Some had been shot and hung by the Gestapo, but the majority had been flung into the vans of the Einsatzgruppen, the SS paramilitary death squads, and poisoned by gas. Seven Russian collaborators had been convicted, and Kazapov had played his part. He'd watched them hang in a Krasnodar city square, in front of a cheering crowd. The fact that the NKVD had invented the vans as an instrument of death in 1936 had remained a state secret.

Kazapov was twenty-three years old, with thick hair the colour of jet, a chalky and unblemished complexion. There was something of the hyena about him. He was prone to move at a trot, tended to scowl, and his eyes were as dark as the mouth of a cave. His colouring had been inherited from his mother, and had been passed to his three younger sisters, too. His father had been a blue-eyed blond.

If only his sisters had had their father's hair and eyes, he often thought.

'Comrade lieutenant,' the lead sniper said.

Kazapov moved over to the sniper's position, the man's right eye fixed to an optical sight on his 7.62mm Mosin sniper rifle, the sight wrapped in an oily rag. He was a diligent soldier, Kazapov knew, a 25-year-old Siberian, his round cheeks the hue of herring bones. His forefinger never left the trigger guard.

'What is it?'

'Movement, comrade lieutenant. Some of our men are coming out of the bunker.'

Five minutes later, after the signalman had informed a major at the NVKD Divisional HQ of the appearance of what was left of the Red Army assault squad, Kazapov watched two military trucks pull up, and a dozen or more NKVD troops disembark. The remnants of the squad were led or carried via field stretchers onto the beds of the trucks and were driven away. The Soviet frontline had already advanced to the point of the bunker, despite the desperate defence of Berlin's every house, every room in a house, by its fated defenders.

The signalman called out to him.

'What is it?' Kazapov said.

'Major Volsky, comrade lieutenant.'

The major ordered Kazapov to apprehend the escaping SS, who'd been under constant observation by a reconnaissance unit, he said.

Kazapov's mother was from Georgia, like Joseph Stalin. Like Lavrentiy Beria, the head of the NKVD. But she'd married his father, a schoolteacher from Stalingrad, and had settled there. His father had died in August 1942, in the first few days of the Nazi offensive on the city, buried in rubble following a multiple Stuka attack. Kazapov had spent too many nights imagining his father's premature death. He'd seen him looking up in terror at the aircrafts' inverted gull wings. He'd seen him hold his head in his hands as he heard the Jericho-Trompete sirens, mounted on the gear legs, as they'd dive-bombed. The Stukas were the wailing heralds of Germany's lightening war. Blitzkrieg.

He'd vowed to kill as many Germans as he could from that day, and he'd kept that promise to himself. Now, he documented the acts of their many war criminals.

CHAPTER FOURTEEN

Outskirts of Berlin, the same day.

Kazapov had outlined his simple plan to the fourteen men now under his command, all hand-picked from an elite NKVD rifle division. They'd just disembarked from a commandeered German half-track APC. A few days ago, it had been hastily painted regulation green, with red stars prominent on the side panels. It was standard practice for all combatants to make use of their enemy's captured military vehicles and ordnance.

Now, Kazapov and his men approached a clearing in a pinewood, a few miles from the city centre. Through underwood and berry bushes, he could just about make out an area of grass, roughly 200 square feet in size. The sky was overcast, an oppressive, pewter grey. It was 6.15 pm. The sky above the city streets had appeared devoid of life, of even the smallest bird or flying insect. But it was different here, despite the grey. There were starlings and butterflies, a hovering sparrow hawk. Fresh tussocks of grass had sprouted, the air redolent. Even the rain had stopped.

The men of the rifle division were part of the military arm of the secret police, called tylova krysa, rear-guard rats, by the frontline troops. They'd beaten malingerers, shot deserters, and carried out mopping-up operations as the Red Army fought its way from deepest Mother Russia to Berlin. They were too enthusiastic in their treatment of the lesser mortals, as far as Kazapov was concerned, but they'd never disobey an order.

In the far corner of the clearing was a single-storey building. Kazapov used his field binoculars to get a better look. The building had been shelled. The windows were blown out and black fire damage all but covered the outer walls. A concrete, bloodstained walkway encircled it. In his mind, he translated the barely intact German sign hanging off the façade: Hitler Youth District Training Centre. Despite this, it would have been a relatively safe sight in war, if it hadn't been for the Waffen-SS military truck, making out to be a Soviet ambulance, parked a few yards away.

The NKVD Divisional HQ had radioed Kazapov again and Major Volsky, who was overseeing the bunker operation, had told him that a Soviet combat convoy, a detachment of a Shock Army, was coming in the opposite direction to the SS truck, about three miles away. Kazapov guessed now that the German officer that had escaped from the bunker had seen it and had decided to veer off and hide the boxes, although he didn't know what they contained. He suspected no one did. But he dared to hope for a breakthrough in respect of the atrocities he was investigating. One, in particular.

He breathed out, focusing now. He vowed that the old, overweight officer and his shameless bunch of SS killers were his for the taking.

'Remember, we need them alive,' Kazapov said to his men. 'If necessary, kill the SS men. But not the colonel. Don't kill the officer, under any circumstances.'

The Soviets had taken prisoners throughout the war, and the NKVD were used to missions with the sole purpose of capturing the enemy. It was part of their role, for military intelligence purposes. But his men weren't told why the German officer had to be captured alive. He reckoned they just thought he must be very important, or very bad, or both.

The Soviet survivors of the recent explosions in the bunker had already verified that Red Army soldiers had been mutilated within it. There was talk of a vat of incense, of discarded papers with a geometric design resembling a swastika. Before Kazapov left, he'd telephoned a man he knew in the ChGK, and had asked him to search the state commission's own records under the SS officer's name — just to be sure. He could barely contain his sense of anticipation.

Kazapov replaced his binoculars into their canvas case and unbuttoned his holster. He took out a TT-30 semi-automatic pistol, attached by a cord to his webbed belt. It was time to act.

*

By the time Kazapov and his NKVD troops had reached the edge of the clearing, an attempt had been made to camouflage the already disguised SS truck with branches and netting. But it was a half-hearted affair and they'd obviously given up part way through the exercise. Kazapov examined it. He saw the peppering of rounds and leaking fuel, two lacerated rear tyres and a buckled wheel. They'd been lucky to get this far, he thought, despite the red crosses and the draped Soviet flag.

About thirty feet from the truck, the five SS men were now throwing papers onto a fire, fuelled by scorched and broken furniture that Kazapov guessed they'd obtained from the Hitler Youth training centre a short while before. It was more of a little camping fire than a full-blown conflagration. They'd slung their Mauser bolt-action carbines and MP40 submachine guns over their shoulders, enabling them to destroy the documents relatively unhampered. But the aged SS colonel held a Walther pistol in his right hand and looked understandably apprehensive.

The fire was struggling to cope with what had become a deluge. Kazapov heard the officer scream at an SS man, whose straw-coloured hair peeked out beneath the rim of his camouflage helmet. The subordinate picked up a large jerry can and began flinging what Kazapov guessed was gas over the flames, increasing the fire's ferocity tenfold.

Kazapov decided they had to move fast. He extended his arms over his head and dropped them to shoulder height: deploy to the right and left.

NKVD intelligence stated that Hitler seemed to have aged almost twenty years in the past few months. Staring at the officer now, he felt the same accelerated deterioration may have afflicted him, though he was rotund rather than frail. Perhaps all of the perpetrators had aged prematurely, he thought. Perhaps their bodies hadn't been able to deal with the singular evil inside them. Perhaps it was bringing an early death upon them, like a cancer.

Two NKVD riflemen kneeled on the flat roof of the training centre, as ordered, and aimed their adapted SVT-40 rifles, fixed with optical sights, at the SS, who had their backs to them. A beefy NKVD man in his early twenties, with wild, joined-up eyebrows, began to sprint the short distance to the officer, his boots kicking up damp clods like a racehorse's hooves.

The other eleven, together with Kazapov, moved out and maintained a jagged line, their rifles and submachine guns raised. They shouted in German to the SS men, demanding they hold up their hands. The SS turned, looked startled. They glanced at one another, then raised their hands, almost as one. They seemed to be glad it was over. But now an ill-looking young man, his limbs lost in the folds of his grey uniform, jerked on his MP40, raising it to hip level.

A shot sounded, echoing repeatedly from the walls of the training centre, as if a volley had been discharged. Hooded crows flew from the trees, their calls, Kazapov thought, ancient and nightmarish. At the far edge of the clearing, a trio of spring rabbits bolted for their burrows. The other Germans stood as frozen as fence posts, even though Kazapov knew that for them, such deaths had been a daily, and sometimes a second-by-second, experience. He knew too that one of the snipers had taken the German out. A spray of blood had erupted from the young man's head and speckled the cheeks and greatcoat of the SS driver next to him. His legs had buckled, and his arms flailed briefly. He lay on the ground now, his feet at right angles, and his body going into spasms.

The SS officer, no longer confused and paralyzed, held his pistol to his temple. But he lunged forward to a box, scooped up what appeared to be last remaining documents and scattered them like confetti over the fire. Standing straight, he raised his pistol to his head again, his expression stoic. The heavy-set Russian got to him just in time, hitting him a little above the pelvic bone with a powerful shoulder barge. They both ended up flat on the grass, the officer breathing heavily. The Russian prized the Walther from his hand and yanked him to his feet. Kazapov noticed that he hadn't put up any resistance, and now looked dazed.

He ordered his men to disarm the remaining Germans.

He walked over to where the young SS man had been felled. Looking down at the corpse, Kazapov saw the entry wound was a black and crimson gash to the side of the head, rather than the sphere the size of a three-kopeck coin that spoke of a clean shot. Fragments of the shattered cranium were showing, jagged like a cat's teeth. The expression was at once perplexed and terrified, as if a god he had forsaken had revealed the measure of his sins to him at the point of his premature death.

Kazapov knew such an impulsive act could have sparked a full-scale bloodletting, and he turned and congratulated the men of the rifle division for their restraint and discipline.

Wiping the stress-induced sweat from his gaunt face, he allowed himself the faintest of smiles now, despite everything. Apart from one death, they'd completed their mission, even if the all the papers had apparently been burned. He was going to the bunker. He would have it searched, brick by broken brick, if necessary. The previous recognition of the SS officer's name had given him a kernel of hope that he may find evidence there of the war crime that haunted him at night, like some crowing succubus.

Then he would orchestrate a session with the SS officer, assuming some heavy-handed NKVD interrogator didn't brain damage the man first. That was something he didn't want to dwell on. The potential brain damage didn't concern him, just the timing of it.

CHAPTER FIFTEEN

Kazapov had ordered the SS colonel, who said his name was Lutz Richter, to be separated from his men. They'd been put into the back of a Mechanized Corps truck that had arrived within ten minutes of their surrender and were now on their way to an improvised NKVD interrogation prison, twenty-five miles east of Berlin — although they didn't know that, yet.

Kazapov led Richter to the side of the road, just as the rear of the convoy heading for the streets around the Brandenburg Gate was passing by. Unlike the elite troops at the front, who rode on standard trucks, the sides of T-34 tanks and artillery tractors, the new recruits at the rear were sitting in filthy carts, pulled by sullen horses.

The animals were not at all an odd sight in the war, Kazapov knew. The Germans had used almost a million in the conflict at any one time. There'd been the horse-drawn supply trains, which had utilized pneumatic tyres on the carts and wagons. The non-mechanized infantry divisions had been dependant on horses, particularly on the Eastern Front. His homeland had mile upon mile of grasslands served only by a crude road network that required horses as a means of effective transport. The Nazis had known this, too. Apart from the horses' usefulness in logistics, there'd been the regular Wehrmacht Heer and the Waffen-SS cavalry, tens of thousands strong. There'd been the mounted Axis Allies, the Hungarians, the Italians, and the Romanians, together with the Russian Don Cossacks of the First SS Cossack Cavalry Division. There'd been the feared Kalmyks, the Buddhist horsemen of Europe.

His mouth became parched and his breath quickened. His neck felt clammy and his eyes blinked repeatedly, as if he'd been suddenly afflicted by a neurological disorder. The echo of the hooves was a dread memory.

The young Soviet soldiers recognized the man standing by the side of the road as an SS colonel, and they began spitting at him. They flicked cigarette butts at his face, called him a fascist beast, a child-murderer, a fucking criminal. Kazapov did his best to shield Richter with his arm, although he sympathized with their feelings.

Behind the last of the carts was a group of boys. Some looked as young as eleven years old. Their faces were covered in dirt, their eyes deadened, and they wore mangy clothes on their drooping and attenuated bodies. Like some of the infantrymen, their feet were wrapped in filthy layers of rags, tied with string and stuffed with straw. The boys were variously armed with long-barrelled revolvers, German officers' daggers, chipped pistols and rusted bayonets.

Kazapov saw Richter looking at them. 'They are orphans,' he explained, in good German. 'They feel safe with us. They clean our boots. Make us porridge.'

The last of the sun was trying to break through the grey sky, the odd beam of muted, golden light. Clumps of flowers, snowdrops and purple crocuses, their petals half closed, adorned the banks of the country road. But the air smelled of a sickening cocktail of spilled fuel, horse dung, body odour and burning tobacco.

'Where will you take me?' Richter said.

'Not I.'

'May I smoke?'

'Yes. But put it out when I say,' Kazapov said.

Richter nodded and opened a silver cigarette case, emblazoned with what Kazapov knew to be a rune. Ancient German writing. The German took out an unfiltered cigarette. Lit it with a matching lighter, inhaling deeply.

'Too late, they are here,' Kazapov said.

A black staff car had appeared from around the verge of the right-hand bend, the horses on the road rearing up as its horn blared. The vehicle was escorted by two motorcycle outriders, wearing the uniforms of NKVD non-commissioned officers, who flapped their arms at the soldiers to move aside.

'Well, I suppose it had to end,' Richter said, tossing the burning cigarette to the ground.

'End? Not for you.'

'Will I be tortured?' he asked as the staff car pulled up beside him.

Kazapov felt it inappropriate to answer.

'I see.'

'You see?' Kazapov wiped thrown-up mud from his sleeve. 'Just tell them everything they want to know.' He looked hard at the German. 'You are not a *real* SS colonel, are you?'

Richter's face was blank.

'No, not a real SS officer at all. What *are* you, then?'

Kazapov had no intention of informing him that he already knew who he was, at least for now.

Two NKVD officers got out of the back of the car, their expressions sternly pinched. They wore regulation mid-length leather jackets and jodhpurs. The blue crowns of their caps and the square black visors were pristine. The red enamel and brass cap badges, with their hammers and sickles, looked as if they'd been polished every hour. Nothing was said. Kazapov knew they weren't in a fighting unit and hadn't seen action, and that fact alone made him a little nervous, although he refused to show it.

'Do you believe in reincarnation?' Richter said.

Kazapov smirked. When they stick wooden splints under your finger-nails and knock out your teeth with a hammer, you will not say such things, he thought.

He heard Richter laugh raucously as he was ushered into the back of the car. The door was slammed hard behind him. The officer seemed unique, at least in his experience. He'd seen many people transported to interrogation centres, and although several had displayed remarkable courage, he'd never heard anyone laugh before.

Watching the car drive off, he felt not a smidgen of pity. All that had happened, all the horrors he had seen, could not be erased from his memory, even if he lived a thousand lifetimes.

CHAPTER SIXTEEN

Federal correctional complex, New York State, 2015, the next day.

Johnny Hockey had been told that he had a female visitor, even though it wasn't visiting time, and he wondered whom it might be. The two officers of the Federal Bureau of Prisons, or BOP, stood in his cell, wearing thin black ties, navy-blue trousers and short-sleeved white shirts, with radios clipped to their left shoulder straps. He watched them as he put on the regulation orange jumpsuit over his white T-shirt and boxer shorts and bent down to slip on a pair of canvas shoes, scowling as he did so.

'I hate this fucking jumpsuit,' he said.

One of the two officers, a black man with a pencil-line goatee, looked like an ex-football player that no longer bench-pressed.

'You know why you gotta wear it,' he said, his teeth glistening. 'Let's say a miracle happened and you escaped. How far you reckon you'd get, dressed as a carrot?'

The white guard, a younger man, with a red-wine birthmark on the left side of his neck, caressed his riot baton and smirked.

You got a point there, Hockey thought.

The black officer shackled him with metal cuffs and leg irons, augmented by a tight-fitting body chain. He'd been gentle, as far as Hockey was concerned, and they all waited patiently for the cell door to open via the remote-control station.

The fastened down bed was made from soldered metal. It had a waterproof mattress, as if Hockey was a child prone to bedwetting. The mirror was stainless steel, like the toilet pan, and cemented into the wall, the sparse furniture all immovable, moulded plastic. The space was little wider than his arm span, a little shorter than a family sedan. The overcooked food tasted of creosote, and the only view was of the opposite wing — and only when the heavy door was opened.

Beyond the prison buildings were the patrolling officers, with rott-weilers and Doberman pinschers. They walked between the parallel mesh fences that were linked into a CCTV system, which triggered the cameras when a perimeter alarm was generated. Next came the fifty-feet-high wall, with guard turrets and yards of concertina razor wire. And beyond the hub of concrete, five straight roads disappeared into a legion of white spruce trees, skeletal and forbidding things. There was no way out and he was stuck in his cell for twenty-three hours a day, the odour of his own body beginning to sicken him.

He decided his visitor had to be May, although he was curious as to how she'd managed to outwit the system. She wore two silver dog tags around her neck. One had her name on it, the other bore the words *one hundred percent Aryan blood*. She had a tattoo above her arse of a sonnenrad, a curved swastika, it was the insignia of the Fifth SS Panzer Division *Wiking,* she proudly said. It had been made up of foreign volunteers. The Nazi paraphernalia in their flat had been acquired by her, online, over a period of four years.

Now he remembered that she'd been to the movies with friends on the evening in question. The feds must know that too, he thought.

He worried that if things didn't go well, he might never touch May's skin again. He loved her in his own way, not least because she shared his beliefs and did things in bed that no one else he'd been with would even consider.

He worried too that he'd become a spider monkey, a con doing hard time. He worried about outbursts of frustrated violence with a shiv by the stress box, the payphone booths, when his guard was down. He worried about the possibility of back door parole: dying in prison. But he'd never do the Dutch: commit suicide, or dry snitch: talk loud enough about another's crimes so that the BOP officers could hear. He wouldn't exploit fish: first timers, or pumpkins: new inmates. He wouldn't have a June bug: a prisoner slave. He wouldn't whistle at a Kitty Kitty: a female officer. He'd just drink mud: coffee, and avoid the porcelain termites: the crazies that smashed up the communal bathrooms.

Hockey shuffled along the wing's concrete corridor, passing the kidnappers, drug kings, gang members and cyber terrorists. Some of them called out to him. A white supremacist shouted, 'Hey brother, keep the faith.' In prison, they were known as the brand, or the rock. The only time he'd interacted with them had been in the exercise yard, a large grass and asphalt area with basic facilities. They'd nodded to him when they'd registered his racist tattoos. One of them had chatted about his joining up, if he got a long sentence.

He relaxed when they were outside the main cell area.

He turned to the black officer. 'My girl's real pretty, isn't she?'

'I'd be surprised if she's your girl.'

'How's that?' Hockey said.

'She's FBI.'

Hockey just grinned.

'You know you don't have to talk to her without your lawyer, son,' the black officer said. 'They're gonna ask you about that first. Don't do what you don't want to. There's no pressure here.'

Hockey wondered why he was being so sympathetic, given the nature of his tattoos. But he guessed they were as common to him as rose tattoos on the outside, and that it didn't bother him anymore. Maybe it was because he knew he was a pre-trial detainee and shouldn't be here at all. He should be in the low-level satellite camp adjacent to the main facilities. Shouldn't he?

He inched through the blue cinder-block hallways, dotted with soft plastic signs highlighting forbidden inmate behaviour, such as refraining from putting hands into pockets. An impossibility for him. He wondered why the FBI were looking to talk to him again so soon after his initial interview. He'd made it clear to them that he didn't know a thing, and even if he had, he'd said he would open his veins and sink into a warm bath like an ancient Roman patrician rather than snitch. They'd looked at one another then, their faces betraying their bemusement. He knew too that everyone there had believed him.

The white officer began humming a tune that Hockey didn't recognize.

He thought now about the choices he'd made that had brought him to this point in his life. He thought about how he'd contacted the white supremacists online ten years ago, and how they'd encouraged him to read Sun Tzu, Niccolò Machiavelli, Friedrich Nietzsche and Miyamoto Musashi, to create the right mindset for the fight. Of how they'd encouraged him to study human anatomy to learn where to strike, and give up 'Molly', the man-made drug MDMA, to get healthy for the fight. They'd even encouraged him to disown his mother because she was a 'skank'. He'd swallowed it all. They'd become a family. They'd made a killer out of the shell he'd been.

They headed towards an office and he thought about his mother.

Once she'd gotten 'meth mouth', the loss of all her teeth, there was no way he could have helped her anyway. There was no way *anyone* could have helped her.

And who can help me now? he wondered.

There was only one man he could think of. A man he only communicated with via intermediaries. César Vezzani. The man who was close to a shadow man. The old man, whom he knew nothing about and guessed no one did but Vezzani. He'd only heard an odd nickname for him, and rumours. And those rumours had been as dark as the eyes of a crow.

CHAPTER SEVENTEEN

The same day.

Carla knew Hockey's father had died prematurely through alcohol abuse, and that his mother was a sex worker. She'd read his previous pre-sentence reports in detail. She'd asked permission to speak to him without an attorney present, as the public defender wasn't available for a couple of days, and she'd viewed the real-time video of him curling up his upper lip in a somewhat ridiculous display of histrionics before he'd said, 'I have nothing to hide.' She'd decided that that was enough to cover her, and she planned to play hardball.

The interview room was little bigger than a walk-in wardrobe. There were no windows, except for one in the door, which was criss-crossed with wire. Hockey and Carla sat on metal chairs at a metal table, all of which were bolted to the floor, and the harsh fluorescent tube lighting lent a bluish hue to their faces. The room smelled goatish and looked as if it hadn't been cleaned in days. Perched above them on the cream stucco wall were three CCTV cameras, covering every angle. The two BOP officers stood outside the door, chatting in half whispers. She'd introduced herself and had told Hockey the reason for her visit.

Licking her teeth now as if she was removing lipstick, Carla said,

'Is your mother still living the American dream, Mr Hockey?' She was goading him.

Hockey remained calm. He said, 'The American dream is a hollow lie peddled by politicians and business people to deprive the electorate of a spiritual and racial truth.' Then he cricked his neck as he jolted it from side to side before looking at her blankly.

It wasn't the answer she'd been expecting, despite what Hank Dawson had said about him. But she had no intention of being drawn into a metaphysical or political argument.

Leaning towards him, she said, 'I'm not interested in your philosophy. As I said, I care about the abomination on that DVD.'

'I don't know what you're talking about, as *I* said.'

His head movement hadn't changed, neither had his breathing pattern. He hadn't shuffled his feet, touched his mouth, or pointed to emphasize the point. She considered the idea that he *could* be telling the truth.

She said, 'Then why steal it?'

'Do you have DNA? Do you have anything at all to incriminate me?'

Carla was silent.

'No, you haven't. Otherwise you wouldn't be here,' he said, his eyes looking her up and down. 'Otherwise why would I have agreed to speak with you without my attorney present?'

Carla said, 'You're facing a double murder one. At the very best, by the time you get out, you won't be able tie your own shoelaces, let alone play footsie with your girl. She'll be long gone in a couple of months anyhow, assuming she's innocent. Now, why did you steal the DVD?'

'Is that the best you can do? For real?'

She sat back, nodding. 'OK. Here's how I see it. I think you're lying. I think you killed the Watsons and stole the DVD to order. But you don't like hurting little blonde girls, do you, Mr Hockey? I mean, killing a grown Jew quickly is one thing, but the prolonged torture of little blonde Aryan girls is something else, right?'

She was taking a risk by lying, figuring that he hadn't watched the DVD. But there was no other way of finding out if he didn't in fact know what was on it. If he *hadn't* watched it, he'd likely stolen it for someone else.

He shook his head. 'I don't hurt little girls. You know that, from my record.'

'So why take it?'

He sucked his teeth.

Ignoring him, she said, 'If you didn't take it, why was it at your place?'

'A lot of people come round my place. They leave all sorts of shit behind.'

'So, someone you know must have stolen it. Is that what you're saying now?'

He grinned.

'Who might that be?'

'Hillbilly Billy,' he said. 'But who is that?'

Carla leaned in again. 'Try harder.'

He strained on the shackles and scratched his inclined head, mocking her as he exaggerated a puzzled look. 'Let me think. Who's been over recently? I remember. Oprah Winfrey and Barack Obama. We had tea and cucumber sandwiches with the crusts cut off and all.'

'No, *you* stole it, which means you killed the Watsons, too.'

Hockey yawned. 'You're boring me. You fuck the way you talk?' He grinned. 'No, I reckon you're a screamer.'

Maintaining her composure, Carla said, 'You're just white trailer trash, after all. Like your girl.'

Hockey stayed silent for perhaps four seconds. Then he roared with such ferocity that his face reddened and his jaw seemed to dislocate. She shrunk back, smarting.

What the hell…, she thought.

The black officer opened the door, told Hockey to hush his mouth and asked if she was OK. She held up a hand, indicating she was, and looked hard at Hockey's face, seeing that it now looked as serene as a cast-iron Buddha head. The black officer left.

'Now that little outburst just then was frustration, I'll admit that much,' Hockey said. 'It is both vain and naïve to think that you can judge a person based on a few words spoken, as if the intricacy of their mind can be reduced to a rapid categorization, or worse, a type. Are you a conceited and shallow woman, Special Agent Romero? I'm giving you the opportunity to defend yourself before I judge you.'

In her mind's eye she saw the face of the young Asian woman who had been the subject of the DVD, the look of innocence and serenity before the horror. She'd interviewed enough felony offenders to know when someone was telling the truth, and although it was obvious that Hockey was convinced she was inept, she had what she'd come for. He *didn't* know what was on the DVD, unless he knew enough about human reactions to stifle the signs of lying. He'd not consciously prevented them either, she decided.

But now she considered that he hadn't answered one question directly, other than that he didn't know what was on the DVD, which meant that he didn't want to lie in her presence. He was smart. His appearance had belied that intelligence and she'd fallen for it. But she figured he had stolen it, or at least was a go-between.

She wouldn't waste any more time on him. He wouldn't tell her more, even if she used medieval thumbscrews on his balls; an idea which, she had to admit, had passed through her mind a few seconds before. As for his guilt or innocence over the murders, that was Hank Dawson's problem.

But where do I go from here? she wondered.

*

Gabriel had emptied the contents of his pockets onto the grey tray that Harry, the desk officer, had pushed over to him. He'd been told he'd have to wait, as Hockey was being interviewed by an FBI agent. He'd visited the complex quite often, due to his private practice, which included working on federal criminal appeals for his well-heeled clients.

'Hockey's mister popular today,' Harry said.

Harry was morbidly obese, his tawny-coloured hair shaved up at the sides and parted on his crown. He wore thin-framed glasses with circular lenses. There was something anachronistic about him, Gabriel always thought, as if he'd strolled out of a 1930s comedy movie.

'Seems so,' Gabriel said.

There was a payphone on the whitewashed wall, a watercooler and a vending machine against it. The walls were otherwise half-covered with various laminated notices that barked important prison visitor protocol at the viewer. Gabriel sat on one of four cheap chairs at a low-slung table, the top scattered with dog-eared magazines and a few yellowing and acceptable paperbacks.

He spent a few minutes reading an article about Yun Du-seo, a Korean painter of the Joseon period. There was a photograph of a *White Horse Under a Willow*. He considered the painting flawless, despite its faded state.

He heard footsteps and looked up. A full-figured woman had walked in, her hair so black it looked to be tinged with violet, like the tail feathers of a magpie. Her individual facial features appeared too generous, flawed even, but taken together those imperfections made for an uncommon beauty. She put her hand on something on the front desk that Harry had stood up to place there. Gabriel couldn't help staring at her.

She looked over at him. 'Do I know you?'

'FBI,' Harry said to Gabriel, nodding at Carla.

'Is the FBI agent interested in anyone in particular?' Gabriel said.

'I'd say that was confidential.'

'No offence, but since I'm here to see Jonathan Hockey and had to wait until you finished with him, I'd say that was conclusive, wouldn't you? Is it normal for the FBI to interview a detainee without an attorney present?'

She shook her head a fraction, betraying her disdain. 'He waived his right.'

'Have a good day,' Gabriel said.

He saw her look at him with a sense of pity and resentment.

'Oh, I will,' she replied.

She turned on her heels and took a few steps before turning back around. 'I recognize you. The Yale professor looking for a cheap sliver of fame. Why didn't you interrupt my interview with Hockey?'

Gabriel guessed she'd seen his interview on CNN, too. He nodded towards Harry. 'Harry got all official on me.'

'Not a good answer,' she said, and left.

Gabriel wasn't used to feeling wrong-footed. It didn't augur well. But it was a symptom of his subterfuge, he imagined.

He took a few minutes before he said he was ready to be escorted to the interview room.

CHAPTER EIGHTEEN

'Who the hell are you?' Hockey asked.

Gabriel eyed his new client. He had an almost shaven head and a mouth that verged on sloppy. His eyes were of robin's egg blue and unusually hooded, given his age, and an inch-long indentation was visible on his forehead. The result of a racist brawl with two East Coast Bloods when he'd been just sixteen, Gabriel had read.

He turned and called to the officers. The white guard stepped in.

'Is this necessary?' Gabriel said, pointing at the shackles.

The officer shrugged disinterestedly.

'Whatever,' Gabriel said, raising his hands.

'I asked you a question,' Hockey said, after the guard had shut the door.

Gabriel sat down opposite him and said, 'You don't watch TV?'

'Idiots watch TV.'

'Didn't the public defender tell you?'

Hockey made a face that said, I wouldn't have asked you if he did, idiot.

'My name is Gabriel Hall. I'm a lawyer. I'm helping the public defender with your case.'

'Helping how?'

'I'm doing this pro bono. For free.'

Hockey's eyes narrowed. 'I know what pro bono means. Why you doing this for free?'

'I'll be honest. I'm a criminal attorney. I get publicity.'

Hockey looked ambivalent. But he said, 'Where's your office?'

Odd question, Gabriel thought. 'Manhattan. I teach at Yale part-time.'

Hockey sniffed.

Gabriel proceeded to tell him that his role was to do research, some intelligent legwork, to help find witnesses and gather information. He got air time, and he was one of the best trial attorneys in the state, all modesty aside.

'Did you see that FBI agent?'

'I saw her,' Gabriel said.

'That ass could squash walnuts, am I right?'

Gabriel nodded, his mouth bunched.

'Yeah, you like her,' Hockey said. 'You work out?'

'Some,' Gabriel said.

'But not with heavy weights, huh?'

'I jog. I do a little hiking these days,' Gabriel said, stating a half truth.

His forearms resembled braided cable, the result of his ongoing mountaineering training that in the past had seen him on the summit of Annapurna I Main. But he'd learned through experience that the less a client knew about his personal life, the better. That rule was particularly important with the likes of Hockey.

Hockey grinned. 'So, you going to get me off?'

'I won't sugar-coat it, but I'll do my best.'

'Looks like Mrs Watson was in the wrong place at the wrong time,' Hockey said.

Gabriel clenched his jaw. 'What about the DVD that was found where you live?'

'That bitch told me about it. I don't watch such things. I despise people who do. They're sick, though. They have mental health issues. Don't they?'

Ignoring him, Gabriel continued. 'Do you have an alibi for the night of the murders?'

'I do. I was drinking with buddies in a loft in Queens.'

Hockey told him the details and Gabriel made a mental note to ask the public defender to file notice of an alibi defence, just in case he hadn't done so already.

He talked to Hockey for a further five minutes. He'd protested his innocence a little *too* often, as far as Gabriel was concerned. But he was intelligent, and not once had he deviated from his story.

'Do you believe me?'

'I do,' Gabriel said, nodding.

'Why?'

'None of the valuables that were taken from the Watsons' apartment were found in yours.'

'Good,' Hockey said, nodding.

'I have to ask you this. How did the DVD end up there?'

Hockey leaned in as close as his restraints allowed. 'Look, I hold things for people. Things I don't need to discuss. But no drugs and no filth. It was just a DVD, to me.'

'Weren't you curious?'

'Curious? I've been curious my whole life. But not about the contents of a DVD.'

'Who left the DVD at your place?'

Hockey's eyes narrowed. 'You're here to represent me, not the prosecution. Besides, you know a snitch's life isn't worth sweat in a place like this.'

Right, Gabriel thought. 'I don't believe you knew what was on the DVD.'

Hockey scratched his belly.

'They call you a neo-Nazi, Johnny. Are they right?'

'What do *you* think?'

'It doesn't matter what *I* think. Besides, it could be important, especially if things don't go to plan.'

Hockey lowered his head. 'Meaning?'

'Mitigation based on the adverse influences on your life.'

'You mean, the neo-Nazis are just hurting for a bunch of reasons, most to do with their own inability to deal with the inadequacy of their upbringing?' he said.

Finding the comment somewhat shrewd, Gabriel gestured with his chin towards the fading blue ink that was visible beneath the three-quarter-length sleeves of Hockey's jumpsuit. 'So, what about the SS tattoo and the Totenkopf?' he said, referring to the death's head.

'Some youngsters get a key to a Porsche and vacations in the Bahamas. Others get tattoos.'

Good answer, Gabriel thought. 'Maybe you should've chosen something less inflammatory.'

'Maybe you're just another Ivy League dick.'

Gabriel felt a modicum of aggression creep over him, which he did his best to mask with a grin.

Hockey smirked back. 'Now that was plain hypocritical of me, given what I just said to that FBI agent.'

'What do you mean by that?'

Hockey rolled his shoulders. 'Don't give it another thought.'

But Gabriel did. He felt as if he was being played.

Hockey craned his neck forward. 'You'll never know what drives me.' He cricked his neck. 'So, what now?'

Gabriel accepted that he had to leave it there, for now at least. 'You'll go before a federal magistrate for a preliminary hearing. If probable cause is made out, you'll most likely be kept in prison. You won't have to testify.'

'How can they find probable cause?'

'As you know now, the Watson family claim that an associate of yours told his girlfriend that you did it. She told them. They told the FBI. Potential probable cause.'

'That isn't probable cause. It's grade A bullshit.' Hockey shook his head.

Gabriel rubbed his palm over his opposite wrist. He said, 'It's called hearsay twice removed and on its own, you'd likely walk. But Jed Watson's print was on the DVD. It might be enough to have you bound over to a grand jury for a federal charge.' He saw hate in Hockey's eyes. 'Someone got a grudge against you, Johnny?'

'A grudge? Are you fucking shittin' me? As you pointed out, I got the death's head and twin sig runes of the SS tattooed on my body, and you're asking if *someone's got a grudge against me*?' He frowned. 'That doesn't fill me with confidence, Mr *Gabriel Hall I teach part-time at Yale.*'

Ignoring the contempt, Gabriel said, 'I don't mean someone who strongly opposes what they think you believe in. But a friend. An associate, as was proffered. The person who gave you the DVD could've done so purposely to frame you. *They* could've killed the Watsons.'

'Could've, yeah. But whoever that might be, they'd better have started running.'

'You part of an organized group?'

'That's it for now. You get to work on the preliminary hearing. We'll talk again.'

'Sure.' Gabriel stood up, straightened his shirtsleeves beneath his suit jacket by jerking on walnut cufflinks.

'Are you a homosexual?'

'No,' Gabriel said as he turned to leave. 'Not that it's any of your business.'

As Gabriel reached the door, Hockey spoke again.

'Wait. Could you give someone a message?'

Turning back around, Gabriel said, 'OK.'

'You'll find him at a bar called Club 88 this afternoon. It's in Queens. In Far Rockaway.'

'I know the area.'

'His name's Jim Saunders.'

'How will I know him?'

Hockey pointed towards his throat with the V of two of his fingers 'He has tarantulas tattooed on either side of his neck.'

Gabriel pursed his lips. 'What's the message?'

'Tell him I need to speak with my father.'

'I thought your father was dead, Johnny.'

'Tell him anyways.'

*

Johnny Hockey's lips cracked a sardonic grin when Gabriel had left the prison interview room. But it drained from his face now, when he thought about the abuse of little blonde Aryan girls. Why the hell did anyone want a DVD like *that*? He couldn't fathom it. Maybe it was one of the victim's parents, looking for revenge. Maybe the DVD could be useful in finding the filthy perpetrator. Maybe.

He'd stolen it, but he hadn't a clue what was on it.

The black officer came in, looking peaceful. He said, 'Forgetting the little outburst with the FBI agent, I figure you've earned an hour in the sun. You wanna work out?'

Hockey nodded.

'Then come on, son.'

In that moment, Hockey knew that the officer was trying to destress him in the hope that he wouldn't do something stupid, although he had no intention of doing such a thing.

'I ain't gonna lose it, if that's what you're thinking,' Hockey said.

The black officer nodded knowingly, like some ancient sage.

*

Three hours later, Carla, wearing aviator shades in her stationary SUV, watched Gabriel Hall walk into a bar called Club 88 in Far Rockaway, Queens. She'd seen his interview on a TV news channel, as she'd admitted to him. She'd called a lawyer friend and had gotten some rudimentary facts about him. After the incident at the federal prison, she'd decided to follow him. The alternative had been to return to the motel she'd checked into, and spend the early evening playing a trite video game on her tablet before driving back to DC in the morning.

Following Gabriel was an unorthodox move, but there was something about him that wasn't right. A hunch, no more than that. Besides, a man like Gabriel Hall didn't do pro bono, at least not for the likes of Johnny Hockey. She didn't buy the rumour that he craved the limelight, even though she'd accused him of it. He acted for rich creeps that shunned publicity. He taught their imperious sons and daughters at Yale, too.

Now the lawyer was visiting a beat-up backstreet bar frequented by the Nazi Lowriders, a 3,000-strong white supremacist motorcycle gang and sworn enemies of the Black Guerrilla Family. She'd first heard about them in a lecture given by a field agent in her rookie days. The 88 in Club 88, she knew, referred to the eighth letter of the alphabet, namely H, and so 88 was a reference to HH, which in the gang's circles was an acronym for Heil Hitler. Known as the Ride, the Lowriders specialized in extortion and prostitution. But there was no way they'd be involved in anything like the DVD. They weren't averse to killing, but not in the manner she'd seen in the photos at the FBI building.

A couple of minutes later, she watched Gabriel Hall emerge from a side exit. He walked around the Harley Davidson choppers parked in the alley, their polished chrome gleaming in the sunshine beyond the shadow. He said something to a huge tattooed man who was smoking outside, dressed in a leather jacket and a denim vest. The man stared at him before Hall walked off.

She decided to find out what was motivating him.

CHAPTER NINETEEN

Two days later, Gabriel left Centre Street in lower Manhattan and walked between two black metal security bollards. He sprinted up the broad granite steps of the Thurgood Marshall Federal Courthouse in Foley Square, a few blocks from the Brooklyn Bridge. Stopping at the top, he put his hand against one of the Corinthian columns of the portico, composing himself before entering the marble-floored main hall.

Hockey was there for his preliminary hearing, which had to take place no later than ten days after his initial appearance. Gabriel guessed that the US attorney's office was under pressure from the mayor and the Department of Justice to expedite the case, not least due to the level of media coverage. It was still regular news on the major networks.

A photo of Gabriel had been shown on a couple of occasions, with statements that he was a Yale professor, a title by which all members of the senior teaching staff were known. He'd thought the images made him look overly hollow-cheeked, his expression harried. He wasn't the only one that had been on TV. Hockey had been taken on a so-called perp walk after his detention hearing, handcuffed and in prison garb, to enable the press to shoot footage. It was a humiliating experience for those who were innocent, but was allowed in the hope of prompting witnesses to come forward.

In contrast to the wood-panelled courtrooms, with their fluted pilasters, the interview room was a dreary space, with a lingering odour of stale tobacco and sweat. Gabriel and Hockey were sitting on metal chairs at a scratch-ridden table. Hockey was dressed in a dark-green jumpsuit, his hands handcuffed in front of him, although the leg irons had been dispensed with. The public defender had gone for a leak. Two armed officers flanked the door outside. One was grey-haired and moustachioed, the other prematurely balding and chunky.

Seeing that Hockey appeared a little tense, Gabriel said, 'It'll be fine in there.'

'You think?' Hockey replied.

'Sure.'

Gabriel thought that Hockey was displaying a trait he'd seen in many tough guys before entering a courtroom. They might have shoved a broken bottle into someone's face a week before, but when faced with the prospect of a judge, most became as soft and pliable as dough. Maybe Hockey was no different. Maybe he was still being a chameleon. What difference does it make? he thought.

Hockey grinned, seemed to relax. 'So, you really think I'll beat this?'

'I do. But don't get your hopes up about today.'

Hockey's face betrayed a hint of misery.

'I'm just telling you the truth in case someone else doesn't.'

'The public defender?'

Gabriel nodded.

Hockey placed his shackled hands on the table, his expression serious. 'Did you give the message to Jim Saunders?'

'I did.'

Hockey nodded, his eyes calculating.

Then there was a knock at the door, it opened, and the middle-aged officer stuck his hairy face in. 'You're on,' he said.

'It was just a test,' Hockey said. 'But you knew that, didn't you?'

*

The sun was at four o'clock, a few grey pigeons pecking in the shade. A middle-aged cop dressed in a dark tie and sports jacket walked past Gabriel, the blue enamel badge visible on his belt. Gabriel thought he heard him say something under his breath, but shrugged it off.

Gabriel descended the court steps nimbly; the hearing had gone well enough, given the circumstances. The federal prosecutor, an assistant US attorney for the district, had exquisite red hair that had accentuated the pallor of her skin and if one looked past the porcelain veneers and the make-up applied with calligraphic precision, there'd been an undeniable, old-money assuredness. In contrast, the public defender was a bearded and somewhat dishevelled-looking political idealist named Victor Beal. He had a sibilant voice, a slight lisp such that he hissed a little after each sentence, and halfway through any that were particularly long. Beal had said the federal prosecutor was just biding her time until she got the opportunity to run for political office. The word 'office' had lasted a full two seconds.

But despite her obvious oratorical abilities, Jed Watson's print on the DVD remained the sole physical evidence. As for the hearsay from the girlfriend of a purported Hockey associate, Gabriel had prompted Beal to protest that it was inadmissible. He knew the Federal Rules of Criminal Procedure allowed hearsay at this stage of proceedings, although it hadn't been taken on-board by the magistrate judge, due to agreement that it was too flimsy, especially as the un-named woman was still at large. But the DVD was something else, and Beal had had to concede that he wasn't claiming it had been an illegal seizure, even though that too could've still been admitted at this stage of the proceedings.

Gabriel stopped to tie his shoelace. He noticed that the dark-haired federal agent, the one who had been at the prison the day he'd first interviewed Hockey, was also leaving the courthouse. She registered his presence at the bottom of the steps, and he watched her veer off to the right, as if she was embarrassed. He'd seen her at the back of the court for the duration.

He'd passed numerous scribbled notes to Beal, that had caught the prosecutor off balance. Hockey had smiled at him on several occasions and had even given him the thumbs up. If the magistrate judge hadn't been such a wily individual, he felt sure he would've gotten Hockey off a finding of probable cause. But, due to the fingerprint, he'd been bound over to a federal grand jury for indictment, which would take place in the next couple of weeks. The indictment, if successful, would state the exact charges, though neither he nor Hockey would be part of that process.

He watched the FBI agent walk across the street to the Metropolitan Correctional Center. In the shadow of the stones, he wondered what she made of him.

CHAPTER TWENTY

The ghost house, near Berlin, the same day.

The old man was sitting in the passenger seat of an eight-year-old station wagon as César Vezzani drove him through the dark lanes to a pine forest situated twenty-three miles east of Berlin. He was still troubled by the events in the US and had decided to visit the ghost house sooner rather than later.

The car was just one of the ways in which he didn't stand out. Something that was important to him. He gave acceptable donations to charities and the local Lutheran church, as if he was a model citizen. He paid his taxes in respect of his legitimate businesses. He'd invested in warehouses in Europe and the US for years and was now worth close to 35,000,000 euro. Not a fortune by the standards of the day, he knew, but enough not to have to worry about decent health care, or, well, anything at all really. At least, not about anything that money could buy.

He'd taken a nap earlier, after strolling around the villa's garden, the only exercise his worn-out body allowed. He'd woken up with a start, saliva dripping from his downturned mouth, as it did so often these days. Fleetingly, he'd seen his numerous female victims suspended, wisp-like, above him. He'd let out a prolonged gasp, the reaction any person would make if they were visited by a shimmering angel or benevolent alien. There'd been nothing distraught about it. These apparent spectral visitations had been happening more frequently, too.

The vehicle stopped outside an isolated and reinforced concrete structure, the size and shape of a pillbox. It was set in a half-acre clearing, the smattering of other buildings unused. Vezzani switched off the headlights. The old man kept his DVDs there, packed in a padlocked metal trunk beneath moveable slabs of granite, three feet down. It was as good a place as any, he'd decided. The contents of safety deposit boxes could be stolen, residences searched on court orders, and isolated farmland excavated without notice. Besides, the ghost house had a sophisticated security system, like the villa, centring on passive infrared beams that sent silent alerts to wireless receptors. The old man watched as Vezzani deactivated them remotely.

But one DVD had gone missing and he'd found out later that the Chechen — a pornographer, opiate addict and near alcoholic — had stolen it. It was his one lapse, a one-off weakness. Vezzani had vouched for the fellow ex-Legionnaire and the old man had allowed him to stay, at both the villa and a nearby farm that he owned, just for a few days. They'd all gotten drunk, and the Chechen had started to boast about his experiences in the Bosnian War in the early 1990s. Of how he'd made the Serbs pay for the atrocities they had visited upon his fellow Muslims, the rapes and tortures, the establishment of concentration camps, the enforced starvations.

These stories had resonated with the old man, and he'd given in to the Chechen's request for a viewing, after Vezzani had hinted at the DVDs' content. He had never told Vezzani why he periodically did the things he did, and Vezzani had never asked the old man. He'd just said that it was necessary. The Chechen had watched quietly, his mouth agape.

It was uncharacteristic for the old man to acquiesce in a viewing, vainglorious even, something his many years on the earth had taught him may prove to be a catalyst for something else, something unexpected and personally devastating. But it was done. Vezzani had been distraught, afterwards. The old man had patted him on the shoulder but said: 'They would have shot you in the neck for vouching for that Chechen thief, in the old days.'

Later, the Chechen had confessed on the telephone that he'd stolen the DVD, in the hope it wouldn't be missed. Vezzani had made it known among other veterans that the Chechen had done a terrible thing for which he would kill him. It was obvious the Chechen hadn't known the old man viewed the DVDs regularly. He was sorry. It was an unforgivable act after the hospitality he'd been shown, he'd added. He would compensate the old man.

The old man hadn't been able to track the Chechen down until a month ago, and then he'd had to do a deal, sparing the Chechen's life in exchange for the whereabouts of the DVD, and his assurance that it hadn't been copied. The Chechen had gone for it, had assured him that he hadn't copied it.

When questioned by the old man, he'd said that Watson's addiction had begun a few years ago, after his participation in peer-to-peer networks accessed via the dark web. Watson had paid for the DVD with an untraceable transfer into an offshore bank account via the Shenzhen Stock Exchange and a spurious trust fund. There wouldn't be any comeback. The old man had believed him and had said that someone had to die in his place, so it would be Jed Watson. He couldn't afford for the situation to be replicated.

The old man took out a portable DVD player from a briefcase, together with a set of keys. 'There's a Thermos in the glove compartment,' he said to Vezzani.

He got out and headed for the structure's rusted metal door, daubed with the graffiti that he'd ordered to be spray canned there. The clearing was dappled with moonlight, but he took out a slim torch to ensure he wouldn't trip on something in the grass. He knew that a fall at his age could debilitate him for months, if not precipitate something far worse.

*

An hour later he walked back to the car. He'd counted the DVDs. He'd selected a few randomly and had checked that none could incriminate him, even though he knew them by heart. They followed the same pattern. The stolen one was the same too, of course.

I am old, he thought. I shouldn't question what I already know to be true. But the fact that they were still all there had made the journey worthwhile, or so he convinced himself.

Although he didn't believe in spectres, he did believe in chain reactions. Watson had been the second link. If only he'd agreed to give it back to the Chechen, all this could have been avoided, he thought. He would have still had Watson killed, but it would have been a clean cut. The man had been addicted to it, he'd decided. It happened, he knew. Besides, Vezzani had said the US Securities Enforcement Division was snooping around, that Watson may have been involved in fraudulent acts. His apartment could be searched. The DVD could be found.

This was the real reason Hockey had killed Watson. The extraction of the DVD had meant to be obscured by the theft of the other expensive items, which had been dumped soon afterwards in the East River. That hadn't gone to plan, and Mrs Watson had been killed, the old man knew, by Hockey's associate, Billy Joe Anderson, in what Hockey had regarded to be a wanton act of unnecessary bloodletting, given that both he and Anderson had been unrecognizable. It was all so unfortunate.

The old man was aware that nothing could stop the forward motion of the chain reaction all the way to the villa. Nothing, that was, except the application of an external force. Newton's first law of motion.

He thought now about the Russian woman.

Vezzani had told him about the story he'd heard about her while he'd been in the Spanish prison. She'd worked on a wayward member of the Galician mafia for two days. She'd done things to him that Vezzani had never heard of before. But the crucial aspect of the story, as far as the old man had been concerned, had been that the Spaniard had confessed his sins within the first three hours under her hands. The old man had decided to use her services, which he required on the rare occasions he felt threatened or compromised, from then on. But there had been nothing to compare to the risk to his safety that he was experiencing now.

He didn't have to continue killing himself. Sometimes he considered giving it up. The scholar in him ached for a purely cerebral life. But it was *part* of him. Nothing compared to it. Nothing at all. He understood Watson's addiction. Besides, his enemies still needed to pay for what they had done to him. Didn't they?

Apart from the killings, Vezzani had been ordered to send all of the DVDs to the relatives of the dead girls after a period of three months following the old man's death. He had promised him that he'd be well taken care of. He didn't doubt that Vezzani would perform that last act. The old man would take his final revenge even as he was rotting in the earth.

'Meet the Russian woman sooner than we spoke about.'

'I will,' Vezzani said.

Encrypted messages would be sent. Electronic funds would be

transferred. That done, the Russian woman would come. The old man's favourite external force.

He wound down the window and looked out at the forest, just to be sure, a habit from days long gone. The slight breeze rippled through the darkened treetops. Nothing more. Satisfied, he inhaled the scent of the pines, his nostrils flaring. The smell of citrus orange mixed with tinges of vanilla and ammonia evoked memories, as it always did. He was overcome by a sense of regret so profound that he felt unable to move or speak.

The killing had to continue, to cleanse himself of guilt too.

This was how he justified his descent into depravity, his conjoining with the darkness.

CHAPTER TWENTY-ONE

Outskirts of Berlin, 1945, two days later.

They came for SS Colonel Lutz Richter early in the morning after his simple breakfast of black tea, a crust of rye bread, a small piece of cheese and half a hard biscuit. He had to admit it had been generous. But the tea had been tepid, the bread and biscuit stale. The cheese had been flecked with green mildew. Still, it had still been a sign, and one he'd taken to heart. Countless people were starving to death in Europe. He knew that a man's importance, especially a prisoner's, could be judged by the amount of food he had to eat each day. It had imbued him with a peculiar sense of optimism, given his predicament.

There were two guards. Stocky and silent. They did not touch him. He was thrown clothes to wear and dressed hastily, and one used a head gesture to prompt him to move. He walked to the cell door, a pair of rubber-soled but tattered slippers on his feet, the navy-blue jacket on his back streaked with paint and reeking of something that he thought was stale vomit.

He passed a door to a courtyard that had been left ajar, purposely so perhaps, halfway down a wooden staircase, and caught a glimpse of the splashes of blood on the far wall where a firing squad had been active at dawn. He heard a distant scream carried by the wind, reminding him of the cry of a mating vixen. He smelled faint wafts of fear-induced human waste. He'd had similar sensory experiences on countless occasions during the past decade. But now he was reduced to a luckless victim, rather than a trusted part of the ruling order.

They carried on down the stairs to what he knew would be an interrogation cell, and the muscles on his face twitched, and he couldn't stop wringing his hands. His optimism had dissipated. The building had been a Gestapo prison, part of the secret state police's network of terror throughout Germany and the occupied territories. Their experience of schadenfreude seemed to linger in the air like foul breath.

At the foot of the stairs there was a long corridor. They walked to the second door on the right. It was made of untreated oak, reinforced with a checked design of iron strips. One of the guards stood beside him, as the other knocked. He heard the harsh voice, and the guards stood either side of the door, and he knew they would remain there for the duration.

This would be his initial interrogation. He'd been held in the filthy, windowless cell for what had seemed like a couple of days already. He stroked his neck and felt the red lesions left by his second failed attempt at suicide, when he'd first been incarcerated at the interrogation centre. He was forced to sleep naked now. The NKVD had removed everything he could use to kill himself.

During the last days, he knew that suicide had become almost a national epidemic. It had even occurred in the bunker. He'd been deprived of that. He'd wanted to die. He'd considered suicide honourable compared to capture by the Jewish Bolsheviks. With the end of National Socialism, there'd been nothing to live for. The Third Reich had been his life. Like many of the leading Nazis, including Hitler and

Goebbels, he'd been a relatively unsuccessful individual before the rise of the party, despite his high level of intelligence. Overlooked, living on hope and disaffected. He'd been on the fringes of society. All that had changed — for a while.

He knew it was all over, yet he wished it wasn't. A guard had shouted to him that Hitler was dead. He hadn't believed it at first, but did now. He'd decided he wouldn't try to commit suicide again, even if he could. He wanted a life. He was already planning his way in the new order. He'd consoled himself by acknowledging that it was a natural reaction.

One of the guards reached over, pulled down on the handle and pushed the door open. Richter felt a sense of menace. He'd been told what the Russians were capable of. And who could blame them? They'd experienced four years of total war since Germany had breached the pact of non-aggression on the twenty-second of June 1941. Then the largest military action in history had been unleashed. Myriad atrocities had taken place in the Soviet Union, as the great force had moved towards Leningrad and Moscow, even by regular army units, many of the German soldiers being little more than boys. They'd acted with an encouraged viciousness that had been tempered on the Western Front. They'd been told that the Russians were subhuman. They were, weren't they? Himmler had said that all 200,000,000 of them should die on the battlefield. Person by person, they should be made to bleed to death. If only it had been so, he now thought.

He steadied himself as best he could and walked into the room.

A man was sitting at a wooden table on a wooden chair. An exceptionally tall, wiry NVKD soldier stood behind him, a couple of feet away. Richter thought the guard looked about nineteen. His skin was as white as oyster flesh, his eyes bright and cerulean. His arms dangled by his sides, and a large leather holster hung on his belt, holding, he guessed, a Nagant revolver. The room was about fifteen feet square. The walls were red brick, the lower ceiling bare stone. The light, coming from a low-voltage bulb, cast an eerie yellow glow.

The man sitting behind the desk gestured with the point of his chin to the empty seat opposite him. Richter walked over to it and sat down. The door closed behind him almost silently, and in that almost silence his thoughts screamed.

CHAPTER TWENTY-TWO

Outskirts of Berlin, the same day.

Joseph Kazapov's temporary NKVD barracks were a collection of three-storey granite buildings that had been built in 1865, according to a brass plaque. He was of insufficient rank to be billeted in a house. The high walls of the perimeter were topped with barbed wire and shards of glass and edged by an asphalt pathway. Fresh-faced Russian troops occupied the wooden guard towers and sentry boxes, the original barrier poles still intact.

He'd first entered the barracks a few days ago, and had thought he'd heard the echoes of the marching feet of the Waffen-SS regiment that had been garrisoned here. He'd looked out at the parade ground that was marked at ten-feet intervals with whitewashed boulders, and it had been empty. The sound had been the wind causing the drainpipes to reverberate.

His first minutes back, after his time on the frontline in the damp and cold of the make-do observation post, had been like returning to a haven. But still the three-inch scar on his left shoulder, which ended at the bottom of his neck, ached, even after he'd taken a painkiller and a drug that he'd found in the hospital block. The German assault troops had taken military-issue pills daily, he'd been told. Methamphetamine and a cocaine-based stimulant. Perhaps that was why they had fought so hard, so recklessly. Perhaps it allowed them to do the things they'd done, or had dulled their humanity enough not to care.

While fighting in the Red Army, he'd escaped unscathed from the battles of Rostov and the Sea of Azov. His scar came from a near-fatal blow from a combat knife, wielded by a Waffen-SS panzergrenadier in hand-to-hand fighting in the Battle of the Caucasus in the summer of 1942. He'd agreed with his comrades when they said, at the time, that if the unknown Soviet sniper hadn't blown the back of the grenadier's head off, he would've had his throat cut. He'd found out two months later that the sniper in question was a mother of three from Kiev named Marta Avdeyev. He'd written her a letter, thanking her for her bravery and the virtuousness of her skill, her devotion to the Motherland.

His office was a cramped, sparsely furnished room with small, lattice windows. Even during the day, he had to turn on his desk lamp to work. He knew that NKVD lieutenants were of little importance. Instantly replaceable, in fact. Ninety per cent of the Red Army's officer class had been murdered or removed during the purges in the 1930s, the Great Terror. After that, the instrument of the purges, the NKVD, had become the subject of a purge. It was insane. No one was safe. A person's continued existence seemed to be ruled by blind chance. But it was something he'd learned to accept.

His life before the war, although subject to the ever-present Stalinist oppression, had still been very different to the monotonous slog of those assigned to the urban factories, or the near servitude of back-breaking work on the rural collective farms. He was fortunate. He had a flair for languages and spoke fluent German and English. His Polish wasn't half bad either. His pushy mother had been eager for him to do well and he'd excelled at school. There'd even been talk of him going into politics, despite his disdain for it.

Sitting at his desk now, he took a shot of vodka from a hip flask and lit a cigarette. The SS officer that had occupied the office previously had owned a 78 rpm record player. It was still working, and he'd found a small collection of records in a wooden box, lying in a cabinet behind his swivel chair.

Taking one out, he put it on. Listened. It was Wagner. He knew that Hitler had said that if anyone wanted to understand National Socialist Germany they must understand Wagner. He'd been told that the last broadcast from Berlin radio was *Siegfried's Funeral March* from Wagner's *Götterdämmerung*. He hadn't doubted it.

The Soviet hierarchy also actively encouraged classical music as an important state mission. Up until a year ago, he'd never understood why that was, given that Stalin wasn't interested in culture other than of a revolutionary nature. But he'd heard a remarkable tale, passed by word of mouth while he'd been fighting in the Caucasus, and which he'd known instinctively hadn't been just another piece of propaganda dreamed up by the fanatical commissars, the political officers.

The most celebrated Russian composer of the time, Dmitri Shostakovich, had composed part of his seventh symphony, *The Leningrad*, amid the 900-day battle for the city. In August 1942, a live performance by the half-starved musicians of the Leningrad Radio Orchestra had been relayed on dozens of loudspeakers. It had revitalized both the army and the civilian population, spurring them on to their eventual victory.

Despite the inspirational aspects of the story, he'd felt morose when he'd first heard it. He still did. For he knew that even high art was nothing more than a tool of the state, as far as his crass masters were concerned.

The grand refrains and mythical leitmotifs of *Götterdämmerung* filled the room, it was an opera he knew, and he turned his head to look out of the window. Beyond the parade ground were grass verges and pools of saplings. There was still no movement on the square, save for a solitary grey squirrel scampering about. Despite the talk of political ambition, he knew his life was worth less than that dumb animal. If he made a mistake, just one, it would mean the end for him. But he was a driven man.

Following his advice, his mother and sisters had travelled south before the momentous assault on Stalingrad, with his father's blessing. He'd guessed that Stalin would not allow the army's lifeblood, the Baku oil fields of Azerbaijan on the south-western shores of the Caspian Sea, to be overrun. He'd encouraged them to attempt a return to his mother's homeland, Georgia, a Soviet republic, via the gap in the Greater Caucasus mountain range at Baku. He'd said that they should follow the Volga River as it flowed south, to go further south from there, down the north-western shores of the Caspian Sea in Kalmykia, a sparsely populated steppe, the home of the Buddhist horsemen. It had still been an autonomous Soviet republic, then. He knew that others had sought refuge there, including Jews

He'd joined the Red Army and then the NKVD because his mother had told him the Germans were beasts and had to be crushed. She'd been right, and he'd been wrong. His sisters and mother had never arrived back in her homeland of Georgia. He suspected they'd never left Kalmykia. To find them was his only purpose, now.

He still dared to hope that the German officer he had captured might in some way help to unravel the mystery of what had happened to his mother and sisters. Lighting another cigarette as soon as the first had burned down to his fingers, he felt the pain of not knowing their fate gnaw at him like the snow and ice of a Russian winter.

CHAPTER TWENTY-THREE

The Russian interrogator had told SS Colonel Lutz Richter that his name was Major Volsky. His NVKD officer's uniform was tight around his neck and revealed his bulging stomach. It was khaki green, with blue piping around the cuffs of his tunic and up the sides of his breeches. His feet were encased in black leather boots that reached above his calves.

Richter had first recognized the uniform at the roadside after the staff car had arrived to bring him here. He knew the NKVD was the notorious People's Commissariat for Internal Affairs, formed eleven years before. They were feared by everyone, including Red Army generals, since the military chain of command was bypassed. The NKVD hierarchy answered directly to its head, Lavrentiy Beria, a man suspected of raping and killing young women. A *sexual sadist*, his SS file had said.

Richter looked at the floor between his knees. He saw an earwig scuttling towards the wall. He noticed spots of dried blood there, and what appeared to be slivers of dead skin. He looked up. High above his head, a meat hook hung from an iron hoop that was bolted to the vaulted ceiling.

'Tell me, German. Why were you so eager to die?' Volsky sucked hard on an untipped cigarette, blew the smoke out of his hairy nostrils. 'Why was that?' He mimicked shooting himself in the head with his stubby thumb and forefinger. 'Nothing but dark oblivion then, German.'

Richter ignored him. He thought the man looked about forty, with receding grey-black hair. His teeth were nicotine-stained, and his breath smelled of tobacco and offal. He was tough-looking and, he imagined, uncouth, his eyes gleaming black onyx, his face pitted by what Richter guessed had been childhood smallpox.

Volsky offered Richter a cigarette and nodded, encouraging him to accept. Richter thought he looked like a seabird, regurgitating food for its young.

Subtlety isn't his strongest point, he thought. But he's no fool.

He took the cigarette and examined it. Put it between his thin lips. Volsky lit it for him with a silver lighter which he then returned to the pocket of his breeches.

It's my lighter, Richter thought.

'You speak good German,' he said.

'Ah, well, I've had a lot of you Germans to practise on.'

'I see.'

'Your name and rank?'

'SS Colonel Lutz Richter.' He inhaled deeply.

Opium, he thought. He inhaled again, as if savouring its intoxicating and addictive fumes. He was a scholar of some note. He'd adhered to the tenets of the Third Reich. But opium was his true love.

'Your regiment?'

'I was not assigned to a specific regiment. I undertook administrative tasks. Only administrative tasks. I am Allgemeine-SS.'

'Allgemeine-SS in the camps?'

'No,' Richter said, shaking his head. He was telling the truth.

'There's an old saying in my country, German. The bird that sings the sweetest song is the last to enter the woodman's pot.'

Richter smiled, grudgingly. Volsky banged his fist on the table. Richter flinched, saw the young guard standing behind Volsky's back smirk.

'The bunker, German. Tell me about the bunker.'

'It was just a bunker.'

Volsky whipped out his hand and caught Richter flush across the face, knocking the cigarette from his lips so that it rolled under the table. He had to force himself not to urinate as his breathing was reduced to hollow gasps.

'Wait, wait,' he said, putting up his hands.

'I see you, German, I see nothing more than a cockroach.'

'I understand,' Richter said, his cheek throbbing.

'For what purpose was the bunker used?'

Richter knew he had to give him something, however small, even at this early stage of the interrogation.

'I used it as a storage facility for certain items brought from the Caucasus and its environs, from the peoples there. Soil and grass samples. Farm machinery. Reports from local farmers and such like. I'm an academic. A bureaucrat. I was doing a research paper for the RSHA, the Reich Security Main Office.'

'SS?'

'Yes, and I have admitted I am an SS officer.'

'A racial project?'

Richter didn't know how to respond at first. He said, 'Not in the sense you are implying. In the broadest sense. Yes, you could say that.'

'You Nazis are obsessed with race. It infects you, like a plague,' Volsky sneered. He wiped what looked like stale snuff from his left nostril. 'We captured an NCO, a young SS man, a short time before we captured you. He was the one who first told us about the bunker.' He stopped, scratched his right nipple. 'He refused to speak at first. He said he would rather die than betray his honour.'

Richter nodded, although he was distinctly ruffled by what he'd just been told. He recited the Waffen-SS oath silently to embolden him: *my honour is called loyalty.*

'He was tortured to find where the bunker was. The exact map co-ordinates. He spoke, of course. For some reason the men who do this vital work like to shave off all body hair before they begin. But who am I to judge such things?' Volsky raised his hands.

Richter shifted his buttocks on the hard chair.

'Tell me about your racial project,' Volsky said.

'It was to ascertain if the Caucasus and its environs would be a fit place for the resettlement of German farmers.'

Blood and soil, Richter thought.

'Lebensraum,' he said. Living space.

'You actually thought you could defeat us and take our land.' Volsky smiled. 'Now we have yours.'

'Indeed.'

'As for race, just think of how many little Jewish communists your Aryan bitches will give birth to.'

Richter felt as if his head would explode, but he held himself in check and merely clenched his fists under the table. What else could he do?

'The SS man we captured said that men from the east were in the bunker.'

'From the east?'

'Yes. He said he heard screaming. He said other things.'

'It had a hospital wing. Of course, he heard screams. Besides, the young have vivid imaginations,' Richter said, wondering what else the NCO had said. Troubled by it.

'Maybe. You, on the other hand, are not young.'

'What?' Richter said.

'Your ears are too big, and your eye bags are too heavy. You look sixty years old.'

'I was a non-combatant.'

He watched Volsky nod.

'I told you. I was assigned specific administrative tasks.'

'We will find out, German. We always find out.'

Richter bowed his head, as if he hoped to placate the major by doing so.

'Why were dead Soviet soldiers in the bunker? We know about them, and we know the SS man wasn't lying. A Red Army assault squad entered it before you left. They saw things too.'

Richter didn't like the way the interrogation was going. He didn't know what the major knew and what he didn't know.

'I will tell you. May I have another cigarette?'

Volsky handed him one and lit it. Richter closed his eyes as he inhaled the smoke, thinking again of his beloved opium.

Volsky sighed, scratched his chin. 'Have you heard a man beg for his life?' He looked Richter up and down. 'Yes, of course you have. You will know most people die crying for their mama.'

Richter watched Volsky's eyes rise to the meat hook. He turned and grinned at the NKVD guard, who grinned back.

'I don't want to be tortured.'

Volsky cocked his head to one side. A look that said: well, tell me then.

'The men were caught in Berlin. Soviets, as you say. The Waffen-SS men in the bunker were sometime camp guards. They said they wanted a little revenge for the destruction of Berlin. Nothing more.'

He felt guilty about what he'd said. He lied, in part, too. But no one could say how they'd react in such circumstances. And the war was over. Wasn't it?

But the Waffen-SS oath came to him once more and he felt desolate.

I need opium, he thought.

CHAPTER TWENTY-FOUR

Three hours later.

Kazapov had been ordered by Major Volsky to take a platoon of 'suitable' NKVD men and extract what was left of the bunker's contents, just as he'd been promised. It was the one place he wanted to be, other than interrogating the German officer, Lutz Richter.

He'd been told that, during the initial interrogation, Richter had said that the bunker was now safe, in the sense that there were no other contingency plans. No booby traps, or mined corridors that could maim or kill. The NKVD had waited until the battle for Berlin was all but over, although as far as the war proper was concerned, the Germans had yet to surrender to the Allies. They were holding out in strength in isolated pockets of Europe, and northern Germany was still under their control. But Volsky had told Kazapov that enough time had elapsed. There were no discernible risks.

Apart from the NCOs, the twenty men Kazapov took with him were young NKVD fanatics, mostly from the Great Steppe, the huge featureless grassy plains of the Motherland. He'd heard them speak of their lives prior to the outbreak of the war. They were goatherds and crop farmers, and such like. Uneducated men who knew the significance of the seasons. They'd been given a weapon each and a semblance of power and now they'd do anything for the state, however extreme. They could be trusted, too.

The platoon also included the remnants of the squad that had stumbled upon the bunker the day that Richter and his four SS men had vacated it. Kazapov knew why. They'd seen things, and they would not be allowed to speak about them, beyond those who were now their comrades. Besides this, their presence was a practical one. They'd been here before. They could point the way. They knew where the corpses of the Red Army soldiers were.

The sergeant's name, he now knew, was Pavel Romasko. He had a youngster with him, whom he called the Kid. He'd asked about their visible injuries and the sergeant had told him that he'd thought he was a goner, but it was just concussion. He'd been given a shot of morphine in his thigh, and his head and left knee had been bandaged. After downing a quarter of a bottle of vodka, a hot meal of potatoes and beans, and having eighteen hours of sleep, he felt remarkably fine, he'd said.

Other than these conscripts and fewer regulars, a platoon of Poles had been assigned to assist with the clearance of the bunker. They were young men too, who'd fought with the Red Army all the way to the Reichstag and Reich Chancellery. They were exhausted and had been told that this was a chance to recuperate from battle, although Kazapov had decided to work them relentlessly. But he'd been ordered not to let them inside the bunker. Volsky had told him that these Polish mules could not be trusted to tell nobody of the things they might otherwise see. Such was the Soviet hierarchy's paranoia concerning the contents of the bunker, their paranoia regarding any contact with the West. Even regular male and female ex-POWs were being tortured by SMERSH, just in case their communist credentials had been damaged by their

German captors. Even heroes. Even the former Russian prisoners at Auschwitz. It was outrageous, Kazapov thought.

Stalin had ordered that no member of the armed forces should surrender, although many divisions had. Kazapov knew that Stalin had established a camp system, separate to the Gulag, for them. It was overseen by the GUPVL, another main administration within the NKVD. He guessed this was Stalin's punishment for those that had survived. It didn't seem to matter that over 3,000,000 had died in captivity. They were deemed traitors by Order Number 270.

He stood inside the doorway of one of the bunker's rooms now, the contents illuminated by torch beams. He saw it filled with a collapsed ceiling and dead bodies, including those of the tortured Soviet men. He also saw what Pavel Romasko had told him was a vat of incense, although it was barely visible. Kazapov had shuddered and fought to control his breathing when he'd been told about it. The last time he'd seen a vat of incense had been in Kalmykia, at the centre of an underground cave that was used as a Buddhist prayer room. One of several that had survived Stalin's frenzy of desecration.

Now, he could still smell the fragrance of incense, even above the stench, which was chokingly rank. The visible corpses were decomposing, and flies and insects moved over them like rippling blankets. He looked around at Pavel and the Kid, at the NKVD men. He knew the sight of the bodies didn't worry them. The savaged earth from Stalingrad to Berlin had been littered with dead people of all ages, and all manner of horrors had been visited upon them.

There was a jarring noise. Dust and small fragments from what was left of the lintel and jagged concrete just inside the door rained down upon them. Glancing back, he saw that the men looked nervous, suddenly unable to maintain their composed stance. A bullet in the stomach was a lingering death. But dying slowly underground, buried by rubble, was worse.

'Collect everything in the bunker,' he said. 'The bodies, furniture, documents. Everything. Cover your mouths with handkerchiefs and wear your gloves. And do it quickly. Ensure that the bodies can't be seen when you take them outside. That vat too.'

The Soviets went about stripping the bunker bare in a methodical manner. They moved in well-organized lines, back and forth to the Poles, who hauled the concealed contents onto numerous trucks parked in what was left of the bomb-damaged street outside. It had been cordoned off with barbed wire, a heavy machine gun at either end. Twenty NKVD troops had also been deployed to ensure it was inaccessible to any unauthorized individual, civilian or military.

CHAPTER TWENTY-FIVE

Two hours later, Pavel found a smouldering wooden crate, lying halfway out of a doorway, and in it a brass casket, about two feet square and smirked by fire. It was secured with an outsized padlock that bore an embossed image of the military eagle, its head turned to the right. He used his torch to make a cursory check of the room, seeing that it contained nothing but ashes and debris. But a brick wall had partially collapsed to the rear, half blocking off an archway that led, he guessed, to another room. He decided that he should take the casket back to the bunker's entrance and hand it to a Pole before investigating the other room.

But after carrying the casket for no more than ten seconds, his curiosity kicked in. That was a bad trait in war, he knew. He lowered the casket and used the butt of his weapon to dislodge the padlock, although it took four blows. Resting his weapon against the wall, he crouched down and lifted the lid the first couple of inches. He winced. There was a peculiar smell, like a mixture of ammonia and preservatives. The unmistakable odour of incense, too.

He pushed the lid against a shattered doorframe and pointed his torch. He saw what appeared to be the ends of scrolls wrapped in something like cowhide. Placing the torch next to his Shpagin, he rummaged about and picked out a metal cylinder. Nothing was written on it. He unscrewed the lid with ease; inside was a reel of film. He put the torch under his armpit and held a frame of the film up to the beam. Vaguely, he saw what he took for a Kazakh or an Uzbek, a man with similar facial features to those butchered thirty yards or so away.

'What the hell do you think you're doing, sergeant?'

Pavel looked to his side. The NKVD officer who'd introduced himself to the men as Lieutenant Kazapov was standing there, his expression furious.

'Put it back.'

Pavel obeyed and wiped the sweat from his forehead. He berated himself. In truth, he didn't care about the bunker. He didn't care about the rest of the war. He'd survived, hadn't he? The Kid had survived, and Doc had been taken to a field hospital and he'd been told that his wounds weren't life-threatening. He'd also been told that after this last task he could go home.

Now all that mattered to him were imagined embraces and imagined kisses. His little Darya and Marat, and his wife, Ludmila. What else was there?

*

Kazapov examined the brass casket, smeared with black smoke. The Red Army sergeant, Pavel Romasko, had stepped back from it after his rebuke. He used the sleeve of his khaki shirt to clean it up a little. It had the regular symbols of the Third Reich embossed on three of its sides. The swastika. The Reich eagle. The twin sig runes of the SS. But there was something else. Something he recognised too. The image looked roughly like a swastika, and was part of the elaborate, circular belt buckle worn by the Kalmücken-Kavallerie-Korps, the Kalmykian Volunteer Cavalry Corps. His breath became shallow and he felt a spasm in his neck.

The corps had been made up of what Kazapov regarded as 5,000 Kalmyk traitors from the surviving, original volunteers, when German Army Group A had retreated from the Caucasus at the end of 1942. The volunteers had originally fought alongside the Heer's Sixteenth Motorized Infantry Corps, despite being Soviet citizens, after the Germans had entered Elista, the capital of the autonomous Soviet republic of Kalmykia, in early August 1942.

He'd volunteered to go to Kalmykia with a ChGK war crimes investigation team in early 1943, after more atrocities had been reported, following the end of the occupation in December 1942. Another round of eyewitness testimonies and exhumations of mass graves had ensued. Another round of listing dead people's names in his logbook. Hundreds of Russian Jews had been murdered by Einsatzgruppe D and their collaborators. There hadn't been any sanctuary on the Kalmyk steppe, the land of the Buddhist horsemen. It had sickened him. But who would have believed the Germans would have reached the shores of the Caspian Sea by September 1942?

However, the real reason he'd joined the NKVD department and had gone to Kalmykia had had nothing to do with atrocities against loyal partisans and persecuted Jews. He'd heard no word from his mother and sisters since a week after they'd entered Kalmykia, and he'd hoped that he might find a trail he could follow in tandem with his official duties. How else would a young man from Stalingrad explain his presence there without being accused of desertion? How else could he have carried out investigative work without being accused of spying?

'Where did you find this?' Kazapov said.

'Poking out of a room down the corridor, comrade lieutenant. It was in the remains of a wooden crate. It was the only thing in it,' Pavel said. 'There'd been a fire in the room. Everything else was burned to ashes. The back wall has collapsed. I didn't go into the room beyond it.'

Kazapov struggled to contain himself. 'Another room?'

'Yes, comrade lieutenant.'

'Show me.'

Kazapov turned to an NKVD soldier who had just appeared in the corridor. 'Take that to my car. Guard it personally,' he said, nodding towards the brass casket.

'Yes, comrade lieutenant,' the soldier said. He had a sturdy frame, his eyebrows singed to little patches, and noticeably bad teeth.

Kazapov's sense of anticipation rose in his chest like a great wave breaking on a cliff's face, although he had no rational reason to believe either the contents of the casket or the room would be significant. There was just a feeling — the same feeling he'd had on several occasions throughout the war. When to duck. When to beat a prisoner and when to give him alcohol. When to speak and when to be silent. When to step to the right rather than the left.

Instinct.

CHAPTER TWENTY-SIX

He followed Pavel Romasko down the corridor, illuminated by the sergeant's torch. They passed several dead SS guards. Some of them had committed suicide by a bullet to their temples or through the roofs of their mouths, as was evident from the Walther PO8 pistols that lay next to their fetid bodies. But some were charred. The familiar smell of burned hair and flesh lingered in the air, a charcoal-like odour, mixed with sulphur and a hint of musky sweetness. Rats emerged from under the stained uniforms, their eyes sparkling. To Kazapov, they were the only living thing that had ultimately prospered from the war. Fat, confident and omnipresent.

Stepping over one of the corpses, he wondered what the revealed room might hold, and he felt dizzy for a second or two.

Further on, the sergeant's torch beam lit up a large space beyond a double doorway. There were galvanized pipes, smeared gurneys, industrial sinks of both porcelain and stainless steel, and operating tables. Translucent bags of now congealed blood were split open, and buckets of water overturned. Amid the dead that had been unsuccessfully operated upon, or who had died subsequently, surgical implements were strewn about: scalpels, hacksaws, a surgeon's shears. Littering the cracked tiled floor by the rear door were an assortment of disposable gloves and syringes, lengths of rubber tubing and hairnets.

The bunker's medical facility, Kazapov thought.

He'd been told by Major Volsky that the SS colonel told him the bunker contained a hospital wing. He hadn't lied about that, at least. It looked to him like a chaotic human abattoir, although it was all but intact. He had an inkling then that the Germans had left it that way, or perhaps the fire had been as indiscriminate in its destruction as the war had been in the lives of the innocents it had snuffed out.

Twenty seconds later, Kazapov walked beside Pavel Romasko through the ash-ridden room where he'd said he'd found the brass casket. The sergeant directed the beam of his torch towards the undamaged section of the bunker that had been revealed by the half-collapsed, red-brick inner wall, damaged by the conflagration. The bricks that were left in the wall were cracked and singed, the rendering like powdered charcoal.

Kazapov scrambled over the bricks and through the archway behind Pavel and, as the torch scanned about, he had to stop himself from gasping.

Together with a handful of investigators from the ChGK, Kazapov had been one of the first NKVD officers to enter Majdanek concentration camp in Poland, close to the Soviet border, in July 1944. It was the first major camp to be liberated. In other camps, he knew, the SS had destroyed the industrial structures of their Final Solution: the gas chambers and crematoria. They'd blown them up and had ordered the remaining inmates to burn the rotting bodies, the victims of typhus, shootings and starvation. But the extent of their vileness had been such that he'd known they couldn't hide it all. They'd left Majdanek relatively undamaged. The truth of what the Germans and their foreign supporters had done in such places had become well-known, even among the lowliest Red Army privates. It had fuelled their desire for revenge.

Looking around him, it was clear to Kazapov that another incident of Nazi panic had occurred in the bunker. The SS had attempted to destroy the passageways, hoping that the worst of sights would remain hidden. Fires had been started nearby. But in their haste, they too had only succeeded partially. He was sure of it now.

As Pavel's torch continued to do its work, Kazapov was rendered speechless. Each item seemed more grotesque than the last. Rosaries hung from hooks on the walls, with human teeth for beads. There were cups crafted from craniums and thigh bones carved in the form of trumpets, with mouthpieces and bells. Elaborately engraved bowls, fashioned from human skulls and containing large stones, lay in a triangular pile on the floor. Kazapov blinked erratically as the light continued to illuminate all manner of other similar horrors.

'Are they relics?' Pavel said. 'Like the bones and hair of the Christian saints. Are they real?'

Kazapov took out a slim torch of his own, guessing the sergeant just wanted to make sense of it all in his mind. But he knew what the musical instruments and receptacles carved from bone were. He knew too that they were real. He knew where they'd come from.

Now he focused, wondering briefly if the shadows cast by the torch beams were playing tricks. But it was not so. There, on a wooden shelf about three feet above the rubble-free floor, was a mummified woman sat upright, encased in a dome-shaped wicker basket. A small woman. From the east.

'Bring some NVKD men. Collect it all. Be careful. Don't spoil anything,' he said to Pavel.

'Yes, comrade lieutenant.'

'Wrap these items in blankets before you do. Put them in crates,' he said, nodding towards the macabre. 'Be sure the Poles don't see this.'

'Yes, comrade.'

'Treat it all with respect.'

'Yes, comrade,' Pavel said.

'And don't mention this to anyone else.'

'The fascists must have hated so much it drove them insane, comrade lieutenant. In Stalingrad, I saw cannibalism. Our men held prisoner in the kessel went mad with the cold and starvation. They ate the warm livers and kidneys of the dead. But I haven't seen anything to compare with *this*, lieutenant. Not even the dismembered in that room down there can compare,' Pavel said, referring to the severed corpses in room with the cauldron of incense. 'Nothing like this violation of the dead.'

But Kazapov had seen and heard of worse things during his time with the ChGK. He didn't say anything, though. What was the point?

'Shut up now and go,' he said.

When Pavel moved off, Kazapov thought the man might be expecting a rebuke, so he called out to him and he turned around obediently. Kazapov shone his own torch onto the wall next to the sergeant.

'Don't speak of such things.'

'Comrade?' Pavel said.

'Cannibalism. It's not what people want to hear. Do you understand me, sergeant?'

In the faint light, Kazapov saw a concerned frown pass over the NCO's face.

'Don't worry. I'll not repeat it. But if you speak of Stalingrad, you will say it was a glorious victory. Nothing less than that,' he said, keeping up the pretence of being a loyal Stalinist.

'Yes, comrade. Thank you, comrade,' Pavel said. 'At Stalingrad, the card-carrying communists led all of the assaults and all-out charges. The commissars brought us chocolate and mandarins, a kind word for us beleaguered soldiers in a trench for a month at a time. The temperature was below minus thirty degrees, comrade. We beat the army that had defeated the Poles and French within weeks. We beat them at Stalingrad. We beat them at Kursk.'

'Yes, yes,' Kazapov said. 'Go on now.'

Kazapov thought there was element of pretence about the sergeant, at least as far as his servility was concerned. He looked as hard and lethal as the bayonet that hung on his belt. He knew the NCO's manner had been born of self-preservation. Regular Red Army soldiers both mistrusted and hated the NKVD, and who could blame them? But it didn't bother him. This hidden room, this chamber, was unexpected.

Pavel Romasko left

And what was on that film I saw him looking at? The film, Kazapov thought. He'd forgotten about it. How could he have?

He let the sergeant slip from his thoughts.

He stepped now over a cranium filled with smooth stones, the narrow torch beam trained on the wicker basket, the mummified woman within. He reached out with his free hand and touched the plaited willow.

He knew that he would never understand the mind of a Kalmyk.

CHAPTER TWENTY-SEVEN

FBI HQ, 2015, the next day.

Sitting at her ash-grey desk, Carla used a mouse to navigate Yale University's website, still convinced that Gabriel Hall's relationship with Johnny Hockey was motivated by something beyond publicity hunting. It intrigued rather than disturbed her, but she was determined to discover the source of that motivation. She was fastidious by nature. She'd spent four months tracing a suspect whom she'd eventually identified thanks to a diamond-shaped mole under his left armpit. She'd tracked down a kidnap victim after a year by sifting through over 10,000 paper documents that were unsuitable for scanning into a computer search programme.

Now, she read with little interest the couple of paragraphs about Gabriel on the university's site and, after reverting to the Google search page, noticed that his name came up on thirty or so other sites. The majority were reports of white-collar criminal cases he'd been defending, and not one revealed his presence on a social or professional media site, which hardened her view that he wasn't representing Hockey to secure the publicity it was generating.

Refusing to wane, she checked the FBI records via SENTINEL,

the software case management system that digitalized investigation workflows.

Her search ended when she read of a suspected case of kidnapping, which had been passed to the NYPD due to lack of evidence. She bit her bottom lip, nodding. Gabriel Hall's niece had gone missing in Central Park eighteen months ago.

She decided to read the NYPD ongoing case notes in detail, knowing it was now one of thousands of missing persons' files.

But first, she rang Section Chief Hester. He was still in the building, even though it was almost 21.00 hours, and she said she needed to see him urgently.

*

Reclining at his desk in a black, high-backed chair, Hester twiddled a pencil above his substantial paunch. He wore cufflinks studded with rubies and behind his head was a framed photo of Georgetown University's waterfront on the Potomac River. Standing, Carla noticed the chocolate bar wrappers in his mesh wastepaper basket beneath the closed Venetian blinds and had to stop herself from lecturing him on the dangers of type 2 diabetes. Evidently, his weight issue was self-inflicted rather than inherited.

'Take a seat,' he said.

'Thank you.'

Carla sat down in front of his beech wood desk on the chair that she supposed he'd placed there purposely for her.

'Let's have it, agent.'

'A defence attorney called Gabriel Hall is acting pro bono on the Hockey case.'

'I know that. Half of New York knows that. Is there a problem?' Hester said, as if he'd be flabbergasted if there were.

'I'm not sure, sir.'

Hester placed the pencil down on his desk, arched both his fingers and his eyebrows. 'Is that it? I was about to go home to my long-suffering wife. She says she sees her pedicurist more often than me.'

She forced a closed-mouth smile. 'Hall's teenage niece went missing in Central Park eighteen months ago, sir. I suspect the NYPD have drawn a blank.'

'So, Gabriel Hall's niece went missing,' he said.

His voice was lethargic, and he looked as if he was about to yawn. Carla couldn't make out if he was overly tired or if he was mocking her. She decided reluctantly that it was a bit of both.

'Yes, sir.'

'And what's your point?' Hester said.

'I attended Hockey's preliminary hearing. Hall and the public defender were present. I saw Hall go into a bar in Queens straight afterward. It's a hangout for bikers and the Nazi Lowriders. Hall said something to a guy there and just walked off. I think he's running errands for Hockey, and Hall's no errand boy. Something's not right.'

He frowned. 'Now, tell me why you followed a New York defence attorney.'

Carla leaned forward, rubbed her forehead and said, 'He's bending over backward for this guy.'

'But that's his vocation,' Hester replied.

She sighed. Hester was clearly frustrated and so was she.

'He acts for people in Watson's social class, not pond life like Hockey. But, Hall has a motive to hate people like Watson and getting close to Hockey is — '

Cutting her off in mid-flow, Hester said, 'How do you know a sex criminal was responsible for his niece going missing?'

Carla nodded. 'The initial investigation was inconclusive, sure. But it cites abduction as a possibility.'

Hester pursed his lips. 'I think Hall is representing Hockey because he believes Hockey killed a man that liked to watch a young woman being murdered, as you say. But if he believes his niece was abducted by a sex criminal, that's just added motivation. That's it. You know your role here, and it has nothing to do with Gabriel Hall. You'll find another lead. Now, I want to go home and eat something with my wife, if that's alright with you, agent?'

She rubbed her thigh, as if straightening out a crease in her trousers. She didn't get up, as she knew she was expected to.

'I'd like to follow Hall, just for a couple of days,' she said.

'Absolutely not.'

'I think — '

He hushed her with a motion of his fleshy hand. 'No. I'm not interested. Focus. Find out who the girl was. Find an existing pattern or an emerging one. Find something that'll stop it, but do it without a federal judge lecturing us for harassing an attorney.'

She stood up. 'Yes, sir.'

As she left the office, she decided that she wouldn't follow Gabriel Hall. Hester, the hard-ass, was right. But she'd purposely left out one crucial detail concerning Hall's niece. She wanted to talk to Hall first, to clarify matters before reporting back to the section chief. Hester hadn't said she couldn't ask the lawyer to lunch.

CHAPTER TWENTY-EIGHT

Yale, the next day.

It was mid-morning and Gabriel poured himself a cup of coffee in a staffroom opposite the Sterling Law Building, the neo-Gothic design of which was based on the English Inns of Court. He sat on an armchair with fading green fabric and glanced at the only other person in the room. The frail male professor, with milky white irises and a forehead as lined as a limpet shell, had the intellect to serve on the Supreme Court, and would have done so, Gabriel knew, if he hadn't been so dismissive of politicians.

The professor was hunched over a table made of fine maple wood, surrounded by piles of papers. His obvious immersion in the minutiae of his work led Gabriel to think that even the fire alarm wouldn't disturb him. But out of respect, he took his smartphone from the pocket of his jeans, put it on vibrate mode and placed it on the arm of the chair.

He saw what he took for dog or cat hairs on the old man's dark-blue blazer, and squinted. He'd been allergic to animal hair, as well as certain foods, since childhood. He thought now about opening one of the windows, but decided he couldn't risk a gust of air spoiling the old man's work.

Gabriel spent half an hour reading a law journal before the mobile started to purr, moving from side to side like a kid's toy running out of battery life. He snatched it up, noting that it wasn't a number on his list of contacts.

He stood up and walked to the narrow, red-brick corridor outside and leaned up against it, in between the two oil portraits of alumni that hung there.

'Hello?'

'Is that Gabriel Hall?'

'Yes. Who's this?'

'My name is Special Agent Carla Romero. We spoke at the federal prison. I was there to see Jonathan Hockey.'

He clasped the back of his head, feeling a little off guard. 'You were at the courthouse, too.'

'Could we meet?'

He thought that might be reckless, but his curiosity kicked in. 'OK.'

'You know Little Italy?'

'I do,' he said, nodding to a colleague, a visiting researcher with blonde hair cut boyishly, as she walked by.

'There's a little bistro on Mulberry Street called Frank's Place,' she said. 'Midday tomorrow suit?'

'What's this about?'

'See you tomorrow,' Carla said.

'Wait,' Gabriel said. 'How did you get my number?'

'Your PA.'

'My PA wouldn't give out my number to just anyone,' he said, frowning.

'She didn't. But I asked her to call me back at the FBI building, so she knew I wasn't a nut job.'

She disconnected, and he arched his back against the wall, images forming involuntarily in his mind, images that he was powerless to reject.

*

A day after Hockey's arrest, Gabriel's smartphone had rung.

The ringtone was the theme tune from a well-known action-adventure movie. Roxana had put it on as a practical joke, hoping, he'd guessed, that it would embarrass him in some rarefied meeting at Yale. But he'd kept it on as a payback. It had infuriated her every time someone had rung him. Now, he just couldn't quite bring himself to change it.

'Hello?' he said.

'Gabriel, it's Abe.'

Abe Murray was an NYPD detective sergeant, and had what Gabriel knew to be an uncommon investigative mind. He was dogged and kind, too. He'd been involved in the investigation into the disappearance of Gabriel's niece after the FBI had passed the file onto the police. The man had worked fifteen-hour days on the case and had reported to Gabriel regularly. Sometimes, he just called to see how Gabriel was, which Gabriel guessed was the case today.

'Abe. It's good to hear from you. How are you?'

'I feel like shit most mornings.'

Gabriel smiled to himself. 'What can I do for you?'

'It's, well, hell Gabriel, I'm sorry to bring this up, but I thought you should know.'

'Know what, Abe?' Gabriel said, confused by the comment.

'The Watson case, you heard of it?'

Gabriel raised his eyebrows, finding the question a little peculiar. 'I'm not Amish, Abe.'

'No, you're not.'

He heard Abe sigh, wondered why the cop was hesitating.

'The douchebag they arrested had a DVD at his place. I'm told it shows a violent murder.'

'I'm listening,' Gabriel said, his gut tightening.

'An expert in such things informed me the victim had the facial features of a Kalmyk girl.'

Gabriel felt bilious and swallowed hard. 'Have you seen it?'

'No, Gabriel.'

'Can you get me a copy?' he said.

'The FBI have jurisdiction.'

'How come?'

'Mrs Watson was a Jew. The suspect is a neo-Nazi type. The victims were both tight with the mayor. You know how it is.'

'Can you get me a damn copy or not?'

Gabriel steadied himself. He sat down at the farmhouse table, putting his free hand to his forehead. He knew what he'd just asked of Abe was impossible. He blamed everyone involved for not finding his niece — because he still blamed himself for letting her out of his sight in Central Park. It haunted him.

'I'm sorry. I didn't mean to snap.'

'As far as I'm concerned, you got every right to.'

'Thanks, Abe. Thanks for calling.'

'No problem, Gabriel. Give my regards to Roxanna.'

'She left.'

'I'm sorry, Gabriel. Real sorry. If it's any consolation, it often happens after something like this.'

No, it's no consolation, Gabriel thought.

Once the IVF treatment had failed, he knew his sister had tried to adopt in the US for some time. It hadn't happened. She'd said she'd

153

read about adopting foreign orphans on the Internet. The most readily available were girls, from infants to six years of age. She'd heard about Americans going to the Republic of Kalmykia, a federal subject of the Russian Federation, to adopt Kalmyk babies and children.

Kalmykia was in the Caucasus, his sister had said, between the Black and Caspian seas to the west and east, and the Don River to the north and the Caucasus Mountains to the south. The nearest known Russian city was Volgograd, formerly named Stalingrad. Kalmykia was once part of the Great Silk Way, she'd said. She'd smiled, then. He'd disapproved of the way she seemed to wallow in the far-flung nature of the place.

His sister and her husband had gone to the capital, Elista, with 20,000 US dollars and had returned with his niece. Her name was Sangmu, a Tibetan name, which meant the kind-hearted one. Gabriel had been angered by that, and entirely sceptical of his sister's motives. But that had changed. For thirteen years, the orphan from Kalmykia, somewhere Gabriel had never heard of before, a child with learning difficulties, had become a focus, and she'd responded to it, becoming noticeably more confident and exceeding expectations. He'd grown to love her in a way that had made him realize how selfish his former life had been.

Sangmu's disability was characterized by impaired intellectual and social functioning, although she had no obvious physical signs. It manifested itself in a weak memory and a lack of social inhibitions. The easily preventable cause, Gabriel had learned, was severe iodine deficiency. His sister had established close links with the American Association on Intellectual and Development Disability, after the diagnosis of her daughter's condition. The child psychologists hadn't been able to decide if the trauma of Sangmu's previous personal circumstances had been exacerbated or lessened by her neurodevelopment disorder. But they'd advised that she should never leave home alone.

He'd known that the chances of the girl in the DVD being Sangmu were 10,000 to one. But a part of him hadn't been able to dismiss the possibility. The possibility too that it might lead to something else if in fact the victim was *not* his niece. In that moment, he'd set his mind to what he would do next: represent the alleged murderer named Johnny Hockey.

*

As Gabriel walked back into the staffroom, the aged professor was struggling to keep his eyes open. He sat back down in the armchair, his head slumped, mirroring the old man. Purposely in his mind, he picked up his three-year-old niece and spun her around, as if he was taking her on a personal carousel ride. She giggled, and her eyes sparkled like black gemstones. He spoke to her softly, naming various mundane objects: a gas oven, a colour TV, a light switch. Things that had been alien to her, and which he'd wanted to become familiar. She had left her previous life behind. She was safe. She was loved. She was a special child.

He had to know what had happened to her. To find her, if she was still alive. Nothing else mattered anymore.

CHAPTER TWENTY-NINE

Brussels, Belgium, the same day.

In 1989, Marc Dutroux, the 'Belgian Beast', was convicted of the rape of five girls. He was sentenced to thirteen years in prison, but only served three. Four years later, in August 1996, he was arrested again, and the police found two girls in a dungeon he'd built in the cellar of one of his houses. They'd been sexually abused, which had been filmed. Two other girls were found buried in the garden of another of his houses. Two further victims were found buried under concrete in a shed close to a third house owned by Dutroux.

Officials were accused of ignoring tip-offs — including letters from Dutroux's mother, who said he was imprisoning girls at his houses — and crucial information from a police informant. A popular investigative judge was dismissed from the case. Dutroux said that he'd been protected by well-connected accomplices, something that was never proved. Others made similar allegations, claiming that Dutroux was part of an organized paedophile network with powerful members.

On the twentieth of October 1996, the White March took place in Brussels. Three hundred thousand Belgians, outraged by what they believed to be at best incompetence, wore or carried something white as a symbol of hope, demanding reform in the police and judicial systems.

Hope was something that Robert Dubois believed in, although sometimes when he walked home late at night, he sensed the old buildings whisper to him, as if they wanted to reveal the horrors that had taken place inside. Sometimes on rainy mornings, after he'd just gotten out of bed, he pulled back the curtains and heard the faint screams of the victims rising from cracks in the pavement. Even if he imagined such things, he knew for sure that wood and stone had some form of memory.

He was forty-two years old, a federal detective chief inspector in Belgium's central directorate of the fight against serious and organized crime. He specialized in combating human trafficking, a crime that had burgeoned into a trade in flesh equalling that in heroin, in terms of both the profits it generated and the misery it caused. Almost twenty years ago, he'd helped arrest the Belgian Beast, and he'd never quite got over the experience.

Tonight, he walked through the Pentagon, the city centre, his six foot three, naturally athletic build and mass of black curly hair giving him a peculiarly animal intensity in movement. It was raining hard and nearing 9.00 pm, and Dubois was heading for an Ibis hotel just off the Grand Place, with its fifteenth century town hall and magnificent market square, illuminated by hundreds of lightbulbs. He had to meet a man who had flown in from Berlin. The man, Finkel, was a member of Grenzschutzgruppe 9 der Bundespolizei, or GSG 9, the special operations unit of the German federal police. They'd talked on the phone, met on occasion, and Dubois liked him.

He eased under the awning of a bar and lit a cigarette with a match. He smoked furiously for ten seconds or so before jerking the cigarette from his lips and throwing it into the rivulet in the gutter. He'd been trying to quit smoking for months and chastised himself each time he succumbed. Moving again, he passed by the shop fronts in the alleyway that led to the plaza and the hotel, thinking that he missed Carla Romero on nights such as these. Every night, if he was honest.

*

The receptionist was standing behind a padded counter of fake leather, a skinny young man with acne, the sleeves of his black suit jacket reaching almost down to his knuckles. The lobby was compact, with an empty bar off to the left. Finkel was sitting alone at a circular wooden table, the half-filled restaurant area behind him. He was in his early thirties, about five eight, bulky, with thinning blond hair, and was wearing jeans and a blue shirt that was damp around the collar. Robert Dubois knew him to be a family man, one with a quirky sense of humour after a few beers. He was familiar with what had gone on in Brussels and had said that it had sickened him. Finkel had two girls of his own.

They shook hands and, after Dubois took off his dripping jacket, he settled himself into a rattan wicker chair opposite Finkel.

'How are you, Robert?'

'Not bad. And Trudi and the kids?'

'They are well, thank you."

Finkel said he had some important information. He grabbed a handful of salted nuts from the ceramic dish on the table.

'It's about the DVD you mentioned,' he said.

Dubois nodded, his ebony eyes fixed.

Finkel rubbed his forehead, took out a photograph from his pocket and placed it on the table, face up.

'The Chechen,' he said.

The Chechen was known to them both, a pornographer of the worst kind. But he'd disappeared, and it was thought that he'd returned to Chechnya, or somewhere equally remote in the Russian Federation. Dubois hadn't seen an up-to-date photo of him for close to ten years. Now he had one in front of him.

Dubois picked up the photograph, looked at it before placing it back down and sliding it over to Finkel. A middle-aged man's face could change a lot in a decade and the Chechen seemed to have aged twenty years. He looked about sixty, with an unkempt beard and straggly, shoulder-length hair. He was wearing a short leather jacket and had a cigarette in his mouth, such that it revealed his little teeth.

They ordered coffee from a waitress who appeared from the bar area, the fat of her neck spilling over her white blouse. She left, and Finkel put his index finger in his mouth, appearing to excavate there for a piece of leftover peanut.

'The Chechen boasted to one of our deep cover officers about supplying a wealthy American with a DVD showing the murder of a young woman, said that he'd been paid well for it,' Finkel said.

'Did he say who?'

Finkel shook his head.

They discussed the meeting the undercover officer had with the Chechen, where it became apparent that his addiction to crack cocaine was a contributing factor in his unintended confession. Plus, the fact that the cop had been masquerading as a purveyor of snuff movies and the Chechen was looking to become a worldwide broker of that appalling merchandize.

The waitress returned, placed the white cups and saucers on the table, smiled and moved away. Finkel picked up a sachet of brown sugar, tapped it against the table, opened it and poured the contents into his cup before stirring it with a metal spoon.

'Anything else?' Dubois said.

In truth, he wasn't that impressed with the intel. He eased back in his chair, felt his body loosen, as it always did when he thought he'd get a lead but instead got nothing much at all.

Finkel took a slurp of coffee and looked at Dubois straight in the eyes. 'The Chechen said the source of the DVD was an old man who lived in Berlin. He said he was a serial killer but has never been convicted of a crime. Not even a speeding ticket.'

'Did he say anything else about the DVD?'

'No.'

'Where is the Chechen now?' Dubois said.

'He's gone to the US. We're leaving it there. At least I'm passing the intel onto you, Robert.'

Dubois stood up. 'Let's get a real drink.'

Finkel remained seated.

'The Chechen also said that the old man is known only by a nickname. One that might interest you, given the photos you sent me.' He slid the photo of the Chechen back across the table top to Dubois. 'You'll want this for your FBI friend.'

*

It was 3.07 am and Robert Dubois was stretched out on a taupe-coloured couch in his ample apartment in Place Sainctelette, close to the incongruous sandpits of Brussels Beach at the Quai des Péniches. During the summer months, the beach played host to ethnic food stalls and Stetson-wearing line dancers, to volleyball tournaments and folk singing. But instead of an ocean there were only the murky waters of the Willebroek Canal. The sand at Brussels Beach hid concrete, just as Dubois' federal police badge hid a near vigilante mindset where sex criminals were concerned. But he bent domestic rules rather than broke them, although he dispensed entirely with international protocol when it came to sharing intel, his meeting with Finkel being but one example. Carla was his equal in this, he knew.

He had become infatuated with Carla within days of meeting her. The infatuation lingered still and often perplexed him.

He'd never married. His home was characterized by minimalism and fine lines. The few pieces of furniture were pinewood. He didn't possess a microwave or TV. When he wasn't working, he liked to cook with fresh ingredients and listen to English rock music.

Dubois had spent twenty minutes going over all the good times he and Carla had enjoyed in their short relationship, before he'd wondered if the relationship she now had with the lawyer named Gabriel Hall was platonic. He'd approved of her reasons when she'd rung to inform him of this development.

Realizing that this was getting him nowhere, other than a maudlin state of mind, he decided to go to bed. He would ring her about the Chechen tomorrow.

CHAPTER THIRTY

Little Italy, the next day.

Frank's Place was on Mulberry Street, between Baxter and Mott, flanked by an Italian cheese shop and a pasta restaurant. The pavement outside was dotted with little round tables and dining chairs, outsized framed menus and elaborate advertising signs. In the shade afforded by the awning of a cigar shop, an old man was sitting on a stool, smoking and drinking coffee. Next to him was a wooden statue of a native American, looking more reminiscent of an Aztec, despite the fake Winchester rifle in its hand. Like the dated streetlights, it was painted in muted red, green and white, the ubiquitous colours of the Italian flag.

The TV above the optics in Frank's Place was an old-fashioned type, as opposed to a flat screen. It was fixed, somewhat precariously it appeared, onto the lime-green wall. A grainy episode of *Friends* was on, the actors as silent as stones. The bar proper had many of its original features, including a brass-plated foot rest and burnished wood-grain panels, with heavy carved feet. There was a laminated marble top, and a stone slab for carving lemons and other citrus fruits.

Gabriel and Carla were sitting in a booth by the window, the midday sun creating shimmering pools on the street and exposing a crimson mote in Carla's left eye. She sipped at a mineral water. Gabriel fiddled with a glass of orange juice, making the ice cubes clink against the thick glass tumbler. After a somewhat awkward introduction, she told him a little about her work and he listened attentively.

Now she said, 'I know you're assisting with Hockey's defence, but I'd like to discuss certain aspects of the case with you. If you're willing.'

He looked at her. Her head was ever so slightly to one side. She wore a dark-grey trouser suit, a russet blouse, minimal make-up and three white gold rings, none of which indicated that she was married.

'I'd like to know your general opinion, before I answer that,' he said.

He leaned back in his chair, brushed off his trousers, dislodging some undefined spots in the process.

She nodded. 'The female victim was likely kidnapped. The DVD is likely one of several. I don't believe Hockey knew what was on it. I don't know if he killed the Watsons. I investigate kidnappings. Female kidnappings. I don't believe that Hockey is a kidnapper, either. But he stole that DVD, I'm pretty sure of that now.'

He looked at her again and found himself momentarily lost in her dark eyes, the remarkable blend of compassion and lack of forgiveness that resided there. She was beguiling. But he knew they were both close to professional misconduct, if they hadn't committed it already.

'Thank you for being candid,' he said. 'Why did you want to meet today? I mean, the real reason.'

She looked down briefly before engaging with him. 'Your niece went missing eighteen months ago, didn't she?'

He clenched his jaw but kept his emotions in check. How did she know that? His name hadn't been mentioned in the few minor press articles. But now he guessed that she'd checked the FBI records.

'Your point is?' he said.

She puckered her lips. 'You're representing Hockey because of your niece. I figure this is all about her.'

'I'd say you are way off the mark.'

'I don't think so, Mr Hall. I think you're trying to get him to say something that will assist you in your search for her.'

'Are you accusing me of acting unprofessionally? Illegally?'

She used her fingers to brush her hair behind her right ear, revealing an opal earring. 'I have a daughter. I understand how you must feel. If someone took her, I'd do anything I could do to find her.'

Sweat had formed beneath his mouth and he wiped his skin dry with the back of his hand.

'I have to go,' he said, standing up.

'Sit down, Mr Hall.'

She said it both with an authority and with a promise of something if he complied. He sat down.

'I can help you. I can help you find your niece. Now — level with me.'

CHAPTER THIRTY-ONE

After her meeting with Gabriel, Carla eased her SUV into the far left-hand corner of a large McDonald's parking lot, next to a line of yellow buckeye trees and sweetspire bushes. She cut the engine, took out her smartphone and called Valentina, the kindly Mexican woman that looked after Monize when she was working late or away from DC. She said that Monize was well-behaved and Carla was not to worry.

Monize's father had left them when she was two years old. But he was a low-level political lobbyist with ambition, and he hadn't moved away from the capital. Monize slept over at his apartment in Columbia Heights once every two weeks, which Carla had consented to, without the need for a court order, and approved of.

She took the standard-issue Glock Model .22, which was loaded with .40 Smith & Wesson cartridges, from the hard-plastic holster on her hip and placed it into the glove compartment. She hadn't used it, apart from on the firing range. The SWAT teams did the killing when necessary. Her Catholic upbringing had left her with a sense that that was always a momentous event, and one she had no desire to experience. She kept it in the glove compartment as often as possible, something to remind her that she was an investigator first and foremost. She didn't want to get too used to a gun being attached to her like a vital thing.

She rang Section Chief Hester on her encrypted FBI smartphone.

'I met with Gabriel Hall this afternoon, sir. His association with Hockey is a front.'

Instead of going into the expected rant, he said, 'Go on.'

'I found out that his missing niece was adopted. She's a Kalmyk.'

'Like the girl in the DVD,' Hester said.

Feeling not a little relieved at his reaction, she said, 'Precisely, sir. Hall said he didn't believe Hockey's story that the DVD was left at his place by someone he knew. Like me, he thinks Hockey stole it to order. That's the reason for the murders, sir. This has nothing to do with anti-Semitism.'

'I see. But this puts Hall in an impossible position. He'll be disbarred.'

'He asked me to get him a copy of the DVD,' she said, turning on the air conditioning and adjusting it to blue.

'Does he think it's his niece?'

Carla rubbed her forehead, 'He wants to know, for sure. But he wants to study it too.'

'And why's that?'

'I told him the killer wears a mask. Like a skull. And dresses in a robe. A Tibetan monk's robe,' she said, screwing up her face.

She'd studied the DVD, which had made her dry retch again. But it hadn't yielded any clue as to the man's identity in terms she was familiar with, nor any motive, beyond sadism. She had a notion, though, that sadism was far too simple an explanation.

'You told him that?' Hester said.

'I had to.'

'No, you didn't.'

'He said he really needs to see it. He thinks there could be a link with the people who took his niece, assuming it isn't her.'

Hester sighed, '*If* his niece was kidnapped. We don't know that.'

'But there must be some connection.'

'Is that you or him speaking now, Agent Romero?'

Ignoring him, Carla told Hester about the message that Hockey had asked Gabriel to give to one of his associates, a man named Jim Saunders, at the bar in Far Rockaway.

'He passed on the message?' Hester said.

'He did.'

Hester coughed, and his breathing became audible.

'Hockey wasn't acting alone and he wants to talk to someone other than his dead father. Hockey would've gotten it out anyway.' She made a face, waiting for his reaction.

'Tell Hall he can't represent Hockey, even in a pro bono capacity with the public defender at the helm. That's a definite.' Hester coughed again, something that quickly descended into a phlegmy wheeze. 'And don't contact him again until I get clearance for this. Is that clear?'

'It is, sir. And thank you.'

'For what?'

She steadied herself. 'I thought you'd, well, that you'd be angry with me for doing this.'

'I *am* angry with you.' Hester sighed. 'But I guess the public defender will get a copy of the DVD disclosed to him sooner or later. You've seen the filth on it. I want those people caught. Just keep it legal.'

'I will.'

'I repeat, I have to get clearance, that's authority from Deputy Director Johnson, so don't go near Hall before I tell you his decision.'

She shook her head, agitatedly.

'And agent, if you disobey me again, I'll have your badge and your pension.'

*

Driving back to DC, she got a call on her personal smartphone, and took it hands-free. The caller, she noticed, was Robert Dubois, whom she'd met during her stint at the NATO HQ in Brussels. They still had mutual professional interests but hadn't been lovers for a few years.

'How are you, Robert?'

'I've been better,' he said.

Knowing he hadn't wanted to break up with her, she quickly moved on to professional matters. 'Have you watched it?'

'I have,' he said.

'What do you think?'

'I think you should come to Brussels to discuss it.'

She made a disappointed face. 'I can't. Least not at the moment. Have you seen anything like it before?'

He hesitated. 'Not in respect of the obvious. No. But I'd say it was genuine.'

If any man could verify that, it was Robert Dubois, she thought. Three hundred violent pornographic videos had been seized in the Belgian Beast's properties, apart from the ones he'd made himself. Dubois had told Carla he'd had to watch every VT, and as result had received two years of counselling from a police psychologist. She hadn't doubted it.

'Listen, Carla,' he said, his voice serious. 'I *do* need to discuss something about the case with you. But not on a phone.'

CHAPTER THIRTY-TWO

That night, after eating a two-egg omelette in the kitchen, Gabriel stood up and strolled to the living room, holding a mug of coffee. The house seemed too large now, and he only used a few of the rooms. He walked over to the window, made a small opening in the crimson curtains and scanned the well-lit street outside. He caught his reflection in the windowpane and thought he looked jaded and morose. The furrows in between his brows had deepened, such that they had taken on the appearance of half faded scars.

A silver sports car hummed by, its polished steel wheels seemingly revolving anticlockwise. A couple stepped out from a late-night sushi bar. Laughing, they walked arm-in-arm towards a parked taxi.

He'd decided to take a two-week break. He knew he couldn't concentrate on new cases or lecturing. He would pass his existing caseload over to a lawyer with a similar practice in the city. A reciprocal relationship.

He'd found himself being candid with Carla at Frank's Place. She'd convinced him that he could trust her. He relied on his intuition in such matters, intuition acquired over years of dealing with liars and truth tellers. By the end of the conversation, which had continued for a further fifteen minutes, she'd said that as a sign of her good faith she would give him a copy of the DVD, although she had to get authorization from her section chief before she did so.

He knew he wouldn't be able to sleep. He looked up for stars in the night sky, but there weren't any.

*

The pasta water had boiled over onto the kitchen tiles and had run through the archway that led to Gabriel's study area. He imagined himself at his laptop in the corner, Roxana sitting on a leather couch, staring at the Picasso print on the wall opposite. *The Old Guitarist* from the blue period, depicting a haunting, emaciated man; it was a painting he knew that she despised. At thirty-eight, she still had the body of an endurance athlete. She took regular yoga classes and was a vegetarian. Her hair, the hue of a raven's breast, was tied back in a chignon and her eyes were as flawless as virgin pearls.

He leaned forward in a swivel chair, clicked the mouse. He'd checked out similar disappearances online and had contacted support groups every night since his niece had gone missing. Any clue had been worth following up. Any pattern. But he'd always reached a dead end. Most of the people he'd contacted had said they'd given up all hope, except for a miracle, and then he'd ask himself why he'd bothered communicating with them.

In his imagination, Roxanna got up and shuffled through the archway to the kitchen to collect a mop. She wore a tie-dyed sarong with a matching pale green, open back halter-neck top. Of all the things he loved about her, it was her back that aroused him most. The colour of burned umber, her shoulder blades inclined towards her spine as the slopes of a distant valley.

'Dinner in five,' she said. 'Once I've mopped up.'

They took turns cooking and doing the household chores.

A few minutes later, he heard her crying. He got up and moved to the kitchen. She was stirring the pasta with a long wooden spoon. He put his arms around her waist, kissed her bare shoulder. She let the spoon stand in the saucepan and squeezed his hands.

'I thought everything would be normal with us, Gabriel. Whatever the hell that means.'

He thought, as he often did, about the years his sister had spent in agonizing IVF treatment that at the time had left her both physically and mentally shot. Despite using some of the ablest doctors in New York City, her money had been wasted. She and her husband had been desperate for a child. They loved Sangmu. Even a blind man could see that. He'd ruined it for them. He couldn't help thinking these things, even as Roxanna's hand went to his inner thigh. He didn't react.

Roxanna had turned and had looked at him.

'You're not the same, Gabriel. You've lost your joy. And I can't bring it back. No one can.'

*

The next day the sky was still overcast, the sun a mere brush stroke of cadmium orange on the western horizon. The single-lane road led to the coast, a few miles east of New Haven and Yale University, south-west Connecticut. Wading birds were scouring the shoreline, as the gulls scavenged among the decomposing clumps of detritus. They squabbled, with wings bent, exposing their red tongues. The wreck of what looked like a wooden yacht or fishing vessel was half-submerged in the pale mud, the hull's rotten planks resembling the green ribs of some prehistoric beast.

Gabriel had been asked by Carla to meet her here. He saw her car parked some distance away, with its lights off. Otherwise the place was empty. Approaching her at no more than five miles per hour, he turned his lights off too. He pulled up beside the SUV and got out of his hybrid sedan, leaving the car unlocked. He opened the passenger door and sat beside her.

'A little Cold War, isn't it?' he said.

'You think?' she said, dismissively. 'I've got the go-ahead from my section chief to allow you to find out what you can. But you report to me. And don't do anything without my say-so. Clear?'

'Clear,' he said. 'You can tone down the authoritarian attitude now.'

Ignoring him, she said, 'But you have to do it from the outside. You can't represent Hockey anymore. Tell him that you've got a tip-off that you're under surveillance for some infringement or other. You're smart. You'll work it out.'

She took out a DVD in a plastic case from a brown envelope and handed it to him.

'Don't tell anyone about this. It's a copy. Watch it, do what you need to do, and then destroy it. Understand?'

'You think I'm indiscreet?'

'If I did, would I be giving you the DVD?'

He shook his head a fraction. 'I suppose not.'

'Did your niece have any distinguishing marks?'

He clenched his jaw. 'No.'

'I should tell you that I checked the FBI computer records yesterday. Twelve young Kalmyk women have gone missing in the US since 1990, including your niece. One every couple of years. On its own that doesn't mean a lot, given the number of people who go missing every year. But —'

Interrupting her, Gabriel said, 'There are only about 3,000 Kalmyks in the US, mostly in New Jersey, so the odds against that are high. Right?'

'Exactly,' she said.

'My sister took Sangmu to language lessons in Howell Township. That's how I know. There are only around a 150,000 Kalmyks in the world. I thought at first that was why she wanted a little Kalmyk. Rare, you see. She likes rare things.'

She touched his forearm, her mood changing. 'Be careful, Gabriel.'

'Do you know something I don't?'

'There's no evidence of serial murders. Not a scrap. But I've talked to a colleague and the DVD is real. There are many forgeries. Of killings, I mean. I'd say that Hockey is on the fringes of a highly organized, tight-knit group. There's a lucrative market for this kind of barbarity. They will protect it, just as they will protect their liberty. I know enough from experience to tell you that these are extraordinarily dangerous people. Their clientele are powerful people, like Watson. They are without mercy. My badge and your association with me will mean nothing to them.'

'You think this is about money?' he said.

'I do. I suspect Watson purchased the DVD.'

But Gabriel was sceptical about that, without knowing why exactly.

She handed him a plastic mobile phone. Pay as you go, disposable.

'It's untraceable. Don't use it for anything else. I'll call in a few days, see if you've come to any conclusions. But don't talk about this on it. We'll meet up again.'

He thought that a little strange, given that the National Security Agency would have better things to do than listen in on an official investigation. But fingering the DVD in his hands, his thoughts focused on the hell he knew he would encounter there, and he shuddered.

CHAPTER THIRTY-THREE

Berlin, 2015, the next day.

An Italian fresco, a Pompeian nude, hung above an empty mantle-piece of pink marble. The fresco portrayed four women of ancient Rome, huddled against a scratched vermillion wall, with seaweed-green pillars. The muted grey and gold stolas curled around their bare feet like anacondas. The old man's most precious piece. It had once been held in a crate within a secure storage room at the Uffizi Gallery, Florence. Now it was covered by a clear polycarbonate sheet, the temperature and humidity adjusted remotely to preserve its exquisite beauty.

César Vezzani had cooked a Corsican meal. Loup de mer, seabream, fritelli castagnini, chestnut flour fritters, and the classic, civet de sanglier, wild boar casserole. He'd poured a fine Patrimonio red wine. The old man had complimented him on the cuisine, saying he should have been a chef de partie at Restaurant Amador in Mannheim, rather than a Sergent chef in the Legion. Vezzani had smiled at that.

They were sitting now in the main living room, opposite each other on oxblood chesterfields. The walls were pale yellow, the curtains a luxuriant green, edged with gold thread. Chopin's *Nocturne in C-sharp minor, Op. 27, No. 1* drifted through the evening air. In his mind's eye, the old man was playing the piece to a well-dressed audience that listened in silent adoration.

Vezzani was an undoubtedly excellent cook, but the old man knew that he always surpassed himself when he had some bad news to impart. The old man blinked slowly, like a lizard waking up in bright sunlight. His forehead became granulated like a walnut shell. He jerked out his chin to indicate that Vezzani should speak, appearing almost emperor-like in his imperiousness.

'An FBI special agent has a strong interest in the case, at least as far as the DVD is concerned. She works out of Washington DC. Her name is Carla Romero.'

'Romero. Brazilian?' the old man said.

'Her grandparents lived in São Paulo.'

'Ah. A city of diasporas.' His breath rattled.

'A New York defence lawyer volunteered to assist the public defender with Hockey's case. Name of Gabriel Hall.'

The old man couldn't risk paying a private practice lawyer to help Hockey. That would've been indiscreet. He smoothed his skull, like a curator caressing the head of an alabaster bust.

'Do we know why?' he said.

'Publicity.'

'Is that credible?' the old man said. It was more of a statement than a question.

Vezzani made a face, his mouth turning down at the sides. His palms swivelled over to communicate: who knows?

The old man stood up and shuffled over to an art nouveau drinks trolley beside the high fireplace. He poured himself a glass of Ducastaing Armagnac, then took a sip of the brandy from the heavy crystal.

'Have you packed?' he said.

'I leave for America tomorrow afternoon.'

'Good.'

The old man walked over to his sandalwood bookshelves. He couldn't decide whether to read Balzac or Voltaire. *Clotilde de Lusignan* or *Micromégas*. His forefinger hovered over both the hardback books before he plumped instead for the eroticism of Goethe's *Roman Elegies*. The old man had amassed a lifetime of learning. The killings aside, he led an oddly monastic life.

He stood still for some moments, lost in the music, both lulled and energized by it. He pondered just one question; how could man create such things when there was no God?

He walked back to his chesterfield and saw that Vezzani had picked up his sewing and was using silver thread to embroider a rune onto a piece of black silk. The old man knew that he'd learned to love sewing during his time in the Legion. It calmed him, he'd said. It had become for him a form of gentle, active meditation, he'd said, like tai chi. The rune was the elf rune, which symbolized loyalty and devotion. It had been worn by Hitler's personal adjutants. He had told Vezzani very little of his past, except that he'd fought in World War Two. That he'd fought in the battles of the Caucasus and Berlin.

The past was as much interwoven with the present as Vezzani's stitching, he thought.

CHAPTER THIRTY-FOUR

Berlin, 1945, the same day.

Major Volsky's scarred face remained dispassionate after Richter said that the Waffen-SS had killed the Red Army soldiers in the bunker out of revenge for the destruction of Berlin, that they'd dismembered and disfigured their victims almost beyond recognition before putting them back together again like a macabre game.

'As an academic, I would never do such a thing to you Russians. The country that gave the world Mily Balakirev, Alexander Borodin and Ivan Shishkin,' Richter said.

'So, you are an academic familiar with Russian culture. So, what? The Nazi Party and the SS are full of academics.'

Richter rebuked himself for such a cheap attempt at flattery. What Volsky had said was true. Even three of the four commanders of the Einsatzgruppen death squads had been doctors of philosophy. And they, together with the German paramilitary Order Police and the various foreign auxiliary police units, had killed as many Jews as had died at Auschwitz-Birkenau, according to the scrupulous records the SS had kept. Over 1,000,000 men, women and children.

He watched Volsky nod to the guard, who walked the few steps to him. He took a semi-automatic pistol from the leather holster. A Mauser C96, with its distinctive thin and elongated barrel. The 'Red 9', issued to the Luftwaffe, rather than the Nagant he'd suspected.

Richter's head was pulled back and he was hit on the bridge of the nose with what he guessed was the steel barrel. He swore aloud. He couldn't stop the hot tears. The blood gushed out and then dropped in clots, the pain an almost detached throb rather than excruciating. But he wondered miserably if the nasal bones were broken.

After a few seconds, Volsky handed him a white handkerchief.

He accepted reluctantly, but said, 'Thank you.'

With one hand holding the handkerchief to his nose, Richter looked around for the second cigarette that had fallen from his spare lips. He picked it off the damp floor. It was still alight. He inhaled deeply and leaned his head back. He blew a cloud of smoke from his mouth and then dabbed some residual tears from his eyes with a clean corner of the otherwise blood-soaked handkerchief.

He was taken back to his cell then, to consider what Volsky saw as his timewasting, he guessed.

Unknown to his captors, Richter had spent the first years of war in the Ahnenerbe-SS. The Ahnenerbe had been founded by, among others, Heinrich Himmler. Its full name had been Forschungs- und Lehrgemeinschaft Das Ahnenerbe e.V, the research and teaching community of the ancestral heritage. Its president had been one Walter Wüst, a dean at the University of Munich and a part-time member of the SS secret service, who'd been known as the orientalist. The unit had ultimately been incorporated into the Allgemeine-SS.

Richter had worked on the Generalplan Ost, the master plan for the east, within the Reich Security Main Office. The plan had foreseen the extermination and ethnic cleansing of central and eastern Europe.

Himmler had said that it was a question of existence, a racial struggle of pitiless severity, in which twenty to thirty million Slavs and Jews would perish through military actions and starvation. This would have meant that Germany would not have suffered another blockade, as had occurred in World War One, with its attendant food shortages.

After the invasion of the Soviet Union, Richter had left the main office and had become a Sonderführer, a so-called skilled leader in the Waffen-SS. Being both mature in years and an SS officer, Richter was a man with special talents who hadn't been content to sit behind a desk and draft reports for the duration of the war.

CHAPTER THIRTY-FIVE

Now, Richter was back in the interrogation cell.

Volsky pulled down the sleeves of his tunic as if he was calming himself. 'How did the contents of the bunker come to be there?'

Richter looked up at the meat hook. He was sweating. He had stomach cramps. He was suffering from both physical and physiological withdrawal systems. He wanted opium.

'Without Himmler, none of this would have come about. He was interested in ancestral history. In the customs and beliefs of ancient peoples.' He bowed his head and covered his eyes with his hands.

'You knew Himmler?'

Richter did his best to straighten up, aware that he had expressed his thoughts and had put himself at risk by doing so.

'Everyone in the SS knew this of Himmler.'

'So, you are not telling me anything of interest.'

Richter coughed, a deep, phlegm-induced hack, and his eyes bulged.

'Some water, perhaps?' Volsky said.

'No, I'm fine.'

What use is water? he thought. Cattle drink water. Horses drink water. Jews and Russian peasants drink water. He wiped an unpleasant mixture of spittle and a more viscous fluid from his chin, embarrassed by it. He craved opium in that moment. He craved it in a way he'd just about managed to suppress until now. He craved it as a new-born craved its mother's breast milk. He felt the urge to wail, but controlled himself just in time. His body was disintegrating, he knew, just as his world had disintegrated.

'The bunker, German. We know about the things that were stored there. Yes, we know. Tell me about the skulls. The other things. Save yourself, German.'

Richter couldn't believe it. How had they survived? He felt lost. Abandoned. Vulnerable. Events were turning against him, his luck was deserting him. But even if I do, you would not understand, he thought. You would not believe me. He watched Volsky's red-rimmed eyes glower at him.

'Sing a sweet song for me, German. Stay out of the woodman's pot.'

'Alright,' he said. 'But this is information you will not want spoken about by a young man with drink inside him.'

Volsky turned to the side and motioned to the door with his chin, prompting the guard to leave the room. He opened a drawer below the table top and took out a notebook, a packet of cigarettes, a small bottle of vodka, an old fountain pen, matches and chocolate bars. He slid all but the notebook and pen over to Richter's side of the table. Richter swallowed some vodka, ate a bar, and lit another cigarette. His craving eased a little.

'The skulls and bones?' Volsky said. 'And the dead woman? All of it was found, even though I am told it looked as if they were meant to be destroyed.'

Richter kept his eyes on the table top. He still couldn't believe it. He rebuked himself for taking the word of a moronic Waffen-SS NCO, who'd told him everything had been incinerated and not to worry about it. How could the man have been so slovenly in the execution of his duties? How could he himself have neglected to check that all was as the man had said?

He knew he would have to be extraordinarily careful. His life depended on it. He put the cigarette to his lips and inhaled. He held the smoke in his lungs, savouring it, before letting it out through his mouth. He thought about making out that they were nothing more than grisly trinkets, but thought better of it. They were so outlandish and incongruous to someone uneducated in their esoteric significance that he knew that could lead to a broken finger, or worse.

'The skull cup is called a kapala. They are anointed and consecrated before use. They appease the wrathful deities.'

Richter coughed again and wiped a sheen of sweat from his forehead with the stinking sleeve of his jacket.

'All of the items are used by Tibetan Buddhist monks to evoke fear and thereby overcome it. To prove to themselves that they understand the Tantras. The sacred texts. The items could be called Tantric paraphernalia.'

'And the woman?' Volsky said, his mouth barely moving.

'The mummified woman was a Tibetan nun. She is referred to as a living Buddha. A Śarīra. A Buddhist relic. Such mummies are incorrupt, without any sign of deliberate mummification. It's a mystery, Major Volsky. I cannot explain it. No one can, at least not in any manner that is coherent to a Western mindset.'

He saw the look in the Russian's eyes after he'd spoken, and he knew his interrogator hadn't expected to hear such things from an SS officer, even one that had emerged from somewhere as outwardly weird as the bunker, and his self-confidence was restored as easily as it had deserted him.

Fuck your woodman's pot, Richter thought. I'll survive this. I can survive anything. Do you know who I am? No, of course you don't. You lapdog of Jews.

He guessed the NKVD didn't even know that Waffen-SS men could be identified by the blood-group tattoos on the underside of their left arms, usually near the armpit. Richter didn't have one. He'd been classed as a non-combatant, as he'd said, at least for a portion of the war. He decided it could be weeks before they found out who he was.

But Volsky's confidence appeared to have been restored too, now. He said, 'And the vat of incense?'

'I had the incense brought from the remnants of a Christmas smoker factory. Silly little hollow figurines invented by toymakers in the Ore Mountains. Cone incense burns down inside the figurines and the smoke emerges from the open mouths. There was a glut of them,' Richter said, truthfully. 'Berliners were shocked and saddened after Stalingrad. But they lost the will to celebrate after the Battle of Kursk. They knew the Red Army was coming. The puerile little incense smokers were redundant, together with the incense they were to hold. Except it didn't go to waste. The vat was taken from a merchant's house. It's from Hong Kong, I think.'

Volsky leaned back in his chair. He said, 'Why go to all the trouble?'

That's a good question, Richter thought.

He stifled a smile. 'To mask the smell.' He eased back in his own chair, lethargically. 'As I said, the men were camp guards before becoming front line troops. They got the taste for it, I suppose. It never leaves you, they say.'

'Now answer my original question. How did they come to be there?'

'I am a professor of contemporary anthropology. I study the lives and customs of ancient peoples that still exist in remote regions of the world. That is the why the items where there. They were for academic study. At my age, I am merely what you might call a sedentary academic. Other people do the legwork for me. I never travelled to the occupied territories. I never left Berlin.'

Richter breathed out, rather pleased with himself.

'You are many things, it seems,' Volsky said. 'You were seen leaving the bunker by an observation post in a bomb-damaged hotel situated over the road. The order was to bring you in alive.'

'I see,' Richter said.

'You *think* you do. We'd organized a force to attack the bunker. There was just an hour's difference between the explosions and our troops being ready. But then again, an hour can be a long time in war, eh German?'

In total war, Richter thought. 'Quite so.'

'They would have shot you. But then it was decided that you should live. We Russians can be fickle. But the past never changes. There can be different interpretations, of course, but what has happened has happened, is that not so?'

'It is.'

'Where did those foul items come from?'

'Kalmykia.' Richter said. 'Buddhist Kalmykia.'

Where else could he have said? It was the only place the Wehrmacht Heer had occupied that they could have come from. It fitted with his academic credentials too, which were themselves real enough.

'With his dying breath, an SS captain told the Red Army assault squad that had stumbled upon the bunker just before you left, that the dead Soviet soldiers were killed because of *Doctor Doll*,' Volsky said.

Richter was flabbergasted. What else did the NKVD know? The uncertainty troubled him deeply. But he would remain calm. Besides, he could see that Volsky didn't have an inkling as to who or what Doctor Doll was.

He said, 'It doesn't mean anything to me. Perhaps the man was simply confused. Perhaps it was just a childhood memory.'

Volsky nodded his head slowly. 'Perhaps.'

CHAPTER THIRTY-SIX

The same day.

Kazapov's head had been filled with the images of the evidence that had been found in the room of death in the bunker, and they'd come to him one after the other, as if viewed through a zoetrope. But he'd had work to do and he'd spent most of the day supervising every aspect of the bunker's clearance. It had been vital that nothing had gone wrong. He'd ensured that the outwardly disturbing items had been covered, as he'd ordered. He'd walked back and forth to the trucks. He'd checked the wooden crates had been secured properly. He'd allowed the men to work in their shirt sleeves. They'd been at it for hours, and the thick, low cloud, the heat from the bricks and the nearby still smouldering fires had transformed what would have been a cold day into a mild one.

But now, as dusk descended and the air cooled, two Poles dropped a crate as it was being lifted onto the bed of a truck, and it shattered. One of the Poles kneeled and pulled back the blanket, to check the condition of the contents, it appeared. A couple of NKVD riflemen ran over to shield the view from the other Poles.

Kazapov raced over to the kneeling man, who looked to be in his early twenties. Kazapov noticed that he was even skinnier than himself.

185

The man wore a Star of David necklace. It poked out from between two buttons on the khaki shirt that he'd put back on. The other Pole had turned his face away. A clever man, Kazapov thought.

'Cover it all up,' he said.

He nodded towards the mummified hand, a skull shaped as a bowl with smooth stones in it, and the disfigured and dismembered corpse of a Soviet soldier.

The Pole did so.

'Your name?'

'Corporal Stolarski, sir.' He saluted.

'Your full name?'

'Icchak Stolarski.'

Kazapov checked the man's shoulder straps. The stupid, clumsy bastard, he thought.

'Report to Sergeant Yeltsin. You're finished for the day.'

'I'm sorry, sir,' Stolarski said.

'What else have you seen?'

'Nothing, sir.'

'You're lying,' Kazapov said, staring hard at him.

'I'm telling the truth, lieutenant.'

Kazapov calmed himself. The last thing he needed to do was to be too overtly harsh on the man. Some of the Poles might become inquisitive. They might think there was something worth stealing. It seemed to him as if the war had turned everyone into a thief.

'Don't worry,' Kazapov said. 'Nothing will come of it. I just can't afford for anything to get broken. You're evidently too exhausted to continue. You've had quite a day.'

'Thank you, sir.'

Kazapov told one of the two NKVD men to wrap the smashed crate and its contents with a tarpaulin and put it on the truck. But Stolarski was still standing there, idling.

'You still here, Stolarski? I told you to report to Sergeant Yeltsin. Now do it.'

'Sorry, sir.'

Kazapov watched him slump off. Idiot, he thought. He would see to it personally that Stolarski received special treatment so that there was no chance of him revealing what he'd seen.

He thought about the glut of other Buddhist ritual items found in the room. He thought too about the film that the Russian sergeant named Pavel Romasko had recovered from the brass casket. He had to watch it. His left eye began to twitch as he had an idea how it might get him in front of the SS colonel he'd captured, Lutz Richter.

Major Volsky disapproved of his investigative work, he knew, considering it a waste of resources. He'd simply shoot everyone vaguely associated with war crimes. Kazapov considered him a dangerous fool.

The world was full of fools.

CHAPTER THIRTY-SEVEN

Major Volsky massaged his temples with his thumb and forefinger of his right hand before bringing the palm down over his nose, mouth and chin. He looked at Lutz Richter now in a manner that suggested he knew he was lying to him. But Richter could see too that he wasn't agitated by it, and this worried him more than anything that had transpired, including the pistol's barrel striking his nose. Richter adjusted his shoulders awkwardly.

Volsky said, 'Most of your kind will never see Germany again. The criminals will hang. Some of the recent POWs will be executed within a few weeks for minor infringements. The others will do twenty-five years in a freezing hellhole. The majority will perish there. If you're lucky, you will avoid such a fate and be one of those who gets back to Berlin within a short time. A Berlin under Soviet rule. But you must co-operate fully. Think on that.'

Richter believed him. The Soviets were capable of expediency on occasion and could be trusted to be true to their word, despite the betrayal by Hitler of the nonaggression pact with Stalin that Operation Barbarossa had brought about. He knew his recent history, and that there was only one sensible interpretation of it.

Ninety-two thousand men had been taken prisoner after the Battle of Stalingrad. The German Sixth Army had been surrounded by nearly 1,000,000 Soviets. Hitler had promoted the commander, General Paulus, to a Field Marshal in the last days of the battle, knowing that no German Field Marshal had allowed himself to be taken alive. It had been a signal, but one that Paulus had rejected. He was first and foremost a pragmatist and had known an ultimate defeat for the Nazis was inevitable. Besides, he'd blamed Hitler for not sending the panzers to relieve his men. He'd been right.

But the capture of Paulus and his twenty-two generals at Stalingrad had been gloomily portentous. The Sixth Army POWs had been sent off to camps in the Soviet Union, to places Richter would now do anything to avoid ending up in. It had been rumoured that many had failed even to survive the initial march, although over 10,000 had defied Paulus's order to surrender. They'd fought to the last man in burned-out houses, cellars and sewers, preferring to die for their Führer. But Paulus had collaborated with his Soviet captors and, over the previous two years, had become a high-profile critic of the Nazis. Richter guessed he'd been treated well enough. The pragmatist.

Richter had spent all his adult life being anything but a pragmatist. But now he wanted to live, and so a pragmatist was what he would become. He knew too that torture was often a crude but well-tried means of obtaining small, specific pieces of easily verifiable information, like a name or a location. But sophisticated intelligence gathering took a lot longer and a lot more work. Real work.

But what else did they want him to make sense of? The thought made him shiver. Had he said too much already? He could be useful to them in other ways though. Couldn't he? He could identify people. Soviet traitors and Jew killers. Would he do such a thing?

Volsky sighed. He looked as if he was about to pick his nose but thought twice about it and scratched his chin instead.

'My father was a professor of mathematics at Moscow State University,' he said. 'In 1926, I told him I had joined the secret police. He begged me to give it up and follow him into the study of mathematics, which he called numerical poetry, and claimed was every bit as beautiful and elaborate as the written poetry of Alexander Pushkin or Vasily Zhukovsky. I said I wasn't interested in mathematics and he called me a communist murderer. I dragged him outside his wooden house, pinned him to the frosted ground with my polished boot, and broke his jaw with a lump of limestone. He had to suck liquid food through a straw for months. I told him he was lucky he had a compassionate son.'

'Ah.'

'The Kalmyk volunteers killed many patriotic partisans. Were you with them in Kalmykia?'

Richter shook his head. If he said yes, he would be hung without delay. He had no doubt of it.

'Say it.'

'No. I've told you this already,' Richter said.

'What happened to the Kalmyk volunteers that followed the retreating Germans?'

'They were formed into a cavalry corp. I was told that many died in the fighting at the Sea of Azov and the right bank of the Dnieper. Many more were killed in the retreat by partisans. The Balkans. Elsewhere. The remnants were sent to Austria, I think, with the surviving family members who'd trailed behind them all the way from the steppe. I don't know what happened to them there.'

'Why did you come to Berlin?' Volsky said.

'I have been here since the beginning, as I said.'

'Why didn't you make your escape earlier?' Volsky said.

'Duty, I suppose. We have that in common at least. Do we not, major?'

Volsky motioned to the vodka with his fat hand. 'Drink, German. Finish it.'

Richter picked up the bottle and drank.

'That will be the last time you taste alcohol.'

Volsky smirked.

CHAPTER THIRTY-EIGHT

Brooklyn Heights, 2015, the same day.

Gabriel had converted his cellar into a gym, six months after he'd bought the house. He'd plastered the brick walls and had laid a hardwood floor, although he'd paid an electrician to wire the strip lighting and had decided he could do without heating.

The floor was strewn now with resistance bands, compact dumbbells, a skipping rope. Mounted on the wall opposite the wooden staircase was a chin-up bar and a mountain climber. Incongruously, a glass-covered print of *The Death of Actaeon* by the Venetian Renaissance master, Titian, hung on the white wall at the foot of the staircase. The goddess Diana changed Actaeon into a stag in revenge for surprising her as she bathed naked in a remote pond. He was ripped to pieces by his own hounds. To remind Gabriel of what? He'd never known. Roxana had said that he was obsessed by tragedy. Was he?

Wearing a T-shirt and joggers, he took a long drink of water from a plastic bottle and towelled his skin. His otherwise symmetrical physiognomy was spoiled by damaged cartilage on the left side of his nose, the result of a climbing accident on the Gift at Red Rock Canyon in Nevada ten years before. He'd never got around to fixing it. Most climbers he knew wore their scars with boyish pride. Besides, Roxanna had told him that it lent a certain mystery to the architecture of his face.

He walked up the wooden staircase, knowing the release of dopamine from his workout wasn't going to ease the stress of watching the DVD, as he'd hoped. He knew too that it wasn't going to ameliorate the memories the sight of a Kalmyk girl would evoke. He'd put off watching the DVD, even though he'd been desperate to get a copy. He knew why. But he decided that after taking a shower, he would force himself to do so.

*

Gabriel had slipped out of bed, thumbed on his smartphone light and had watched Roxana for a few seconds.

She looked beautiful, he thought, the lovely contours of her sculpted neck, the peace that had descended on her sleeping face. He considered kissing her forehead, but walked over to the door and unhooked his bathrobe. He knew she couldn't even hate him anymore for the distance he'd placed between them.

He ambled along the balcony to the stairs, heading for the kitchen. Reaching it, he made himself a cup of green tea and carried it into the living room.

Seven months had passed since his niece had gone missing, and as usual he couldn't rest. He decided to watch some TV and sat on a couch. He channel-surfed until he found a programme he felt able to watch, a black and white documentary featuring several jazz musicians in New Orleans.

An hour later, after the film had finished, he got up and walked slowly to the stairs. He took them one at a time, feeling wretched. At the top of the staircase, he turned right and headed for the bedroom she'd slept in the night before she'd disappeared, as if in a dream state. His sister and her husband worked away from home quite often, both employed in the commercial insurance business, and he and Roxanna had said they'd be pleased to look after Sangmu when their own schedules allowed.

He hesitated at the door that still had her name on it, as if he was some superstitious archaeologist about to encounter the contents of a cursed and ancient tomb.

A couple of seconds later, he turned the brass knob and entered, flicking down the light switch on the wall. The room hadn't changed at all. He and Roxana had agreed on it, even if this was the only thing they did agree on, now. He stepped almost reverently over the pale carpet to her bed. He sat down on the soft duvet and took the framed photograph from the white bedside table. It was the first photograph his sister had given him of Sangmu. One where she was still in her native Kalmykia, a poverty-stricken region of mostly barren steppe, he now knew.

She wore a pair of cheap joggers that looked stained and worn at the knees. Her skinny upper body was clothed in a threadbare green jumper, which appeared three sizes too big. He rubbed his thumb over the image of her face. In contrast to her body, her cheeks were chubby. They looked sunburned. His sister had said that Sangmu's surviving relations were pleased that she'd been adopted by a couple from the US, especially after they'd been assured that they'd be sent regular updates on her progress and that every few years she'd be brought home, so that she would always know where she was from and who her extended family were. He'd come to believe that, before her disappearance.

He forced a smile as he stared at her dusty black hair in a bob; her fringe wasn't quite straight, and it was too high on her forehead, as if she'd cut it herself. She was smiling, despite her predicament, revealing large lopsided teeth. Her lips were full, her eyes vital. She was barefoot and stood on the edge of arid scrubland in the north of her homeland.

There was the culmination of generations of desire for something better in those eyes, he'd thought.

*

In his study, sitting in front of his laptop, Gabriel viewed about twenty minutes of the two-hour-long DVD before he thumbed the pause button on his remote and began to weep silently. The only sound that had been on the DVD had been something he'd recognized. Something primordial that had resonated, as if it had triggered a genetic memory of sound made aeons ago. It had been occasionally accompanied by what he'd regarded as an artificial wailing.

Beyond the brutality and subjugation, he'd noticed something peculiar. The abuse had looked dance-like, at times almost tender. But there'd been something else too. It hadn't been simply perverted sexual gratification. Something akin to a ritual had been evident.

He'd looked intently at her in freeze frame, and he'd kept on freeze framing at specific moments. But the photography had been such that the girl's whole face had been shown rarely. For the most part, all that had been visible had been an eye, a partial profile, itself half shrouded by her black hair. He hadn't recognised her, save to say her individual features had looked classically Kalmyk.

Carla had been right about the killer. He was dressed in the robe of a Tibetan monk and wore a skull-like mask. Apart from the swastika emblem, the back of the robe was embroidered with an animal that had looked to him like a hybrid. The body of a hound and the head of a lion. The reared-up body and head were pearlescent, the flamboyant tail and mane turquoise. The roaring mouth, flailing tongue and flared nostrils, a flaming red, and the eyes yellow sapphires.

Gabriel stood up now and half-stumbled to the bathroom, whereupon he washed his face with water, cupping it to his skin, again and again and again. He was a criminal lawyer, but his clients weren't physically violent. He lived in Brooklyn, but in an affluent neighbourhood. He hadn't experienced anything like the DVD, and he wondered if he could continue to watch it. But he knew he would. He knew he had to.

He thought the mask was both repellent and extraordinary. He guessed it represented some sort of demon, with a mouth like a toad's and rows of square teeth, together with four huge fangs. There was no nose, only two small holes. The eye sockets were deep, but appeared to have eyes at the base, which were painted scarlet. Five miniature versions of the mask were attached to the head, with the same sunken red eyes. Two wing-like flaps protruded from the neck area, like misplaced ears, the same colour as the eyes. In the centre of the forehead was a larger eye, with a blue iris, surrounded by a white eyeball, the third eye of Buddhism. The rest of the mask was a dull yellow hue.

He wondered if it was a tribal death mask, or an elaborate, eastern image of the Devil. He wondered who this man was and who the girl had been. He didn't know if finding the makers of the DVD would lead him to Sangmu. But the outside chance was enough to energize him. To shut down those who were doing such damage to innocents, too. But first he had to become familiar with what he had seen, and work forward from that.

He brought up his search engine and moved his mouse rapidly. He found images of the lion-like creature on the robe quickly enough.

A few further minutes later, he was staring at an image of an identical mask.

CHAPTER THIRTY-NINE

New York City, two days later.

The Russians had flown into JFK on a standard Aeroflot scheduled flight from Moscow's Sheremetyevo International Airport. There were three men in their early twenties and the woman, who was thirty-two. She spoke broken English. She'd told immigration control that they were in the entertainment business, but that their visit was partly for pleasure and partly in the hope of making some contacts, that they intended to stay for one week only. They had return tickets and just enough US dollars not to arouse any overt suspicion, despite their appearances.

She'd acted for the old man on a few occasions, although they were not friends, not even acquaintances. She had never met him, nor did she know anything about him. She was unaware of the source of his obvious wealth, the money he used to pay for her services, of his collection of DVDs at the ghost house.

César Vezzani had met them at a hotel, as agreed. The Morning Inn was a bland, red-brick tower in Long Island, Queens, just under two miles from the airport. The lobby was all off-white tiles and opalescent glass, the staff mostly recent immigrants for whom English was a second language. He'd learned that meetings such as this were often best conducted in public areas. They didn't appear out of keeping, if the other people present and the nature of the space meant that a high degree of anonymity was assured. A hotel lobby met those objectives.

He'd always thought the Russian woman had excellent cheekbones. The straight blonde hair was shaved up on one side, the remainder mainly worn in a ponytail, especially while she was working. Her hair was closer to the colour of milk than wheat, he thought. The eyes were acid green, like those of a Persian cat and her body seemed out of kilter with her face. Her neck was muscular. She exuded strength but wasn't freakish. She looked like a powerful female athlete, a sprinter, perhaps, with the height of a rower. He knew she was a consummate killer, with or without a weapon.

Today, she was wearing a leather jacket and well-cut jeans. Her red blouse matched the flat-heeled, blood-red boots. Her nickname was Fury, after the chief torturers of the underworld, the bringers of vengeance. He'd always thought it an apt moniker.

They sat in the lobby and began drinking vodka. The young men talked Russian to one another. Vezzani thought they looked remarkably similar: black suits drawn taut over heavy frames, with granite-like, clean-shaven faces.

He handed Fury a flight bag. The contents included four disposable mobile phones, contact numbers, addresses suitable to stay at, 10,000 dollars in used notes for expenses and a sealed white envelope. She unzipped the bag and peered in, then rummaged around, obviously looking for firearms. He watched her, not a little fascinated.

'There is mistake,' she said. 'No guns in here.'

Vezzani shook his head. 'No mistake.'

'It joke? Yes?'

'No joke.'

'Then we buy our own.'

He moved forward and grasped her forearm. 'He won't like that,' he said, referring to the old man.

He saw her flinch. A man with no past and no profile, who was not averse to paying for torture and murder, was a man to be feared, even by a contract killer like Fury.

One of the young Russian men looked at Fury. 'You got a problem with pig face?' he said, in his mother tongue, referring to Vezzani.

'Pig face would knock your teeth out before you got to your feet,' she said, speaking back to him in Russian.

Vezzani removed his hand and sank back into the pleather couch, not knowing what had been said. But the acerbic atmosphere was clear enough. Not that it bothered him. Combined with his solid physique were years of perfecting the art of savate, the French martial art that utilized vicious kicks and disorientating slaps with the open hand. It had been developed by sailors in Marseilles in the early nineteenth century, when the use of a clenched fist in a fight had been outlawed. He was lethal too.

The Russian smirked, and he dug out a red and white packet of CCCPs. Vezzani was familiar with the cigarette brand and clenched his jaw. The Russian wiggled the packet in his hand, and he and the other two got up and walked to the glass entrance doors.

'I don't like that brand,' Vezzani said, referring to the Russian initials for the Union of Socialist Soviet Republics.

'It iron,' Fury said, and flicked her ponytail with a wave of her long fingers.

Vezzani grinned. 'Irony.'

'Irony. Yes.'

He didn't believe her. Russians like those who had just left were oddly nostalgic for the Soviet Union, or at least the power it had represented. He wondered why the old man used such people, even given his admiration for the woman.

He said she should spring Hockey when he was going back to the prison after a visit to court. Nearly half of all escapes occurred during transport, he said. And of those, nearly three-quarters were from vehicles. The brunette called Charlene Rimes, with the tattoo on her back, and her big-mouthed boyfriend, Billy Joe Anderson, should be questioned after that.

Hockey had gotten a message to Vezzani via Jim Saunders, who had visited him in prison, that had informed the Corsican where Rimes and Anderson lived, and provided other useful information, such as their smartphone numbers. Vezzani knew the authorities didn't have a clue who they were, for now at least, and that meant he was one step ahead.

'Kill them any way you like,' Vezzani said.

She didn't even blink.

'As for Hockey, the envelope contains the names of relevant federal officers, their duty rosters and home addresses,' he said. 'We checked the state records and the ones that live with women are ticked.'

'And the soon to be dead people?'

'There is a short list of questions we need them to answer.'

She nodded.

'There's also a list of people you can trust in the US. Use them. They'll get you vehicles. They'll help you out. They've been told to take orders from you. Only you. He holds you in high regard,' he said. He looked at her beautiful and pitiless eyes. 'I hold you in high regard. Are we OK?'

'We OK.'

'Guns?' he asked, hoping for the right answer and demanding it with his own eyes.

'No guns, César Vezzani,' she said.

He nodded. 'Don't kill any cops. Or federal officers. Clear?'

She smiled, her large, symmetrical teeth the colour of coconut flesh.

'It's vital,' Vezzani said.

'Too much heat already?' she said.

He couldn't stop a troubled look clouding his face.

'Tell him price doubled,' she said.

CHAPTER FORTY

Brooklyn Heights, the same day.

Gabriel now knew that the hybrid animal on the back of the killer's robe in the DVD was a snow lion, a mythological beast that had been the emblem of Tibet on postage stamps and currency, and adorned its military flag between 1912 and 1950. It represented fearlessness, the protector of Buddha in paintings. Sculptures of it, fashioned from bronze and stone, were to be found guarding what remained of Tibet's temples and holy sites. It was a celestial creature that was said to leap from one Himalayan peak to another.

He knew too that the mask worn by the killer was a wooden Tibetan demon mask, the making of which was a religious art form. Such masks were often worn in monastic rituals, a yellow mask depicting profound knowledge. Wearers of demon masks were deemed able to communicate with the deities. It was a Citipati mask, a wrathful deity, a reminder of the eternal cycle of life and death.

The sound he'd recognized had been made by the elongated dharma trumpets of Tibetan monks, the sound sometimes referred to as singing elephants. The wailing that had accompanied it had been the music of the femur trumpet, crafted from a human leg bone.

He'd begun scouring obscure online journals and specialist websites, the images from the DVD still flitting through his mind like fragments of a nightmare. He was convinced that there had to be a link between what the killer wore and the victim, a Kalmyk. The Kalmyk people were Tibetan Buddhists, he knew, which meant that the man in the mask was either a Kalmyk or someone disturbed enough to dress as a monk of their religion in order to murder one of them.

*

Gabriel saw Roxanna in the living room, curled up on the couch. She wore a pair of white shorts and a light blue T-shirt. She was watching a French film: *Pierrot le Fou*. The Blu-ray covers of *Les Enfants du Paradis* and *L'Atalante* lay on the glass-top coffee table.

'I thought we were going out to lunch,' he said.

'I'm going away for a few days,' she said, matter-of-factly.

Standing, he felt inept.

She bolted upright. 'You've left me already, Gabriel. You can see that, can't you?'

Roxana left him that afternoon, taking with her a compact suitcase of clothes.

The double blow had left him reeling. He'd walked around outside, ghost-like, for weeks, seeing people in the streets like him. People whose wrecked lives showed in their eyes, in the pallor of their skin, their gait and demeanour. Hopeless, broken people. Hollow people. He'd gotten drunk often. He'd pulled off the highway and put his head to the steering wheel. He'd sat in public places, lost in his misery. He'd punched more than one wall.

CHAPTER FORTY-ONE

The Bronx, New York City, two days later.

She left a fast-food restaurant at 12.45 pm, holding the glass door open for some rowdy school kids. Her hormones were raging, her appetite skewed and insatiable. She'd covered her cheese burger with mayonnaise and had gulped it down in half a dozen mouthfuls.

The sky was a dowdy patchwork of white puffs and grey streaks, but it was humid, and she wore a floral maternity dress that seemed to amplify her already enormous bump. It was a ten-minute walk to home. Blue-collar workers used to gaze at her when she walked by. From the windows of trucks and holes in the road. From ladders and scaffolding. Now, they didn't, or if they did, it was with a curious closed-mouth smile that she figured was half sympathy and half affection. But nothing remotely sexual, except for the odd pervert. This lack of acceptable attention pissed her off. She was a soft-featured Italian, her thick hair the colour of sable fur, her sensuous mouth the colour of plums.

The brown-brick houses she passed had jerry-built porches and lean-to garages made from inexpensive, mismatched materials. The lack of visual amenity was exacerbated by occasional litter-strewn gardens and paved yards. Even the thick cables attached to the obtrusive telephone poles dipped heavily in the middle.

She walked on past the blocks of flats and deserted warehouses, all but a few shop fronts boarded up. But she knew a lot of people in the neighbourhood and it was home. It had always been so. Her name was Francesca Carpenter. Fran, to her friends.

She came to a piece of waste ground, with a calcified wheelbarrow and a rusted, portable cement mixer the only signs of the abandoned building site. She heard a vehicle pull up a few yards behind her. It began to creep forward, making her feel nervous.

A black SUV appeared in her peripheral vision, the front passenger window down.

The woman had blonde hair in a ponytail and eyes like green quartz. No, like a seagull's, she thought. Cruel. Her black leather jacket was zipped up to her chin, despite the heat. She knew instinctively that something wasn't right. But it was the middle of day. Nothing could happen to her here.

'Excuse me,' the woman said. 'We look for Fordham Road. Shopping. Yes.'

Fran detected that her accent was Russian. They'd moved into the outskirts of the neighbourhood in recent years.

'It's a long way away.'

'So, we way off, eh?' the Russian said.

'Yeah, what I said.'

She felt frightened now without knowing why. The thing about a tough neighbourhood was that locals were generally safe, and visitors generally weren't. But somehow the roles had been reversed, even though the woman hadn't threatened her in any way.

'Can you show me, on map?'

The Russian unfolded a map and half pushed it out of the window.

'Sure,' Fran said, although she wondered why a vehicle like that didn't have sat nav.

She moved forward, so that her swollen belly was almost touching the car's shiny, metallic black paint. Two guys sprang out from the back doors, and she turned towards them.

'What the hell?'

Turning her head had exposed her fleshy neck. She felt a pinprick, but as she raised her hand instinctively, it was gripped hard by the Russian, and she gasped, her only response to the sudden, violent contact.

Almost instantly, she felt queasy, her surroundings becoming vague and disjointed. It was as if she'd drunk too much red wine. She tried to scream, but no noise came out, as in a dream. Feeling faint, her eyes glazing over and watering, she saw the road undulate, like a film she'd seen of a suspension bridge as an earthquake struck. The ugly houses became fluid things and she realized she was falling.

My baby, she thought. My precious baby.

But she didn't hit the pavement.

In her mind now, she was suspended in the depths of a black ocean, her body enveloped by the muscly arms of an enormous octopus.

CHAPTER FORTY-TWO

Fury saw a young man run out of a hardware shop, just as Fran was being bundled onto the back seat. He had floppy blond hair, like the photos she'd seen of Californian surfers, and wore a mustard-coloured apron.

The few cars that had passed by had been placated by the bar of red and blue LED light, which flickered atop the SUV's rear windscreen. The road didn't lead to anywhere useful, save other houses. But Surfer was standing in the middle of it now. He started to wave his arms about, in a vain attempt to attract attention to what he'd seen happen, apparently.

Now he lowered his hands. He stood still, staring.

'He's checking the number plate,' Fury said in Russian to the driver.

'We can change them,' he said.

She frowned. 'Not quickly enough.' She glanced around. The road was clear. 'Take him out.'

The Russian floored the accelerator and Surfer ran for the pavement up from the shop. Here, it abutted a twelve-feet high wire mesh fence, which sectioned off a derelict basketball pitch. The SUV mounted the kerb and Surfer started sprinting. He glimpsed over his shoulder every few seconds, a look of wild fear on his fresh face, as if he was a primitive seeing a motor vehicle for the first time.

The SUV was so close to the fence that a flurry of sparks flew out, like ignited sparklers. The SUV's alloy bumper bar hit him with a distinctive *thud* and he somersaulted over the windscreen, as stiff as a shop mannequin.

'Stop,' Fury said.

The SUV skidded to a standstill, little puffs of dirt mingling with the faint blue rubber smoke.

'Reverse.'

Four seconds later the sensation reminded her of the time she'd run over a deer in the Black Forest. She'd thought then it would feel like going over a speed hump. It hadn't.

Just the same.

She'd used a needle on the pregnant woman because she knew a Taser would have been an unacceptable risk. The woman might miscarry, or worse. The electronic current produced involuntary muscle spasms. Too dangerous. She wanted both the woman and the unborn child unharmed.

The SUV sped away and she checked the rear-view mirror. Surfer's body was mangled, a leg bent up to his ribcage, the back of his head resembling cat food. Blood was leaching from three of his limbs. He looked as if he'd just jumped off a ten-storey building.

Her eyes slid to her own reflection. Her name was Anna Belova. She covered a burn mark that ran from her left temple to her jawline with expensive foundation cream. The worst of the ugliness had been removed by plastic surgery in Hong Kong. But still it left a reddish marble on her skin. She fingered it at night, after she'd removed her make-up.

Her uncle had abused her from the age of eight. She'd decided to take her revenge on her sixteenth birthday, with a steam iron. He'd managed to yank it from her in the struggle and had slammed it back into her face. The searing heat had made had her faint. After she'd come to, she'd taken the iron from the kitchen worktop and had stabbed its metal point into the back of his skull as he'd been watching TV. They'd found him three days later. His erstwhile good looks had morphed horribly into something reminiscent of a cheese and tomato pizza. She'd reheated the iron and used it to hit him in the face more than thirty times, although she'd lost count after a dozen blows.

A week after that she'd entered a squalid block of flats in Moscow and had started to hang out with skinheads, who treated her with respect. Some were followers of neopaganism and the white power groups. Others, members of the People's National Party, which at the time was xenophobic and anti-Semitic, regarding Hitler as an idol. They'd spoken openly of extermination. Women had been welcomed into their ranks.

She'd seen the packs of abandoned homeless children that lived underground like troglodytes. She'd given them a handful of roubles at first, but a skinhead had said she'd just be feeding their drug habits. She'd gotten part-time work at an extremist publisher and the skinheads had taught her to pump iron. She'd told herself that no man would touch her without her consent again.

Now, her ideology was limited to Putinism — at least, its near lawless capitalist aspects — her work to instances of international criminality.

Still looking in the rear-view mirror, she applied some more make-up.

CHAPTER FORTY-THREE

Yale, the same day.

Gabriel walked past the neoclassical Hewitt University quadrangle in the centre of the grounds, glancing at the World War One cenotaph in memory of the 'Men of Yale' situated in front of the stately colonnade. He looked down at the sunken courtyard garden of the Beinecke Rare Book and Manuscript Library, and at the three minimalist sculptures by Isamu Noguchi of a pyramid, a globe and a cube, which were said to represent time, the sun, and chance. The heat hadn't abated, and the only creatures moving at speed were small birds, hunting winged bugs.

Gabriel had done as much research as he could in the short time that had elapsed since he'd watched the DVD, but still he didn't know whether the Kalmyk religion could have anything to do with its hideous contents. He had to find out, and that was why he was on his way to see Professor Boris Iliev. That was why he knew he had to be frank with him, to an acceptable degree, at least. It would be a wasted exchange if he just skirted around the central issue.

Gabriel knew his sister had been anxious to teach Sangmu about her cultural and religious roots, as much as was possible, and she'd taken advantage of events such as the New Jersey Folk Festival, which for one day in April 2011 had centred on the Kalmyk people. They'd started to migrate to the eastern state in the late 1950s, due to the sponsorship of Russian émigrés and the Tolstoy Foundation. His sister had been invited to Rashi Gempil-Ling, a Kalmyk Tibetan Buddhist temple just off Route 9. She'd told Gabriel that the smaller of its two buildings, which smelled of incense, had been empty save for an enormous prayer wheel, a lavishly decorated device that a Tibetan monk had said contained a million printed prayers wrapped around an engraved, brass core. A gift to the world.

And who could blame them for coming? Kalmykia was one of Europe's most deprived and under-developed regions. The Dalai Lama had sent a high lama to minister to them, but Stalin's agricultural policy, the disastrous irrigation projects, the relentless ploughing and grazing, including the introduction of robust sheep from the Caucasus mountains, all had reduced the dark soil of the once fertile steppe to a near desert. There was no industry, except for a trifling amount of food processing, fishing and wool washing, and the average wage was little more than fifty US dollars a month. Who could live on that?

Elista had few shops, his sister said, and fewer restaurants. She'd been true to her word and had taken Sangmu back to Kalmykia every few years to visit what was left of her family. The capital, ramshackle as it was, compared favourably to the rest of Kalmykia, she'd said. But despite the hardships only a relative few had come to America. Now, Moscow didn't bother them much in their restored autonomous republic. They had their own land, albeit in a poor state. Their language, abolished in 1924 by the Bolsheviks, was once more being taught in the few schools that existed. Traditional musical instruments were made from imported Mongolian timber and domestic animal skins. They were making the best of it. All this Gabriel knew, but it didn't explain a thing.

The library building was a six-storey, windowless, off-white oblong, the walls of which were made of translucent marble and appeared to glow orange in the half-light of dawn and dusk. It had closed for months of renovation works. Normally the interior was cavernous, with subdued lighting and the feel of an ultra-modern place of worship, the valuable books in tiers of glass cabinets, their antique pages illuminated by hundreds of jaundiced lightbulbs. Gabriel had always thought it looked like an outsized and extravagant beehive.

Now it was all but empty, the cathedral of learning rendered prosaic by rusted and paint-stained scaffolding, by enormous dust sheets and hung polythene dividers.

It was off-limits to the students who usually filled every available work surface, every recess. But Boris Iliev, a Bulgarian, had refused to work anywhere else and had been granted a concession. He'd published a dozen books on his specialty and was widely regarded as the leading expert in his field. He was in the religious studies department and specialized in Tibetan Buddhism, although he also had a penchant for Kalmyk history.

If any man could make sense of it, it was Boris Iliev.

CHAPTER FORTY-FOUR

New York State, the same day.

Johnny Hockey had entered a not guilty plea when the case was heard before a district judge at his arraignment, following the return of the grand jury indictment. The public defender had told him beforehand that it was normal to plead not guilty at this stage of the proceedings. It allowed sufficient time for the disclosure of detailed evidence to take place. Hockey had shrugged nonchalantly. He wasn't going back to federal prison in any case. Word had gotten to him that today was 'game day'.

Federal prisoner transport was the responsibility of the US Marshals Service. The transport vehicle was a white van, reinforced with blast-proof doors, side impact bars, wire mesh and bulletproof windows. It was doing a steady thirty miles per hour as it carried Hockey and two prisoners from the federal courthouse back to the remote correctional facility. They were held in segregated compartments that were little more than claustrophobic cages, which smelled vaguely of bleach and beeswax. To mask the stink of previous passengers, Hockey knew.

The sun was a peach-coloured glow atop a grassy hill, the country road a mere two-lane track without white markings. At a junction, a black station wagon approached from around the nearest bend. It skidded to a halt in front of the van. Simultaneously, two dark-green SUVs and a mail van, which had been travelling behind, boxed it in, like police cars corralling a drunk driver on a motorway. Two at the sides, preventing the van's left-hand doors from opening, and one at the rear. Reversing wasn't an option and the right-hand doors were all but jammed in by an overgrown bank. The vehicles had tinted windscreens and opaque windows — even the mail van.

The driver was Carl Carpenter, thirty-two, a big-boned ex-Navy man, with a widow's peak. He wore wraparound shades. He'd watched the vehicles on and off, a little warily, in the wing mirror for the past five minutes or so, but had put his fears of their significance down to an overactive imagination, a decision he now regretted. The air conditioning was on full blast and he reached over to the dial and turned it down, silencing the airflow.

'Jesus,' Kowalski said.

He was a squat, middle-aged guy, with a foot fetish he couldn't keep to himself, and a bad case of halitosis that made Carpenter wince. In truth, Carpenter didn't know which disgusted him the most. They were both dressed in general issue black padded jackets, Kowalski with a baseball cap on his meaty head. Their holsters held Glock 22 .40 calibre pistols.

'Stay calm,' Carpenter said. 'Call it in.'

Kowalski picked up the VHF radio handset and reported what had happened. He said they had a potential life-threatening hijack situation, and added that he wasn't sure exactly what was going down, but if they didn't receive emergency backup soon, there could be fatalities.

For a few seconds, it was as if they were merely waiting at a red light, except there was no passing traffic. Carpenter wondered if the roads had been blocked with fake maintenance works. Maybe there just wasn't any traffic. It was isolated enough.

He looked around him. He watched, almost casually in the circumstances, a buzzard struggling to hover above a swaying cornfield, buffeted by the high wind. But his thoughts were dark, and who knew what lurked in the blackness?

Kowalski went for his Glock.

'Wait, you wanna get killed for *these*?' Carpenter said, referring to their human cargo. 'Let's just see how this pans out.'

Carpenter wanted to live. He *had* to live. His wife, Fran, was eight months pregnant.

His personal smartphone rang. He put his hand into his cargo pocket, pulled it out. The number was unknown. He took it anyway.

'Who's this?'

'Just shut fuckup. Watch video on phone. If you love wife, watch.'

It was a woman's voice, a little staccato due to the shaky connection. An accent he wasn't sure about due to the quality, but had sounded Eastern European.

'What the hell's going on?' he said.

But he checked his mobile hurriedly. A video had been sent. He thumbed it open. He heard the screaming first. It was Fran. His eyes widened and sweat broke out on his forehead. His breath quickened, and he found himself clasping the smartphone so hard that a vein popped up on the back of his hand.

Fran was on her back. It looked like a bedroom, but he'd nearly gone into shock. A man was standing over her, wearing blue denim overalls that looked strewn with paint and oil. His face was obscured by a white, full-face ski mask, making identification impossible. He held a knife with a long, serrated blade. Fran's arms were over her head, her hands and forearms out of view. Her legs were splayed, as if she was going into labour. The bump of her stomach seemed to have increased in size, such that it dominated the small screen. She looked as vulnerable as a wing-damaged sparrow.

'Open back door, Carpenter,' the woman's voice said. 'I don't tell you again.'

Carpenter hit two buttons instantly. The back door unlocked. He was whimpering and shaking.

The radio crackled. A voice said, 'A state trooper is twenty seconds away. Don't get out of the vehicle.'

Carpenter fingered the silver Saint Christopher next to his pulsating throat, which he regarded more as an agnostic amulet than a symbol of faith. He didn't hear a siren. He adjusted the wing mirror electronically. The road that rose to the hill behind him was empty. He started pleading to God with a new-found piety for his wife's deliverance.

CHAPTER FORTY-FIVE

Yale, the same day.

Professor Boris Iliev was in a poky basement office. He was a tall man, perhaps six three, with an elongated neck, pallid skin and wiry grey hair. A pair of thick, black-rimmed glasses were perched halfway down his hawkish nose. He wore a woollen, pale green blazer, with buttons that looked like hazelnuts. The tone of his voice was guttural, almost comically so, as if he spent his days trading in scrap iron rather than poring over ancient and sacred texts for a living.

Sitting at a wooden desk, they exchanged pleasantries and Gabriel said that he had been shown a video of the horrific abuse and murder of a young Kalmyk woman in which the man wore a Tibetan demon mask and a Buddhist monk's robe. He didn't mention Sangmu, but he could see by the look on Iliev's face that he had an inkling of what this was all about, given he'd met Sangmu on a few occasions, knew she was a Kalmyk and that she'd disappeared in Central Park eighteen months before. Thankfully, he was too much of a gentleman to enquire further.

'I'd be grateful if this conversation was kept private,' Gabriel said.

'Of course, Gabriel.'

'Thank you.'

Iliev took off his glasses and began to stroke his left cheek at the tip of the left temple. 'How can I help you?'

Gabriel clasped his hands, forming a steeple above the desktop with his index fingers, which he pointed downwards. 'I know the Kalmyk people are Tibetan Buddhists, but that's just about all I know about their religion. Is there anything in their belief system that might allow what I just referred to?'

Iliev raised an eyebrow, as if he found the question a little impudent.

'I have to eliminate all possibilities,' Gabriel said, truthfully.

Iliev said that the Kalmyks followed the newest of the schools of Tibetan Buddhism known as Gelugpa, which some called the Yellow Hats. It had been founded over 700 years ago. The Gelugpa monks had allied themselves with the Mongols in 1577 and, over time, their spiritual practices had been adopted by those feared horsemen. In turn, that connection had propelled the school to pre-eminence in Tibet, which had been awash with warring Buddhist sects. Monks from the different factions had tortured and murdered one another.

'This was not the Tibet portrayed by Western culture, but rather a land overseen by monks that repressed the local peasantry. There was a class of untouchables, called ragyaba. Whippings that often led to death. Capital punishment was rife, as were penal amputations.'

Gabriel nodded rather sullenly. 'When did that stop?'

'Officially — in 1913. But severe lashings and judicial mutilations are documented up to the date of the Chinese invasion of Tibet in 1950.'

Iliev smiled, revealing gaps in his teeth. He eased his head back and breathed out. He remained silent for a few seconds.

'Often a single example speaks loudest, does it not? In 1934, Tsepon Lungshar, a not insubstantial Tibetan official, was blinded for advocating political reform in his Buddhist homeland. The untouchables tightened two yak knucklebones onto his temples by means of leather thongs attached to the bones, and a stick above the crown of his poor head, which they simply twisted. The pressure was too much for one of his eyes. The other was gouged out. His empty eye sockets were cauterized with boiling water.'

Gabriel thought Iliev sounded as if he was describing something as innocuous as how to tie a cravat. Maybe it was just the way his accent jarred, the way it seemed to lack any intonation, any compassion.

'The Chinese invaders weren't any better, of course,' he went on. 'I'm merely pointing out the reality. It was no Shangri-La.'

Images from the DVD and the blinding of the Tibetan official jostled for dominance in Gabriel's mind, and he felt a strong urge to hit a bar and order a double Jack and Coke. He wanted to drink so much that he would lose himself in it. But he managed to remain outwardly objective.

He said, 'And what about the Kalmyks? Is their Tibetan Buddhism any different?'

'Historically, many Kalmyk monks trained in Tibet. They established portable monasteries and travelled with the nomadic people. Human rights weren't a priority.'

Based on what Iliev had said, the fact that he had portrayed the history of Tibetan Buddhism as a history of violence, Gabriel felt anxious, not least because it had substantiated what little he did in fact know.

He said, 'Is there anything in Tibetan Buddhism today that could explain the torture and murder of a young Kalmyk woman by someone dressed as a monk?'

Iliev shook his head a little. 'No. I'd say not. There is some controversy around a text called the Kalachakra Tantra, which is an apocalyptic vision. There are certain references to sex magic rites, wherein women are perceived as energy donors. But most academics regard these as allegorical in nature. Is there a record of human sacrifice in the last century? Or in this one? Absolutely not.' Iliev drummed his fingers on the desk. 'What I'm trying to say is that being a Tibetan Buddhist does not mean that you are from a pacifist tradition. But the culture of Kalmykia is no longer what we might term *medieval*.'

He paused, as if lost in thought, as if he was running an imaginary finger down the pages of an arcane document.

Gabriel rubbed his thigh, agitatedly. 'There was a ritualistic element in the DVD. At least that's what it seemed to be, to me.'

'I see.'

For some reason Gabriel found difficult to understand, he just couldn't bring himself to explore that any further.

He said, 'So the murderer could be a Tibetan Buddhist, a Kalmyk?'

Iliev's mouth formed a sphere. He said, 'Or an orthodox Jew, or a Roman Catholic. An atheist, perhaps. I'm not an expert on such things, Gabriel. Are you?'

'No, I'm not.'

Iliev's mobile rang. He took out an old model and made an apologetic face before answering it.

'Of course, my dear. No, I won't be late tonight. And yes, I'll pick up some milk on my way home.' He put his hands up. 'Now, if you don't mind, Gabriel.' He waved across the books and papers in front of him. 'Got to get a little more work done before I leave.'

'I understand. You've been very helpful. Thanks, Boris.'

Gabriel stood up to leave. Iliev looked up at him, his eyes squinting. He put his forefinger beside his head and it vibrated there. He looked a little vexed.

'I was giving a series of lectures at Harvard, a couple of years back. The influence of the Kalachakra Tantra on the Chilean diplomat and founder of Esoteric Hitlerism, Miguel Serrano, and the place of Tantric paraphernalia in ritual and magic. The last lecture was on a short history of Tibetan Buddhism in Kalmykia. An old man attended that lecture, though not the others, he confessed. We spoke after the lecture. We had coffee. He said his elder brother had told him that he saw something akin to the items that the Chinese had put on display in the Dalai Lama's Potala Palace after the invasion. The so-called Tibetan chamber of horrors.'

Gabriel nodded, knowing the reference.

Iliev sneered. 'Crude propaganda. The Chinese were just trying to justify the unjustifiable through fostering ignorant prejudice.'

Iliev dismissed it with a flick of his long hand.

'The old man said his brother had seen these things taken from a bunker in Berlin at the end of World War Two. He said that his brother had been one of several Poles that were ordered to carry out the gruesome task of loading the waiting trucks with the contents of the bunker. His brother was sent to the Gulag to keep him quiet and it killed him, he said.'

He paused. He grimaced.

'Does the DVD show the severing of limbs? The nose and ears?'

Gabriel hesitated. Then said, 'Yes, it does.'

'As I said, such things were typical punishments in pre-1950 Tibet for common criminals or those deemed enemies of the state. But in 1945 the victims were Red Army soldiers fighting Nazis in Berlin,' Iliev said. 'It was an unusual way to kill someone, though. In your DVD was the cranium severed and filled with smooth stones?'

'The same,' Gabriel said. His left leg began to vibrate involuntarily.

Iliev nodded, as if to himself.

'Is it a case you're working on, Gabriel?' he said, as if he was hoping it wasn't personal.

Gabriel knew that the world of commercial television, let alone social media, was simply of no interest to Boris Iliev. He'd likely never heard of Jed and Esfir Watson or Johnny Hockey.

'Yes,' Gabriel said.

'Thank God.'

Iliev made a face that confirmed that he was glad to be immersed in matters some concerned esoteric and irrelevant.

'Does the old man live in the US?' Gabriel said.

'He did at that time, or so he said.'

Gabriel knew that any other form of torture or the mutilation of a corpse could have been replicated perhaps twenty times. But this was different. If what the man had said to Iliev was true, it might be a lead. He had to believe it. And yet men had been the victims. Red Army soldiers. Not Kalmyk women. But he felt there had to be a link. Besides, he had nothing else to go on. Not a damn thing. If he didn't feel so desolate, he would have been excited.

'He only agreed to speak with me if I agreed to contact him if I came across anything like it,' Iliev said. 'I thought, why not? But that is odd. No?'

It is, Gabriel thought.

'I will speak with him. I'll tell him about the DVD, within reason.'

Boris Iliev nodded a fraction. 'OK, Gabriel. His name was Bronislaw Stolarski.'

'Do you have his address or phone number?

'No, he refused to give me them. That's strange too, I suppose. I never saw him again. He could be dead. He looked half dead then, come to think of it.'

'Could the DVD be part of an ongoing punishment for a crime? An old crime? A lingering dispute perhaps?' Gabriel said, thinking about the missing Kalmyk girls from New Jersey.

'I don't know, Gabriel. I really don't know.'

Gabriel saw Boris Iliev look at him with a mixture of sympathy and incredulity, as if he couldn't understand why a fellow intellectual would want to become involved in such a thing. Gabriel repeated the name, Bronislaw Stolarski, in his mind. An old Jewish man, he thought.

CHAPTER FORTY-SIX

Twelve feet behind Carpenter, Johnny Hockey knew that the heavy bolts securing the back doors had released. No doubt about it. The wind had eased the doors open just enough for him to see two guys running from the back of an SUV. One had a gas-powered metal cutter in his hands, like those used by firefighters, the other, binoculars and a radio. They were dressed in khaki fatigues, black ice hockey goalie masks and military boots. The two prisoners on either side of him shook their cages and jumped up and down like aroused apes. Hockey stayed silent and motionless, his shackled hands in his lap.

The man with the cutter let it hang down in one hand as he used the other to swing open the doors. He scrambled into the back of the van, saying nothing. Hockey felt the warm air, smelled the bilious sweetness of the corn.

'The steel's not that thick,' he said, finally.

He heard the engine of the station wagon in front start up, then it took off. He couldn't make sense of it. But now he saw the flickering LED lights on the road to the rear, the faint noise of the siren, like a hog chased on a farm.

The second masked guy, who was still outside the van, spoke briefly into the radio before laying the binoculars on the floor. He pulled a piece from an ankle holster; a small revolver by the look of it, Hockey thought. He held it barrel up and fidgeted agitatedly, staring at the fast-approaching state trooper's black and gold vehicle. He put the radio to his ear briefly and turned and shouted at the man with the cutter to abort. Hockey felt the urge to swear, like someone afflicted with Tourette's, but instead he just concentrated on his breathing.

He saw a third person exit the SUV at speed, dressed as the other two. But he noticed the end of a ponytail jutting out from the collar of the plaid shirt worn under the fatigues. Ponytail walked purposely towards the man with the revolver and, grabbing the wrist of his gun hand, jerked him forward and drove a knee into his groin. He doubled over, gasping. Ponytail, still holding the wrist, slid a boot behind his right ankle and drove the free palm into his right shoulder. He fell backwards. But Ponytail didn't let go of the wrist and twisted it viciously as he toppled. There was a sickening *crack*, a branch snapping, and the revolver was snatched away deftly before he was halfway to the uneven aggregate. The man howled.

Ponytail crouched down, putting a knee onto the man's chest. The action seemed to stifle his writhing. The mask was yanked off his face, the trigger cocked, and he was shot through the forehead with his own weapon. A little grey smoke, a louder *crack*. The revolver had bucked a fraction. The man's head had bounced off the dusty surface as the round impacted. Blood spurted out from the entry wound like water from a drinking fountain, subsiding after a second or two.

It drenched his face now, the blackened wound like barbequed meat. Ponytail and the guy with the cutter walked back to their vehicle, with a nonchalance Hockey knew most would find disconcerting. He saw Ponytail take one last glance at the police cruiser before getting back into the SUV.

A couple of seconds later, the remaining vehicles screeched away, fishtailing as puffs of blue tyre smoke rose about the wheel arches. The two prisoners opposite Hockey slumped down on their metal seats, dejected.

Hockey inhaled the fecund smell of the farmland, the dry air almost burning the back of his throat. He nodded, accepting the events that had transpired.

*

Fury had arranged for two vehicle changes in the hour that had elapsed since the aborted mission, leaving the redundant cars in isolated barns. She'd thrown the revolver out of the open window, into a drainage ditch. The Russian driver of the white SUV they were now in pulled off the road at a gas station that had four pumps positioned under a roof supported by flaking cream-coloured pillars.

The wooden shop to the left was painted a drab green. There were no other vehicles. Dusk had fallen, the temperature had dropped by almost six degrees already. The Russian driver parked up next to a pump and Fury got out. She told the three Russians not to move until she got back. She strolled over the cracked and dirty forecourt to a payphone and rang the American that had worn the mask in the video of Fran Carpenter, the pregnant woman.

'She OK?' she said.

'No physical harm has come to her. What now?'

'End it quick,' Fury said.

'Yes, ma'am.'

The woman had seen her face and it was always going to end this way. Fury replaced the receiver before checking her make-up in the shiny stainless steel around the handset, as if she'd merely ordered a takeaway.

She dialled César Vezzani's number next and reported all that had transpired. He expressed his disappointment but told her that they had located the brunette called Charlene Rimes. He gave her an address and she heard him hang up. They'd used the code names that Vezzani had put in the flight bag at the Morning Inn, although she thought they were so basic that he must have made them up in less than a minute while he was shaving, or something similarly mundane. *Hen. Rooster. Pullet.* And so on. Maybe he'd been watching a documentary about chickens at the time, or was just fond of them. Maybe he like the taste of chicken meat. What did it matter?

Surfer's death was an irrelevance to her. The guy that had pulled the revolver was a liability. She'd killed him because he'd disobeyed her direct order. She decided she'd only use her own people from now on. The state trooper was random and sheer bad luck, she decided. If there'd been a leak, the roads would've been choked with FBI vehicles, the sky filled with the sound of their helicopters before they could make good their escape.

She walked back to the SUV and an attendant came up. He was about thirty-five, with a huge gut and a patchy beard. He wore a stained red T-shirt with a profile portrait of Marilyn Monroe on it. He had a half-eaten doughnut in his hand. She remained outside the vehicle.

'Hey, buddy. You gonna use the pump or what?' he said to the driver.

Fury noticed his overcrowded teeth and weak jaw, the scar that indicated he'd been born with a harelip.

'Урод,' the driver said, leaning towards him. *A real ugly man.*

She knew he was pissed off at their failure to rescue Hockey and had wanted to take it out on someone. But she rebuked him in Russian: *ублюдок. A real bastard.*

Turning to the open-mouthed attendant, she said, 'All men are pigs, yes. But not you. You are not pig.'

He stood there, his expression changing from gratitude to one of mild concern, the way men looked when they registered her physical strength, its jarring juxtaposition with her facial beauty. He was silent for a few seconds. Nothing seemed to move, as if there was a fissure in time.

'No, ma'am. I'm no pig.'

She walked over to him and stretched out her hand and he flinched, his head titling back, but there was no threat in it. She touched his lip lightly, almost tenderly, with two of her fingertips.

'My cousin in Omsk has lip like you.' She half smiled. 'We do not need pump. OK?'

He trembled a little and walked away, turning back once after he'd gotten a few feet from the door of the shop, his face betraying his bemusement and anxiety.

She turned to the driver, who looked to be sulking. 'Cheer up, Afanasy. We're going a long way north to play with a bitch pindo,' she said, referring to a slutty American woman.

He grinned.

Then they all started grinning.

CHAPTER FORTY-SEVEN

Berlin, 1945, the next day.

The NKVD major general's office dwarfed Kazapov's, with a French First Empire chandelier in lacquered bronze at its centre, the supporting chains attached to the necks of the nine gold-plated imperial eagle heads. There were decanters of the finest Godet cognac, and exquisite rugs worth more than it cost to construct a house in pre-war Moscow. All of it stolen goods. It smelled of cigar smoke and sandalwood aftershave balm and had been previously occupied by the Waffen-SS commanding officer, a Prussian count. A man who died at Stalingrad.

The general's uniform was of fine khaki cloth, trimmed in blue silk and embroidered with the insignia of the internal troops of the NKVD. The tunic had gold buttons and an erect collar, edged with crimson where it reached his fleshy chin. He was examining the brass casket that had been retrieved from the bunker. Kazapov had purposely replaced the padlock with another, which he'd blackened with a cigarette lighter.

The general crouched over it now, with his hands on the rim, his legs slightly bent. He'd refused to allow Kazapov to place it on his antique desk when he'd entered the office a few minutes before. He'd pointed to a bare patch of the polished wooden floor, about three feet from a

Louis XV console table that was pressed against the wall. The table had a photograph on it of what Kazapov guessed was his family back in Georgia; a stern-looking wife, her black hair in a bun, and five teenage children standing in front of a wood-panelled dacha beside a frozen lake. Kazapov had recognized the general's accent as being the same as his own mother's, and smarted a little when he'd first heard him speak.

The general was a small man with ample cheeks. Below his bald, suntanned head, his eyebrows were thick and wiry, his nose short and broad. But his rank demanded respect from everyone but the highest members of the Party. Kazapov knew that the general had arrived in Berlin from Moscow a couple of days ago. He suspected that Comrade Beria had sent him. He knew that Beria, and more importantly, Stalin, liked their own kind in places of power, especially after the purges.

The general straightened up and placed his palms on his lower back.

'Mutilated Red Army soldiers. Macabre items. That mummified woman. This mysterious box,' he said, pointing his round chin at the casket. 'Major Volsky says he won't find out anything else from the German officer and that he should be handed over to the experts.' He raised an unkempt eyebrow.

Kazapov remained silent and still, conscious that the general could be testing him.

The general shook his head before walking over to his fine desk. He placed his right palm there, raising his chin into the air imperiously.

'Well, do you have any idea what this is about, Kazapov?'

'Not yet, comrade general. It would be most helpful if I was allowed access to the SS colonel. I think I can help in deciphering all of this quickly.'

'So, you don't believe what he said to Major Volsky?'

'With respect, comrade general, the major is used to dealing with military prisoners, and the German, whoever he is and whatever he knows, is not a military type, at least that is not the essence of the man.'

'That smacks of insubordination, Kazapov, which is a dangerous trait in peacetime and a very dangerous one in wartime.' He looked quizzical. 'Where are you from?

'I was brought up in Stalingrad. My father died there in a Stuka attack. My mother is Georgian.'

'I see. Georgian, eh. Good. Well, I can't see the harm in it. You are authorized to investigate such things?'

Kazapov nodded. 'I am assigned to the ChGK.'

'Indeed. But it will form part of my report to Commissar Beria.' The general's face took on a mischievous expression. 'He might call for you.'

'It would be an honour, comrade general.'

Kazapov saw the general look at him as if he was a maniac. He knew that most young NKVD officers did their utmost to keep their distance from the unpredictable and sadistic Beria.

'But I must warn you that you don't have much time. Now take the box, open it and speak with the German. Then you will report to me,' the general said. He waved a meaty finger at the casket. 'I don't have to tell you to photograph the contents and document them.'

'Shall I open it here, comrade general? It's the reason I came to see you, after all.'

'Here? Absolutely not. I imagine you'll find something disgusting in it, and the benefit of being an NKVD general is that I don't have to see disgusting things any more if I don't choose to. Nor partake in disgusting acts. Do you understand me, Kazapov?'

Kazapov nodded once. 'I do, comrade general.'

'Get to the bottom of all this and you might even get transferred from the ChGK. A hideous business.'

The general's face looked as he he'd sniffed ammonia.

Kazapov didn't tell him that he'd volunteered for the role. He walked over to the casket and reached down for it, feeling most pleased with himself. He had the general's consent to question Richter, which was his purpose. The casket was a sideshow, an excuse to be in his presence, even though he was desperate to examine its contents thoroughly, the film too, of course. He lifted the casket, which wasn't heavy, and turned towards the oak double doors, with their intricate gold-leaf knobs. There was a knock at the doors.

'Yes,' the general said.

An NKVD captain opened the doors and peered in.

'Fräulein Bayer, comrade general.'

The general smiled, revealing his uneven teeth.

A young woman entered, wearing high heels, sheer stockings and a long coat trimmed with fox fur. She had soft features, blonde hair that curled at the ends and a full mouth, accentuated by crimson lipstick. Kazapov was amazed. Until that moment, the Berlin women he'd seen had looked dishevelled, soot-ridden and ravaged by war. Wizened and ghostly, even.

'I hope I'm not disturbing you, general,' the woman said. Her Russian was passable.

'Not at all, my dear. Lieutenant Kazapov was just leaving. With his box.'

She turned to Kazapov and smiled.

'You. I saw you in Berlin.'

'You did?' Kazapov said, feeling anxious.

'Yes. You saved an old German woman from being molested. I was driving by in a staff car.'

Kazapov saw the general glance at her.

'On the way to visit *you*, my darling,' she said to the general.

The general smiled weakly.

'I did what I thought was right, comrade general,' Kazapov said.

'No doubt,' the general said.

'I saw some drunken men attack a woman in a headscarf, so frail she stooped. I thought it was an affront to the revolution. A disgrace to Stalin and our glorious leaders.'

The orders had come from Moscow that rape was to be frowned upon rather than encouraged. Kazapov thought that Moscow had become concerned about post-war repercussions now their revenge on the German fascists had been all but exacted.

'Quite so. You acted correctly, young man.'

'You are sweet,' Fräulein Bayer said. 'You remind me of someone I once knew.'

Trying not to stare, Kazapov told himself that even being fucked by the general had to be better than being gang-raped by stinking, drunken conscripts. He doubted she would have survived if it hadn't been for the old man.

He brought his heels together and nodded to her, catching a whiff of her perfume as he left.

CHAPTER FORTY-EIGHT

Kazapov had returned to his own office, with the brass casket, feeling frustrated for more than one reason. Apart from his unsettling meeting with Fräulein Bayer, he'd also been told that Lutz Richter had been taken to the infirmary with breathing problems. That worried him, but he'd been assured that they weren't life-threatening complications.

Sitting at his desk, he considered now whether Fräulein Bayer was as charming and complex as a Saint-Saëns piano concerto. He couldn't decide. She was just a distraction. Wasn't she? Yes, indeed. Just a beautiful image to compete with the ugly images of war that were in danger of sending him half mad, he knew. It was imperative that he remained lucid and rational. The alternative was to do something spontaneous. But to do something spontaneous in Berlin was to end up dead or in Siberia, where a man might as well be dead. He couldn't find out what happened to his mother and sisters then.

He sensed that he was close. He couldn't fathom why exactly, apart from what he now knew about the religious items from Kalmykia in the bunker, and that he'd studied the typed transcripts of Major Volsky's interrogation of the SS colonel in detail, using his ChGK credentials as a pretext. The reference to Doctor Doll had simply heightened his sense of anticipation, rather than perplex him.

He realized now that an image of Fräulein Bayer wasn't enough. He wasn't a rapist. He was young, and he hadn't had sex for over six months. He'd pulled a young Jew from a cellar in a village, twenty miles south of the city of Stanisławów in western Ukraine.

Over the following three days, he'd taken her statement as he was billeted temporarily in the area. She'd been hiding from the Ordnungspolizei and her fellow Ukrainians in the auxiliary police. She'd offered herself to him. It wasn't gratitude, she'd said. She'd just wanted to feel the warmth of human skin against hers, after living like a rat for months. She was clever and pretty and courageous and alone. She'd said she'd wait for him. Part of him had wanted to say that he would come back to her. But, how could he?

He realized he wanted Fräulein Bayer for different reasons. She'd made eyes at him, hadn't she? She was a prostitute, wasn't she? At least, one with a single customer. He needed to try, at least. The memory of her would be just another torment unless he did. He would have to wait until a projector could be found to view the film. Why waste time speculating? The throb in his breeches had become undeniable.

I must see her again, he thought.

He wanted to forget the war for one night.

*

Kazapov had bribed a Red Army military police sergeant to find out where Fräulein Bayer lived. The man was, he'd said, a former cook in a state-run hotel in Moscow. Now he supplied the willing German prostitutes with the legs of wild rabbits and a few potatoes. The odd duck egg for the women who were prepared to do the things the others wouldn't. They were living in a converted mansion house on the eastern edge of the defeated city.

Kazapov stood now in front of the house, a three-storey baroque structure, built with natural stone. There were bullet holes in the brown brick around the rose window, which was above the oak-panelled door. The window was boarded up, as were all the others. There were chunks of lime plaster lying about the uneven pavement, the result of a howitzer shell exploding on the edge of the second floor, he reasoned. But it was essentially cosmetic damage and the building looked habitable enough.

The house was situated in a street that was off-limits to the ranks. A notice had been nailed to the door, stating that the building was under the protection of Stavka, the Soviet High Command. Anyone that entered without specific authorization would be shot. Kazapov knew that this was no hollow threat.

He moved across the street and concealed himself in the remnants of a large townhouse opposite. He crouched down beside a brick wall, smirched by black smoke. He could see the darkening sky through a massive hole in the ceiling and roof. Wasn't this a spontaneous act? No, reckless, perhaps, but not spontaneous. There was a difference.

The street had been cleared of Germans a week before and now appeared lifeless. Nothing stirred. Not even a rat. It was as if the area had been subjected to a massive deposit of lethal gas. Just then, he heard an approaching vehicle.

Twenty seconds later, he saw a black NKVD staff car travelling slowly up the street, avoiding the craters and larger pieces of broken masonry that still littered it, although it was obvious that an attempt had been made to clear a passageway through the worst of the rubble. It stopped outside the mansion and Fräulein Bayer was helped from the back seat by a fellow NKVD lieutenant, who saluted after she'd stepped onto the pavement. She pulled her fur collar up around her elegant neck. The evening air had a steely quality to it.

Kazapov held his breath.

The car drove off and he watched her open her purse and remove what he guessed was a door key. He emerged from his hiding place and walked across the street. She heard his boots on the rubble, he knew, because she hesitated as she got to the top of the cracked entrance steps but didn't turn around.

'Fräulein Bayer,' he said in German.

She turned. 'Yes. Who is it?'

'Lieutenant Kazapov. We met in the general's office earlier today.'

'Oh yes,' she said, smiling. 'What on earth are you doing here?'

He didn't reply. He just kept looking at her.

'You know you shouldn't be here,' she said, twisting at the waist and pointing to the notice behind her before turning back. 'But I'll tell you a secret. No one ever comes here to check. I suppose the sign is enough of a deterrent. Except for you, that is.'

'I needed to see you,' Kazapov said.

She giggled. It wasn't a nervous reaction, but rather the response of a woman that was used to such comments. He had simply validated the power she had, even in a city where German women were defence-less victims.

'Needed?'

He nodded. 'Yes, needed.'

'Do you drink tea? The tea is worse than average and there is no milk.' She turned and unlocked the door without waiting for an answer.

There was only one possible answer, after all.

CHAPTER FORTY-NINE

The smoke rose sluggishly to the dull-white ceiling. No lights were allowed at this hour, the small room illuminated only by the lazy inhalations on their cigarettes. Her given name was Brigitte. She'd been a minor stage actress prior to the last months of the war, and Kazapov liked her sense of self-deprecation. When she'd taken off her navy-blue and white polka dot dress, that was worn below the knee, she wore a whalebone corset of crimson silk. She left her high heels on as she walked over to him. He'd felt as if he could've floated.

'Do you know why you are lying here with me?' she said.

He shook his head. 'No. I don't'

'Remember in the general's office I said that you reminded me of someone?'

'I remember.'

She sighed. 'He was called Kurt. He was a Luftwaffe pilot. He was shot down two years ago. He was my first real boyfriend. Do you know why you remind me of him?'

'How could I?'

'Because he would have helped that old woman too, despite the danger. And because he was the only boy who had the courage to ask me out. A bit like you. Does that upset you?'

'Not at all.'

She inhaled deeply and exhaled the smoke audibly.

'What will happen to us?' she said.

Stroking her firm breast beneath the single white sheet, Kazapov said, 'I really don't know. The world is like a playground for madmen. And yet every cell in my body is heightened by it, as if I'm in a constant state of sexual excitement.'

Brigitte's body stiffened, and she pushed her head back into the pillow.

'That scares me, Joseph.'

He felt a deep guilt rise from the pit of his stomach. Why had he said such a thing, after all he had seen? The horror of it. He knew then for perhaps the first time that he was changed. Forever changed.

'Will you act again?' he said, wishing to change the subject.

'Oh, no. After all that has happened, how could anyone waste their life acting? I will simply live a decent life. How could anyone want anything else after so many have suffered and perished? Just the simple things will be enough. Enough fresh food to eat. A walk in the open without wondering if you will be raped or murdered. The simple things.'

They finished their cigarettes, stubbed them out in the heavy glass ashtray between their thighs.

'The general said you too will be a general one day. That's if you learn to court your superiors rather than antagonize them. He sees something in you.'

'The old man is a clown.'

She nodded, her expression wistful. 'What part of Russia are you from?' she said, propping herself up on the pillow, such that her breasts were visible.

He told her. He told her about his father's death in Stalingrad and his mother and sisters too, that he suspected that they'd never left Kalmykia. His deepest fear, he said, and one that dominated his inner dialogue.

He had to tell someone, he thought, although he found it both cathartic and at odds with the reason he believed he was here in her bed.

He began to tell her something of his work, but she asked him to stop. She said she'd seen enough already. He chastised himself silently.

'Do you have a photograph?' he said.

'I was an actress. I have scores of photographs. Would you like one?'

'Thank you.'

'But I want something from you too,' she said. 'Just to remind me that tenderness existed, even here.'

He nodded. He'd kept a few photographs of his time in the previous occupied territories in his wallet as solemn mementoes.

She reached over to the bedside table and, after he'd gotten out of bed and had gone to his jacket slung over a chair, they made an exchange. He returned to the warmth of the bed, of her silky body.

Her hand hovered above his bandaged shoulder. He could tell that she was resisting asking him about it. This was the nature of war, he thought. In the thick of it, you wanted to be anywhere else. When you were somewhere else, you couldn't help returning to it in your mind. She asked him then, despite her previous statement, and he told her.

The deep wound he'd sustained by the knife-wielding Waffen-SS panzergrenadier had been exacerbated when he and a platoon of NVKD troops had first entered Berlin. They'd been ambushed by a group of Hitler Youth that had ridden around the smashed city on bicycles, hunting Soviet tanks. Each one had had a couple of panzerfausts, a recoilless metal tube used to launch a high explosive warhead, clipped to their handlebars, like outsized fishing rods. The little bastards.

The NKVD men had unleashed a volley from their small arms after a panzerfaust shell had exploded against a pitched roof, a few feet above Kazapov's head. He'd been showered by sludge before a sharp edge from a careering piece of shattered guttering had embedded itself into his already slashed shoulder. He'd half-staggered into a ravaged house. The medic had patched him up, sewing the sutures without the benefit of an anaesthetic. He'd been told that he would be left with an ugly and permanent scar from the end of his right shoulder to the bottom of his neck.

'Can I see you again?' he said.

'You must know that if it wasn't for the war, we would not be here together. The war makes one do extraordinary things. I'm no whore.'

'I know that,' he said, lying. 'How could anyone presume you a whore?'

'The general,' she said, desperately.

'You are merely saving yourself from death. I do the same. Your weapon is beauty. Mine is the NKVD uniform I wear.'

She snuggled into his chest.

'Will you see me again?' he said.

'This is a dream wrapped in a nightmare and I need to wake up,' she said.

Kazapov jerked away from her and, lifting his side of the bedsheet, stepped out of the bed again and walked towards the armchair where he'd placed his clothes.

'I must go,' he said.

'If you must.'

'You will never speak of the things we discussed to anyone.'

'Of course, not,' she said,

'I can rely on you then?'

'Really, Joseph. How could I have survived all this by repeating the things I overhear?'

Her voice betrayed her rising fear. After her easy dismissal of a relationship, however brief, he savoured it.

CHAPTER FIFTY

Back in his office, Kazapov had placed the brass casket onto the centre of his ink-stained desk. He'd cleaned it meticulously with methylated spirits.

He lit one of the strong cigarettes that were already starting to make him cough in the mornings, which he obstinately put down to the war's ill effect on his health. Inhaling, he put his cigarette on the corner of an amber, art deco ashtray, and rummaged around in the left-hand drawer of the desk before laying his hand on the small magnifying glass he'd placed there when he'd first been assigned the office. He took it out, put it on the desktop.

He unlocked the replacement padlock. Opening the lid, he smelled the remnants of the exotic odours. He lifted out the scrolls and parchments within and placed them on the desk. Beneath them was the metal cylinder.

He unwrapped one of the scrolls and stared at the writing. It looked simplistic and was indecipherable. There was a double X, an inverted R, a childlike b and backward 3. He recognized it as the Cyrillic script of Kalmyk Oirat.

Frustrated, he took out the cylinder and unscrewed the lid. He knew from experience that films had been made of the savage German advance into the Soviet Union, of the torture and murder of camp inmates and Axis traitors, too. The worst of the Nazis liked to watch them for ghoulish entertainment, the survivors had said.

He held a frame of the film up to the desk lamp and used the magnifying glass to get a better look. He saw the Kalmyk volunteer in his ushanka, or woollen hat, a Reichsadler adorning it. He was astride his Panje horse.

Now another Kalmyk volunteer, whose wild-looking hat was made of some long fur he didn't recognize. This man had a merciless face, with an unkempt and drooping moustache, a bandana of cartridges slung across his uniformed chest. Kazapov's breath quickened.

He knew the history of the Kalmyk people had long been one of violence. They had originated from Oirats, western Mongolians, who migrated from the steppes of southern Siberia to the lower Volga region of the then Russian Empire in the 1600s. They'd continued their nomadic lifestyle, living in felt yurts south of the Don River, and wintered on the western shores of the Caspian Sea.

They'd fought for the imperial tsars against Napoleon, against the British in the Crimea and the Turks in the Ottoman wars. Prior to the Russian Revolution, parts of their land had been overtaken by settlers, and some 200,000 had left for their ancestral home. The remainder had built fixed settlements, including Elista. But they'd continued their allegiance to the tsars and had fought for the White Army in the Russian Civil War. A few had escaped the Bolshevik backlash and settled in Belgrade with the Russian émigrés, where they'd constructed the first Buddhist temple in Western Europe.

For those Kalmyks that had decided to stay put, there had followed repressive years in which Stalin executed their leaders, desecrated their temples and burned their religious texts. They'd become impoverished peasant farmers. Monks and leading Kalmyks were deported to Siberia. Sixty thousand had died in the great famine of 1931–2. A time when the state had had to remind its citizens that it was a crime to eat their own children, or other people's children.

When the Great Patriotic War had broken out against the Nazis, it became clear that some Kalmyks had never forgiven their treatment by the Bolsheviks. They had collaborated with the Germans, hoping for a degree of freedom, Kazapov guessed, although thousands more had fought for the Red Army. He knew it wasn't uncommon for even ethnic Russian populations to be split in their allegiances.

In February 1943, three months after Kalmykia was 'liberated' by the Red Army and loyal partisans, Kazapov had gone there as part of the ChGK team investigating war crimes. He'd spoken with an elderly farmer, an eyewitness to some of the atrocities. The farmer had also informed him that he'd allowed a Russian woman and her three teenage daughters to hide in his barn. They'd been left behind by a small group of partisans. They'd been hunted by mounted Kalmyks allied to the Germans, and the females hadn't been able keep up. They looked like Jews, he said. Kazapov had been only too aware that his mother and sister could be taken for Jews.

A squad of Kalmyks had searched the barn soon afterwards. The four females had been found, of course. They'd been put into one of the farmer's own carts and had been pulled away by two of his own mules. The farmer had put up his hands and had shrugged when he'd been questioned further. He'd told Kazapov that he'd thought he was going to be shot, but for some reason they'd spared his life and left hurriedly. He'd guessed they were eager to molest the women.

Upon hearing this first-hand, Kazapov had puked up his breakfast in front of the farmer and had trembled to such an extent that the farmer's toothless wife insisted that he rest awhile and drink some goat's milk laced with vodka and eat some salted fish to rejuvenate him. Kazapov had wished then that Stalin had made corpses of every Kalmyk.

Later, he'd convinced himself that the women the farmer had spoken about were not his mother and sisters. Many mass graves had been uncovered in Kalmykia and the corpses exhumed had included numerous women, not all of them Jews. None had been identified as his mother or sisters.

He convinced himself of it still. There were millions of displaced refugees wandering around in Europe. They could be anywhere.

Now Kazapov put down the reel of film, his eyes moistening.

If he believed that, then why had he volunteered for the bunker detachment?

He reached for another cigarette, decided he needed vodka.

PART TWO

REVELATION

CHAPTER FIFTY-ONE

Virginia, 2015, the next day.

Gabriel had driven for nearly four hours. Darkness had fallen slowly, the cloud on the horizon ribboned and fiery. Carla had called him on the mobile she'd given him in Connecticut, and he said he had things to tell her and she said likewise. She'd asked him to meet her at her home a few miles from Arlington County.

He parked the sedan and got out. He walked over the flint-ridden path to the three-storey farmhouse, glancing at the apple orchard, silhouetted against the eastern skyline like a giant spider's web. There was a little lake or slurry pit out there amid cattle pasture, and it was surrounded by a split-level fence. He could just about make out a patch of the oleaginous water, the moonlight playing on it.

He knocked on the oak door, feeling oddly nervous. The hall light went on. She was barefoot and wore a flowing white linen dress that all but hid her shapely body. Her hair was up, a few strands cupping her chin, and a gold crucifix hung from her neck.

'Please come in,' Carla said.

She led him through the hallway and he noticed a walk clock with Roman numerals, and the framed photos of, he guessed, Amazonian tribespeople. The living room was commodious, with dark-wood furniture and brass table lamps of irregular design. The room smelled of a mixture of rosehip and lavender water. They sat opposite each other on armchairs, the upholstery's ornate embroidery pleasing to him.

'Did you hear about the attempt to free Hockey?' she said.

He nodded, morosely. 'Yes.'

'The officer is a psychological wreck. They haven't found his wife yet.'

Gabriel breathed out hard. 'I know.'

'Have you told Hockey you can't represent him anymore?' she said.

'No. But I will.'

She pulled the hem of her dress down. 'So, what have you got for me?'

He told her about the snow lion emblem and the Tibetan demon mask. She said that she knew about those things, and she said it in a way that bordered on irritation. He gave her a summary of his talk with Boris Iliev, although he left out the part about Bronislaw Stolarski and his brother in World War Two. He wanted to speak with Stolarski first, if he consented and was up to it. In truth, he'd found the story questionable and wanted to confirm or reject that suspicion face-to-face. Then he realized he didn't even know if he was still alive.

She grabbed her knee, awkwardly, as if she was suffering from rheumatism. 'The girl in the DVD wasn't your niece, was she?'

He winced. 'No. I'm sure of that, at least.'

He knew that this was the main reason she'd allowed him to watch the DVD. It was the main reason he had watched it, too, if he was being honest.

'Why would someone do that?' he said.

'There could be many reasons.'

There were a few seconds of silence between them.

She said, 'I told you at Frank's Place that if you helped me, I would help you. I meant that.'

She told him about her telephone conversation with Robert Dubois, stating that he was her counterpart in Brussels. She didn't mention their love affair.

She stood up and walked slowly over to an antique drinks cabinet made of yew wood, as if she couldn't take it all in, or wasn't inclined to. She unscrewed the lid from a bottle of red wine. 'Drink?'

'Thanks.'

She poured two glasses. She came back and handed him one. She remained standing in front of him.

'Robert Dubois has asked me to meet him in Brussels. He has some information.'

Her tone had become coldly practical, he thought.

'I'm hoping to meet with a man that might have some information too. It's sketchy for now,' he said, referring to Bronislaw Stolarski.

He'd half changed his mind. He wanted to give her some hope, but he wouldn't say more about it.

She rubbed her temple with a palm, as if she was trying to extricate herself from an immersion in dark, inner thoughts.

CHAPTER FIFTY-TWO

New York State, the same day.

Charlene Rimes had checked into a thirty-dollars-a-night motel, with chipboard walls and orange curtains. It was situated on the outskirts of a little town called Alexandria in Jefferson County, a couple of miles south of the US–Canadian border. She knew that it wouldn't be long before the feds identified her as the person who struck a deal with the Watson family after snitching on Johnny Hockey.

The Watson family lawyer had asked her to keep her smartphone on her until they were forced to reveal her name. She was concerned about that, but Billy Joe had assured her that he and Hockey had acted alone and had killed the Watsons for the possessions they'd stolen — and she'd believed him. There was no one else involved in the acts. He hadn't rung her since. Hockey had been arrested. Why worry?

When the call from the lawyer did come, she figured she could evade the authorities by slipping over the longest border in the world, into southern Ontario. She could spend some time moving between the so-called Thousand Islands, a vast archipelago in the St Lawrence River as it emerged from the lake. It could take a year or more to find someone in there, and she guessed they wouldn't waste their resources.

She had no intention of entering a witness protection programme, to be wet-nursed by the US Marshals Service for the rest of her life.

She'd had a bowl of chili with rice in a restaurant about eighty yards from the motel, and was now walking back along a dirt track, which abutted the minor road, to avoid being struck by a vehicle. There were no streetlights, but the moon was as white as the belly of a flatfish, the sky brocaded with clusters of luminous stars. She felt good, having downed a carafe of Californian red with her meal.

If Hockey was convicted, the money from the Watson family would be transferred into a private bank on the Isle of Man, although she didn't have a clue where *that* was. Like it mattered, she'd thought. They'd said their lawyer would form a company and she'd be authorized to draw on the cash via a secure online account. But she knew that depended on the emergence of more evidence against Hockey.

She'd only agreed to talk to the Watsons on the understanding that she wouldn't have to testify. But the FBI had other plans, she knew. She'd been given 6,000 dollars to cover her expenses over the next few weeks, and felt like she'd won a lottery. But she was too cute to blow it on extravagant living. She still wore a retro leather mini-skirt, a faded denim jacket and scuffed gold trainers. She felt guilty about what her betrayal might mean for her now ex-boyfriend, Billy Joe. She consoled herself by thinking she was just taking advantage of a once-in-a-lifetime opportunity that had dropped, as if from Heaven, into her otherwise poverty-stricken hill girl lap. He was a vicious jerk, anyways.

She got parallel with a telephone pole and a white SUV passed her at speed but slowed down and stopped about ten yards ahead. She thought about running and then thought better of it. If the authorities had somehow tracked her this far, she figured she would have to accept her fate. She put her right hand on her hip as the SUV reversed.

When the vehicle was revving by her side, the electric front window came down. She saw a white woman about ten years older than herself in the passenger seat, a muscular young man driving. The woman turned her head and smiled. She wore what looked like a silk scarf around her neck and her blonde hair was in a ponytail.

'FBI?' Charlene said.

The woman nodded.

The back doors opened, and two cropped-haired young guys got out, wearing well-tailored suits. She hadn't done time, but she'd been around white supremacists and felony offenders long enough to know instinctively that they weren't FBI. They had a look about them that spoke of criminal brutality. There was a sugar beet field to her left. She'd never smoked and had even dreamed of becoming an athlete in her youth. She might have a chance. What other choice was there?

She took off at a sprint, heard the woman shout something. The earth was wet and slippery, from irrigation, she guessed. But the crop was short, the green leaves no hindrance. She got a full thirty-five yards before she tripped on something, something that sent her sprawling face first into the slushy topsoil. She tried to get up, but realized she'd sprained her ankle, or broken it. What was certain was that she wasn't going anywhere. She heard the footfalls behind her and gritted her teeth, hoping that the woman would temper the aggression that had all but oozed from the young men.

Three seconds later, the woman and the three men circled her, as if they were African wild dogs surrounding felled prey.

'Where is boyfriend?' the woman asked.

'What are you, Germans?' Charlene said.

'You stupid. Dress like whore.'

'What did you say to me?' Charlene said, screwing up her face.

She lay in the mud, among the sugar beet, looking at the woman who had bad-mouthed her. She'd removed her scarf, she noticed. She's got the biggest neck for a lady, she thought. Compared to hers it was the difference between a pony's neck and that of a thoroughbred race-horse. Like the ones she'd seen once down at the Kentucky Downs in Franklin. She wondered if the woman was in fact one of them filthy transvestites. But no. She was too damn beautiful.

'Enough. Where is he?'

'How did you find me?' Charlene said.

Then she knew how. Her smartphone. Had the Watson family betrayed her? What the hell was happening?

'Where?'

'I dunno. Useful as a mink coat in the desert, anyways,' Charlene said, referring to Billy Joe.

She saw the woman frown.

Charlene hadn't been overtly threatened and no physical violence had been used against her, so she reckoned a slice of humour wouldn't go amiss. It had worked for her before, when rednecks had gotten a little rough. But after the woman had said something foreign, the men moved forward. On her back, she flinched, her mood changing. She saw their pitiless eyes and recoiled like a beaten mongrel.

Crouching down, two of the men grasped an ankle each. She grimaced and cried out, the searing pain careering up her calf. Her ankle had swollen badly already, resembling half a tennis ball. The third man sat down behind her. He grabbed her wrists and pulled her arms back over her head, and manoeuvred his mud-streaked boots by her pierced ears. She felt them pressing into her shoulders.

Her body was straightened out. It felt as if she was on a human rack.

In this vulnerable state, the fear of what might be visited upon her next eclipsed the pain in her joints, the agony in her ankle, even.

'Don't hurt me, please. Please don't hurt me, lady.'

'One more time, that is all. Where is boyfriend?'

'He took off. He likely hates me now for the reward and all.'

Charlene watched the woman reach into her jacket pocket and take out a length of lead piping. From her other pocket, she removed a long, rusted nail, the type used on fence posts. She held them both up.

'Choose,' she said.

CHAPTER FIFTY-THREE

Gabriel looked over at Carla's grey stone fireplace. There was a framed photograph on it of a young girl. He pointed to it.

'May I?' he said, anxious to change the mood.

'Sure,' she said.

He strolled over to it and picked it up. 'She's pretty.'

Carla came over to him. 'My daughter, Monize. Her father still sees her a lot, which is good.'

'Is she with him tonight?'

'Yes. Maybe you'd like to stay for dinner?'

She half laughed and shook her head, as if she'd embarrassed herself.

He hesitated. He couldn't figure her out.

But said, 'I'd like that.'

'I'll cook pato no tucupi. My grandmother taught me. She also left me this house, in case you were wondering how I could afford it on an FBI salary.'

He nodded, his mouth in a pout. 'Food sounds good.'

'You speak Portuguese?' she said.

He shook his head as playfully as he could muster.

'Then you haven't got a clue what it is, have you?'

'Actually, no.'

She smiled, weakly. 'Boiled duck in a broth of scalded cassava.'

'Right.'

'You'll love it. Besides, I can't have you driving back to New York without feeding you.'

'I'm staying over at a motel. I'm seeing Hockey tomorrow morning.'

'That's settled then. I'll start dinner. Help yourself to wine.'

She turned and walked towards the doorway.

'Just so you know I'm not hiding anything from you, I should tell you that I followed you to that bar in Far Rockaway.'

He had a feeling she was hiding more.

'OK.'

*

They talked about the ongoing investigation throughout the meal. He hadn't been able to stop the images of the dead Kalmyk girl from flashing through his mind. The fragments of the nightmare.

Now he forced himself to speak. 'The duck was delicious.'

He reached for a glass of water on the bare wood of the dining room table.

'And the cassava?'

'Yes.'

'You're lying,' Carla said. She wiped the corner of her mouth with the linen napkin and placed it beside her plate. 'So, tell me, what do you like doing when you're not being a lawyer?'

He took another sip of water.

'I like art. I like looking at a thing of real beauty, like a Pissarro or Castellini.'

He spoke passionately about his love of art for the next few minutes.

She smiled in a manner that suggested she was wondering if he was tough enough for what he'd gotten himself into. Maybe that was why she was acting odd, he thought.

'I'll leave the dishes till morning. A nightcap? I have a really fine port that I usually keep for special occasions,' she said, standing up.

Her frostiness was beginning to irritate him. He had an inkling that she was conflicted. But then he realized it didn't have anything to do with him. It was all about her daughter. He understood that. Her line of work meant that her daughter could be put at risk, at least to a vastly greater extent than the child of, say, an accountant. Her current assignment had no doubt escalated that fear.

He stood up too and walked around the table, meeting her by the cabinet. She turned to look at him. His eyes lingered almost involuntarily over the rich contours of her face. He was close enough to smell her again, a mixture of almonds and grapefruit, he thought. The cream she used on her skin, the lotion for her hair. She wasn't wearing perfume.

'It must be tough, having to deal with this for a living,' he said.

Ignoring him, she said, 'You can sleep over in the spare room. I'll bring you breakfast.'

He decided it would be impolite to refuse. 'If you're sure?'

She nodded.

'Thank you.'

She looked at him, her beautiful eyes stern yet sympathetic. 'Sangmu's date of birth is September thirtieth, isn't it?'

'Yes,' he said, figuring she'd read it in the FBI case notes.

'And she's seventeen now, right?'

'Yes. Eighteen in a couple of weeks.' The skin on his cheekbones quivered and he clenched his right fist. 'What is it, Carla?'

She blinked, and her eyes shifted to his midriff. 'All of the victims in New Jersey disappeared before their eighteenth birthdays. We don't know why.'

'But you think their eighteenth birthday is significant, don't you?'

'Yes,' she said.

He knew she wouldn't say that she thought they were murdered on their eighteenth birthdays.

'I'm sorry I've been a bad hostess. It's just one of those days, and this is just awful, isn't it?'

He breathed out. 'You haven't been a bad hostess, Carla.'

She touched his cheek with two of her fingers. 'We'll find her, Gabriel. I promise.'

He wished he could believer her. He couldn't remember a time he had felt more desolate, and there'd been many times he'd felt that emotion.

CHAPTER FIFTY-FOUR

Warm tears had welled in Charlene's eyes. She shook her head, almost imperceptibly. The woman crouched down beside her, and she trembled like the leveret she'd chased down in a ditch as a child.

'He's in Alabama. His mama lives there,' Charlene said, referring to Billy Joe Anderson.

'Zip code?' the woman said.

She blurted out, '36765.'

She watched the woman stand up and put her vicious implements away. She took out a smartphone and played around with it with her thumb. She squatted down again. Charlene saw the online satellite image.

'Point where. Exact.'

She felt her body relax as the human rack unfurled. Even the throbbing pain in her ankle appeared to lessen. The man behind her let go of her right arm. She felt a tingling sensation there but dismissed it. She moved the image around with her forefinger.

'There,' she said, pointing to a field.

She reached forward and was permitted to feel the outline of her swollen ankle, and her tears fell onto the soil.

'Explain,' the woman said.

'He always bolts home. His daddy built a shelter,' she said, without pronouncing the 'r'. 'Underground. He thought the world was going to end. He died of moonshine. Guess it did for him.'

'Moonshine?'

'Liquor. Alcohol.'

'He thought there be nuclear war?' the woman said.

'No, he thought the four horses of the apocalypse were on their way. Did for most of his life, Billy Joe said.'

The woman shook her head, as if she didn't understand what had been said.

'What else he tell you?'

'He said that Johnny Hockey and him killed the Watson guy, but he alone killed the Jewish wife,' Charlene said, compliant now.

'Did he say why?'

'He said the Watsons were rich, which they was. He said he'd take me to Vegas. He didn't though. Can I go now?'

'What else?'

'What do you mean, what else?' Charlene said.

'Who did they give the stolen goods to?'

Charlene shook her head. 'I don't know, except Johnny said there was a foreign guy Hockey knew.'

'His name?'

'He didn't say his name.'

The woman said, 'Did you speak of this to anyone? To the Watson family when they say they give you money?'

'No. I swear on my grandma's grave.'

'You not lie, girl. I know you not lie.'

'I was brought up right. Told not to lie. I just told the Watson family Hockey's address. I'm sorry. Real sorry. Now can I go?'

'Sure, you go,' the woman said.

The woman raised her hand, like some ancient warlord, and the men stood up. They stepped back. She watched the woman move behind her.

'I might need crutches,' Charlene said.

'No, do not think so. I help you up.'

Charlene only felt the hands on her head for a second. It was how she'd been grasped by a faith healer once. Dreamlike, she heard the muted *crack*. For the briefest moment, an intense, white-hot pain shot through her neck and upper spine, like a trapped nerve multiplied a hundredfold. The last thing she saw was a bolt of lightning in a crimson sky.

CHAPTER FIFTY-FIVE

Federal correctional complex, the next day.

Gabriel interlinked his fingers. He glanced down at the metal table in the prison interview room before looking up at Johnny Hockey.

He said, 'They came for you, didn't they?'

'I don't follow,' Hockey said.

'Yes, you do. The attempted escape.'

Hockey grinned. 'They were after the bank robber. He's known as Clay Bob in here on account of the fact his name is Bob and Jesse James was from Clay County, Missouri. A nod to the master, you might say.'

Gabriel pressed the tip of his tongue against the roof of his mouth to stop himself from yawning, although he wanted to shout at Hockey and call him a liar, too. He couldn't tell which the dominant desire was. But he'd mimicked a southern accent with a certain aplomb, he'd give him that much.

Carla had brought him crispy bacon and scrambled eggs, after she'd asked him how he'd like his cooked breakfast. He'd put on fresh clothes, which he'd taken from a bag he'd put in the boot of his car before driving to Carla's house, cargo trousers and a cotton shirt, rather than a suit, and had set out on the long drive to the federal prison. He hadn't slept more than an hour last night. He'd had nightmares. They weren't recurrent, but took the form of sequential episodes. The monk hadn't featured, but a vicious dog had.

'Listen, Johnny,' he said. 'I can't represent you anymore.'

'Because you still think they were out to free me?'

Gabriel shook his head. 'I got a tipoff that the FBI are looking at my bank records.'

Hockey bent over and pinched his nose. 'Do they have a reason?'

'I got sloppy,' Gabriel said, feigning concern.

'Sloppy how?'

'I had a relationship with a futures trader. A client.'

Hockey snorted like a wildebeest. 'Did you fuck her to find out which way the stock market was heading?'

Gabriel took a sip of water from a disposable cup on the desk between them.

'It's complicated,' he said.

Hockey scratched his flat stomach like a primate.

'No, it isn't. A mathematical equation used to explain an aspect of theoretical physics is complicated. You think I'm a dumb fuck, don't you?'

Gabriel couldn't be bothered to comment. He looked over his shoulder at the BOP officers. They had no interest in what was going on in the interview room. He turned back and saw that Hockey was glaring at him. He thought he was going to tell him to get the hell out of here.

But Hockey said, 'There's a storm coming. All you believe in is doomed.'

Hockey's eyes went blank. There was nothing in them. Not fear, nor hate. Not joy or wisdom.

It chilled Gabriel.

CHAPTER FIFTY-SIX

Newbern, Hale County, Alabama, the same day.

The white SUV had been left at a garage in Tennessee and exchanged for a similar model in metallic grey. Keeping the same car but a different colour was an old trick that Fury had learned. For some reason she didn't understand and had no wish to, it was less likely to be considered a getaway car than any other. It was more likely that a different car of the same colour would be stopped. She didn't understand that, either.

The SUV entered the outskirts of Newbern at 3.10 pm, although the bruise-coloured clouds made it feel like dusk. The town sign that declared a population of 223 lay among switchgrass. A few yards down, a pack of dogs mounted one another in front of the remnants of a little white-washed church. It was raining. The warm, torrential rain of a southern storm. Thunder boomed, and lightening streaked across the eastern horizon above a pine forest.

Moving at no more than ten miles per hour, the SUV zigzagged to avoid the debris on the road. Piles of twigs and branches, broken slate roof tiles, flung wooden panels and chunks of dislodged masonry. Lead pipes had been snapped like balsawood, the timber frame houses reduced to tangled heaps. Many of the oak and willow trees had been rendered blackened stumps, and the crops of cereals and legumes they passed in the surrounding fields had been flattened or torn asunder. Cars and trucks littered the edges of the roads, upturned and windowless. Families were living in small caravans and tents. Some old people were just sitting on the indented remnants of the pavements, among the piles of sodden leaves, weeping or staring into the distance, like the insane.

Fury had pocketed Charlene's smartphone as she'd strolled back to the SUV. She'd taken out the battery and SIM card, then tossed the phone out of the window halfway from the murder site to Newbern. Charlene's body had been burned with gas and her smouldering corpse buried amid a copse of spruce trees, ten miles from where she'd died. Fury had chosen the site having seen, online, a photograph of the spruce trees that were opposite the prison where Hockey was held. It was fitting, she'd thought.

'What happened here?' the driver said.

'Tornado,' Fury said.

'Looks like the aftermath of a bombing raid.'

It does, she thought. While some buildings were destroyed, others seemed remarkably intact.

They reached the southern outskirts, and the residences that hadn't been decimated rapidly deteriorated in size and construction. Fury hadn't seen an inhabited corrugated-roofed shack since she'd done a hit in a shithole near Dimitrovgrad a couple of years ago.

Here, the people sitting on those open porches that hadn't collapsed looked either bloated or unhealthily skinny. Indolent too, she thought. They seemed to lack even a modicum of vitality or purpose, as if they acted purely on whimsies. Except for a black girl who was weaving in and out of the debris in bare feet, her white cotton dress streaked with mud, a stick in her hand, her legs the rich golden brown of brandy.

Ten minutes later, Fury located the field easily enough. Satellite navigation was a tool sent from the gods, she thought, although whose gods, she wasn't sure. But she would wait until dark before pinpointing the spot where she hoped to find Billy Joe Anderson.

*

The SUV pulled up beside an irrigation ditch. The rain that had half-filled it was still pouring. There'd been a hail storm, the solid pellets the size of marbles. Electricity shot out of the clouds with a neon glow. Fury told the men to get out and bring the pickaxe and shovels they'd used to dig a grave for Charlene Rimes from the boot. They wore oilskin jackets and wadding boots, she a padded ski jacket, zipped up to her chin, together with a green, wide-brimmed hat, and baggy Gore-Tex trousers.

The moonlight was muted by scudding storm clouds. They leaped over the narrow ditch and trudged through the mud and grass. The field was isolated, about four miles from the town. There was a shed in the far corner, nailed together with what appeared to be odd pieces of wood and thin metal sheets. It had survived the storm, somehow. The rainwater danced on it and rusty old farm machinery lay about it.

Roughly ten yards away, she saw that a segment of the field was slightly raised along the periphery. It wasn't too obvious, but it looked unnatural, an almost perfect square. Twenty-five feet square, she guessed. It sagged a little in the middle too.

The shelter, she thought.

She wiped the heavy raindrops from her face and thought about the kill. If he said he hadn't told anyone else about the hit on the Watsons, or didn't answer convincingly the other questions Vezzani had written down and handed to her at the hotel, she felt that she would have to play with him, just to be sure. Then she realized she wanted to play with him anyway. It had been a while since she'd tortured someone. She had to admit that she had lost the taste for it with Charlene Rimes, and that was why she'd dispatched her swiftly by breaking her neck.

She trusted the men with her, but things would be done to Billy Joe Anderson. She didn't want anyone leaving their puke in the shelter or attempting to intervene, even verbally. That had happened before on a job with a different crew. Was there anything worse? She decided to take them back to the ditch and speak to them. To let them know what to expect. She *hated* losing her rhythm while she worked.

CHAPTER FIFTY-SEVEN

Billy Joe Anderson was a skinhead, with a small-boned frame and an addiction to sugar-laden drinks that were already starting to make his back teeth rot. Dressed in a T-shirt and jeans, he was sitting in the shelter, stirring a saucepan of beans on a portable gas stove as the sauce bubbled. A battery-operated LED light hung from a hook in the roof.

The roof was made from plywood, with a layer of sand and polythene as a form of waterproofing. Any heavier and the roof would've been a bigger hazard than an outside explosion. Any lighter and the shelter might as well have been open to the stars.

The underground shelter was, in fact, an in-ground swimming pool. Or to be more precise, the concrete frame of one. Billy's dead daddy had told him that he'd gotten the idea from a survival magazine he subscribed to. A shelter proper could set a man back nearly five times as much, he'd said. Billy had thought that it was just about the only sensible thing the old sonofabitch had done in his otherwise useless life. There was no way a redworm would bother his sleep in here.

He'd first hooked up with Hockey a couple of years ago. Hockey had told him he was sure he could kill people, although up until then his antics hadn't gone beyond assaulting dark-skinned immigrants. Plus a couple of late-night arson attacks on unoccupied Muslim-owned shops in Albany. Now he was a killer, too.

He knew that Hockey had been against killing the wife, Esfir Watson, but Billy Joe had felt an overwhelming desire to satisfy the bloodlust that the death of Jed Watson had engendered in him. He hadn't been able to stop himself. She'd just walked through the front door as they were collecting the valuables. It hadn't been planned.

He'd gone on the run as soon as he'd heard that Hockey had been incarcerated. He'd bought a motorcycle off a Nazi Lowrider acquaintance, a guy named Jim Saunders, a friend of Johnny Hockey. He'd considered trying his luck over the border in Tijuana, Mexico. He'd figured he'd slip over a part of the border that wasn't patrolled on a regular basis and avoid the fence, all 640 miles of it. He knew that less than half of the border was secure. But Tijuana had an ugly twelve-feet-high structure running down the length of the beach. It even extended into the ocean. Then he'd decided that a gringo with white supremacist tattoos wouldn't exactly blend in, and the thought of doing any time in a Mexican jail was about as appealing as running naked through a bunch of organ pipe cactus plants. Besides, it was fucking chaos down there. Everyone said so.

And so, he'd run home. There was nowhere else he felt safe.

He knew Hockey would never snitch, but shit happened. Besides, Hockey had been his only source of work, so he figured that after it had all calmed down, he might go freelance for a while. He knew nobody would find him in Newbern. He'd dropped his smartphone in a skip in the Bronx before he left New York and hadn't told anyone where he was going. Charlene had given information to the Watson family that had done for Hockey, but she'd never give *him* up, he thought. He hadn't contacted her, as it could compromise him. He'd decided to stay put for a week or two, although he had enough non-perishable food for a month.

He stopped stirring the beans, left the wooden spoon in the saucepan and raised his head slowly, as a stag did when he was hunting it. He'd thought he'd heard something, even above the fading storm. An unfamiliar vibration that meant the source was heavier than a muskrat, but not as heavy as a stray cow. It produced a form of paranoia that played with his mind and made him jittery. He grabbed his daddy's old shotgun, that was resting against the plastered wall, put it in his lap. It was the only thing daddy left him, apart from a rusted harmonica.

Maybe it's just the wind and rain, he thought.

Then again, maybe not.

CHAPTER FIFTY-EIGHT

Berlin, 1945.

Now, five hours later and in the early hours of the morning, Kazapov leaned over a long bench in a large cellar beneath the barracks. The air was surprisingly dry and smelled of something akin to baked bread. There was a lightbulb above his head, with a tin shade painted white. Many of the items held previously in the Nazi bunker had been stored there. It was guarded by four NVKD internal troops.

A makeshift screen had been rigged up, a canvas sheet tied to an iron bar that ran the length of the ceiling. The sheet had been secured crudely to the floor with nails. A box projector had been salvaged from a Berlin institute. Kazapov had acquired it from a corporal for a near pristine pair of jackboots and a gold signet ring he'd taken from a dead German officer in East Prussia. Wartime souvenirs he could do without.

Resting his elbows on the bench, Kazapov leaned forward and propped his chin up with his clasped hands. He watched as the flickering black and white images came into view. There were the smiling faces of the Heer, officers and NCOs, who stood about a half-track on barren land, smoking and holding aluminium field drinking cups.

They were obvious veterans, who were likely regular German soldiers rather than conscripts.

He stopped the projector. There was a man standing to the left, his profile partly obscured by another man's head and his officer's visor cap. He played the two-second clip time and again until he satisfied himself. He clenched his jaw and nodded a fraction.

He continued viewing the film. There were the smiling faces of the Kalmyk volunteers, mingling with the Germans, and their backs were slapped in a congratulatory fashion. The Kalmyks examined what looked like their new European rifles to replace the old Soviet ones, as if they were orphan street children who'd just been handed chocolate bars.

The images changed. Battle preparations. Makeshift firing ranges and stick grenade drills. Rudimentary explosives training.

The images changed. Actual combat scenes — and the smiles were no longer perceptible.

The images changed. Retribution for those Russian partisans taken alive. Violent interrogations. Hangings. Shootings.

The images changed. A group of what looked like Russian Jews rounded up by a dozen or more Einsatzgruppen and herded onto trucks.

The images changed. A farm cart and huge-jawed mules, with their heads bowed.

He averted his wet eyes for a few seconds.

His mother and sisters were huddling together beside the wooden spokes of a wheel, about to undergo a terrible ordeal before their deaths, he had no doubt of that.

He looked back, but he could not bear it. He grabbed his head in his hands, and screamed silently, as if a trapped insect was burrowing its way along his ear canal. But he had to know.

It took a long time before they died. And in that time, part of Kazapov died too.

*

An hour later, Kazapov had managed to calm himself sufficiently to stand up. He knew he must remain calm, despite the brain-numbing pain he felt. If he did something rash or unexpected, it would be noticed. He would not be able to fulfil what he saw as his duty to his deceased family then. And that was the only duty he recognized now. He would speak with the German officer as soon as possible.

He stumbled forward, his legs shaking. He put his hand against a support beam and had to stifle a howl.

He'd reported his mother and sisters missing in Kalmykia as a separate report to the ChGK. He'd hoped that would lead to a breakthrough. It hadn't, of course. He knew that in the future the one-page report would be kept in a crate in a cellar somewhere remote, buried underneath other unconfirmed missing persons' reports. They would be forgotten about. Greater crimes than anyone had ever seen before had taken place, after all. Not just imagined ones. He would not report what he now knew to be the truth. No one would know but him. No one would make a connection. He'd already decided to take a personal revenge.

He walked over to remove the sheet and had something akin to a terrible epiphany. He knew he'd never recover from what he'd seen. It was as if the world had become a prison that had shuttered up its windows to the sun forever.

CHAPTER FIFTY-NINE

'It's you?' Richter said, sitting in the interrogation cell.

He'd recognized the young man as soon as he'd entered the room, even though he wore a spotless NKVD officer's uniform, as opposed to the unwashed camouflage he'd had on when he'd led the Russian troops that had captured him.

'My name is Lieutenant Joseph Kazapov. I am to discuss certain matters with you,' he said. 'Have you recovered from your illness?'

'I feel a little better.'

'What happened to your nose?'

A large blue-black bruise was visible on the bridge of Richter's nose.

Richter shrugged. 'Where is Volsky?'

Kazapov frowned. 'Major Volsky has been assigned other duties. They intend to move you from here, and soon.'

The word 'they' was not lost on Richter. An inclusive 'we' would have meant more of the same, but the lieutenant had consciously sought to detach himself from the NKVD and Richter wondered why. He decided to test that notion.

Richter spoke softly. 'What's happening in the city?'

Kazapov was silent for a few seconds.

'The birds are returning,' he said. 'In those areas that have been under occupation for some time, the roads are being cleared, little by little, by large groups of Berlin women. We call them rubble women. They are no longer being raped indiscriminately. There seems to be a semblance of normality, even here. Even after all that has transpired. I suppose they feel that being ruled by the Soviet state is preferable to the unbridled chaos of the last days.'

'I see,' Richter said, nodding.

He watched Kazapov put his hand into his pocket and take out a piece of paper. Kazapov unfolded it, placed it on the table and slid it over to him. Richter looked down at it. He had to stop his mind from drifting back to what had been the most fulfilling months of his life after he'd seen what had been drawn there.

Kazapov prodded his long finger at the paper. 'You know what this is, don't you?'

'It's a belt buckle.'

'Tell me about it?'

But Richter's mind was elsewhere now. The memories were too vital. Too potent.

Kazapov leaned forward and snapped his fingers close to Richter's face. 'Are you listening to me?'

Richter nodded. He focused. He knew that the longer he survived the initial outbreak of violent reprisals, the more chance he had of staying alive. The arrival of this young lieutenant had just made that all seem more likely, he thought.

'I'm interested in this,' Kazapov said, pointing at the belt buckle again. 'I'm interested in the papers you were so eager to burn.'

'The buckle was worn by the Kalmyks who fought for the German

Army, but I suspect you know that. The papers were just reports,' Richter said, with a dismissive motion of his hand.

'The few papers in the street outside the bunker and on its floors, bore the same design,' Kazapov said. 'I know they detailed the map coordinates of installations. Ordnance and logistical matters. Of little use now. That means the papers you took with you were something different.'

'They weren't, I can assure you.'

He'd lied. The papers had been comprehensive reports of the Kalmyks' military activities for the Germans. Dates, names, locations.

Kazapov looked down at his hands, rotating them, as if he had just committed some awful crime. Richter didn't doubt that he'd done his fair share. He was NKVD, after all. A front line officer, he suspected.

Kazapov said, 'Do you know the Kalmyk language?'

'Do you have a cigarette?'

Kazapov took a packet out of his breeches, together with a matchbox and handed them to Richter. He smiled. 'Please answer my question.'

'Yes.' Richter said. 'I know the Kalmyk language.' He smiled back. 'Am I to be transferred to one of your camps?'

But it was Kazapov's turn to ignore a question. 'Were your language skills one of the reasons you were assigned to Kalmykia?'

Richter flinched. There was no doubt in his mind that Kazapov knew the truth. He'd been found out. He knew too that there was no point in denying it.

'How do *you* know what your superior officer is ignorant of?'

Ignoring him again, Kazapov said, 'The Kalmyk traitors were known for their brutality and ruthlessness, especially on the steppe. Did you see any of those things?'

Richter had personally intervened to stop numerous atrocities in

Kalmykia. The Buddhist horsemen had gone too far on occasion, even by the standards of the day. They had had the bloodlust. The Russian partisans they'd fought against had not been afforded a modicum of mercy. Things had been done that could not be undone. This he knew.

But he said, 'Of matters that took place out on the far steppe, I cannot say. I never left Elista, the capital.'

He saw a look in Kazapov's dark eyes that demanded more.

He told him that the volunteers had joined up with a small band of Kalmyks from Belgrade that had advanced into the Caucasus with a motorized corps known as Windhund. He said that it had reached as far east as twenty miles from Astrakhan on the northern shores of the Caspian Sea. The Kalmyk volunteers had been mainly used to protect the flanks of Wehrmacht units, to kill partisans and guard installations and lines of communication. Those that had refused to remain on the steppe as the Wehrmacht Heer retreated in 1943 had formed the Kalmücken-Kavallerie-Korps. They wore the belt buckle. Their families followed the Germans home, too. Thousands of women and children and old people. Some sat atride camels. A marvellous and tragic sight.

'I have read Major Volsky's report,' Kazapov said. 'You lied to him. You said you'd never left Berlin.'

'I am only supposed to tell you my name and rank.'

Kazapov nodded, sagely. 'I have it on good authority that all the Kalmyk traitors will be forcibly deported back to us, with their families. You know what will happen to them then. Let me tell you what happened to your precious Kalmyks that remained in Kalmykia after you retreated.'

Richter had heard a few rumours, but he didn't know for sure. He didn't know why Kazapov wanted to tell him either. Perhaps he had misjudged him.

'On the twenty-seventh of December 1943, Soviet authorities declared the Kalmyk people guilty of co-operation with the German Army and ordered the deportation of the entire population, even those who had served with the Red Army and the loyal partisan units. Even the 8,000 that had received medals for battle merit and for courage. Everyone was sent to various locations in Siberia. In conjunction with the deportation, the Kalmyk autonomous republic was abolished. Stalin has obliterated all trace of the Kalmyk people there. He even ordered the renaming of their towns and villages.'

Kazapov filled in the details. 'They were transported in trucks from their homes to the local railway stations, where they were loaded in cattle wagons. They had no prior notification and no time to collect their belongings or warm clothes. Men and women, the old and the young, were rammed into the wagons, which had no sanitation or food. Water fell through the cracks in the roofs and froze at their feet. The suffering was so bad en route to the east that many of the oldest and youngest did not survive the journey.'

He paused, wiped his mouth.

'Your beloved Kalmyks are scattered like chaff in a wind. A cold Siberian wind, that is. Half or more will die in that unforgiving place.'

Richter felt a knot in his stomach and put his hand to his forehead. He did not speak. He could not. One hundred thousand Kalmyk families had trekked west for forty-two years before reaching the Volga steppe. Peter the Great of Russia had given them a khanate. But the Russian Revolution had been the beginning of the end for them, just as Stalingrad had been the beginning of the end for the Reich. He mourned the fallen, silently.

'They want to take you to Moscow,' Kazapov said. 'They want to take you to the mincing machine.'

Richter sensed his blood draining from his face and he clenched his jaw to stop himself from panting. He'd heard of the terrifying nickname for Moscow's notorious NKVD HQ that doubled up as the most feared prison in the Soviet Union. The Soviet intelligence gathering centre was incomparable in its brutality to any other. Lubyanka building. The mincing machine.

'Do you believe in a god?' Kazapov said.

Richter only heard a vague noise. 'What did you say?'

Kazapov repeated the question and said, 'You can seek guidance, if you wish. Strength.'

'Everything I believed in has turned to ashes. To dust. Perhaps it would be better if I went to Moscow, after all,' he said.

Only now did he realize that he had spoken the words he'd been thinking. But he didn't believe that, let alone want it to transpire. The very thought of the mincing machine filled him with dread.

'It is not a good way to die,' Kazapov said. 'The NKVD torturers are known by the implements they use. Hammer. Axe. They do the vilest acts to Russian men, women and even children. Imagine what they'll do to you.'

Richter sat with his mouth agape.

'There may be a way out, even now. I will ask you some questions and you will answer me truthfully. We may be able to do a deal between us. Only between us. I may have to take you on a drive to verify an important piece of information. Do you understand me?'

Richter was silent.

'Take you time and gather your thoughts,' Kazapov said.

He got up and left the room.

In truth, Richter didn't know how he felt. But he'd seen enough emotional pain in his life to know that Lieutenant Kazapov was dying inside, despite his attempt to hide it. He had enough curiosity left — his dominant trait since childhood — to wonder why, despite his predicament.

CHAPTER SIXTY

Ten minutes later and after returning to the interrogation cell, Kazapov said, 'I know Doctor Doll was a codename for Othmar Rudolf Werba, a military intelligence officer in the Abwehr. I know that he spent three years working with the German consulate in Odessa, that, like you, he was a speaker of the Kalmyk language. I know he commanded the Kalmüken Verband and that he died in the retreat. I know these things because I went to Kalmykia to investigate the atrocities that took place there. This is my role within the NKVD.'

Kazapov watched as Richter tried unsuccessfully to mask his astonishment. But he wasn't finished yet.

'I know you are a Sonderführer. I know you were an officer under Doctor Doll, that you helped lead the Kalmyk volunteers. I know that you had the Red Army soldiers, Kazakhs and Uzbeks, killed in the bunker in that way because they were Muslims, the historic enemies of the Buddhist Kalmyk. For Doctor Doll and the Kalmyks loyal to Germany too, perhaps. You learned to kill like that from the Buddhist horsemen. Punishment amputations and disfigurements. A bullet to the back of the neck. I saw it on the steppe, I suspect that you assisted Einsatzgruppe D in finding the Jews that were murdered in Kalmykia too. A place you loved.'

Kazapov paused. He lit two cigarettes in his mouth and handed one to Richter, who accepted willingly. Kazapov saw that the German's hand was shaking.

'I volunteered to go with the snipers to the observation post over-looking the bunker because the captured SS sergeant who had the coordinates beaten and burned out of him had a handwritten letter on him. The letter was signed by you, Lutz Richter. I had heard the name once before while I was in Kalmykia. I contacted my superior in the ChGK and he confirmed it. And then I saw you there.'

Richter sucked hard on the cigarette, letting the smoke out in little billows. 'How, may I ask?'

Kazapov said, 'I found the reel of film in the bunker. It was in a brass casket with some ancient parchments and scrolls. I saw your face on the Kalmyk steppe. There is no doubt who you are. And if you go to Lubyanka there will be no doubt there, either.'

'I did not assist the Einsatzgruppen,' Richter said. 'The parchments and scrolls are wrapped in yak hide. Brought from Lhasa in Tibet to Elista via Siberia and the Volga region. They are as useful to you as the documents I burned.'

He paused. His face was almost hidden by a cloud of smoke. 'I couldn't leave those items you found in the bunker in Elista for Stalin to burn either,' he said. 'I took them to the bunker to safeguard them.'

He snorted and shock his head.

'So much for that. But I disapproved of the — '

Ignoring him, Kazapov said, 'Only I have watched the film.'

Richter tugged the cigarette from his lips. 'It was all meant to be destroyed. Strict instructions were given. Fucking incompetent bastards. I should have checked. I should have, it's true. But I didn't, young man. Always check. Always.'

He looked to have aged five years, Kazapov thought, as he watched him suck hard on the cigarette once more.

'The Einsatzgruppen officers were young men of letters,' Richter said. 'Orators, who could encourage the murder. They were helped by uniformed volunteers from the auxiliary police forces in the occupied territories. In Lithuania, the Einsatzgruppen were outnumbered ten to one by the locals. They gathered up the watches and rings as payment. Ukrainian civilians travelled far to kill Jews in this manner. It's no surprise Ukrainians were the guards at Treblinka, other death camps too.

'In Romania, Bulgaria and Hungary, the fascist administrations killed their Jews without our help at first. They killed Roma women and children, even those whose male kin were fighting in the army. In other parts of the Soviet Union, the pogroms against the Jews started as soon as we invaded. The local populations did the gruesome work as the SS just looked on. But it was a messy and uncoordinated affair. German thoroughness was called for.

'But what the Einsatzgruppen did was incremental. A stage at a time. The men first. Then the women and children. The officers organized grotesque processions of Jews, even mock Passion Plays before the slaughter. Himmler stopped the shootings due to the psychological effects on his men. This led to Himmler bringing the gas vans in. This led to the industrial destruction of the Jews, did it not? A detachment from the act itself. Was it not so?'

Richter hung his head in his hands, his breath becoming erratic.

Kazapov put his hand on the Sonderführer's forearm. 'Calm yourself. We will not speak of generalities again,' he said. 'There is only one atrocity that interests me. You will tell me the names of the Kalmyk volunteers involved and you will tell me the name of the Einsatzgruppen film maker. All the other known German and Kalmyk officers are dead or dispersed. You know this.'

Kazapov removed his hand and stiffened up. 'Four women. They looked like Jews but were not. A middle-aged woman and her three daughters. They were hiding in a barn. But the Einsatzgruppen didn't kill them. Maybe they had revolvers on them. Maybe not. Maybe the Kalmyks thought they were partisans. Maybe not. You destroyed the useful records you had in that fire. But the film is now mine. I must have the names. You gave up the Waffen-SS in the bunker easily enough. I suspect that you won't want to give up the Kalmyks as lightly, but you know you will.'

He paused.

'Why did you keep the film?'

Richter looked up. His eyes were red rimmed, his lips quivering. 'I didn't order them killed, I swear.' His voice was little more than a warbling whisper. 'I kept it to remind me of those times, to remind me that the Kalmyks had a savage side too. It was meant to be destroyed in the fire.' He cleared his throat and he lowered his eyes again. 'Will you ensure that I survive this?'

'I have offered you a deal. But I must have the names,' Kazapov said.

He'd done his best to stop from screaming the words.

Ignoring him, Richter said, 'So, the women on the film were your mother and your sisters.' Richter fingered the thin strands of his own hair and blinked. 'The colouring. I'm right, aren't I?' he said.

'If you speak to me like that again I will beat you to death myself,' Kazapov said.

Richter began to wheeze. Sweat broke out on his forehead. The cigarette fell from his fingers. He grasped his collar, jerking at it. He hugged his body with his other hand and doubled over.

Kazapov left his chair and moved over to him, calling out for a guard worriedly. The German seemed to be experiencing a terrible cramp, a closing over of his airways.

The door opened. Two NKVD captains were standing there. Not what Kazapov had expected. By the look on their pale faces, he knew Richter's time was up, and he cursed himself for not obtaining the information he desperately wanted.

He attempted to remonstrate with them, but they just glared at him as if he was barely human. If he attempted to bribe them, he'd likely beat Richter to Lubyanka. But he had to do something, even if not immediately.

'He needs a medic. He needs one now,' he said.

CHAPTER SIXTY-ONE

Shafts of sunlight fell through the lattice windows and Richter felt somewhat pleased with himself. He could see the bluish-grey sky, the high branches of a spruce tree. The office was lined with oak bookshelves and a few mundane items, a decanter, spirit glasses, a desk lamp. He believed that his tactical approach was beginning to pay off, especially with the arrival of Joseph Kazapov.

A deal, he thought. He'd jump at it, but he would play it soberly. He'd feigned breathing problems, on that occasion at least, simply because he'd needed time to think. It had all become rather too emotional. The fate of the Kalmyks had genuinely disturbed him. But he was lucid now. He saw things clearly again.

He'd been attended to by a Red Army medical officer, and got a shot of morphine after he said that he was a narcotics user and was suffering from withdrawal symptoms. One of the guards at the cell block had been called in and had attested to the fact that he often moaned himself to sleep due to stomach cramps, and that he often stumbled and sweated excessively. It was true. But he hadn't expected this treatment. He decided that these NKVD were as soft as cotton wool.

The two officers that had escorted him from the medical centre had remained outside the office, he knew. His new environment was a positive sign too, he believed. He expected Lieutenant Kazapov to enter at any moment.

Now he thought: why were captains on guard duty for a lieutenant? Especially as they were NKVD. Perhaps it was because he was a war crimes investigator. Perhaps not.

The wooden double doors hadn't been closed. The man that entered and walked stiffly to the window, overlooking the tree where a wood pigeon now preened itself, had a gaunt and stony face. He wore an NKVD officer's uniform that hugged his lean body, which to Richter's eyes verged on emaciated. He looked about thirty, with fine, swept-back hair. His eyes were large and lifeless. They were dark green and flecked with umber.

'We are going to Moscow, you and me, Nazi,' he said.

'Moscow? But I don't want to go to Moscow.' It was all he could think of saying.

'Comrade Beria has ordered it.'

'Beria? Beria knows about me?' Richter said, his expression fearful.

He stepped forward a couple of paces, almost involuntarily, as if breaking a fall.

'Are you going to torture me in Moscow?'

'You are an old fool,' the man said.

The officer pulled out a padded chair from the desk, sat on it. He put his high leather boots onto the desktop, twiddled a pencil he'd picked up there in his right hand.

'Comrade Stalin hates the Kalmyk people for their betrayal. Following your testimony, Comrade Beria will describe to him in detail all the things they did for you German fascists and all the things the NKVD will do to the Kalmyk people in exile for that betrayal, and Comrade Stalin will nod, and Comrade Beria will continue to be Comrade Beria.'

'Where is Lieutenant Kazapov?' Richter said, his breath quickening.

'It seems that Comrade Beria's general has a soft spot for him. But when Comrade Beria hears what I have to say, Lieutenant Kazapov will be digging ditches in Siberia for the next twenty years. Comrade Beria is my uncle and he despises insubordination above all things.'

Richter felt petrified and his cheeks began to quiver.

'But there's no need. I'll tell you everything. Important things. Ask Kazapov.'

'Did you tell Kazapov anything other than you told Major Volsky?'

Richter thought about that. If he said yes, his one chance of survival may be thwarted. If he said no, he'd confirm that Kazapov was just an insubordinate officer with too high an opinion of himself. He suspected that Kazapov had engineered his session with him. He knew why. He suspected too that Major Volsky wasn't pleased about that. An insubstantial snub, no doubt. But an insubstantial snub in the NKVD was enough to finish a man, something that Beria's nephew had just confirmed.

Before he had a chance to answer, the two officers outside the door appeared. They each grabbed one of Richter's arms, steadying him. A trickle of frothy saliva ran from the corner of his mouth to his chin, and his body started to quake.

Opium, he thought. I need my opium. The morphine had drained from him, its demise accelerated by the shock of this turn of events.

Beria's nephew took a clean white handkerchief from the left-hand pocket of his breeches, rolled it up and tossed it to one of the guards.

'Clean him up. My uncle likes his meat fresh. We leave in twenty minutes.'

CHAPTER SIXTY-TWO

Hale County — Berlin, 2015, the same day.

Fury was standing in the rain, about three feet from the shelter, knowing the roof would be secured from the inside. Their only option was to remove the wet sods and smash their way through unless Billy Joe Anderson surrendered once the excavation had begun. But she decided that that was unlikely.

'Dig him out,' she said.

Her voice was contemptuous. She stood still, expectant, vicious, as if she'd morphed into a ratter that was waiting for a rodent to be unearthed. The three soaked men proceeded with the manual work, digging out the sods with pickaxe and shovel.

Just as they got to the makeshift waterproofing, a blast sounded, splintering the wood and causing a flurry of shredded polythene, a disorientating cloud of sand. One of the men caught many of the discharged pellets full in the face, causing eruptions on his skin. Fury, temporarily stunned, watched him spring back, his feet leaving the ground. Lying on the wet grass, he looked as if he'd been assaulted with a cheese grater, so shredded and bloodied were his cheeks.

Regaining her composure within a second, she knew that Billy Joe

Anderson had one more shell, unless he'd used a pump-action shotgun. But a pump had a distinctive sound. One she hadn't heard.

'Pick him up. Pass him over the hole,' she said in Russian.

The two men did so, holding the obviously fatally wounded man by his wrists and ankles as they swung him back and forth over the partially shattered roof. The next shot hit him in the middle of his spine, causing a bloody rupture of bone and tissue. The two Russians just managed to hold him in place, even though they were smarting.

'Drop him,' Fury said, taking off her hat.

The moment the body hit the jagged hole she leaped into the air and landed feet first onto the now dead man's stomach, sending them both careering through the weakened roof with the force of a propelled boulder.

*

Billy Joe sidestepped as he saw the body he'd obviously shot at fall through what remained of the roof, but he wasn't fast enough to avoid it hitting him. He heard his shoulder pop, and felt a strangely detached numbing pain, just before he landed on the filthy carpeted floor.

Dazed, he vaguely registered a heavy weight on his chest among the rising dust: the hideous-looking corpse. He looked around. Hazily, he saw the shotgun three feet away. A good-looking blonde, who seemed to have come from nowhere, picked it up, smashed it against the wall. He breathed deeply, saw two men appear in the hole in the roof. They were big, able to handle themselves. One had a shovel in his hand. The woman said something to the men that sounded to him like Polish. He'd never left the US. The man with the shovel let it fall from his hand and the woman caught it by the handle.

The two men dropped down into the shelter like crazed predators.

They pulled the dead man from him and lay the wet and ravaged corpse against the wall opposite. The rain was coming through the massive hole in the roof. He could see a black cloud rolling by.

Suddenly, it felt unreal, as if he would wake up in a sweat.

'Strip him,' she said in English.

He knew she'd used English purposely. He didn't doubt it. He saw the two men glower at him before producing thin-bladed knives from leather sheaths attached to their now exposed belts. He figured the stiff had been a friend.

They began to slice at his jeans and T-shirt with a deftness that was disconcerting, as if they were fishmongers boning a prize catch. They ignored his groans and winces, and he knew in that moment that their trade was killing. He just prayed it would be quick. But something told him it wouldn't be, and he had to force himself not to weep openly.

The woman put the shovel against the wall and removed her rain jacket. She bent over him from the side, about six inches from his head.

As if reading his mind, she said, 'I work on you for hours.'

He glanced at her. Up close, he saw that she was muscular, her green eyes shimmering like sunlight on a pond.

'Wait. Just hold up. I'll tell you anything you wanna know.'

She backed off and, bending down again, took a pair of scissors from her discarded jacket pocket. He thought they looked like dressmaker's scissors. Like the ones his mama used. Heavy and cutthroat sharp. She stared hard at him.

'You get drunk in bar. Tell friends you big man. You killed Watsons. Yes?'

'Jesus, no. I won't.'

'Snow Lion,' the woman said.

Billy Joe flinched. He couldn't help it. Hockey had mentioned the name on several occasions.

'And, Vezzani?' she said.

He hesitated but knew he must speak if there was a chance of saving himself.

'Hockey just said that he was gonna pay us for doing things.'

'What things?'

'Like killing the Watsons.'

She eased down beside his head, stroking his damp forehead with her free hand. He felt a gnawing sensation on the left side of his face. He lifted his hand instinctively. He had no earlobe, just a raw unevenness that paralyzed him. Blood gushed down onto his neck to the floor. Desolate, he let the tears flow too.

*

Billy Joe was an unrecognisable pulp, barely alive. What was left of his face was no longer contorted in agony, and instead of the screams all that left his swollen mouth was a trickle of yellow vomit streaked with blood.

Fury knew now that he didn't know anything of significance and that he hadn't told anyone about the Watsons other than his girlfriend, after all. But that was enough. Wasn't it? Besides, he'd heard the name Snow Lion, and knew that Vezzani had been the paymaster.

A frail moan emerged from the pulp. A finger twitched. Nothing more. Picking up the shovel, she thrust the sharp metal blade into the flayed neck, before pushing down with her mud-splattered boot, as if she was about to dig a grave.

*

They stopped at a payphone on Main Street in Greensboro, still in Hale County, one hour later. The tornado damage was far less than in

Newbern, as if it had skirted around the small city. The street was still bordered by two-storey buildings, mostly whitewashed retail shops with red-brick accommodation above. Some of them looked ransacked rather than ruined. The rain had stopped.

The payphone had no dial tone, which didn't surprise Fury. She took out her smartphone, thumbed in a number.

Three seconds later, she said, 'The rooster and hen dead.'

'Did they know anything?' César Vezzani said.

'Some.'

'I need a full report.'

'Report, yes.'

'Stand down now.' Vezzani said.

She smirked.

*

In his Berlin villa, the old man was informed by César Vezzani that the country and western singers, Rimes and Anderson, were dead, and that he'd sent Fury and the Russians home.

The old man used his thumb and forefinger to stroke his earlobe. 'No. Tell her to come to Berlin with her boys. Don't tell her why. Let it cook a bit. In truth, I don't know why myself. But always be prepared. Good soldiers are always prepared.'

He had a feeling in his bowels, and it wasn't a pleasant one.

Vezzani said, 'Carla Romero has a four-year-old daughter. Gabriel Hall is unmarried and childless. He teaches at Yale.'

The old man's bald head nodded.

He thought about his nickname. It had meant to conjure up something not quite human. Something elusive and mysterious. Something to be used only by those who served him, or at least that he paid for their services. There was nothing in it that could link him to his actions unless someone who knew his nickname also saw one of his DVDs. That may well have happened or may happen now, in the future. This was the real reason he had had the country and western singers killed.

He began to grind his back teeth with a mixture of frustration and anxiety. It was a habit he'd started after the war. Like his desire for revenge, it had never left him.

CHAPTER SIXTY-THREE

Brussels, the same day.

Robert Dubois sipped the second Leffe Blonde he'd ordered in a bar just down from Bruxelles-Central railway and metro station, where the waiters wore long masonic-like aprons and black ties. He took off his suit jacket and unbuttoned the top two buttons of his white shirt. It was a balmy night, and he plumped to sit on one of a row of brightly coloured deckchairs on the pavement outside. He checked his wristwatch. She was twenty minutes late. Nothing changes, he thought.

'Robert.'

The voice was unmistakable. He turned and saw Carla leaning against the bar's façade of grey, cast-iron window jambs and red brick. She wore an apricot-coloured blouse and had what looked like a green yoga bag slung over her shoulder. The last time he'd seen her had been almost two years ago.

He stood up as she walked over to him. He kissed her on both cheeks, inhaling her musky perfume. Her hair was held up with an elaborate gold hairpin that was decorated with embossed kanji, and he had to stop himself from running his tongue over her caramel neck.

He thanked her for coming and paid for the drinks. They walked to the edge of the pavement and he hailed a cab.

'Rue Lesbroussart,' he said to the Arabic driver, who had his window down.

He'd decided they'd have dinner at an expensive Vietnamese restaurant there, although he knew his lack of communication on such matters, his inability to share mundane decision making, was but one of his idiosyncrasies she disliked. But he did it anyway. Perhaps he deserved to be on his own, he thought.

*

They were sitting across from each other at a teak table with a fine lace tablecloth. The lighting was dim, the pearl-coloured wallpaper made of silk. Bright watercolours of Ha Long Bay hung there, the limestone pillars topped with rainforest reflecting in the emerald Gulf of Tonkin. Carla found herself gazing at the islet of Stone Dog, the depiction of a junk passing by it.

'Where the dragon descends into the sea,' Dubois said, smiling.

She knew he was referring to the local legend of the creation of the islets. They had spent a week on holiday at the nearby Cat Ba Beach Resort. It felt like a thousand years ago.

The first time Carla had come to this restaurant, she'd loved it. It was an undeniably happy time. But tonight, she was at best unsure of her emotions. She'd travelled to Brussels to get answers from Robert Dubois, and for that reason alone. She asked him to order for her and when he asked her if she was sure, she snapped at him.

The minutes before the food arrived passed in relative silence, punctuated only by rather brusque exchanges between them. It was a relief when the tiny, smiling waitress, clad from neck to toes in a bridal-white dress, brought them their meal, placing the plates of food beside a small lazy Susan that held the condiments. She remembered that they'd eaten the same dishes when they'd been here before, and Dubois's lack of subtlety irritated her.

She'd first met him a year before that, and they first made love in a medieval house that had been converted into a bespoke hotel in Bruges, an hour's train ride from Brussels. She'd woken up to the sound of ducks on the canal outside the lattice windows.

They'd become lovers almost instantly. For her, it was a visceral passion that had erupted just at the sight of him. He'd occupied her thoughts every day. When they touched, she had felt, what seemed to her sensations, something which no other person could possibly have felt.

But she had known from early on that their relationship would be short. Dubois was unable to mask his rapacious nature. She'd ended it. She'd said it was due to the physical distance between them, since she'd moved to Washington by then. It had become too intense, as she'd known it would, and Dubois showed signs of an increasing jealousy. She'd been conscious of not wanting to exacerbate that to a potentially dangerous level. She'd missed him terribly, although it had been the right thing to do, for both their sakes. She'd never doubted that and still didn't.

They talked about the past for a few minutes. The good times. The bad. Carla brought up Gabriel and Dubois quizzed her about him so relentlessly that in the end she told him to back off. When he didn't, she told him to shut the hell up. They didn't talk for a while, after that.

The waitress appeared at the table without sound.

'Coffee?' she said.

'Yes, thank you,' Carla said.

Dubois nodded and looked out of the window. Carla followed his gaze.

'What information do you have for me, Robert?' she said.

He told her what Finkel had told him about the Chechen. He said that the Chechen had talked to a deep-cover operative about an old man who lived in Berlin, a serial killer, albeit the Chechen had been under the influence of crack cocaine at the time. He told her about the DVD that the Chechen claimed he'd sold to a wealthy American.

Was it the same one? she thought. It had to be, didn't it?

He took out a white envelope and passed it over to her.

'You must ensure that the Chechen is found in the US, that as many resources as possible are mobilized. His recent photograph,' he said, nodding towards the envelope.

She didn't find that patronizing. How could she? She knew what motivated Dubois. When they'd been lovers, they'd talked of what they might do together in the fight against the murder of girls and young women, and now they were doing it. Weren't they?

'There is something else,' he said. 'The Chechen said the old man was known as Snow Lion.'

'Snow Lion,' she said, her mouth bunching.

She had to stop herself from emitting a little squeal, to celebrate this breakthrough.

'Is the Chechen to be believed?'

'Finkel thinks he is,' Dubois said. 'In this, at least.'

She knew the German and she accepted that.

'Thank you, Robert.'

'My pleasure.'

She saw him looking at her, a hint of a sneer on his handsome face. He was noble, and he was weak in equal measure, she thought.

She called the waitress over and asked for the cheque. He looked disappointedly at her.

'I have a flight back to DC in three hours,' she said.

'I see.'

'My treat,' she said, passing the back of her open hand over the table. 'It's the least I can do.'

She smiled, and he nodded, knowingly, she could tell.

'Could you ask Finkel to check Berlin records for missing Kalmyk girls going back, well, going back sixty years?'

'The old man in Berlin, huh? Yes, I will.'

'Thank you, Robert.'

*

In a cab to Brussels Airport, she rang Hester. She'd already found out the material facts relating to the disappearances of young Kalmyk women in New Jersey, and since her discussion with Dubois, her investigative imagination had fired up and she'd decided that all possible angles had to be covered.

Six hours behind Brussels time, Hester was still in his office. He was diligent and tenacious, even as he was physically slothful, she thought.

'It's Carla Romero, sir.'

'It's late,' he said.

'Are relationships still frosty with the FSB?' she said, referring to the Federal Security Service of the Russian Federation.

She heard Hester sigh.

'Why, Agent Romero?'

'Are they, sir?'

'Officially.'

'And unofficially? Do you have a contact there?'

'Where's this going?'

She told him the relevant details about the Chechen, the Berlin connection and her thought process, the fact that she worried the disappearances of Kalmyk girls could go back way beyond the timeline established in New Jersey. She didn't mention Dubois, although she'd been authorized to go to Brussels as part of her ongoing investigation.

'I'll make the call,' he said

She smelled a waft of her perfume. She knew why she'd worn it, and felt stupid. A fraud, even.

CHAPTER SIXTY-FOUR

Brooklyn Heights, three days later.

Gabriel got out of bed and walked to the bathroom in his boxer shorts. He'd overslept. He took a shower and had a bowl of porridge, then, following a second cup of coffee, he got a call on his smartphone from a private investigator he'd contacted named Sam Cartwright. Sam did the leg work for Gabriel, serving court documents, occasional surveillance and the kind of digging around in other people's lives that up until now Gabriel had deemed inappropriate for a lawyer.

Sam was an ex-cop, but had been suspended for an alleged assault on an underage drug dealer in a police cell. The kid was the son of a successful businessman from Rochester in Upstate New York. The charges against the kid had been dropped on the proviso that Sam resigned. He'd told Gabriel that at that time his career prospects had been about as healthy as a ketamine addict's bladder — but he was now regarded as one of the most proficient PIs in the state and had confided in Gabriel that his earnings had trebled since he'd worn the blue. Gabriel was pleased for him.

He gave Gabriel the address he'd asked for and said that the man was still named Bronislaw Stolarski, that he'd changed addresses three times in the last eight years and had no credit history or private pension.

He's still alive, Gabriel thought.

'Thanks, Sam.'

'Hey, forget about it. You've always been good to me, Gabriel.'

'Thanks anyway. Be sure to send me an invoice.'

Gabriel figured that Stolarski was no older than his late seventies, which was relatively young by today's standards. He now knew that he lived in the White Mountains.

He leaned back in his chair, his mind unable to join the dots. What connection could there be, with what had happened in Berlin in 1945 and the disappearances of Kalmyk girls? There was only the similar manner of death of the young woman in the DVD and what had allegedly been inflicted on Red Army soldiers back then.

He decided he would visit Stolarski in the next couple of days and see if he'd talk. Sam had said that the man didn't have a mobile or landline number and only received mail twice a week.

His smartphone rang again. Thinking it was Sam and that he'd forgotten to tell him something important, he picked it up agitatedly. But it was Beal, the federal public defender. He said he'd filed a pre-trial motion to test the validity of the prosecution evidence. He also said that Hockey would like Gabriel to be there. Gabriel said that he wasn't representing him, as he well knew, and that the last time he'd seen Hockey he'd told him that face-to-face, and he hadn't taken it too well. Beal said he could simply sit at the back of the court as an interested observer. Hockey had asked if Gabriel could ring him after the hearing and fill him in on the legal details, which he could do legitimately as a non-participant.

Disconnecting, Gabriel rubbed the back of his head and clenched his jaw. He guessed he couldn't afford not to keep up the pretence. Hockey might say something to someone that could prompt a dangerous investigation into him. It hadn't worked out the way he'd once hoped it might. Hockey would rather languish in prison than give even a hint of the whereabouts of those who bankrolled him.

He consoled himself with the knowledge that if he hadn't offered to help Beal with the defence of Hockey, he would never have met Carla. If he hadn't met Carla, he wouldn't have seen a copy of the DVD, and if he hadn't seen the DVD, he wouldn't have spoken with Professor Boris Iliev. That, he dared to think, might lead to something else, something positive, if he managed to have a meaningful conversation with Bronislaw Stolarski.

*

The next day, Gabriel left the court room at 3.46 pm. He walked over to a payphone and called Hockey in prison. He told him that the motion had gone well enough and that Beal was up to the job. Hockey sniffed at that and said he didn't understand legal procedure but thanked him for going as he'd asked. It was good of him, he said.

Now Hockey said: 'You know, I had a dream yesterday. I was tied down on a beach. The waves were crashing in. I could smell the salt and the seaweed. Then people came. Just random people. But they began shoving live fish in my mouth. I couldn't breathe. I was dying. They were killing me. You ever had a dream like that?'

Gabriel shivered, wondering if that was a threat.

He said, 'No, Johnny. Can't say I have.'

'They're moving me.'

'Where?'

'Some army base in a few days. They still think that failed attempt to hijack the prison truck had something to do with me, I guess.'

'I see.'

'You don't see shit,' Hockey said.

Gabriel ended the call.

CHAPTER SIXTY-FIVE

The farm, Bezirk Potsdam, East Germany, 1988 — The farm, near Potsdam, German Federal State of Brandenburg, 2015.

She'd been kidnapped off the mud-caked street of a small village ten miles from Elista, the capital of Kalmykia, a month ago. Her kidnappers had been three middle-aged men, wearing trainers and baseball caps, that she'd suspected had been in the Soviet military. Everyone spoke of the fact that they were untrustworthy and corrupt. Who else would do such a thing?

Gagged and bound, she'd been driven overnight to a teeming city that she hadn't recognized. For two days, she was held in a damp cellar that had smelled of blocked drains, where night and day were indistinguishable. She'd been drugged by a man that had looked to her like a bandit. Thickset and tattooed, with little eyes like a Dalmatian pelican. He'd put a needle in her thigh and had grinned. She'd woken up in the back of a truck, bleary-eyed and nauseous. Vaguely, she'd seen another man, whose countenance had been equally terrifying, as he'd crouched by her legs, and she'd lapsed into unconsciousness again. The journey from her homeland had taken close to eight days and she'd been kept alive by drip-feed.

The farm was fifteen miles from Berlin's city centre. It had two stacks of chimneys, and a large black flue jutted out from one side. There were no discernible security systems, although they existed. It was owned, on paper at least, by offshore companies. The names of the shareholders were dead people, the victims of posthumous identity theft.

She'd been held in one of several bare brick cellars, tethered to the wall like a medieval prisoner, except her restraints had been padded so as not to mark her skin by chaffing. She was put in what the old man called 'the hole', a dry well that had been built around years before and left intact, and fed liquidized food laced with drugs through a garden hose. She was seventeen years old. She'd spent the time wringing her little hands before being brought back to the cellar.

She'd started crying and begging to be set free when the door had opened. She'd called her mother's name. Her chains had been removed. She'd been blindfolded and coaxed to her feet by her elbows. Weak through lack of exercise, she'd wobbled like a day-old lamb. Then, she was lifted into the air and felt movement.

She'd been washed in a porcelain bath scented with oils and chrysanthemum petals. Her hair rinsed with rosewater, her nails shaped and buffed. Any moles, other blemishes or distinguishing marks had been concealed with cinematic make-up. She'd been drugged with Rohypnol, which had caused delayed sedation, muscle relaxation, reduced anxiety and partial amnesia.

Her blindfold had been removed about ten minutes previously. She was woozy now, her body drained. The room was unlike the one she'd been held prisoner in. Sticks of aromatic incense rose from iron pots that were half-filled with sand. The room was thick with it. The floor was strewn with ornate silk cushions and multi-coloured rugs. There were bright lights and 8mm movie cameras attached to tripods.

The door opened and someone scuttled in. The hands were gloved, the face covered by a ghastly mask, one that she thought she recognized, even above the haze in her head. She decided it must be a man, because the person wore the maroon and yellow robe of a Tibetan monk. It had the old Buddhist symbol of Tibetan Buddhism embroidered on it, a swastika, with a dot in each of the four quadrants.

'Please sir,' she said in Kalmyk Oirat.

The unmistakable dour scent of burning juniper floated in from the adjacent room he'd come from, the smell of a Tibetan funeral pyre, mixing now with the incense.

He said something to her that she didn't understand. She shook her head.

The man lifted his mask somewhat, but enough to reveal what looked to her like a barnacled neck the circumference of a black stork's. To her, he appeared as an ancient man, whose teeth she imagined, were jagged and fang-like, his eyes, sunken rubies.

He bent down, grasping the robe above the hem and lifted it up. His legs, she thought, were as thin as those of an ibex or wild sheep. He spread his arms so that the robe resembled the wings of a great bat. He made small circles with his outstretched arms, such that the splayed material began to undulate.

He turned gracefully, and as he did so, the room was filled with sound, the deep, haunting notes of a dungchen, a Tibetan horn, and above it, the eerie wailing of the femur trumpet. The back of the robe was all but covered by something unmistakable that made her smile, despite the drug and the mild uncertainty brought about by his antics and her surroundings. It was a holy creature, one of the four dignities, sacred in her homeland. It was leaping.

A snow lion.

*

Nearly thirty years later now, the old man, dressed in a silk bathrobe, walked falteringly over to a battered chest, positioned against a red-brick wall at the farmhouse, the lingering smell of incense making his hairy nostrils flare.

A few hours ago, he'd been thinking of that time back in 1988. He'd thought about how many times Jed Watson must have watched the converted 8mm cine film before Johnny Hockey killed him. Many, he'd guessed.

He'd finished converting all the old films to DVDs flawlessly, using professional imaging equipment to scan and transfer each frame. He'd kept the original films at the ghost house so that he could update them via state-of-the-art technology when it became available.

Now he stopped for a few moments in front of the gilded Renaissance mirror above the chest, licking his blotchy forefinger. He lifted his oval glasses and shaped his meagre eyebrows. He wanted to look his best for her.

He bent over, flipped open the brass clasps. It had been decades since he'd seen her, so long, in fact, that he sometimes wondered if that time had been imagined. But when he took out the black and white photograph, marred and fading, beneath his old military uniform, it was if it had all happened a few days before.

You were so beautiful, he thought.

This was the only aspect of his war that had brought forth life into the world instead of death.

CHAPTER SIXTY-SIX

Outskirts of Berlin, 1945, the same day.

Sonderführer Lutz Richter was sitting in the back of an NKVD staff car, like the one that had first taken him to the temporary interrogation centre. He was on his way to an isolated airstrip, where he'd be flown the thousand miles to Moscow. He knew that all the airstrips for miles around had been destroyed by the months of Allied air force raids and two weeks of near constant Soviet rocket and artillery bombardment. He knew too that his specific destination was Lubyanka Square and the NKVD HQ, an imposing nineteenth century neo-baroque building, with a distinctive yellow brick façade.

The administrative centre and Beria's third-floor office had expensive parquet flooring and spotless pale green walls. The mincing machine, the notorious prison section, did not. He wondered why both Beria and Himmler had wanted their offices so close to the torture cells.

Himmler's office had been at Prinz-Albrecht-Strasse, Berlin, the headquarters of the Reich Security Main Office, the Gestapo and the SS. It had once been an art museum. El Greco and Bellini had hung there. Then prisoners had hung there, their wrists tied behind their backs so that their shoulders had dislocated. It had been renamed the

311

house of horror by the locals. Passers-by reported screams coming from within. The prisoners were subjected to repeated near drownings in a tin bathtub filled with ice-cold water, to electric shocks, to beatings with rubber batons and cow-hide whips, to the burning of flesh with soldering irons.

Do these things now await me at Lubyanka? Richter thought.

What he did know was that few survived the mincing machine, and even if they did, they were no longer of any use to anyone.

Squeezed between the two NKVD guards, behind the driver and with Beria's nephew occupying the front passenger seat, Richter's visibility was marginal, although he knew there were two motorcycle outriders up front.

Straining for a view of the city, he caught glimpses of the aftermath of the devastation. People were scavenging what they could from near demolished houses and offices. There were little groups of female civilians, dishevelled and flustered, with scrawny children at the roadsides, pulling small carts of ragged clothes, pushing prams full of firewood, the odd tin of food. The injured and the infirm were transported in wheelbarrows.

A few nuns in filthy habits were doing what they could, which was nothing at all as far as Richter could see. The occasional bicycle was ridden. Nothing more. Not one living animal was to be seen. Just the carcass of a donkey or nag, the flesh stripped from it, half the bones too.

Further on, endless lines of male POWs, the teenagers and the old, shuffled along the edges of the piles of debris, grey and dejected, like endlessly wandering wraiths. Anyone in uniform had been taken. Even firemen, air raid wardens and ambulance drivers. He knew many would perish en route to the east, and many more in the prison camps. The capture of Berlin was Stalin's reward, a tactic Richter felt was sound.

Karl Marx had said almost one hundred years before: *He who possesses Berlin, controls Europe.*

The vehicle reached the outskirts of the bombed city where a group of five Red Army women soldiers was gathered beside a blackened Soviet T-34 tank, its turret scalped. Their heavy woollen dresses were mud-splattered, their berets askew. They were screaming and kicking a grey-haired member of the Volkssturm to death, his skinny body hidden in a voluminous greatcoat.

As the car approached them, one of the women bent down and started to strangle him. Seemingly bored, she finished him off with a bullet to the side of the neck. His head was tossed back and forth by the impact, like a fairground punch ball. The women clambered over the rubble and disappeared into a hollow building, with a crumbling rococo façade, as if they'd been finally rendered ashamed of their actions.

Fucking banshees, Richter thought.

CHAPTER SIXTY-SEVEN

Now the road was narrower, the sides less littered with burned-out military vehicles, the air cleaner and all but silent, save for the odd transport and cargo aircraft. They had left Berlin behind. No one spoke to Richter in the car.

Thinking of the past, he wondered momentarily if the choices he had made in his life had been terrible mistakes. Had the Reich been a hopeless dream from its inception?

Suddenly, the car was full of concerned shouts from the driver and Beria's nephew.

The vehicle turned abruptly onto a grass verge and came to a jolting stop as the brakes were applied too heavily, the car's metal grille impacting with the bank of earth that abutted the verge.

Richter lurched forward, banging his injured nose on the front seat. It began to bleed again. Straightening up, his eyes streaming, he could just make out the two outriders sprawled on the road ahead, and the bizarre sight of their motorcycles rolling forward without them. The concerned shouts were replaced by awkward action, with arms flung randomly about. In the barely subdued panic, his guards struggled to free their TT-33 pistols from their leather holsters.

Richter knew that the outriders had been dislodged from their motorcycles by a thick piece of taut wire, which, he guessed, had been positioned at neck level, or at least as near as could be estimated. But it had done the job spectacularly well. It lay on the road now, half curled up, like an outsized viper.

He heard heavy footfalls behind him and looked around. There was a dozen or so men spanning the road, about three yards away. They wore long leather or tweed coats and civilian hats. More men appeared from over the bank, similarly attired. They all carried German MP40 submachine guns, Mauser rifles, or pistols. Two had stick grenades tucked into their belts.

No shots were fired, but Richter vaguely heard voices speaking in German.

The driver was pinned in by the bank, but Beria's nephew managed to half scramble out. He was knocked unconscious by the butt of a carbine to the back of his head. The two guards either side of Richter were aiming their pistols at the men milling about with remarkable calm outside the closed windows. The car was surrounded, its occupants outnumbered and outgunned.

The guard on the left exited the vehicle on all fours. He fired once before he was hit by a volley of at least ten rounds, the empty brass casings clattering on the asphalt like a set of bar chimes struck discordantly. He appeared to shiver with the impact and pitched forward, blood bubbling from his mouth as if, amused, he was spilling something he'd drunk.

The guard to Richter's right grabbed him around the neck and pulled him down, placing the pistol's muzzle to his temple. Accepting his fate, Richter started to mumble a Tantric prayer to himself.

The window nearest Richter shattered, the sound like a howitzer discharging, the shards of glass mere patters as they cascaded onto the grassy verge. The guard holding Richter down jerked back up, releasing him in the process. Richter looked sideways at him, still fearful for his life. But the man's head was moving this way and that, and his teeth were chattering. In that moment, Richter knew he had never seen action and the thought eased his anxiety a little, although he knew the man could act erratically out of sheer despair.

A hand clad in a leather glove was thrust through the jagged remains of the window, imbedding a serrated blade into the guard's jugular. He squealed like a distressed sow. The blade was eased out and little geysers of blood squirted from the entry wound in one-second intervals, covering the seat in front, the roof, the windscreen. The man went rigid and shook before falling against the door.

Wiping the thick blood from his own face, Richter knew the wound was fatal. He felt oddly detached from it all now. The guard was no longer a man, after all, but rather just blood-splattered wax, motionless and pale, the eyes unblinking. The door was pulled open and the man in a trilby hat and a woollen overcoat jerked on the guard's arm and let him topple to the grass to bleed out.

'Komm schnell,' the man said.

Hearing his native language spoken to him directly by a German helped propel Richter from the NKVD vehicle. Bursts of submachine-gun fire signalled the premature deaths of the driver and Beria's nephew, and the rear leather seats were peppered in a flurry that flung padding and severed springs about amid the muzzle smoke. Richter looked over at the nephew. His feet were still inside the car and a trail of blood was leaching from his lower back. It was obvious that he'd regained consciousness after the bludgeoning. He was making a faint mewing sound now, like a puppy snatched from its mother's dog basket. A fitting end, Richter thought.

Three unmarked cars pulled up behind. But the threat of an execution had taken its toll and Richter had to be assisted, his upper arms held as two young men all but dragged him to the rear vehicle. He glanced back. The NKVD staff car looked as if a bloody mist had descended upon it.

He was folded onto the back seat, the aroma of fresh leather wafting over him. He managed to straighten up as the car began to reverse at speed. The man in the front passenger seat turned around and offered Richter a stainless-steel canteen.

'Drink?' he said.

It sounded more like a command than a question, but Richter took it just the same. He wiped blood from his lips and chin, but it was still oozing from his stinging nose. He'd expected water; this was schnapps, and it warmed the back of his throat. Nothing calmed him like opium, but this came a close second, given the circumstances. The man who had handed him the canteen was handsome, with a lean face and eyes the colour of violets.

'Who are you?' Richter said.

'SS Hauptsturmführer Walter Basse.'

'But the war is over,' Richter said. 'Isn't it?'

'Not for everyone,' Basse said.

Basse began to unbutton his overcoat. He pulled it down over his right shoulder, revealing something that made Richter grin. Under the Waffen-SS camouflage jacket, on a field grey uniform, was a rune on a shoulder strap, one worn by the Second SS Panzer Division, Das Reich. It was the Wolfsangel, or wolf hook, said to be a powerful talisman that warded off danger.

'Das Reich?' Richter said.

'Nein. Werwolf.'

Richter knew that in the autumn of 1944, Himmler had set up

Operation Werwolf as a potential SS guerrilla movement, and that in March 1945, Dr Goebbels had given the 'Werwolf' speech, urging every German to fight to the death.

'It's not the end?' Richter said.

'No,' Basse said. 'Berlin has fallen. But Army Group Centre fights on in Czechoslovakia. We hold out in Denmark and the north. Elsewhere, too.'

'I had no idea. And Himmler?'

'Has escaped Berlin.'

Richter rubbed his forehead with the thumb and forefinger of his left hand, disbelievingly.

'How did you know I'd be here?' he said.

'We didn't. We were after prisoners for intelligence purposes. A barter, if it came to it. When I saw the Russian grab you and his pistol went down, I ordered your rescue.'

In that moment, Richter convinced himself that the Tantric prayer had played its part.

CHAPTER SIXTY-EIGHT

The NKVD general stood with Kazapov and Volsky in one of the bunker's corridors, outside the room that had held the savaged and dismembered corpses of the Red Army soldiers. Hurricane lamps hung at intervals, the leaking pipes bound with grey tape, used to patch-up tanks.

'So, this is where it happened,' the general said. 'The smell is unbearable. Like those foul camps. I knew I shouldn't have come. But curiosity is a demanding mistress.'

Kazapov thought about the general's other mistress, Brigitte Bayer, and winced. Volsky went to put his hand on the general's right tricep, but evidently thought better of it.

'I think we should go, comrade general. The ceilings aren't safe,' he said.

'The major is right, comrade general. The ceilings could collapse at any time, the sappers warned,' Kazapov said.

He guessed that the general was lying, and that Beria had told him to report personally on the matter, and that though he disliked such places as an affront to his senses, to disobey or to try to fool Beria was a mistake a man only made once.

The general nodded. 'Alright. I've seen enough. But do you smell that fragrance in the air?'

He looked as if he was remembering something from his past, a memory that had been fanned into life by the aroma.

'Fragrance, comrade general?' Volsky said.

'Yes. It never leaves you. Not after all these years. Not after all that has taken place.'

The general looked down, searching with his dark eyes for something among the debris.

'General, please. We must go,' Volsky said.

Ignoring him, the general said, 'And do you know what it is?'

'Incense. It's incense,' Kazapov said.

'Yes, indeed,' the general said.

An NKVD captain came up the dust-strewn corridor towards them. He saluted the general, breathing erratically. Kazapov noticed that his skin was unusually pallid, that he was stick thin and had watery eyes.

'I'm sorry, comrade general, but I have bad news.'

'What is it?' the general said.

'The SS colonel, Lutz Richter, has escaped.'

'Escaped?'

'I'm afraid so, general. There are no survivors.'

The general's face creased. 'Fucking shit! Beria will be apoplectic.' He stared at the captain. 'How?'

'We don't know, for sure, comrade general. A group of renegades, perhaps.'

He sighed. 'Beria will be apoplectic,' he said, repeating himself. 'His nephew was in that car.'

'We have fifty men looking for him, general,' the captain said.

'Double the number. Do it now.'

'Yes, comrade general.'

'Triple it.'

'Yes, comrade general.'

The captain saluted and shuffled off. Kazapov couldn't believe what he'd just heard. But it was so. He raked his brain to find a way to take advantage of the fact that Richter had escaped. If he could get to him, he would be able to get the names of the Kalmyks shown in the film he'd viewed. Those who had murdered his mother and sisters.

The general took out a cigarette, which Volsky lit for him obsequiously. The general began to smoke with furious puffs.

'We need to find this man, and quickly,' he said.

Kazapov nodded. 'Please, comrade general. I would like to take a squad and hunt for him.'

The general removed his cigarette. 'Why would you?'

'It's my duty, general.'

The general shook his head. 'You are too eager, Kazapov. Your eagerness will get you killed. Nevertheless, take some Poles, if you must. If you find him I will promote you personally.'

'Thank you, comrade general.'

The general stubbed out his cigarette, as if he'd suddenly decided that smoking was a risky thing to do in the bunker. He took some snuff from a silver box, sniffed it from the back of his hand.

'Let's not fret too much. They will all hang. The only thing that will survive this is our beloved communism. The future.'

But Kazapov knew the general wasn't the fanatical Stalinist he liked people to think he was. Who was? Kazapov figured he was simply trying to keep himself alive like everyone else.

'Still,' the general said. 'Beria will have *someone's* balls for this. Just not mine.'

As they walked away, Volsky whispered to Kazapov. 'Don't think his nephew's death means you're off the hook, little man.'

CHAPTER SIXTY-NINE

Oranienburg. north of Berlin, the same day.

A light drizzle was falling, and the fading light was exacerbated by charcoal-black clouds that hung low in the sky.

Joseph Kazapov's head was pressed hard against the side of a bomb crater, with only the thin material of his cloth forage cap between them. He'd lost his helmet when a mine had exploded nearby a couple of minutes before. The Polish squad he'd ordered to help him find Richter was pinned down by a sniper. Every time they moved, a bullet hit the crater-ridden, sludge-filled road — or a recruit. Three young men already lay dead among the debris.

He'd received a radio message from an NKVD signalman who'd stated that a group of plainclothes Germans had smashed their way through a roadblock and had shot at Red Army soldiers. He'd said an old man had been seen in the back of the car who'd fitted Lutz Richter's description. They were in the ancient town of Oranienburg, about twenty miles north of Berlin. It seemed they'd been heading for the far north, which was still under German control. They had abandoned the vehicle due to the burst tyres. Kazapov had ordered that no further action should be taken until he arrived on the scene.

When he had, he'd been shown the building where the few men that had survived the gun battle were holed up. But there was an active sniper there, too.

Gas pipes had been shot through and fires started. The resultant explosions had taken out a Red Army squad. Dynamite had been rigged up in an old garage that had killed another five men. Flaming wooden beams had crashed to the ground, sending sparks and black ash flying and had badly injured two more comrades. Brave young men that had fought at the siege of Leningrad against the Germans, Italians, Finns and Spanish. The surviving men had looked to Kazapov to be both furious and not a little wary.

He now knew that the sniper was on the fourth floor of the building, a Mercedes-Benz office complex, eighty yards ahead. Using his field binoculars, a split second after a shot had been fired, he saw the red brick walls peppered with bullet holes. All but a few windows were shattered, but it hadn't been gutted. There was no sign of the German sniper, not even a muzzle blast or a single fleeting and muted reflection from the optical scope glass.

He pushed three hand grenades inside his belt and put a fresh, circular magazine into the well of his Shpagin. The grenades were cylindrical and nine inches long, including the handle. He knew that once he'd released the firing lever that jutted out from the handle the time delay was four seconds.

The five men with him, the remnants of the squad, were bunched in the shallow bomb crater. They were all privates in the First Infantry Division and wore tarpaulin jackets, drill pants and their old Red Army-issue helmets emblazoned with the Polish military eagle, the Piast Eagle. Apart from their rifles, two were armed with RPG-1 anti-tank grenades. He knew they could take out the sniper, but that wouldn't serve his purpose.

He looked at them in turn. Ash-grey faces. Filthy uniforms. Young minds warped and twisted, he could tell. Young hands that had brought death into the world.

The legacy of war, Kazapov thought. Of all wars. Of my war.

One was a lad from Warsaw, with a hooked nose. The bare skin on his neck bore rope marks. He swore every other word. A metal joist had embedded itself in his shin. Now he cursed the indiscriminate nature of war, and said he'd had enough and was going home. He stood up and let his German M-09 ammo pouches fall. He limped forward, using his 7.62 Mosin rifle to bear his weight.

As the others started to scream at him to get down, a high-calibre bullet hit him in the cheek, whirling him around on his makeshift crutch like a spinning top. Then he dropped. In the open. In the dead zone. His helmet was still on, but his body was splayed. He was as vulnerable as a beached starfish. The second bullet penetrated his neck. He coughed and whimpered. His hands grasped his throat, his fingers trembling as they tried in vain to stem the arterial spurts of blood. It took him less than a minute to die, the blood mingling with the earth.

Kazapov thought briefly that the earth from Berlin to Moscow must be drenched in it.

Some said prayers. Others cursed his stupidity. Kazapov looked on with fascination. The boy was a Jew from the Warsaw ghetto. His mother had been sent to Treblinka, he'd said. His father had fought with the partisans. Kazapov couldn't imagine what had made him commit suicide. For suicide it had been.

He knew too that in July 1944, the Polish First Army had been ordered by Stalin to halt at the Vistula River for no logical reason other than to allow the Germans to savagely put down an uprising by the Polish Home Army and civilian resistance in the capital,

Warsaw. Kazapov had been told that Hitler had ordered the population to be expelled and the city destroyed. The Poles in the city had thought they would be aiding the Red Army. But Stalin had let the Germans do his work for him. He'd rule Poland unopposed now. Most of the east and the Balkans too. Kazapov guessed it had all become too much for the lad from Warsaw. And he himself had had enough, too.

'I'm going to kill that German sniper,' he said.

'You're crazy, lieutenant,' one said; a skinny wretch with broken teeth, who smelled even worse than the rest.

'When I move, cover me,' Kazapov said.

'Go on, lieutenant. Kill the bastard,' another said.

Then the others joined in, screaming and baring their yellow teeth like madmen.

Kazapov watched them, faintly amused. It was easy to rouse the young to violence. For him, it was his last chance to get to Richter and obtain the names he craved. A company of NKVD troops from a rifle division were on their way, he knew. Sent by the general in the hope of placating Comrade Beria for his loss.

He crawled forward and readied himself for the dash. The four remaining privates flung themselves towards the lip of the crater, aiming their weapons with a newfound relish.

CHAPTER SEVENTY

Kazapov wiped the grainy rain from his gaunt face and, after springing up and rushing behind a burned-out Wehrmacht staff car, he raced forward again, slaloming to avoid the craters, jagged metal, strewn masonry and smouldering timbers. He clenched his jaw and murmured to himself. He spoke of revenge, of the things he would do to those that had killed his mother and sisters, of how he would make it last, the Poles' covering fire a discordant accompaniment.

A bullet hit an oil drum less than six inches to his right as he sprinted past. He forced himself to ignore it, pounding through the foul puddles and leaping over the mounds of rubble, mortar holes and disfigured corpses. Soft ash floated down from the sky, covering them in a grey shroud.

Another bullet ricocheted off a boulder an inch from his left foot and he grimaced, but the red-brick wall of the Mercedes building was less than five feet away now. Reaching it, he bent over and gasped for breath before edging towards the nearest entranceway. He was safe — at least, for a while.

The entranceway had been hit by mortar fire. A lintel hung down in front of him like broken signage. The walls were blood splattered, the floor a mixture of cigarette butts and discarded ration packs. He reckoned the entranceway had seen more than its fair share of war.

Further up, about three yards away, lay the corpse of a pregnant woman, riddled with mortar fragments. A patchwork scarf half covered her head so that it was impossible to tell what colour her hair had been. Not that it mattered, he thought. The street ahead seemed devoid of life.

The dark blue wooden door hung inwards from its bottom hinges. He kicked it down and ran in, his Shpagin raised to his shoulder, with both hands steadying it. He scanned the entrance hall. The floor was wet and covered with debris and discarded personal items: a satchel, a woman's hat, a black bicycle. The staircase leading from the hall's rear had a bulky wooden and metal banister that still looked robust. Kazapov knew that the sniper was waiting for him above.

As he began to ascend the stairs, a door on the ground floor was flung open. Three plainclothes men rushed through, firing their MP40s somewhat haphazardly in his general direction, their vision hampered by the bannister. The bullets embedded themselves deep into the blue walls of the staircase and ricocheted off the lattice ironwork beneath the rail, causing flashes of sparks. The sound was deafening, adding to the sense of chaos as pieces of concrete, wood and plaster careered through the air about him.

Pressing his body hard to the stairs, he fingered his belt for a grenade. He pulled the lever and tossed it over the staircase. Then he did the same with a second and a third grenade, in rapid succession.

The first grenade exploded with a resounding force, accentuated by the confined space of the entrance hall. To Kazapov, it felt like diving into water from a great height. It seemed to hammer his head and burn his chest, all at once.

With blood oozing from his ears and shards of plaster and wood cutting into his face, he took aim through the middle of an iron swirl and discharged at least thirty-five rounds from his submachine gun. He rolled sideways, waiting for the other grenades to detonate.

A couple of seconds after hearing the blasts, he rolled back and let off another long burst, hitting the thighs, chests and heads of the men who'd been blown off their feet or lacerated by grenade fragments. Their screams and wailings degenerated into pitiful moans.

Kazapov wiped the blood from his forehead, the protective tears from his eyes, and moved down to the floor, which was slippery with fresh blood. All the men were dead. One had a gaping hole where his stomach had been, a scarlet chasm with strands of bloody tissue hanging down, like a crimson jellyfish.

He guessed that Richter was behind the door through which the men had charged.

The sniper, he thought.

If he went for Richter first, the sniper might come for him from behind. Richter couldn't go anywhere, since if he did, the Poles or one of the other soldiers would surely kill him. He checked himself, turned and began to ascend the stairs again, one at a time, his Shpagin raised before him.

He stopped at the top of the first staircase. There were two more floors.

He called out in German, 'Come down, we will escape through the sewers underneath the cellars.'

He heard a noise above, a scuffling that could have been a rat, but was more likely to have been the sniper repositioning himself.

He isn't going to fall for it, he thought. And he decided his accent must have been atrocious. It had been a stupid idea.

The upper floors were solid, like the rest of the building. Built with precision, built to last. It hadn't sustained a direct hit in a bombing raid, that much was clear. He discounted spraying the floors above him with bullets.

Two minutes later, he reached the top of the staircase on the third floor. Two men, dressed in smart trousers and overcoats, were half slumped against a wall. Both were middle-aged. One moustachioed. There was no way of knowing how they'd died, or when, except that they didn't smell bad, so he decided it couldn't have been that long ago. There didn't appear to be any wounds on their bodies. But he'd seen enough dead men to know there was no mistake. It was a mystery, but one he had no interest in. He waited.

There was a massive, ground-level explosion, which shook the building and made him cover his head instinctively. But no masonry fell. Too well built. And he guessed it was another gas explosion.

'I have radioed for flamethrowers,' he said in German.

The flammable liquid fried a man to cinders. The Soviet version had three backpack fuel tanks that shot out a trio of flames. He knew soldiers on all sides feared death by a flamethrower as much as they feared being buried alive.

'OK, Ivan. I'm coming out. Don't shoot.'

There was a corridor that looked remarkably pristine. On either side, there were four doors. The third on the left, facing the street, opened, and a plainclothes man appeared. He looked to be in his early twenties, but his body had been ravaged by war. His cheeks were concave, his blue eyes bloodshot and glazed. His hands were empty, raised above his bare head. The light brown hair was matted with sweat.

Kazapov said, 'Now we go down.'

He motioned with his Shpagin: walk ahead of me. The German obeyed, clearly knowing that the war was over for him and choosing to surrender rather than face certain death by flamethrowers.

Kazapov shot him in the back after the sniper's foot had hit the third step. He felt the weapon buck in his hands and pump against his shoulder muscle. The impact of the bullets flung the sniper down the staircase and left him sprawled on the second-floor landing. His eyes and mouth were wide open, as if he'd just seen something astonishing.

The smoke rose in curls from the entry holes before dissipating.

CHAPTER SEVENTY-ONE

Kazapov had searched the rooms on the ground floor but he hadn't found Richter. He hadn't panicked though. There was only one place he could be now. The cellar.

Twenty seconds later, Kazapov lowered his torch.

He said, 'It is me, Lieutenant Joseph Kazapov.'

There was silence for a few seconds.

'I can't go back with you, young man. I would rather die here, than in Moscow.'

'Where are you?'

'Over here,' Richter said.

Kazapov raised his torch and saw Richter huddled against a damp-blackened wall, his crouching body half covered by a wooden ladder, some stacked pallets and crunched newspaper.

Kazapov said, 'We could leave together. For the West. The Allied lines aren't far. We can surrender together.'

'We'd never make it,' Richter said.

'Not so,' Kazapov said. 'You will be a prisoner of an NKVD officer. No one will question us on the way.'

'Why would you do this?'

'You know why.'

'The deal is still on?' Richter said.

'It is. But you will write the names before we leave the building. I have a pen and paper. The Kalmyks who murdered my mother and sisters. The Einsatzgruppen filmmaker.'

Richter nodded in the white glow of the torch beam.

*

Kazapov and Richter had waited for twenty minutes before crawling out of a back door and on towards some long grass and a ditch, outwitting the few troops at the rear in the process. The road they'd scrambled up to was ridden with shell craters and strewn with broken tree branches and burned-out military vehicles.

Further on, they'd watched two Polish officers wearing rogatywka, the distinctive four-pointed peaked caps, execute three Waffen-SS men with their pistols. They'd passed columns of refugees, trudging silently through muddy verges, their heads bowed like nags ploughing fields. Even the old women couldn't cry any more. They'd walked to the end of the cordoned-off road on the outskirts of the town.

A gnarled log was used as a makeshift barrier, the ends lying across two rusted oil drums. Tangles of barbed wire filled the ditches on either side of the roadblock. Beyond the ditches was dense pine forest. A frail mist still hung between the branches, like shreds of gossamer.

Richter now wore the civilian clothes of one of the dead men at the Mercedes-Benz factory. Kazapov had worried that the SS uniform would be too inflammatory. He'd tied Richter's hands behind his back with rope. The old Sonderführer had agreed to be punched in the right eye. It was swelling, a livid bruise beneath that resembled a crescent of raw meat. Kazapov knew that such an injury would likely prevent anything similar happening; it was how things were in war, when the victors saw a subdued and beaten enemy.

The guards by the barrier weren't front line troops. They looked to Kazapov like ineffectual peasants from the Urals. But they also looked like the types known to shoot Red Army officers in drunken confrontations. Not well-disciplined, political troops. He wasn't particularly worried, though. They appeared sober and their Shpagins and carbines were slung over their shoulders. They kept them there as he approached.

'Papers, comrade lieutenant, if you please.'

The man that spoke was a corporal, his exposed skin windburned, his nose askew. He held out his filthy hand. Kazapov passed him his ID papers, keeping a stern face.

'Who's this?' the corporal said, gesturing to Richter.

'A suspect.'

'Papers.'

'He doesn't have papers. He's suspected of being in the SS. Now open that fucking barrier before I report you personally to Comrade Beria.'

The men hurried to lift the barrier and said no more. Kazapov was NKVD, and he guessed they'd rather embrace the Devil they still likely believed in, than face Beria's wrath. His raping of teenage girls abducted from the streets of Moscow by his henchmen was a state secret, but most Russians were too terrified to even mention his name. He wasn't the most feared and hated man in the Soviet Union for nothing.

Kazapov and Richter walked past the Soviet roadblock and on down the road between the endless pine trees that infused the dusk air with their scent. They heard the songs of small birds.

Richter said, 'Where are we going?'

'There's an NKVD checkpoint about four miles ahead. They don't trust Red Army troops to be so close to the Americans and British.

They might defect for a chocolate bar or a packet of cigarettes. We'll skirt around it.'

Richter shook his head and Kazapov knew that such behaviour was alien to him, even now. It was, he believed, a simple matter of the German having felt a part of something larger than himself. The Reich. That had changed.

All things change, he thought.

At the inception of Operation Barbarossa, the progress of the Germans had been so swift that many of the Gulag labour camps in western Russia had been abandoned by the NKVD in a state of panic. Fearing that those labourers that remained may be used by the Germans or defect to them, they'd been systematically murdered, to a man. That was the system he himself was a part of, and but one reason over a million Soviets had joined the German army in one capacity or another.

They walked on for a further two miles or more, keeping to the road so as not to arouse unnecessary suspicion. Kazapov had said that an NKVD officer would not walk a prisoner through mud when he had a road to travel on, even if it was crater-ridden. It would have appeared clandestine.

Now, Kazapov put out his arm, halting Richter.

'Cossacks,' he said.

CHAPTER SEVENTY-TWO

They'd emerged from the forest; twenty or more astride their Russian Don war horses. Like the Kalmyks, the Don Cossacks had suffered greatly under Stalin. Consequently, some had fought for the Nazis, Kazapov knew. The traitors had been formed into SS cavalry regiments and fearsome anti-partisan units.

But these Cossacks were loyal to the Motherland, and that helped to ease his concern, although he had seen their tactics in East Prussia at the beginning of the year, when as part of the Red Army, some 2,500,000 strong, he'd crossed Germany's outer borders. Sitting astride their mounts, laughing and screaming, the Cossacks had used their curved sabres to butcher small groups of civilian refugees attempting to reach the inner Reich. They'd even sliced off the outstretched arms of the surrendering Wehrmacht Heer. But they'd been renowned for their bravery for all that and had helped prevent the Nazis from entering the vital Caucasus oil fields during the Battle of Stalingrad. They'd galloped out of the frozen mists like ghost riders to sever the Germans' horse-drawn supply lines. He watched them trot up.

'Comrade,' a lean sergeant said, nodding his head slightly.

He had black eyes and a wiry, grey moustache. He fingered the hilt of his sabre, that was sheathed beside his left leg. He wore a blue overcoat, black boots and a woollen pillbox hat. Kazapov breathed out through his nostrils, attempting to relax.

'We search for Nazis and deserters, comrade.' The Cossack removed a tin box from his coat pocket. He took out some tobacco, bit into it and began chewing. 'And you, comrade?' He smiled broadly, revealing a gap where his two front teeth should have been.

'I have this prisoner. I have orders to swap him for an SS camp guard held by the Americans. The guard was responsible for murdering Russian POWs. He'll hang by the gates of that place.'

'And this one is what?'

'He ordered the shooting of captured Americans.'

'Why don't you let us take the Nazi for you, comrade?' the sergeant said, looking at Richter the way a Siberian tiger might eye a lame goat.

'I can't do that, sergeant. I have strict instructions to make the swap personally.'

Kazapov sensed Richter trembling beside him.

'I think it's not safe out here, comrade lieutenant. Many SS and traitors. The Nazi will be safer with us.'

Slowly, Kazapov removed his pistol. The Cossacks had Mosin carbines, but they were slung over their backs to allow them to ride unfettered.

'I said I can't do that, sergeant,' Kazapov said, raising the pistol and pointing it at the Cossack's horse. 'Now be on your way and I'll forget all about it. If you're not gone very quickly, you will be walking all the way back to the Don steppe. And that's a long way to walk.' He knew a war horse was a Cossack's most prized possession.

The sergeant grinned and brought his heels into his mount and trotted off. Kazapov lowered his pistol. The Cossacks spat at Richter as they passed by him and a couple even kicked out at him. The last of them jerked on his reins so that the horse reared up and Kazapov found himself gulping saliva. The Cossacks never really did take to anyone giving them orders; apart from their ancestral leaders.

'Thank you,' Richter said.

'You would have been better off in Moscow than with them.'

'So, the war is over for me?' Richter said.

Ignoring him, Kazapov said, 'You shouldn't have come to my country.'

Richter looked down at his feet. 'I know that now. And history will judge us harshly because of it.'

'I can't take you to the Americans or the British,' Kazapov said.

Richter's eyes narrowed. 'But we have an agreement.'

Kazapov raised his pistol.

Richter's face softened and he looked remarkably calm.

He said, 'You should have seen Berlin in the summer of thirty-eight.'

Kazapov lowered the pistol, so that he could see Richter's face clearly.

Richter said, 'Every one of you Soviets will continue to live in constant fear, despite winning the war.' He nodded. 'We believed in something. What do you believe in, Joseph Kazapov?'

Kazapov knew that Richter had spoken the truth. But what did it matter? He would remain in the NKVD or whatever replaced it. He could kill with impunity. He couldn't risk doing what he'd set his mind to outside of the major system of order in the Soviet state, even if he did it alone and without consent.

'Revenge,' Kazapov said. 'I believe in revenge.'

The faintest of smiles passed over Richter's lips.

'Do you have a last cigarette for me?' he said.

'No more cigarettes.'

Kazapov decided now that he couldn't risk shooting Richter in the forehead, as he'd planned to. He would smash his skull in once the

Cossacks were out of earshot. It wasn't what he'd just said. Kazapov knew that his family would be alive if it wasn't for the likes of Richter. But the man's death wouldn't ease his own pain, the feeling in his gut like a smoking cannonball, the feeling in his head like a blistering sun.

He would bury the body in the forest. He would smoke a cigarette as he squatted beside the unmarked grave. He would walk off towards the checkpoint where he'd file his report, each paragraph laced with untruths.

That done, he would murder Major Volsky before he left Berlin and blame it on some unsuspecting member of the Volkssturm, who'd be executed without a fuss.

CHAPTER SEVENTY-THREE

Baton Rouge, Louisiana, 2015, the next day.

The Chechen had to be taken alive.

The sun had just risen, casting long shadows, but the humidity was stifling already. Carla had flown down from DC aboard an FBI, eight-seater jet, the black fuselage without identifying insignia.

The detached, rundown house was about twenty yards back from the residential street, surrounded by a rusted wire-mesh fence. It had a wooden façade that looked as if it had been subject to termite damage, and a tin roof, a little terrace area. For the last twenty-four hours, the property had been under surveillance via satellite imagery by FBI special agents on alternating eight-hour shifts, and a physical stakeout had been ordered as soon as the Chechen had been identified as an occupant.

On the other side of the house was an abandoned, red brick veterinary clinic. To the rear, a private cemetery, the overgrown branches of moss-strewn willow and cedar trees touching the elaborate sarcophagi, the marble coated with damp lichen.

The front garden was unkempt, a mass of yellowing elephant ear, wild azaleas and purple thistles, with withered palm fronds and bamboo among the carpet-grass. There was no garage, but a pickup truck, with dimpled orange bodywork, was parked on the cracked cement driveway to the right of the house. The two chrome exhaust pipes shone in parts like luminous stars, as shafts of sunlight caught them. Muted, intermittent laughter could be heard coming from the front room, above the songs of blue jays and waterthrush, the constant chirping of cicadas.

Carla wore an FBI baseball cap and a T-shirt, both of which were already wet with sweat. She crouched beside an unmarked SUV, with tinted windscreens, just far enough away to avoid ricochets off the bonnet and wheel arches. Both ends of the street, which were out of eyeshot, had been cordoned off with rolls of yellow tape, and patrol cars belonging to the local police department.

A small black, FBI SWAT truck, which had moved at a crawl up the opposite side of the street to Carla, halted now, and the helmeted, seven-person team disembarked from the back doors. They hunched down, and duckwalked beside a stone wall that led up to the curtilage of the house.

The issue wasn't who would win a shootout, but rather how to avoid one happening. She had impressed on the SWAT team the necessity of taking the Chechen alive. Anything else would be regarded as failure. Other lives depended on it, she knew. Young Kalmyk women's lives.

The SWAT team reached the end of the wall and the lead agent opened the gate, which hung from a piece of frayed rope lassoed around an iron post. They bolted upright and rushed forward. A pair jogged to the rear of the property, where the parish PD had already ensured a no-escape zone. Two others headed for the flanks. The remaining three would go through the front entrance once the wooden door had been taken care of.

Carla edged closer, to get an unencumbered view of the frontage. The metal ram impacted the door three times before it swung inwards. But a second later, a chrome folding chair crashed through the front window, raining shards of glass onto the garden. A skinny white man, naked as a new-born, leaped from the jagged opening and landed among the foliage. He had a shaved head and looked to be in his mid-twenties. His muscular body was heavily tattooed with blue crescents and geometric designs. He began screaming, his right hand brandishing a machete.

Carla thought he resembled some deranged pagan warrior.

The smashed glass had sent the three SWAT agents to the ground. Now they radioed warnings to their unseen colleagues, their various weapons raised. Machete still stood among the elephant ear, contorting his features and shouting out threats and obscenities. The agents assumed kneeling positions behind a blast shield.

Carla knew from the photograph Dubois had given her in Brussels that Machete wasn't the Chechen. She confirmed that to the SWAT team via her own radio. She drew her Glock and jogged forward.

She squatted down by the edge of the abutting wall, aiming the pistol with her finger across the trigger guard, her other hand holding her radio over her chest. She had no intention of shooting anyone, including Machete.

The three agents had got up, and the one with a Remington 870 twelve-gauge shotgun edged forward now and shouted out to Machete to drop the weapon and lie on the ground. But Machete was either psychotic or, more likely, high, Carla thought. With two submachine guns pointing at the house, the damn fool ran at the agent with the pump, the machete above his head, glinting in the morning sunlight. She almost called out, but held her tongue. *She* wasn't the one who could lose the use of a limb in a fracas.

The shotgun discharged, the tens of pellets hitting Machete's torso and spinning him to the ground. He lay on his side, his arms dog-legged over his head. Thin grey smoke rose about him, as if his soul had just departed from his body. She heard screaming inside before her radio crackled. The ground floor had been secured from the rear.

She didn't move again until she got the all-clear.

Standing, she saw two Caucasian women of similar age to Machete as they were bundled from the front doorway, their hands cuffed behind them. They wore brightly-coloured bikinis, their bodies pierced and tattooed with matching scarlet chrysanthemums entwined in grey barbed wire. They both had blonde hair, thickly lacquered, such that it reminded her of sheaves of corn. When they saw Machete's horizontal and bloody body, they began to wail.

Carla holstered her sidearm and walked to the gateway. She headed up the garden, little puffs of pollen rising about her trainers. She reached Machete and bent down, putting two fingers to his throat just below the jawline. Unsurprisingly, there was no pulse. She saw that his powder-blue eyes were like spoiled scallops, the gaping entry hole blackened. Blood leaked from the corpse like red sludge from a sack. Two fire ants were already crawling over his pale face.

She stood up and wiped her slick forehead with the back of her hand. She walked a few yards to the doorway, the sound of emergency vehicles flooding her ears. Peering into the shadowed hallway, she waited for the Chechen to appear.

He came out a few seconds later, his shoulder-length hair dishevelled, his beard cut to a satanic goatee. He wore baggy trousers, with a splattered paint design. He was bare-chested, his upper body covered from shoulders to navel in wiry hair. When he was bundled past her by two SWAT agents, she smelled the stale cigarette smoke and alcohol.

She watched him as he was manhandled down to the fence, his demands for a lawyer met with silence.

The unit chief, a lofty black man named Elmore du Preez, came up to Carla's shoulder.

He said, 'I sure hope he was worth it.'

Me too, she thought.

CHAPTER SEVENTY-FOUR

Federal correctional complex, the next day.

Hockey lay on a padded bench while a tattooed training partner helped him place the barbell back onto the vertical stands. The mixture of an endorphin rush and exhaustion was heady.

It was a cloudless afternoon, engendering a rare moment of civility into the place. Even the BOP officers, holding their sniper rifles and shotguns in the viewing turrets, situated strategically around the exercise yard, looked relaxed. They rested their forearms on the safety barriers. They wore shades and chewed gum.

A group of black men played basketball. The Mexicans were gathered around a tier of benches. Each group had its own distinctive set of tattoos, together with the generic ones. A spider's web on the elbow meant a long sentence, a teardrop a murder. Playing cards meant a gambler, and EWMN on the fingers was an acronym for 'Evil, Wicked, Mean, Nasty'. But the vehemently opposed racial groups weren't allowed to exercise together. They were either segregated by fences, or simply came out at different times.

Hockey strolled across his portion of the yard after his workout, his muscles pumped, the veins protruding like elvers under the surface of his skin. Dressed in an orange undershirt and joggers, a checked bandana around his sweaty head, he mourned the passing of his hour of relative freedom outside the cell. He craved the outside.

An officer came up to him. He was a squat man, with several chins and a well-trimmed moustache, who wore aviator shades.

'After your shower, you'll be escorted to the library,' he said.

'Why's that?' Hockey said.

'Your cell's being searched.'

'There's nothing there,' Hockey said, truthfully.

'Shower and library.'

Hockey knew shakedowns for drugs, a miniature smartphone or a shiv happened intermittently, so he just nodded, knowing there wasn't anything else he could do.

A few minutes later, after removing his clothes in the changing room, he walked into the shower area. He was careful not to slip on the wet tiled floor, even though there were only a few innocuous-looking inmates about. He couldn't afford to show any sign of weakness, especially here.

Things happened in the shower area. It was a platitude, almost an urban myth. But it was a fact. The reason was simple. When they were in their individual cells, they couldn't get at one another. In the yard, there were CCTV cameras everywhere. There were the officers in the turrets, the riot control officers nearby. Only those that were multiple lifers, those that had no chance of getting out, killed in the yard, and then only the inmates that were members of their own gang, or racial grouping. A hit ordered from the outside, or a stabbing in revenge for what had occurred on the inside, something that would be regarded a trifling snub by law-abiding people.

When he got to his chosen shower head, he picked up the bar of soap from the wire cradle affixed to the wall and broke it in half. The last time he'd been in prison, someone told him that a Crip had been rushed to the hospital block, his hands leaching blood. The soap had contained three razor blades, snapped into little pieces. But this bar was safe. Just soap.

The warm water felt good on his skin as he washed the sweat from his hard body. He put his head back, allowing the water to wet his cropped hair and cover his face. Then, pressing his hands against the tiled wall, he let the water career down his back and over his buttocks.

After dressing, he was led from the changing rooms by a single officer to a cinder-block corridor. Hockey waited for him to unlock the green circulation door, the metal flecked with rust, that led to a grille gate about twenty feet away. He walked past an office door to his left and the guard slunk forward. He was tall man, with a thin, high-ridged nose and a small, pale pink scar on his jawline. He wasn't adroit, Hockey knew, but he wasn't a dumb-ass either.

'Wait up there,' he said, pointing to the gate.

Hockey walked the few steps to it and the guard motioned for him to put his hands through the grille so that he could secure them with double-lock handcuffs. Hockey reckoned he was afraid he'd grope one of the female civilian staff in the office, or worse.

'Just got to collect some paperwork,' he said.

The guard went into the office behind him.

Hockey thought about the fuckup. He'd been told not to watch the DVD. He'd been told to hold up for three days and then take a flight to France and deposit the DVD in a safety-deposit box in a private bank in La Défense, the main Paris business district, at precisely 10.00 am local time. He'd been given a smartphone number to ring when the job was completed. The FBI raid on his flat had thwarted that.

Later, while in prison, when he thought he'd been told what was on the DVD by the female FBI agent, he received a message. It had nothing to do with little blonde Aryan girls. She'd lied to him. But it *was* a snuff movie. His employer had been framed by the Albanian mafia, they said. A complicated matter and one he need not know the details of. The message had come from César Vezzani. He'd believed it. He hadn't snitched to the authorities. He hadn't given them anything.

Five seconds later, he heard the door open behind him and the steps of what he thought was the guard. It wasn't. But there was no way he could see the Russian inmate, a prison kitchen porter, a man heavy-boned but lean, his eyes the colour of cedar wood, with plump lips and a goatee. There was no way he could've seen him exhale a slither of metal from his nasal cavity to pick the lock in the circulation door. There was no way he could've seen him squat down to remove the shiv from his rectum. There was no way he could've seen the dagger tattoo on the man's shoulder, the tip dripping blood, the elaborate rendition of a Russian Orthodox church on his back, or the cross on the chest denoting the prince of thieves, a symbol of a respected member of the Russian mafia. Tattoos acquired in a prison thousands of miles away, cut with an improvised razor and ink made from a mixture of urine, ash and scorched rubber.

Hockey merely glimpsed the tattooed and muscular forearm flash under his eyes, the glint of metal caused by the fluorescent strip lighting on the shiv protruding from the calloused hand. He felt the makeshift knife slice deep into his neck. Then — again and again in a kind of frenzied sawing action, severing his windpipe and carotid artery to bring about an expedited exsanguination, a quick bleed out.

He collapsed, with a mixture of bodily shock and disbelief, hanging from his secured hands like a suspended puppet. Giddily, he became conscious of the thick blood bubbling out of the gash. His eyes widened involuntarily as he sensed his body going into a spasm. He felt as if he was drowning. He gasped for air, but there was none. He panted like a dog. There was still no air.

The pain he felt was cool and distant. His head had slumped to his chin. The severed windpipe and artery had destroyed all muscle control there. His brain began to shut down and the corridor went red-black.

Unconsciousness occurred within thirty seconds, his death within eighty.

His pale face had been dappled with blood at first, but his limp body was so drenched with it now that when the guard left the office with a black file under his arm he thought someone had thrown a tin of red paint over Hockey, as a sign of something he wasn't yet aware of. Something like a tar and feathering, perhaps.

When he got closer, he rushed forward, seeing the gruesomeness of Hockey's death, the futility of it. He thought about trying to stem the blood flow. But as he crouched down to Hockey's face, he grimaced. He knew that the catastrophic blood loss had led to cardiac arrest. Even the eyes were filled with blood.

CHAPTER SEVENTY-FIVE

Central Park, Manhattan, the same day.

It was more than a year after Sangmu's disappearance before Gabriel could bring himself to run five times around the one and half mile Reservoir Circuit again. At first, he'd stumbled on a couple of occasions every time he did so, the memories of that day causing a physiological breakdown. It was, he'd imagined, something analogous to what the bereaved felt upon visiting the sight of a fatal car accident or house fire. But part of him, albeit a small and very optimistic part, had thought she might suddenly appear one day.

Now, somehow, with the late afternoon sunshine on his back, the light breeze fingering the leaves of the elm trees, he considered that he was getting closer to her abductors, and the thought both excited and burdened him. He admitted to himself that the burden was born of fear. She could be dead already. He could become a victim too. But he felt he had no choice but to continue with what he'd set out to do. How could he live with himself otherwise?

He sensed the mobile given to him by Carla vibrate in his hand. He continued jogging and held the phone to his ear, without speaking.

'Gabriel?' Carla said.

'What is it?'

'Are you driving? It's a bad connection.'

'I'm jogging in Central Park.'

'Could you stop for a moment? It's important.'

He stopped, wiped the sweat from his face. He looked out at the oil-black water beyond the iron railings and grassy bank. The breeze had picked up and the ducks bobbed about on the lake as if they were plastic toys.

'What is it, Carla?'

'Johnny Hockey died in prison today.'

He winced. 'How?'

'His throat was cut. He — '

He pressed the disconnect button. He knew Hockey was a criminal, but he hadn't wished him dead.

He didn't know what left the body at the point of death, although he believed that something eternal did. Maybe it was the soul. But whatever it was, he wished it peace. He knew that in life Hockey hadn't known what peace was, and he sympathized with that. He deserved it in death, at least.

Gabriel passed under a walkway nearby, a little suspension bridge, walked to a public bench and sat down, trying to compose himself. A homeless man was sitting on another bench opposite him. He had greasy hair and a few days' growth on his chin and wore camouflage trousers and was wrapped in a mouldy blanket. He kept swearing at a red squirrel that was hopping about on the grass to the left of him.

The mobile vibrated again.

He took the call.

'I'm in Manhattan. I'll meet you by the fountain in an hour,' Carla said.

*

351

Walking over the herringbone Roman brick that marked the edge of the Bethesda Terrace, Gabriel caught sight of Carla looking up at the Angel of Waters, the fountain's eight-feet bronze sculpture situated in the middle of an ornamental pool amid lily pads. She wore black jeans, a white T-shirt and a patterned serape.

She looked nervous, he thought, her eyes scanning the immediate area and the tree line beyond. She saw him and moved off.

He followed her under the terrace's overhang into a red brick tunnel with a vaulted ceiling that retained some of the original Minton tiles. The tunnel was lit by enormous globe-shaped lightbulbs and had the ambiance of a Victorian grotto. He saw that the Mexican-style shawl that hung to her waist was made of cotton rather than wool, that her beautiful eyes were darting about.

'Who killed Hockey?' he said.

'A Russian gang member.'

'I don't understand.'

'A murderer with no hope of parole. It could be as simple as someone thinking the case was going bad for Hockey. The longer he was inside, the more chance there was of him cracking. He could've been murdered for some other, unrelated reason.'

She looked acquiescent, he thought.

'Are you OK, Carla?'

She nodded.

He rubbed his brow. 'He told me he was being sent to an army base.'

'A Marine base,' she said. 'The FBI were consulted.'

'Looks like that signed his death warrant,' he said, solemnly.

'I didn't think you'd take it so badly.'

'You think I'm in this for revenge? Is that what you think?

'I don't know.'

He shook his head. 'So, the same people could be responsible?' he said, referring to those that had made the DVD.

'It's a high possibility, yes.'

She told him what Dubois had said about the old serial killer in Berlin nicknamed Snow Lion and his stomach tensed. She told him about the capture of the Chechen. She said that he couldn't repeat that to anyone, that she would lose her badge if he did. He told her the information was safe with him.

'Think back,' she said, leaning towards him. 'What happened in 1989?'

Gabriel didn't know what to make of the question, but guessed it wasn't something random.

'I don't know what you're referring to.'

'Yes, you do. Think about what I just told you.'

He racked his brain. He got it. 'The Berlin Wall came down.'

'Exactly. And thousands streamed over the border from East Berlin. We know that Kalmyk girls went missing every couple of years in New Jersey from 1990. We checked the records with the FSB. Sometimes they're reticent about such things, but they owe the FBI for favours I don't need to go into, and my section chief called in one of those favours. Long and short, from 1958 to 1989, fifteen young Kalmyk females went missing in Kalmykia. All under the age of eighteen. One every couple of years. They were never found. And then it stopped. Except it didn't. It started up again in 1990 in New Jersey.'

He felt a chill go through him, as if the man in the demon mask had ran a long, yellowing fingernail down his spine.

'Sixty years,' he said. 'It could be the same man. The old man. The serial killer in Berlin.'

He felt like puking.

'It could be, yes.' She pushed the fingers of her right hand through the hair on her crown. 'It could be a coincidence.' She nodded, as if to herself. 'But we checked the Berlin records too from 1990. Only a few hundred Kalmyks live there now. Three Kalmyk young women have gone missing, so it's a pattern, I believe.'

Gabriel's mind was in danger of overloading with it all.

He said, 'The Kalmyks returned to south of the Volga, Kalmykia that is, in 1957, after Khrushchev pardoned them.'

He told her why they'd been banished from their land and something of their history, partly to ease the worry and the pain he was experiencing, he supposed. To have a handle on it too, even a vague one.

He said, 'It has to be linked to *something*. Something at least sixty years ago.'

She nodded. 'There's often a trigger.'

'I'm going to see the man I mentioned,' he said, referring to the old Jew, Bronislaw Stolarski. 'I'll contact you afterward.'

'OK, Gabriel.'

'And you?'

'Interviewing the Chechen with my section chief.'

'Let me know how it goes.'

'I will.'

Gabriel turned and left.

Carla wanted to call out to him, to tell him that Section Chief Hester had informed her that Assistant Director Johnson had deemed the request that she shared information with a criminal defence lawyer inappropriate, especially since he'd acted for the alleged perpetrator, Johnny Hockey.

But she didn't tell Gabriel that Hester hadn't given her permission to work with him. There was an upside and a downside to that, she thought. The downside was that her own conscience was troubled by it, and that it wouldn't engender what might otherwise be a healthy degree of caution in his actions. The upside was that he might otherwise refuse to continue to feed her useful information. He might do something unpredictable and alone that would put them all in danger.

CHAPTER SEVENTY-SIX

The White Mountains, the next day.

Gabriel drove past a little wooden sugar house that was used to boil down sap to produce maple syrup. The foliage — green ash, scarlet oak and European beech — was already fading. Travelling out of the canopy, he saw a deep ravine and a thunderous waterfall, and to the right, a river canyon leading out of glacial cirque. The Whites were almost a six-hour drive from New York City. Part of the greater Appalachian range, the mountains covered a quarter of New Hampshire. It was a landscape of exceptional beauty, he thought.

Using his sat nav, he turned left off a furrowed back road onto a mud track, a few miles from Interstate 93. It had been raining heavily a couple of hours before and the track was hard going. He knew the car's tyres and lower bodywork would be covered in pale-brown mud by the time he arrived at his destination. He still had no idea what Bronislaw Stolarski would be like, or even if the old man would consent to talking with him.

The sky was dough coloured and just the odd speck of rain fell. The small bungalow was surrounded by rusted vehicles, empty chicken houses, windowless outbuildings and piles of household junk. A pair of grey and white huskies snarled and barked ferociously. Gabriel was glad to see they'd been chained to a sturdy iron pole impaled in the ground. His dark-tan brogues slid on the wet grass as he stepped out of the car and he had to hold onto the bonnet to stop his sand-coloured trousers from being ruined.

Steadying himself, he inhaled the warm air, fecund with the sweet smell of the mountains.

'It's OK,' a man's voice said. 'They only bite if you get within range.'

'Don't worry, I won't,' Gabriel said.

The black man looked about sixty years old. He was sitting on a wooden chair on an uneven porch, with a make-do plastic-sheet roof. A hunting rifle was propped up against a tin box, within an arm's reach. He stood up as Gabriel approached the porch. He wore a knee-length raincoat and a white collarless shirt.

Up close, the man was enormous, around six five, with thick limbs and a neck like a mule's.

'We don't get visitors,' he said. 'Don't want to neither, truth be told.'

'I apologize for intruding on your peace,' Gabriel said. 'I've come to see Mr Stolarski.'

'Who is it, Ned?'

It was a wheezy voice and had come from inside the bungalow.

Gabriel watched Ned eye him up and down.

'Ned, who is it?'

'Just some fella from the city.'

'Well wheel him in.'

*

They were alone. Gabriel guessed Ned had resumed his position on the porch. Bronislaw Stolarski was sitting in an armchair, its maroon fabric dulled by sunlight and age. Stroking a large ginger cat, curled up on his lap, purring, he used a handkerchief in his other hand to dab his sallow eyes.

'Throat cancer,' he said, fingering his bandaged neck now. 'I've had all the chemo they can throw at me. I go for check-ups to the Norris Cotton Center down in Grafton County. A little place called Lebanon. Waste of time, you ask me.'

He smiled, showing perhaps a dozen half-rotten teeth.

Gabriel nodded, smiling back. The accent had a hint of eastern Europe, although it was obvious that he'd been in the US for long enough to pick up the vernacular.

'Well, sit down.'

The interior was as ramshackle and chaotic as the exterior. There were piles of yellowing magazines and dirty laundry, the window panes were grimy and the odour musty. The few pieces of furniture were dated and dust-ridden. Even the porcelain sink was piled high with used dishes and cutlery.

Gabriel picked up a crumpled jumper and sat on a lime-green couch, with a pale red bedsheet draped over the back, wondering if he'd attract fleas. He felt his nose itch, his eyes too. Myriad cat hairs were visible.

'Don't worry about Ned,' Stolarski said. He put his finger to his parched-looking lips. 'Vietnam vet. PTSD. Like me, he's not fond of city life. He was a recon sniper. He killed more enemy than a platoon of eager marines. He can shoot the ears of a squirrel from 100 yards.'

'I see.'

'He's as strong as my knees are weak. I read to him nights. He doesn't read too good. Together, we'd make a formidable man. Ned likes me to read fairy tales. No military history for him. I suppose fairy tales speak loudly about a chasm between good and evil. One that doesn't exist. Does it?'

'I guess not,' Gabriel said.

Stolarski was dressed in creased jeans, a pair of scuffed brown loafers and a stained cardigan, his skin seemingly wafer thin and pallid. He was bald, but steely hairs protruded from his large nostrils. His eyes were speckled with burst veins. His body was both stooped and concave.

The cancer, Gabriel thought. He wondered why he'd been so open with him. Perhaps it was because he hadn't spoken with anyone else but Ned in a long time. Maybe he was just made that way. It didn't matter, but it was a good sign.

'What can I do for you?'

'My name is Gabriel Hall. I'm a criminal defence attorney. I spoke recently with Boris Iliev.'

Gabriel sneezed and apologized.

Stolarski rubbed his chin with a thumb and forefinger. 'I remember. Smart guy. Yale professor,' he said, pointing a long-nailed finger before retracting it immediately, as if to emphasize the point.

'A colleague of mine. He told me what you'd said about your elder brother. About the Berlin bunker at the end of World War Two. He said your brother died in the Gulag. He said you asked him to contact you if he ever saw anything like the things you described again.'

Stolarski nodded before looking at Gabriel a little warily. 'That's right.'

'I don't mean to be rude, but how did your brother tell you this if he was sent to a forced labour camp and died there?'

Stolarski's eyes narrowed. 'No mystery, young man. My brother was let out after he got uranium poisoning. It was common in the mine. He died two months later. The Gulag killed him. No question. To be precise, he told my mother what had happened to him and she told me. I was too young at the time.'

'Again, no offence, but you didn't give Boris Iliev any contact details. How did you expect him to find you if he had some information, as you'd requested?'

'*You* did.'

Gabriel couldn't argue with that. Besides, Stolarski had moved around a lot, Sam Cartwright had said, and had no landline or smartphone, so what good would it have been anyway?

'Now, you've proved yourself to be a lawyer, but what exactly are you doing here?'

Gabriel wiped a bead of sweat from under his chin. It was uncomfortably warm in the bungalow. There was no fan, let alone air conditioning. The warm air was exacerbating his allergic reaction and he felt his left eye begin to close over.

He said, 'I told Boris Iliev that I would tell you that I saw something like your brother had seen.'

'Is that so?' Stolarski said.

His eyes suddenly became more intense, more vital.

Gabriel nodded.

'Well, guess you've driven a long way. But me and Ned don't go out much. We don't drive now. I rely on the cancer centre for transport, in case you were wondering. Why don't we take a drive? Grab something to eat at a place I know? I can still eat, you know. If it isn't too chewy. Not steaks and such. Besides, if your allergy to cat hair gets any worse, you won't be able to see shit.'

'It would be my pleasure,' Gabriel said.

'That's settled then.' He made a noise in the back of his throat that sounded as if he was retching. 'We can talk there. It never gets busy. Don't know how it survives, tell the truth.'

Gabriel smiled a closed-mouthed smile.

'I should tell you that I told you about my brother and the uranium mine because I could see right off that you are a serious man, otherwise I would've called to Ned and he would've thrown you out.'

'That's fair comment.'

Gabriel could tell from the tone of Stolarski's voice that he was a serious man too, and he didn't doubt what he'd said about Ned was a fact.

Stolarski clasped his hands as if he was about to pray. 'You will tell me where you saw the things you speak of before we go.'

Gabriel knew he had to, otherwise it would have been a wasted journey.

He said, 'It was on a DVD taken from a murdered man's apartment.'

CHAPTER SEVENTY-SEVEN

The secret prison, the same day.

Carla and Section Chief Hester were sitting in the back of an unmarked, metallic silver FBI SUV as it approached the secret prison that held the Chechen, with his ongoing consent. The two prostitutes that had been with him in Baton Rouge were Latvian illegals. They were being held in segregated cells in a remote detention centre prior to deportation.

The sky was almost obscured by the overlapping branches of mature beech trees, their leaves dulling to the colour of red ochre and apricots. The single lane, asphalt road led to a chain link fence, with thousands of yards of concertina razor wire atop it, which surrounded the 100 acres of what was ostensibly a military base. Metal Department of Defense signs had been placed at twenty-five-yard intervals and warned of the consequences of unauthorized access.

'They say there are snipers in the woods. They say they can release armed drones if they have a mind to,' Hester said. 'I know for a fact that there are people where we're going who have one million plus on their heads. They know it. They know too that they're not safe anywhere else.'

Carla nodded. Hester straightened his silk tie. He looked to be wearing expensive Italian cloth on his ample frame.

The Chechen's whereabouts had been kept confidential, save from those few federal officials involved in his arrest and those who had given permission for his unorthodox incarceration. A lawyer from the Attorney General's office at the Justice Department had informed the Chechen that if he waived the right to an attorney and agreed to an incommunicado existence at the secret prison, he would likely walk, if he was co-operative. The Chechen had not been charged with any federal felony, and was in truth free to leave. But he'd been told that if he *did* choose to leave, he would be rearrested and charged, and would have to take his chances in the regular prison system like everyone else.

Carla had not heard of such an arrangement before, but Hester assured her that such instances had occurred in the past, especially when an individual could be crucial in an investigation into matters as serious as those they were involved in. The detection and apprehension of serial killers, especially where there was a suspected racial motive, meant the justice system could, on occasion, be flexible in the execution of its duty.

'Put your badge on view,' Hester said to Carla. 'They'll take your weapon. They'll scan you. Don't bitch about it.'

She nodded again.

The entrance was secured by an electronic pole, with a metal and Perspex box to the right. Two cement blockhouses were situated either side of the box, like relics from a different age. Here, the razor wire was exposed to the sun and it glinted and shimmered, creating a mirage effect. Three helmeted US Army Military Police in combat uniforms, with grey Velcro patches on their left arms that bore the legend 'MP' in black, were guarding the entrance. One was sitting inside the box and two were standing either side of the pole.

The MP closest to the driver, a black man with the physique of a wrestler, wore shades, carried an M4 carbine and had a 9mm Beretta M9 holstered on his right thigh. The MP on the other side, another black man but with a leaner frame, held an M249 light machine gun to his chest.

The FBI driver was ordered to turn off the ignition and did so without complaint. The MP came up to the window, which lowered without sound. He took the papers that the driver handed over and read them in a thorough manner before looking at Carla and Hester, who took off his shades and stiffened up. The man had fingers like fat cigars, although the other standing MP's hands were gloved, Carla had noticed.

The MP walked over to the box and brought back a grey tray, which he thrust through the front window. The driver collected their weapons and the MP took them back to the box. He returned with a hand-held metal detector and, after motioning for them to disembark, waved it over each of them in turn, checking a silver-plated pen and a car keyring when the detector had buzzed, and a red light had blinked.

A flat-top, four-wheeled remote device about the size of a dinner plate came from around the back of the box. It was controlled by the MP in the box with a joystick, as he looked at what Carla could see was a flat screen. She knew it would be checking the wheel arches and the chassis for suspect objects, for heat and noise signatures.

Ten seconds later, it reversed from under the SUV and moved in sharp angles back to its position.

The MP said, 'Return to the vehicle.'

He raised his palm and the pole lifted. The SUV pulled away, keeping to the mandatory five miles per hour. Carla glimpsed the nozzle of a heavy machine gun in the centre of the six-inch wide aperture of the blockhouse to the right. She looked at the seated MP inside the box, a white man with deep lines in his forehead. He glanced back at her, his expression cynical, as if there was no escape for those that entered, including himself.

Carla saw exercise yards and what looked like red-brick military barracks inside the fence. APCs and jeeps were parked outside a central, two-storey building, with a colonnade of cement pillars. There was a checkerboard pattern of roadways and grass lawns, as immaculate as bowling greens, to its rear, where other low-level buildings of various design and construction were dotted about. An empty flagpole stood at the edge of a parade ground to the far left. There were no military insignias, nor signage. No more than five armed soldiers were visible.

'I'd appreciate it if you left the talking to me,' Hester said.

'You want me to take minutes?' Carla said, regretting her retort immediately.

Hester shook his head.

CHAPTER SEVENTY-EIGHT

The restaurant was just off the highway, twenty miles from Concord. There was a dozen or so tables, finished in light-blue Formica, with a bunch of laminated menus in red plastic holders and glass-held condiments placed upon them. Gabriel had helped Stolarski take off his overcoat and they sat at a booth by the window.

Gabriel sipped coffee from an off-white mug. Stolarski hadn't touched his glass of milk. They'd both ordered waffles with maple syrup.

On the way over, Stolarski had explained how he and Ned had teamed up after meeting at a rehabilitation facility Stolarski worked in as a psychiatric nurse. It was a profession he'd entered to try to make sense of the world, he said. But it hadn't helped him on that search, so he'd read the Greek philosophers and Marcus Aurelius, but they hadn't helped either. The old man was intriguing, Gabriel thought, on several levels.

'I need to take a leak,' Stolarski said.

Gabriel smiled, weakly.

Stolarski stood up and walked totteringly towards the toilets to their left. Gabriel looked around. A middle-aged waitress, with hair like pink candyfloss, was taking a food order from a young mother with noisy kids.

Behind her, a couple of truckers were sitting on stools at the counter, eating their way through corn dogs stacked like freshly-sawn lumber.

Stolarski returned to the table after a few minutes. He massaged his forehead with the palm of his left hand as the waffles arrived, brought by a girl who looked too young to be working. She placed the white plates down on the table.

'Enjoy,' she said.

After she'd returned to the counter to collect another order, Stolarski said, 'She should be in school.' He shuffled on his plastic seat.

'Can we talk about Berlin?' Gabriel said.

'Later,' Stolarski said, his tone brusque.

Stolarski began to eat his food, his movements slow and determined. But the syrup on his waffle ran over his chin and Gabriel turned away, seeing his own outline reflected in the large windowpane, and beyond, the tree-clad mountain, the sky that had turned from dough to sapphire in the time it had taken them to get here.

When he turned back, Stolarski was staring at the middle-aged waitress.

'You ever seen hair like that before?'

Ignoring him, Gabriel said, 'We need to talk about Berlin.'

Stolarski put his knife and fork down and looked at Gabriel. His eyes had narrowed, and his chin was raised. 'When you show me a copy of that DVD,' he said.

'I can't do that,' Gabriel said, shaking his head to emphasize his words. 'Why do you want to see a thing like that anyway?' He was troubled by the request.

Stolarski's already deeply lined brow furrowed to the point that it resembled something other than skin, something synthetic. 'To know you're not stringing me along, is all.'

'I can't show it to you. That's a red line.'

'OK. But I want details and I will give you details,' Stolarski said.

'Do I have your world you won't repeat anything I tell you?'

Stolarski nodded.

'Say it for me.'

'You have my word.'

Gabriel felt he could tell him some of the details. He had to, didn't he?

When he mentioned the snow lion embroidered on the back of the Tibetan monk's robe and the fact that the young victim was a Kalmyk, Stolarski's gaunt face tightened, such that Gabriel thought it looked like a skull clothed in gossamer. A ghost.

There were wastelands in his eyes.

CHAPTER SEVENTY-NINE

Stolarski had talked for five minutes or more. He'd told Gabriel about his childhood, his beautiful mother and sister and his intellectual elder brother, Icchak, who'd read Leontiev, Jung and Luria, had studied medicine at university and hoped to become a psychiatrist. He seemed to have transformed into something more noble and erudite. He was still surprising Gabriel.

'We were living in Lublin in 1939. He was eighteen years old. A good student. We Poles got hit from both sides then, the Germans from the west and the Soviets from the east. We found ourselves in the ghetto. Most of the Jews were sent to Belzec and Majdanek death camps after the Ordnungspolizei, the German Order Police, hunted them down in the cellars. But there were escape routes for those young and healthy enough to try. My brother got me and my mother out of Lublin and we joined the Jewish partisans, who were fighting the Nazis from the forests. But we had nothing to speak of. Friends that were injured died of their wounds. The Germans flattened the ghetto after their evil work was done. My father had died early on, fighting the advancing Germans in a cavalry regiment.'

Stolarski stopped speaking and drank some water from a glass that he'd asked the girl to bring over. He still hadn't touched his milk.

'My brother, Icchak, joined the Polish Home Army and fought at his beloved Lublin in July 1944. He fought the Germans and the Hungarians. He fought the Kalmyk cavalry.'

Gabriel's pupils dilated, his chest heaved.

He said, 'Kalmyk cavalry?'

'Yes,' Stolarski said. 'That's why I reacted the way I did earlier.'

'I see.'

'When the Red Army arrived,' he went on, 'my brother joined the newly-formed Polish First Army. Those communist sonsofbitches sent the defeated Poles to POW camps after they'd invaded. They killed thousands of our officers and intellectuals in the Katyn massacre in 1940. Doctors, and such like. Lawyers, like you. Beria, the head of the NKVD, had agreed to the invasion from the east with the Gestapo at a conference in Zakopane. Still, my brother fought for the Soviets. The Nazis were beasts. At least the Soviets hadn't gassed the children or smashed their little heads in with rifle butts.

'There were some 80,000 like my brother. They fought all the way to Berlin, to the Reichstag and the Reich Chancellery. He was told to help clear a bunker by carrying the items from its entrance onto waiting trucks.'

He confirmed what Gabriel had been told by Boris Iliev at Yale. Gabriel didn't doubt he was telling the truth.

'There's a name that might interest you,' Stolarski said.

He reached for the glass of milk. He put it to his lips and drank.

He said, 'It's the name of a young man back then, and I will never forget it. My mother told me that Lieutenant Joseph Kazapov of the NKVD turned my brother over to SMERSH officers before he was sent to the Gulag. They interrogated him for days. Knocked three of his teeth out. Did other things, my mother said, that he wouldn't repeat, not even to a priest. You heard of SMERSH?'

'I have a vague memory,' Gabriel said.

'It's an acronym for Smert Shpioam. It means 'death to spies'. A name thought up by Stalin. But in the war years in the Soviet Union, spies were said to be everywhere. Not that the details would matter much. SMERSH had a human quota of Soviet ex-POWs to torture and either deport to the frozen tundra or subject to extrajudicial killings. Icchak Stolarski was in the wrong place at the wrong time. They wanted to kill him. He was in no doubt about it. But for some reason, they didn't. He told my mother he knew enough about psychology to convince them that he hadn't said or thought anything anti-revolutionary or traitorous. I guess that was the reason.

'At first, he was sent to a lumber camp in Siberia. My brother was skinny but still managed to lose another thirty pounds. He lost four toes to frostbite.' He sighed. 'If it had stopped there he might have survived. But he was sent to a uranium mine. They said the uranium mines were the longest torture the NKVD could think up. My brother said it was Kazapov's doing and I don't doubt it. It was because of what he'd seen outside the bunker.'

Stolarski finished his waffles, wiped his mouth clean with a paper napkin.

'You haven't touched yours.'

'Not hungry,' Gabriel said.

'One thing I will always carry from my past as a young refugee in New York. I never leave a scrap.'

Gabriel wanted to confide in someone now. It was a natural reaction to share his pain after hearing so much of someone else's, he supposed.

It was a desire to empathize. Besides, they had an agreement to recip-rocate, didn't they? It was the right thing to do.

'My sister adopted a Kalmyk girl,' he said.

Stolarski pursed his lips and nodded, as if he wasn't surprised by what Gabriel had just said.

'She disappeared.'

'Was it your niece in the DVD?' Stolarski said.

'No.'

'Then what is the reason for all your questions?' Stolarski said.

'The same people responsible for the DVD could've taken my niece. Tell me, what happened to Lieutenant Kazapov?'

'Some of my brother's old comrades that I managed to track down years after said that nobody knew. They never heard of him again. Some said they guessed he'd died after the war, or in the last moments of it.'

Stolarski burped. 'Well, best get back. Ned doesn't like being on his own for long.'

'Are you OK?'

Stolarski nodded. But his eyes were sparkling with tears.

But Gabriel wanted more answers. 'How did you find out about Boris Iliev's lecture?'

Stolarski looked worn out. He said, 'Are you taping this?'

'Absolutely not,' Gabriel said.

'They have a computer at the treatment centre I mentioned to you. They showed me how to use it. I've read a couple of Iliev's books too. I've done my research, Mr Hall. I know where those Tibetan Buddhist things come from.'

'But why were you interested? You know Kazapov wasn't responsible for what was in the bunker or the death of the Red Army soldiers.'

Stolarski looked a little taken aback before he rested his hands on the table top and nodded a fraction. 'Are you a prosecutor? A government man?'

Gabriel sat back and put his open hands up to his shoulders. 'You can check me out. I've got some ID if you want to see it.'

Stolarski shook his head. 'That won't be necessary, and put your hands down.' He rubbed his mouth and nose with one hand before putting in his lap. 'I'll be honest with you. I wanted to find Kazapov, but there was no way I would've gone to the Soviet Union. I would've been shot if I went snooping around after him there. I knew that. So, I waited. But by the time the iron curtain came tumbling down, he'd disappeared completely.'

'He resurfaced before then?'

Stolarski sighed. 'Are you gonna let me tell it the way it was or not?'

'I'm sorry.'

'Five years ago, I was on one of those ex-military chatrooms on the Internet, down at the treatment centre, which was my purpose in learning how to use it, in point of fact. Anyway, I was still searching for Kazapov, although I'll admit I was on the point of giving up, when I was contacted by a real old guy, a Russian who was now living in Nebraska. He'd been a guard at Lubyanka in Moscow, the headquarters of the NKVD in the days before Stalin died. He was a minor defector in the 1960s after he'd been in security in the nuclear programme. He wasn't worried about retribution after the old guard died.'

Stolarski made a face, as if he wasn't sure if he should continue, but didn't have a good enough reason not to.

'He said a major called Joseph Kazapov liked to cut the noses and ears off the women there. Said he called it penal amputation. Apparently, Kazapov got drunk one night and said the Tibetan Buddhists used to do it, and that it was something the Kalmyks had done in the war. Worse than that too, he said. That's what led me to Iliev. It was a long shot, I knew. A dead end. Except after what you've told me, maybe it wasn't.'

Gabriel felt his stomach tense, his hands knot. 'What was the defector's name?'

Stolarski sniffed. 'He died about three years back.'

Gabriel was apologetic for his previous tone and his questioning. Stolarski was dying, after all. But had he tried to mislead me earlier? he thought. He gave him the benefit of the doubt and decided the old man would've opened up to him at some point, maybe on the way back to the bungalow he lived in with Ned.

'Don't worry about it. I know it looks like me and Ned are off the radar, that we live like pigs, but we like it that way. We've done regular jobs. I still got my US passport and enough money to get by. Ned's got an inheritance and a military pension. We're doing OK. We're still alive.'

'You think Kazapov is?' Gabriel said.

Stolarski was silent for a few seconds.

'I honestly don't know.'

CHAPTER EIGHTY

They were sitting at the back of a rectangular mess hall. The dining facility's tables and chairs had been stacked with an almost obsessive precision against the breezeblock side walls, which were painted an ivory colour. Four MPs stood in each corner of the facility.

The Chechen had refused to give his real name. The house in Baton Rouge he'd been extracted from had been searched and, apart from the drugs and pornography, four false passports had been found, all with different names and all bearing the Chechen's photograph. There were no weapons, other than the machete. The Chechen had no record of violence. But Carla suspected he was a violent man. She could smell it on him now too.

He sat across from Carla and Hester on a dining bench at a long wooden table with metal legs. He smoked a hand-rolled cigarette, using a plastic cup of water as an ashtray.

Even here, he has no sense of propriety, she thought.

Hester said, 'Where did you obtain the DVD?'

'From an old serial killer in Berlin,' the Chechen said, inhaling smoke.

'Who did you sell it to?'

'An American.'

'What was his name?'

The Chechen grinned and tapped the cigarette on the edge of the cup. 'Jed Watson,' he said.

Carla did her best to keep her poker face.

'Do *you* want to end up with your throat slit by a member of the Russian mafia in a high security federal prison?' Hester said, making a reference to Johnny Hockey.

The Chechen dropped his cigarette into the cup and scratched his goatee. 'No.'

'That's good, because I can help you with that. Do you need any more cigarettes?'

'No.'

Hester coughed into a fist and rested his forearms on the table top, a shoulder width apart. 'Who is Snow Lion?'

'The old serial killer in Berlin.'

'What is his name?'

The Chechen grinned again and turned to Carla. 'What do you think of his interrogation technique?'

Carla was silent.

'Have you heard of Hanns Joachim Scharff?' the Chechen asked her.

She glanced at Hester. He was gritting his teeth.

She said, 'I'm not here to be interviewed.'

Ignoring her, the Chechen continued. 'He was a Luftwaffe interrogator in World War Two. He was known as the master interrogator of Nazi Germany, and as you can imagine, there was a lot of competition. He was charged with interrogating US Air Force pilots. He was even used to interrogate VIPs, very important prisoners. He was so good that his methods shaped US intelligence techniques during the Cold War. Many of his methods are still used by US Army intelligence. He was successful because he didn't once use physical torture to obtain the information he wanted.'

He looked at her, his eyes demanding a response.

'That's very interesting,' she said.

'Hanns Joachim Scharff made the POWs think he was their greatest asset. They were told that if they didn't pass over information, they would be deemed a spy and handed over to the Gestapo. He said that there was no way he'd allow that to happen and shared jokes and food with them. He spoke fluent English and new the social mores of the day in the US. He asked them questions he knew the answers to and then asked them a question he didn't know the answer to. They often told him the answer, thinking he knew that answer too, believing they weren't betraying a secret, but rather they would obtain more favourable treatment.'

'That's enough,' Hester said.

'Is it?' the Chechen said. 'In 1948, Scharff was invited to the US and gave lectures to the US Air Force. He was granted immigration status, even though his former paymasters were the enemies of the US. In the decades that followed, he became a world-renowned artist in mosaics. His works hang in the Epcot Center and in the Cinderella Castle at Walt Disney World, Florida. A happy ending.'

Hester said, 'The only thing *you* will get is a continuation of the status quo.'

Ignoring him, the Chechen said, 'I'm prepared to tell you today what type of house you will buy for me in Miami Beach and how much you will deposit in a bank account in my new but legal name, here in the US, at least. I will tell you the new hairstyle I want and the shape of my new nose.' He fingered his fleshy nose. 'Perhaps I will go from a Muslim from the North Caucasus to a Christian from Boston. Perhaps not.'

'As I said, I'll pass,' Hester said. 'You think the US government is Santa Claus?'

The Chechen smirked. 'When you're authorized to trade, come back. Otherwise, don't bother.'

The Chechen gathered up his cigarette papers and tobacco pouch. He looked right through Hester as if he was made of glass. He stood up and walked away.

Carla knew Hester didn't have authority to trade.

When the Chechen was out of earshot, she said, 'We've got to trade with him.'

Hester sighed. 'I mentioned him to the FSB. They said he's a child pornographer. A paedophile. Tell me you can't see a problem.'

CHAPTER EIGHTY-ONE

Ministry of internal affairs special camp, Irkutsk region, east Siberia, March 1953.

They emerged into the cold air, squinting despite the dullness.

In truth, the recent dead could only be separated from the exhausted living when no sound or movement came from their wasted bodies, following a beating for supposedly malingering. But even if they could withstand a beating without movement or sound, it wouldn't do them any good. The bodies were dragged away by the MVD, the skulls crushed with hammers to ensure that no one was feigning death. The guards flung the corpses down a disused mineshaft that was subsequently covered with clumps of frosted dirt. There were no mistakes in the special camp. There was no mercy or compassion.

Some prisoners were Ukrainians, who'd been rounded up in 1942, due to Stalin's paranoia over potential collaborators. They'd aged twenty-five years in half that time. They were the forgotten ones. There were Latvians, Lithuanians, Finns, Estonians, Poles, Belarusians. They knew that thousands of others had been shot by the NKVD in abandoned prisons and forced labour camps, those closest to the German advance in 1941;

shot rather than being allowed to defect. But no one here thought they themselves were the lucky ones.

There were political prisoners. There were those deported for their ethnicity or religious views. There were sometime convicts, kulaks. There were the habitual 'thieves in law'. There was Icchak Stolarski.

Staraya Chara uranium mine had an ideal location for a forced labour camp. It was a canyon bordered on three sides by towering rock faces. The fourth was a craggy slope that was fastidiously guarded, day and night. No one had ever escaped. Escape to what? the prisoners said. The bitter cold made for swollen chilblains inside the confines of the mine. Outside it, a man would freeze to death in hours amid the windswept bleakness of a landscape made up of rock fragments and icy lakes.

In winter, the temperature dropped to minus fifty degrees Fahrenheit in the Siberian taiga. Only the nomadic tribes of reindeer herders could survive out there, and they were bought easily enough with the promise of substantial rewards for aiding the guards in capturing an escapee. There was even talk of a guard becoming an inmate if his negligence was responsible for a runaway. Everyone agreed that there was no more incentive for diligence than that.

Some prisoners reduced themselves to spying for the guards. Some got a threadbare coat for it. Some got murdered in the mine with a pickaxe by the half-crazed convicts for the symbolism of the coat.

Most prisoners worked in rags, held in place with string. They wore rubber boots made from useless tyres. They ate potato peelings and bits of bony and salted fish off studded tin plates. They drank stale water from studded tin mugs. They were put into roofless, stone punishment cells, with studded wooden doors. The food was rancid there.

They pushed barrows of rock for fifteen hours a day. They sweated the water from their bodies at hundreds of feet below ground. They died from tuberculosis, leukaemia, lung cancer. Cancers with no names yet. Uranium ore wasn't the problem, but rather the radon gas it emitted when mined. None of them knew this.

Some took to suicide, blowing themselves up with dynamite. Some were shot for minor transgressions. Hundreds died in the frenzy for atomic bombs. Thousands.

In December 1944, the secret police had been assigned to supervise the Soviet atomic bomb project, known as Task Number One, which led to the first testing five years later. The Gulag uranium mines were integral to that and to the mass production of atomic weapons, which was ongoing.

*

It was night time and Icchak lay awake on his bunk of slatted wood, staring at the corroded studs on the cell door. His mind was scarred now. He no longer led men as a trusted NCO. He no longer had a modicum of respect from others, or for himself. He was no longer a man in any meaningful sense of the word. The tips of his toes were black, the rank cloth his head was wrapped in as useless against the cold as a match in a hurricane.

When he'd asked a guard if he could contact his family within the first hour of his arrival, the man had sneered at him and had had said to forget he ever had a family, that he would never see them again. When Icchak had spoken of his army service against their mutual enemy, the guard beat him with a rubber truncheon. The pain in his body had been eclipsed tenfold by the agony he experienced via his imagination. He'd vowed then, not to think of his family again.

Below him the eighteen-year-old boy was whimpering. Icchak didn't have the energy to tell him to sleep. He barely had the energy to breathe. The man to Icchak's left had said he'd been there since the beginning, just after the end of the war. Most of the inmates, including Icchak, had been to lumber camps and other non-toxic mines before coming here.

The man, whose name was Vasily Popov, had said he'd been crammed into a small transport plane with a dozen others, and had been told that they were to set up a mine. He'd said they'd looked at one another with bemusement and trepidation. The aircraft had landed on the right bank of the Sakukan River, around ten miles from the canyon, which he referred to as 'the pit'. They'd crossed the frigid river with the aid of ropes and had trekked through the stark landscape. Icchak had just shaken his shaven head at that. Vasily was the only man he trusted in the camp, apart from the handful of other Poles.

He, like the others, coughed up blood in the tunnels. The guards just smirked. They would all die here, wouldn't they?

Early each morning, all the prisoners, or zeks, lined up in the unrelenting cold for the rollcall, which happened twice a day. This morning the air numbed their bodies and their minds. Those that had gone insane with the cold, or because of their predicament, or both, made little noises like children, like monkeys. The guards thinned them out on a periodic basis.

Icchak's dulled brain registered three men dressed in civilian winter clothes standing to the side of an MVD officer. Dimly, he wondered if a new war had started, or if the MVD had been replaced by something even more sinister and brutal, something these men represented. Was that possible?

Snow fell in glops from the rock faces. The prisoners shivered in silence.

'Prisoners,' the officer said. 'I have terrible news and I have other news.'

Icchak stared at the hard dirt. He didn't know what could be terrible news. This was terrible. What else could be? Even burning to death meant he would be warm for a while.

'These men are from the MGB, the Ministry of State Security. Our glorious leader, Comrade Stalin, is dead.'

The prisoners just shivered in silence still.

'You will be freed.'

Five seconds passed.

Some wept. Some shook their heads, thinking it was a vile game, Icchak knew. Some collapsed. Some began to murmur. Icchak waited.

A few weeks later, the survivors found out that the men from the MGB had been sent to Siberia from Moscow to shut down the mine and murder the zeks to a man, just like in 1941. But they had received an urgent message at a fuelling station. Stalin's death had meant they'd lived. It had been an almost comical piece of luck.

Today, the day Icchak was told he was free, he went to the camp infirmary, which was a pitiable and ineffectual place, a stone-built building the size of the communal latrine. There were no doctors, just a couple of ex-army medics.

Ignoring the stench, Icchak walked to his wooden bed and laid down on it. His ulcers bled daily and were the size of scallops. But these were the least of his physical problems. There'd been no diagnosis of his illnesses, but he knew instinctively that they were fatal, or at least one of them was. He knew nothing could be done for him, but still he'd come here.

He cradled his head.

He thought: I'm dying and I'm free.

A man he knew came into the infirmary, wincing at the sickly smells that pervaded it, he could see. He walked towards Icchak.

He bent down to Icchak's head and spoke to him for a minute or more.

When he'd finished, Icchak tried to speak but his breath was rattling. He just nodded. The man put a small piece of salted fish into his hand and left.

CHAPTER EIGHTY-TWO

West Berlin, 1954.

West Berlin was a city that had existed for five years, an enclave surrounded by communist East Germany. Its two million population was split into the French, American and British occupation sectors, although the border with East Berlin was still open and people travelled between the two with ease.

Kazapov was in the north, the French sector, dressed impeccably in the fashion of the day: a broad-shouldered, double-breasted grey flannel suit with cuffs. His hair was parted to the right, slicked down with cream. He wore browline glasses. He might have been mistaken for an up-and-coming architect, with a passion for Bach and Proust, perhaps.

He'd been told by the MVD, the Russian Ministry of Internal Affairs, the renamed NKVD in which he was now a major, that this was a rare dispensation. Two days. No more. False papers. No weapons. If caught, he would be shot by the French. The MVD didn't have to tell him that if he didn't return to the USSR, they'd find him. They'd kill him. He didn't doubt it. But he'd said he didn't need two days. One would suffice.

But the communist state didn't like personal revenge, he knew. Even considering such an act was deemed an offence, despite Stalin's death.

A man or woman thinking for themselves was a dangerous habit, after all. Imagine what it could lead to.

He'd made up a plausible story as to why he'd wanted to come here. He was valued by the state now. He didn't know when he could get to those Kalmyks that had fled. But the day would come. He had no doubt of that. He looked up at the brick façade of the terraced house.

Brigitte Bayer walked towards it ten minutes later. The sun was bright above the reconstructed church steeples and birds were singing in the chestnut trees across the road in a little park.

She is still beautiful, Kazapov thought.

She held a girl's hand. The girl was blonde, like her mother, and wore a navy-blue skirt and a yellow-coloured blouse buttoned up to her neck. He skulked behind a small parked car, but heard the girl call her mother, 'mama'. His eyes caught a glint of a ring on Brigitte's right hand. He remembered it being there. He steadied himself.

This would be the hardest test, he thought.

*

He waited for two hours before the child left. On some errand, he guessed. Or to play in the park. He took off his glasses and crossed the street. He walked leisurely up the short flight of mottled steps.

Half a minute later, Brigitte Bayer put her hand to her mouth when she opened the door. 'It's you,' she said. 'Is it really you, Joseph? My God, I thought you were dead!'

'No. I — '

'Come in, come in,' she said, beckoning him with her hand.

She wore a short front-pleated white dress, adorned with red flowers. Her hair was up, and she glowed with a now natural beauty. She led him to the living room, with white wallpaper embossed with a yellow diamond pattern, and gestured to a red-satin couch and asked him if he wanted a drink. He said no.

She sat beside him. There was a plate of unfinished food on a box frame coffee table, together with a half-empty glass of water. The walnut-framed radio was on. Sender Freies Berlin was playing Edith Piaf's *Le Vagabond*, the sound oddly distant and crackly.

They talked for five minutes or so. She confirmed that she hadn't married. She worked as a secretary for a burgeoning magazine. She was doing well, she said. He didn't doubt it. She would do well anywhere. People were drawn to her as if she held a secret that could transform their lives into something more splendid and interesting.

'The general was executed by firing squad two years ago,' Kazapov said, offhandedly. 'The child?'

'You saw her?'

He nodded.

'She's your daughter, Joseph,' she said, placing her hand on his forearm.

'Please don't be angry at me, but how can you be so sure?'

'The general couldn't get it up,' she said, without a hint of a blush. 'He just liked to watch me undress, as he puffed on a huge cigar. The sad old man. But at least he protected me from being raped. There was only you, Joseph. Kurt died before I met you, as you know. I was an actress, but never a whore. That's how I'm sure. And I wanted a child. I wanted something good and pure to come out of that madness. You can understand that, can't you?'

'Yes,' he said.

'She's a wonderful child. Musical and good-tempered. You'll love her — ' She looked down at her lap. 'I'm sorry, I didn't mean to presume. What will you do, Joseph?'

'Do?'

'Now you're in West Berlin.'

'I can't stay long.'

'Oh.' She looked disappointed.

'I'm sorry, Brigitte.'

'Sorry?'

'For telling you about my mother and sisters.'

'I don't understand,' she said.

He picked up a cushion and slammed it into her face. He pushed her head back onto the arm of the couch where there was no give. She made muffled sounds. Kicked out. Scratched his hands. Then she didn't move. He kept up the pressure for a further minute before getting up to go, leaving the cushion in place.

She could recognize him. She knew his name. But more than this, he'd foolishly told her about his family in Kalmykia. A possible link could be made. He couldn't risk it. She had to die. He felt wretched about it, even though he burned, drowned, maimed and murdered all manner of people for the state now. Even though his specialty was young women.

He walked out of the room and heard the front door open and looked about for something to use as a weapon. He saw a metal torch on a table against the wall. But he drew his hand back when he heard his daughter call out, 'Mama, mama. I forgot — '

He looked down at her. She looked quizzical.

'Where's my mama?'

'She's resting.'

'Who are you?' she said.

'Please forgive me.'

He saw her looking behind him. She ran past him and heard her calling 'mama' repeatedly, pitiably.

Leaving, he heard his daughter screaming.

CHAPTER EIGHTY-THREE

East Berlin, the same day.

In East Berlin, the Soviet sector, the wind was picking up and the sun was fading inch by inch behind the blocks of flats, the concrete monoliths of Stalinist architecture. Kazapov had bought a rib-knit balaclava from an open-fronted shop. He didn't want it to keep his ears warm.

Five minutes later, he placed a few Deutsche Marks into the hand of a teenage crook with dirty fingernails and bad teeth, who peddled flick knives from the lining of his black overcoat.

He walked past the dead trees, their fat trunks clothed in dried lichen, and sat down on a slab of granite in the remnants of an overgrown cemetery. He waited until he was alone and took out the knife and balaclava. He placed his hand into the face opening of the balaclava and stretched the wool that covered the back of the head with his fingers. He cut two eye slits and placed the balaclava and knife back into his jacket pocket. Standing, he checked the time on his wristwatch and walked off along the pebbled, weed-ridden path.

*

According to the nameplate beneath a doorbell, the man, Conrad Weber, lived on the third floor of a converted merchant's house. It had survived the Allied bombing raids in 1945. The east of the city had been targeted less than the west, Kazapov knew.

The MVD intelligence files he'd accessed stated that Weber was unemployed and had taken to drink. He was separated from his wife and two children and lived alone. He'd spent the war as an official SS photographer and filmmaker and had joined the Einsatzgruppen der Sicherheitspolizei und des SD in October 1939. When the Germans had advanced into occupied western Poland, he'd photographed the executions in the town of Kórnik. In 1942, he'd travelled to Kalmykia.

He would surely die if he fell from that height, Kazapov thought.

He waited until an old woman carrying a small dog under her arm had gotten halfway out of the front door, the light-blue paint flaking. Then he vaulted the flagstone entrance steps and grabbed the door just before it closed. He'd turned away from her so that she couldn't recognize him.

He crouched down beside a beige wall inside the hallway. It was quiet. The staircase had an elaborate banister, but it was chipped here and there. The air smelled vaguely of damp and cat piss. The property was well past its prime.

He reached the second-floor landing and fetched out the flick knife and pushed it up the sleeve of his shirt, which was held tight to his wrist by a silver cufflink. He put on the balaclava backwards and knocked on the door, clenching his teeth with anticipation. He didn't want to use the knife and would only do so if something went wrong. He didn't want to get blood on his clothing and draw attention to himself.

The door opened. Conrad Weber was unshaven, his eyes reddened. He wore a pair of baggy trousers and a grease-stained undershirt. His

SS blood-group tattoo had been burned off his upper arm, leaving a wrinkled piece of eggshell-coloured skin.

He registered the balaclava and tried to slam the door shut. But Kazapov had stuck his black leather shoe against the frame. He burst through. Weber retreated to the compact living room and onto the French windows that led out to the small balcony.

He turned, his arms outstretched before him, pleading for his life. Kazapov held up the knife, the blade shimmering, and told him to shut up or he'd stab him to death.

The man looked to be in his mid-thirties, with a flabby stomach. He was swaying on his feet. Kazapov could smell the cheap alcohol on his breath. His cheeks were speckled with red-spider veins.

'I have gold coins and silverware. In a bank, close by. You can have it all.'

Kazapov saw that Weber was sweating and shaking. He couldn't tell if it was fear or the alcohol.

'Did the Russian Jews in Kalmykia offer you gold and silver?'

Weber's eyes lowered to the fraying carpet. 'I have nightmares,' he said.

'I know,' Kazapov said. 'But you weren't forced to do what you did. You could have gone home. You weren't under any threat if you *didn't* murder children and pregnant women.'

'I couldn't let my friends do all the dirty work. But I wish to God I had. The nightmares never stop.'

'You won't have nightmares tonight.'

Kazapov inched towards him, the knife held at head height.

'I'm going to gut you like a fish,' he said.

Weber turned, pushed open the French windows and staggered forward. He flipped over the balcony silently, a dull thud and a scream from a female passer-by testament to his suicide.

Kazapov put the knife in his jacket pocket and walked past a cracked wall mirror. He stopped and turned to look at his reflection. His black eyes were dull and pitiless. There was not one vestige of humanity left in them.

CHAPTER EIGHTY-FOUR

Brooklyn, 2015, the next day.

Carla's SUV was stationary in a parking lot at the foot of Atlantic Avenue, the main truck route through the borough, about a mile southeast of Gabriel's home in Brooklyn Heights. The parking lot was a stone's throw from the South Ferry waterfront and opposite an Arabic mosque, with a selection of antique shops, pastel-coloured rowhouses, red brick office buildings and Middle Eastern restaurants to the rear. It was 5.35 pm, the sun still high in the west, the landscape criss-crossed with shadows, and the tarmac was emptying of vans and station wagons, the drivers pulling on cigarettes and talking into smartphones.

Gabriel got out of his sedan and sat in the SUV's front passenger seat. Carla had called him that morning and asked to meet with him. He would normally have taken a cab or walked, but she'd told him not to.

During the short drive, he'd had the feeling that he was becoming lost in something like a lethal maze. He didn't have a rational explanation for that, other than his not having a clue which direction to go in next, and all the previous day's talk of torture and death with Bronislaw Stolarski was playing on his mind. He wasn't sleeping more than a few hours a night. As for Joseph Kazapov, he had no idea how or whether to investigate him further at this stage. He was probably dead, anyhow.

'It's good to see you,' Carla said.

'You too, Carla. What do you have for me?'

'It's good news, up to a point. But I must say this first. The operational secrecy I'm acting under on this is of the highest level. Do you understand that, Gabriel?'

'I'm a lawyer. Keeping confidences is second nature to me.'

Haven't we had this conversation before? he thought.

'That's what I hoped you'd say. I have to believe it.' Her tone was almost remorseful.

He watched her close her eyes briefly. She breathed deeply through her nose, as if willing herself to speak.

'The Chechen confirmed that he sold the DVD to Jed Watson.'

'This is a real breakthrough, Carla.'

'It is. But that's not all. I was informed yesterday that Jed Watson was under investigation by the SEC Division of Enforcement," she said.

'Go on.'

'They intimated that he might have been involved in a major financial fraud. It's early days,' she said.

She brushed her black hair away from the side of her head, kept it up for a moment, as if she was overheating, before letting it cascade down over her shoulders.

Gabriel rubbed his face with his palms. 'So, Watson was vulnerable to an arrest and to having his property searched, in which case the DVD would be found. Then a link might be made,' he said, clarifying it in his own mind. 'And that's where Johnny Hockey came in.'

'Right. I suspect Hockey was told to do a hit and get a DVD, so he did a hit and got a DVD.'

'Did the Chechen confirm that Hockey did it?' Gabriel said.

'He wasn't asked that question. Not yet at least.'

'What about the girlfriend of the Hockey associate, the one who wants the reward?'

Carla shook her head. 'There's been no sign of her.'

'And have the FBI subpoenaed the Watson family?' Gabriel said.

'Yes. Her name is Charlene Rimes. She was twenty-two years old.'

'So you think she's dead already?'

'Yes, I do,' she said, nodding solemnly.

Gabriel interlocked his fingers and placed them over his nose, as if he was a child that had smelled something awful.

A white van with tinted windows slowed down on the opposite side of the road in front of them and he watched Carla check it out. When what looked like a co-worker was dropped off at the pavement, the tension in the side of her neck subsided.

'Do you think the Chechen knows Snow Lion's name?' he said.

'He won't say it, at least not for the present. He's keeping a lot back until he's offered the option of turning state's evidence to get immunity from prosecution, although he'll spend the rest of his life in a witness protection programme. He wants a chunk of real estate and a chunk of cash. His face will have to change. His identity. He knows that if he gives up Snow Lion, he will be a marked man.'

'And will he be offered those things?' Gabriel said.

'I don't know, Gabriel. My boss is adamant that he won't give in to the Chechen's demands.'

'But he must,' Gabriel said. 'Tell him he has to. Jesus Christ. What's his name?'

She hesitated, and it worried him, although he didn't know why.

'Hester. Section Chief Hester. But he said the FSB told him the

Chechen is a child pornographer. It's more complicated than you think. Besides, it's above Hester's paygrade. Have you met with that man you mentioned?'

'Yes,' he said.

He felt sure now that Bronislaw Stolarski had been telling the truth about his brother, Icchak, and after what Carla had told him about the Chechen, he felt it was only right to tell her. He did so, without mentioning his name. He told her about Lieutenant Joseph Kazapov of the NKVD, too.

'It's a long shot, but could Hester contact the FSB again and see if they have any information on the wartime service record of Joseph Kazapov?' he said. 'He might have survived. He could still be alive. It's possible, isn't it?'

He wanted to verify Stolarski's opinion that Kazapov had survived the war, if that was possible. Besides, he had a nagging feeling he couldn't pin down about Stolarski and a burgeoning one about Kazapov — although if he was still alive there was no connection to the disappearances that he knew of, and no motive.

Her eyes seemed fixed on the traffic, on people emerging from the doors of businesses and homes. She wasn't looking for anyone she knew, he thought. She was looking for someone she should be wary of.

'Carla. Did you hear me?'

CHAPTER EIGHTY-FIVE

Carla's house, the same day.

Carla had gone to bed early, tired after her long drive back from New York. She had a headache and had taken a couple of painkillers with a glass of Argentinian Malbec. Not a sensible thing to do, she realized, but she hadn't felt like doing the sensible thing.

Monize was staying over at her father's house in DC. Carla had rung her a couple of hours before from the car on her hands-free, and her daughter had said that she'd been to the movies and had eaten a tub of buttered popcorn. Carla had smiled to herself then.

Now, her eyelids flicked open. Her bedroom was dark, without a hint of street or moonlight, due to her heavy curtains and the farmhouse's remote location, and she blinked hard, once, to focus. She sensed that her hair was damp at the nape of her neck. She stroked her belly and thighs. It seemed her whole body was clammy.

The creaking sound had come, she guessed, from the maple staircase. It swamped her senses, and she tensed as the adrenalin pumped through her. But it could've come from anywhere. Couldn't it?

Part of her decided it was the old house settling down. Another part of her didn't.

Slowly, her right hand moved towards the mahogany bedside cabinet. Three of her fingers eased open the top drawer that held her Glock 22. She kept it there at night in a secure metal box. She couldn't risk Monize finding it and squeezing off a round. It had a full magazine in place. It *always* had a full magazine in place. The key was kept on a piece of string around her neck. She lifted the box out and rested it on her belly.

Five seconds later, the empty box was back in the drawer and she was holding the Glock close to her chest. She felt all of the weapon's thirty-four ounces. She knew the trigger pull was 5.5 pounds. It bucked, but there was good shock adsorption. There was no traditional safety lever, save for the small one built into the trigger proper.

Her backup, a Glock 26 9mm, the so-called Baby Glock, was in the standing wardrobe. It was strapped to her ankle when she was on active service. But before she could retrieve the backup, she saw what appeared to be the beam from a torch beneath the bottom of her bedroom door. She sensed her heart rate escalate and had to force herself not to scream.

She threw back the duvet and swung her legs around. She picked up her slippers with her free hand. They had good soles, having been purchased with the bare floorboards of her home in mind. She thought about shooting at the door, but had no idea if anyone was behind it. She thought about walking to the wardrobe and squatting there. She decided to grab her smartphone and run. By the time she was outside and had cleared the curtilage, she could risk slowing down and speaking into it.

Three seconds before her bedroom door was flung open, she'd reached her en suite bathroom, her motion silent and fluid. She locked the door and put on her slippers. She opened the window that led to a portion of the rear fire escape and the walkway beneath, which extended for some six hundred yards to a sparely lit and barely populated minor road.

She heard heavy footsteps heading for the bathroom. She tucked the

Glock and the mobile into the waistband of her pyjama trousers, then grasped the nearest fire-escape rail and swung her body over feet first. Swivelling around, she almost galloped down its steel steps, which were perforated to aid drainage and stability in movement.

She reached the walkway, sweat dampening her T-shirt, which bore an image of Rio's Christ the Redeemer on the front. Both the Glock and the smartphone were pointing upwards in her hands now. She ran, her eyes fixed ahead.

She couldn't remember when she had ever been so swift, when her body had felt so light, although her sense of fear was palpable. Her hands were shaking, her gaping mouth dry. She had an ache in her abdomen and the sweat was running into her eyes.

A few seconds later, she heard heavy breathing and multiple pounding feet about twenty feet behind her. She didn't want to slow down to use her phone. It would be twenty minutes minimum before a patrol car turned up, longer for a SWAT team. By that time, it would be over.

Her eyelids stretched to their limit, her lungs heaved. The fear was on the brink of crippling her. She knew she couldn't outrun them. But now her training kicked in.

Stop, she thought. Turn. Assume the firing position.

She didn't need any motivation other than the threat of capture. Grabbed by the back of her flowing hair, perhaps, and flung to the hard surface. Or worse, hit with a bullet, as if they were culling an animal. A bullet might sever the femoral artery in her thigh, in which case she knew she'd bleed out in a few minutes. A bullet might irreparably shatter the ball and socket joint in her shoulder. It didn't matter. She had decided to face them.

She saw them in the half light of the moon and illuminated by intermittent iron lampposts, but she found it hard to focus on individuals.

There were three of them. No, four. She thought she saw a baseball bat, but it could have been a pump-action shotgun. She couldn't tell if they were all Caucasians. That didn't matter, either.

She positioned herself onto her right knee in what felt like one movement, placing the smartphone face up on the asphalt. She held the Glock at eye level, with one hand on the handle, one steadying the grip. She adjusted the rear white sight so that it aligned with the front dot.

Fifteen rounds, she thought. Enough, even if she wasted half a dozen.

She blinked. She didn't understand why. Her hands began to tremble.

'Fucking shoot!'

The sound of the man's voice reverberated in her head. He wasn't talking to her. She heard the buzzing. She felt the fifty thousand volts in her back, overriding her central nervous system and causing the uncontrollable contraction of her muscle tissue. The spasm debilitated her.

Taser darts.

She lay in the foetal position. She was shaking now, and fluid was dripping from her nose. Her lips were parted. and she was mouthing something.

Monize.

CHAPTER EIGHTY-SIX

Yale, the same day.

Gabriel had asked a male student to meet him at Yale, a German national named Berne Lange, with red hair and freckles. He was an affable young man who was a conscientious, if not brilliant, student. He arrived at Gabriel's small office at 9.35 pm, wearing tanned trousers and a turtleneck sweater on his lanky frame.

After what Stolarski had told him, and what he'd said to Carla about asking Hester to contact the FSB to search their own archives for Joseph Kazapov's service record, Gabriel had come up with an idea a few hours ago. It wasn't a particularly creative one, he knew, but it was an idea for all that. Besides, he had no further leads to go on at present.

Gabriel had consciously left the blinds open and he made Berne a cup of espresso using his portable coffee machine. He invited him to sit at his old writing desk, in his high-backed computer chair, telling him what he wanted. He asked him to keep it between them. There was nothing sinister about it, he said. It was simply an academic paper he was working on.

Berne said, 'Sure, Professor Hall. Does this mean I'm going to get a few extra marks this term?'

'No, Berne, it doesn't.'

Berne's pianist-like fingers moved nimbly over the laptop's keyboard.

He checked the wealth of historic newspaper archives online. He told Gabriel that the Berlin State Library, in conjunction with Germany's Centre for Contemporary History and the Fraunhofer Society, a research organization, had spent four years digitizing every issue of East Germany's newspapers published between 1945 and 1990, including *Neue Zeit, Berliner Zeitung* and *Neues Deutschland.*

Berne searched diligently. Gabriel refilled his coffee cup a couple of times and spent the rest of the time pacing the oak floorboards until Berne politely asked him to stop. Not wanting to distract him, he did so, and instead sat in an armchair and rubbed his upper lip with his forefinger.

A couple of hours later, Berne said, 'Wow.'

'You have something?'

'Listen to this, Professor. It's about the workers' uprising on June seventeenth, 1953. The East German government called in Soviet tanks and open fired on crowds of peaceful demonstrators. An edition of the *Berliner Zeitung* blamed the uprising on fascist elements from West Berlin. *Neues Deutschland* said the government had protected the city from agents of foreign powers. Outrageous propaganda, huh. I won't find anything that compromises the laughable legitimacy of the Soviet Union here,' Berne said.

'Where else can we look?'

'There are several West German newspapers and periodicals online too.'

'I'm not sure. It's getting late,' Gabriel said.

'OK.'

Berne sounded disappointed.

'Just a little longer then,' Gabriel said. 'If you're sure?'

Berne nodded, without taking his eyes from the screen.

Berne found a site for *Der Spiegel*, the popular German weekly news magazine that had been founded in the late 1940s by a British Army officer and a former Wehrmacht radio operator. It was known for its investigative journalism. The site had records going back to its inception.

'Try up to 1960,' Gabriel said.

'It has a decent search facility.'

Three cups of espresso later, Berne said, 'Ah-hah.'

'Another workers' uprising?'

'No, Professor Hall.'

Gabriel moved over to the plasma screen.

'What is it?' he said.

'A human-interest story with potential political ramifications. It happened in West Berlin in 1954. There was one witness to a murder. That witness was an eight-year-old girl, the female victim's daughter. The child's name was Helma. It makes out there was a happy ending. She was adopted by a US military attaché and his wife, a man named Peter Honey. It appears that wasn't an uncommon practice. She got out of the enclave. There's mention of an affidavit by the mother, signed in 1945.'

Berne ran his finger down the online article and pointed to a name.

'There,' he said.

Gabriel squinted at the small font size.

'The name you're looking for, Professor.'

Gabriel saw the name: Joseph Kazapov.

CHAPTER EIGHTY-SEVEN

Virginia — Brussels, the next day.

The station wagon was parked under a flyover, next to an all but stagnant, coffee-coloured stream. The first thing Carla noticed was that her hands were cuffed to a steering wheel. She knew she'd been drugged. She felt nauseous, her vision blurred. She had little memory of how she'd gotten here.

Vaguely, she heard a police siren in the distance, but realized it was travelling away from her.

They're not coming for me, she thought.

'Nice sleep?'

The voice came from behind her. She tried to turn around, but the flex-cuffs restricted her movement. She only caught a glimpse of him. He looked big, but was nothing more than a dark bulk, without definition. She turned back to face forward and noticed that the sun was shining. The windscreen was smeared, and the sun created a glare effect. She squinted.

The car was uncomfortably warm and musty, even though the heater was off, and she bent her head down to wipe the sweat from her forehead. Somebody had dressed her in a white, disposable hazmat suit. She saw drops of blood on the sleeves, on that part of the whole-body garment covering her knees. The stench of her own sweat and the smell of the sweet aftershave coming from the man behind was repugnant.

'You've been a naughty girl.'

Tears flooded her eyes.

'You've got the wrong person,' she said.

'Why do people always say that?' he snorted. 'You know that's a lie. Don't go lying to me, naughty girl.'

She still had the wits to determine a Caucasian accent. A mountain accent, with a hint of a Californian twang.

'What do you want with me?'

'We're going for a walk.'

'I don't want to go for walk.'

She shook her head and sweat and nasal mucous flew off her skin.

'No, you'll walk.'

His tone didn't have a trace of uncertainty to it.

Sweet Mary, she thought. Help me Mother. Help me Virgin Mother.

But hers was a faith based on dogma and tradition, her prayers for a form of deliverance as half-hearted and learned as a child's.

*

He'd removed the flex-cuffs with a hunting knife and manhandled her from the car. The cuffs had been replaced with fresh ones. When she'd flopped to her knees from a mixture of disorientation, fatigue and a modicum of stubbornness, he'd dragged her up by the hair. Facing her, he'd led her down a grassy slope, preventing her from falling forward by his rough hands. The slope levelled off at the riverbank. She'd seen a scruffy heron flap its seemingly outsized wings and fly off, circling over the flyover to the thick woodland just beyond. She would have given anything, almost anything, to have sprouted wings.

The man was indeed huge, with thick, unwashed hair to his shoulders and a greying goatee. He wore stained jeans, dirty military boots, a denim vest with a black T-shirt underneath. He had tattooed blue dots for eyebrows and a black tarantula spider on each side of his thick neck. A large vein under the skin around his right temple looked like the outline of a curled-up earthworm.

He walked away from her and she saw the initials NLR tattooed on the back of his neck in between two sets of SS tattoos. A Nazi Lowrider. She'd seen him before.

Suddenly, she remembered where. He was the man that Gabriel Hall had spoken to outside Club 88 in Far Rockaway. The man he had said was named Jim Saunders. Momentarily, she felt betrayed.

He was bending over now, fixing what looked like a small digital camcorder onto a three-feet-high tripod that had been placed there when she'd been in her drug-induced sleep, she guessed. She wanted to cry out, but bit her lip instead, even as the photographs from the DVD floated through her mind, as potentially injurious to her sanity in those moments as slithers of asbestos would be to her lungs.

Through watery eyes she saw him walking back to her. She was on her knees on the grass where he'd placed her. He grabbed her by the hair again, lifted her half off the ground and pointed to the camcorder, thrusting her head towards it at the same time.

'You just keep looking at the lens.'

She nodded, whimpering.

'They told me to film you die. They told me to cut you. They said to tell you that you'd know how and where.'

'I have a daughter,' she said, green fluid dribbling from her nose.

'You want me to get the poultry shears now? You want me to?'

'No,' she said, her voice a whisper.

'You keep looking at the lens and you tell the story. You tell all of it and it'll end right then. In that moment.'

*

Three hours later, she was sitting naked in a wet room, with off-white tiles. She'd washed herself then scrubbed her body with a nylon nail brush, such that her skin was left mottled and tender.

She hugged her knees to her breasts now, her still dripping hair shielding her face, as if she was a foundling brought in from the wilds.

*

After work at a federal police office in Berlin, Finkel had driven to Brussels via Düsseldorf to meet with Robert Dubois in a downtown bar that was famous for its live jazz. It hadn't been a social visit. Dubois had told him, with a look of bewildered bleakness, that Carla Romero had gone into hiding. He hadn't seemed to know all the details, or if he had, he hadn't divulged them. He'd said simply that she'd rung him on his private smartphone.

Travelling home to Berlin, Finkel had experienced the beginnings of a tension in his shoulders that he hadn't put down to the long journey, and a nervy feeling which had jarred with his usual professional equanimity.

But upon his return to the capital, he'd gone immediately to a somewhat nefarious pensioner he'd come across in his time in GSG 9, a wizened-looking man with extravagant eyebrows who lived in a near dilapidated cottage in Potsdam. The man had worked for the former East German Ministry for State Security, the Stasi, and Finkel had procured for himself an object once used to pass secrets from the French to the

Soviet sector of Berlin in the days before the wall had been demolished by popular demand.

That purchase had not fully abated his nervousness, nor had it cured the tension, but it had eased them, although in a manner that a civilian would have found morbid, defeatist even.

CHAPTER EIGHTY-EIGHT

California, the next day.

The main house had a red-tiled roof, a tasteful colonnade and a cream façade. It was a five acre site, with three guest houses, two swimming pools, a tennis court, and well-tended gardens. The residential estate was surrounded by a wall that was fifteen feet high, the entrance an electronically controlled, wrought-iron gate.

Gabriel had asked Sam Cartwright to locate the whereabouts of the woman that Berne had read about online, named Helma. By now she would be a septuagenarian, if she was still alive. He'd given Sam the details of her legal parents, Peter and Mary Honey. Sam had located her relatively quickly, and commented that it was the easiest assignment he'd had in weeks, so he wouldn't be sending an invoice. Instead, Gabriel could buy him a couple of beers the next time they saw each other. Gabriel had felt it would be impolite to argue.

Sam had said that Helma's parents had changed her given name, that she was now named Barbara. She'd been married to a Wall Street banker and was seriously rich. Old money and new. The banker's name was Walt Murray He'd died of a heart attack on a golf course three years

409

ago, and Mrs Barbara Murray now lived in the Coachella Valley area of California, near Palm Springs.

Feeling the sweat against his baseball cap, the visor shielding his eyes from the intense sunlight, Gabriel walked up the drive of sandstone paving slabs towards the gate, noticing the tips of Chilean mesquites and willow acacia.

As he rang the gate's intercom, a blood-red open-top sports car passed by, the waft of air welcomed.

'State your business,' a male voice said.

'My name is Gabriel Hall. I'm a New York attorney. I'm here to see Mrs Barbara Murray.'

Following a pause, the voice said, 'You're not on our list of appointments.'

'It's very important,' he said.

'Ring and make an appointment and take your hat off.'

Gabriel removed his baseball cap.

'Tell Mrs Murray it's about her father.'

There was silence for a few seconds.

'Wait there.'

Gabriel wondered why the security was as hot as the weather, despite Barbara Murray's wealth.

A couple of minutes later, Gabriel watched a slim young woman stroll down the drive towards him. She wore a canary yellow T-shirt and shorts. Her blonde hair was cut in a messy bob.

When she reached the other side of the gate, he said, 'You don't look like security.'

'No. I'm Mrs Murray's assistant. I'm also her accountant.'

He noticed her gleaming white teeth, a hint of make-up. She had a laminated identity badge hanging between her breasts. Her name was Candy Shinwell.

Smiling, he handed her his business card.

'People can buy these for the price of a coffee,' she said.

'That's true. But I'm not a fake.'

'Really? You look like a smartass conman to me.'

Gabriel forced a smile. 'Ouch.'

Grinning cynically, she said, 'I'm going to call security unless you're out of here real quick.'

'Why didn't they come down?'

'They watch screens. They have low IQs. They can't tell the difference between a lawyer and someone who wants to sell my employer a shitty insurance policy.'

'You always so spiky, Ms Shinwell?'

'I worked in Washington for three years. I saw your kind every hour of every day. Good day, Mr Hall, assuming that's your real name.'

She turned on her heels and began to walk up the slight incline of the drive that was flanked at the top by chitalpa, with their lush pink blooms.

'Hey, gatekeeper,' Gabriel called out.

She looked back, her face scrunched up. 'What's with you?'

'Give this to Mrs Murray,' he said, thrusting a white envelope through the bars. 'She'll want to read it. You'll know that the twenty-third amendment doesn't grant the residents of the District of Columbia representation in Congress,' he said, hoping to prove his credentials as a lawyer. 'Did that bother you?'

'You're persistent. I'll give you that.'

'Give it to her. And don't read it on the way,' he said.

She walked back, snatched the envelope from him and glanced at it. 'If you're some kind of nut, I'll call the police.'

'Just give it to her.'

Three minutes later the gate opened.

CHAPTER EIGHTY-NINE

Ms Shinwell led Gabriel into a naturally well-lit room that he took for a study, then left without speaking. There were silver-framed photographs on what looked like an antique desk of French design, photographs of smiling family faces. There was one that he guessed was Mrs Murray in an haute couture evening dress of emerald-green silk, with her tanned husband sporting a tailored white dinner jacket.

His eyes shifted to the wall-to-ceiling glass doors and the terrace beyond, which was festooned with climbing vines and clematis. A couple of marble cherubs stood on plinths beside an ornamental pond. Mrs Murray was living in rare splendour, he thought.

A few seconds later, the woman in the photograph opened the door. She had dyed auburn hair and her skin was clear and unlined. She wore a beige trouser suit that hugged her trim body. Gabriel figured she'd kept a plastic surgeon busy for years. She sat on a pearl-white couch.

'Please sit down,' she said.

'Thank you.'

He settled himself into a doughnut-shaped rattan wicker chair with massive cushions.

'My assistant says it's about money. *Is* it about money, Mr Hall?' she said, glancing at his business card in her hand.

'Money?'

'I've read the note. Are you going to blackmail me?' she said, her eyes fixed on him.

'Of course not, Mrs Murray.'

Her head moved slightly to one side.

'So, how did you find me?'

'A private investigator I use professionally. He doesn't know anything, in case you're worried.'

He saw her body shift nervously.

'I talked with a Jewish man who told me that his Polish brother was sent to a Soviet forced labour camp after the war. A uranium mine. Part of the Gulag. A lingering death sentence.'

'That's tragic, I'm sure. But what does it have to do with me?'

Her eyes betrayed her unease.

'The man responsible was a lieutenant in the NKVD. Your biological father. Joseph Kazapov.'

She blinked, twice. He saw her clench her right hand.

They talked for half an hour. She had the type of intelligence that was born of experience rather than an expensive education. But there was an undeniable vulnerability there too, Gabriel thought. He told her as much of his own story as he could, and had felt good for doing so. He told her about the online edition of *Der Spiegel*. She'd looked at first sympathetic, then ashamed. She'd opened up to him, and after she'd done so, he understood why the security was so tight.

She got up and walked over to a walnut cabinet. She unlocked a drawer with a brass key, took out a large envelope and handed it to him.

'A copy of my birth mother's one-page affidavit. Brigitte Bayer. A black and white photograph of him in his NKVD uniform. I don't know why

I've kept them so long. Perhaps you are the reason, Mr Hall.' She looked out to the terrace. 'I don't know what he calls himself now, or where he lives. I have no desire to see him, of course. Quite the contrary, in fact. I hope and pray you find him. When you get to my age, you don't care about scandal anymore. It doesn't frighten you. But *he* still does.'

'So, he's definitely still alive?'

She nodded. 'Up until about eight months ago, yes.'

'But you haven't seen him since 1954 in Berlin?'

'Do you want me to sign an affidavit too, Mr Hall?'

He looked down at the parquet flooring momentarily.

'No. That won't be necessary. But can you think of any reason why he's doing what he's doing, assuming he's responsible?' he said.

He had to remind himself that he still had no evidence at all, and part of him found his own question a little obscene because of it.

She looked morose, her head bowed.

'You've read the article,' she said. 'What else is there to know? I believe he's insane.'

Gabriel thanked her and left, thinking that was too simple an explanation, even if he did manage to prove Kazapov's guilt. But the fact that there was no doubt now that he'd killed Brigitte Bayer, and that he was alive was something, at least.

*

Gabriel was sitting in the back of a cab, travelling to Palm Springs International Airport, two miles east of the desert resort city, to board one of a meagre number of scheduled flights at that time of year to JFK. The turquoise sky was flecked by a few high, translucent clouds, the air conditioning evaporating the film of sweat that had covered his body within a minute of exposure to the heat. He studied the folds of skin on the middle-aged driver's neck, that reminded him of a slab of pork belly.

He'd read the affidavit, which had been translated into English. He'd studied the old photograph. Joseph Kazapov just looked like a skinny young man. It offered no clue as to what he would look like now, or how he might be identified, unless the man was standing naked in front of him — the document referred to a long scar on his shoulder.

The mobile phone Carla had given him rang and he fetched it out from the pocket of his black trousers.

'Gabriel Hall?'

It was a man's voice. One he didn't recognize. A gruff French accent, he believed. He didn't know how to react, so he kept silent.

'Where did she give you the phone?'

Gabriel didn't answer.

'Tell me, please.'

Gabriel felt trapped. If he said where, he could be putting Carla in danger. If he said nothing, he could be missing an opportunity *and* putting her in danger. Thinking of Sangmu, he made up his mind.

'In southwest Connecticut. A few miles from Yale.'

'Thank you. My name is Robert Dubois. I'm in Brussels. There's been a breakthrough. I can't discuss an ongoing investigation on the phone, even one that is likely clean.'

Gabriel felt numb, but he remembered Carla mentioning the Belgian federal police officer. He knew most Belgians spoke French as a first language. But why wasn't *she* ringing him? As if reading his thoughts, Dubois clarified the position.

'Carla is in hiding. She was threatened by Jim Saunders, the man the late Johnny Hockey asked you to give a message to at Club 88 in Far Rockaway. Don't worry. She's in an FBI safe house. She is well protected. She gave me this number and asked me to inform you of these things.'

Confused and more than a little nervous, Gabriel put his free hand to his forehead and began to massage it with his palm.

'Will you come to Brussels? I will meet with you.'

'For what purpose?'

'I can't discuss it, as I said. But I have contacts with the German federal police, as you would expect. In Berlin, to be precise.'

Gabriel exhaled deeply and felt his hand trembling. The sweat reappeared.

'Can you just tell me if…if someone's died. I need to know,' he said.

'No one has died, Mr Hall.'

'Thank God.'

'If there if a God, Mr Hall, He played no part in this, unless He is a diabolical entity. Will you come? I'll let you know the details.'

'Of course I will.'

'One more thing, Mr Hall. Carla told me to tell you that the FSB informed her boss that Joseph Kazapov died in a town called Oranienburg in Brandenburg in 1945, just after the formal surrender of Berlin.'

CHAPTER NINTY

Berlin, the same day.

It was Sunday, and Finkel had just watched a subtitled Chinese martial arts film at a theatre off Oranienburger Strasse that still had metal ashtrays screwed to the backs of the wine-coloured seats. He'd had a fizzy drink and popcorn.

He left the shabby art nouveau building, cleared his throat and inhaled the warm afternoon air. He walked along the uncluttered pavement to an outdoor parking lot a short distance away, replaying the balletic fight scenes and lavish imagery in his mind. He'd loved martial arts films since his teenage years. Then it had been an ideal. Now it was escapism.

There were a few vehicles scattered about, but apart from a middle-aged woman placing a bag of groceries into the boot of her small car, he seemed to be alone. He decided to make a call before driving home via an off licence. He'd drink a few beers and go to bed early. He lived with his wife of ten years, Trudi, and their two daughters, in a spacious, three-bedroom apartment on the edge of a recreational park in Berlin.

Watching the woman get into her car and reverse, he took out his smartphone from a back pocket. Trudi and his girls had gone hiking in the French ski resort of Chamonix. He and Trudi had a good marriage.

Trudi was a devoted mother and their sex life had gone from eager to experimental, which pleased him. He considered himself a fortunate man.

Now his wife's smartphone was answered.

'Hallo,' Trudi said.

'How's it going there?'

'Fantastic. You should've come with us.'

'Are the girls missing me?' Finkel said.

'Of course, darling.' She snickered. 'They have little crushes on one particular Italian tour guide. Don't tell them I said that.'

'Can't wait to see you all.'

She put the girls on and he told them he loved them, and they kissed down the phone. The call ended with all three of them saying 'Tschüss' to him in unison.

A small bird landed about ten feet from him. A sparrow, its wing injured, the primary feathers touching the ground. It hopped about in the sunlight, attempting to fly, but only managed about three yards before falling to the ground. He suddenly felt alone. He turned, pressed the key fob and strolled towards his red sedan. He pulled on the door handle, bent down to get in.

'Don't turn round. If have concealed weapon, lose it.'

It was a woman's voice. Eastern European. Likely Russian, he thought. It was a serious voice. He knew when to take someone seriously and when to call their bluff.

He was wearing a short-sleeved shirt and blue jeans, so he guessed she could see he didn't have a pistol.

'I have a pocket knife,' he said.

'Lose it.'

Feeling the first tendrils of panic, he put his hand in his front, right-hand pocket and took out the small knife, its steel blade folded into the handle, and with it the object he'd acquired in Potsdam after his meeting with Robert Dubois.

He tossed the knife to the side and, as it landed, he coughed and put his hand to his mouth and swallowed. He immediately put his hands up and said he felt faint, hoping that she hadn't seen what he'd done and wanting to appear timid.

'You Western cops. Pussies. Yes?' she said.

He breathed slow and hard. He still hadn't seen her face or how many others might be with her. He guessed she had others with her or was armed herself.

'Hands on roof. Wife and girls be home soon. So, no hero. OK, cop?'

He gritted his teeth and nodded.

CHAPTER NINTY-ONE

The farm, near Potsdam.

Finkel had been bundled into the back of a silver van at the parking lot, his hands and feet secured with nylon flex-cuffs. Black gaffer tape had been wrapped several times around his quivering mouth and a hood that had smelled of rotten apples placed over his sweaty head. His shoes had been removed, his watch, smartphone, key fob, wallet and wedding ring all taken.

By the time he arrived at his unknown destination, he'd calculated that he'd been driven for less than an hour. Upon arrival, someone had dragged him by his extended arms across what felt like cobblestones. A door had banged open, then another. He'd been flung to the floor and pulled by his feet over a cold surface before yet another door had opened loudly. They'd thrown him down a flight of steps then, and he'd lost consciousness when his head first hit the natural stone.

*

A cold sweat covered his naked and trembling body now. He heard someone enter the room, which he couldn't discern in any meaningful detail. His mouth tasted of metal, his head throbbed. His cracked skull had, in fact, shifted to an abnormal position, such that it protruded from his forehead, giving him the grotesque look of an extinct humanoid.

'You look older. Uglier.'

He recognized the voice as the woman at the parking lot, but he struggled to understand what had been said. She squatted down by his head and jabbed one of her fingers into the pressure point under his Adam's apple, where the trachea passed just under the surface of the skin. He gasped and panted. The shock of the sudden pain kick-started his senses, as he guessed was its purpose.

She stood up. She wore a red sports vest that showed her biceps and forearms lined with visible veins, as if she'd wrapped them in ivy leaves. Hands akimbo, her beautiful mouth cracked a lazy grin.

'I keep you alive for whole week with blood transfusion and drug. Then your wife and daughters suffer same. I promise you this, cop.'

Finkel heard her even as he heard a grating noise inside his head, as if his cranium had become active tectonic plates. The fact that she knew about his family, that she'd threatened to torture them, terrified him and he became almost immediately compliant. All this was unnecessary. He'd tell her what she wanted to know. He'd tell her anything, now.

The woman took a long pair of scissors from her back pocket and bent down again.

'Close eyes,' she said.

*

The cellar smelled like a rodent's cage. Finkel lay in his own half-congealed blood, barely conscious. Before Fury had taken his lips, he'd said he had no idea of the old man's name, except that he was known by some as Snow Lion. A serial killer that had never been prosecuted for a crime. He lived in Berlin, the Chechen had said. He confessed that he'd given an up-to-date photo of the Chechen to Robert Dubois, a Belgian police officer, to hand on to Carla Romero, an FBI agent. Dubois' investigation wasn't linked to any international organization like Interpol, he'd said, adding that their work hadn't been sanctioned by any cross-border initiative. They were acting out of moral outrage, he'd said, and alone.

An intended plea for his life had been reduced to a mere muffled word that had degenerated into a pitiable wheeze. A thought of remarkable clarity, given the state he'd been in, had risen above the maelstrom: he would die here, in his own filth.

What had been left of his rational mind had deserted him then. He'd felt something on his throat. He hadn't known what it was. It had pressed harder. It had not relented. His starved lungs had felt as if they would burst out of his sternum. He'd dry retched. His final sensation had been of a petrifying descent into oblivion.

*

The old man had told Vezzani to order Fury to dismember Finkel's corpse, weigh down the body parts and dump them in a local freshwater lake that he knew of. The lungfish and catfish it was stocked with were voracious carnivores, it was said. There'd be nothing left to identify by means of DNA before long. He couldn't afford to have the corpse disposed of at the farm. He didn't want cadaver dogs finding it in the forest. In the circumstances, he'd deemed the lake the best option.

Finkel had been the fifth person he'd murdered by proxy in just a few days. The risk of Hockey remaining in prison had been too high. As Vezzani had said, he could have chosen to speak out. He'd doubted it, but he *could* have. He had been Vezzani's choice, but one he himself had agreed with. Another smokescreen to hide his identity. Fury had said that Hockey's Russian murderer was already serving multiple life sentences, and it would be his family that would benefit from the payments that Vezzani would organize. The young woman, Charlene Rimes, had little more worth than a domestic animal.

But he considered now Billy Joe Anderson and the motorcycle thug, Jim Saunders. The neo-Nazis. They were dead too, Saunders by a recent hit that Vezzani had arranged. His body had been chopped up and buried in Arizona. Or had it been New Mexico? He didn't know the details. He didn't need to. It was just part of a clean-up, which hadn't finished yet.

The neo-Nazis were odd beings, he thought. He regarded them as ridiculous shadows of those they wished to emulate. The Nazis had killed with a scientific purpose, with a spiritual intensity, with a craving for death that he'd not seen since they sought to rule the earth. With the proliferation of nuclear weapons, he doubted their malign ambition would ever be replicated. Total war in the modern age meant destruction for all combatants and their families, after all.

CHAPTER NINTY-TWO

Brooklyn Heights — Washington DC, the next day.

Gabriel was still worried about the call from Robert Dubois, not least because of what he'd said about Carla, and the fact that the FSB had stated that Joseph Kazapov had died seventy years ago. He wondered who'd been lying and why. Was the FSB protecting Kazapov out of some misplaced loyalty? Had Barbara Murray been duped? Stolarski too? And what was the breakthrough in the investigation? Had Dubois been convinced by new evidence that Joseph Kazapov had survived the war, that he lived still? Had he been found? Was Dubois luring him into something? Had Sangmu been found?

He was catching an early flight to Brussels the next day and rather than waste the intervening time asking himself the same questions, which after all he couldn't answer, he'd decided to try to find out the answer to the one question that didn't present any conflicting evidence. There wasn't any evidence at all, in fact. That question was, what was the motivation for the killing of young Kalmyk women? Following the success online that Berne Lange had enjoyed, Gabriel decided to check what other online sources there might be.

Sitting in his study area, he viewed on his laptop a black and white film of Kalmyks in Germany in the 1950s, likely collaborators and their families that had escaped from the Soviets, he thought. The films showed unique and fascinating footage of their daily lives and Buddhist worship. He'd wondered, briefly, if he'd been watching a victim of Snow Lion.

Due to his discussions with Bronislaw Stolarski and Barbara Murray, together with his own rising suspicions, he was as sure as he could be that the historic disappearances of the Kalmyk girls, including his niece, Sangmu, weren't the result of a random hatred. Something personal *had* happened to the murderer, decades ago. He had more than an inkling now that it was linked to something earlier than the 1950's, that something had happened during World War Two. So many terrible things had happened then that it seemed like a good place to start.

Now, he clicked on the website of the United States Memorial Holocaust Museum in Washington DC. After a rudimentary search, he read an extraordinary fact that made him sit up and shake his head.

The museum had obtained documents from the Kalmyk Republic of the Russian Federation. The reports detailed seven previously unknown mass executions of Jews and other Russians in the republic during World War Two. The massacres had been conducted by Einsatzgruppe D, during the republic's occupation by German and Romanian armies between August and December 1942. The documents had been held previously in the Kalmyk state archives.

Gabriel read that the archives included a list of names of victims, eyewitness testimonies and exhumation reports of mass graves. The site also stated that before World War Two, only a few Jews had lived in Kalmykia. Following the Nazi invasion of the Soviet Union, hundreds of Jews had fled there, seeking refuge. But the Nazis had been as tenacious in their desire to exterminate European Jewry as they'd been grimly efficient. An estimated 700 Jews had been murdered by the Germans and their collaborators in Kalmykia.

The museum's library and archives were available to the public in set-aside reading rooms. Gabriel thought he had the option of searching further online or paying for an in-situ research assistant. But after accessing the relevant webpages, he realized that the details were limited.

The reading rooms were on the fifth floor of the museum building and were open to the public on weekdays from 10.00 am to 5.00 pm, he read. It wasn't necessary to make an appointment, but he rang ahead as suggested and asked one of the reference staff to reserve the specific materials he wanted to view. He'd decided to drive down to the capital and do the research himself.

He'd learned from the site that there was no single list of civilian victims or survivors of the war, and normally tracing an individual through the Holocaust entailed searching through a variety of sources, beginning with the name of the town the person had resided in before the war. At least he didn't have *that* to contend with, he thought.

He decided to change his airline ticket, to fly out of Washington instead of Boston on a direct Lufthansa flight.

*

The United States Holocaust Memorial Museum was America's national institution for the study and dissemination of Holocaust history, and served as the country's memorial to the millions of victims murdered and otherwise oppressed during that period. It opened in April 1993, since when the museum had been visited by more than 15,000,000 people, all of whom were encouraged to reflect upon the moral issues in the context of their own lives.

The museum was adjacent to the National Mall in the south-west of the capital, its entrance a neoclassical portico on Fourteenth Street. Upon entering, Gabriel completed a form and showed his photo ID in the form of his driver's licence.

The interior was evocative of those dark times. There was a replica of a freight wagon used to transport Jews to the death camps, a shaft of light cutting through it. There was the Tower of Faces, showing Jewish women in evening dresses and their everyday lives before their annihilation, an image that was devastating in its simplicity.

The museum had hundreds of staff and volunteers, almost 13,000 artefacts and 40,000,000 pages of archived documents. Gabriel sat at a table with a fixed reading light. He had located four relevant video and document archives under the search for 'Kalmyk'. One was a film of the Germans advancing towards Stalingrad, although the exact location was unclear. Another was a foreign language oral history interview, documenting, among other things, the increased use of violence by the Kalmyks in 1942. The second film focused on the ethnic diversity of the Soviet Union at the outbreak of the war, including Kalmyks. The fourth archive, which he'd seen referred to online but had been limited there to a summary, was entitled: *Selected Records of the Soviet State Extraordinary Commission to Investigate the Crimes Committed by the Nazis and their Collaborators on the territory of the Kalmyk Republic during WWII.* This was the document that had recently come to light. The researcher he'd rung had stated that the hard copies contained lists of both Jewish and other Soviets who had perished or had gone missing.

The woman who brought the three files wore conservative clothes, spoke in whispers and had the palest skin he'd seen in years. He began looking for one surname — Kazapov.

After a short time, he found what he was looking for. He checked it twice. He even took a photo of it on his smartphone. Four women with the surname Kazapova, the female form of Kazapov, were recorded missing in Kalmykia. The person who'd documented their names was Lieutenant Joseph Kazapov of the NKVD, attached to the state commission in Kalmykia.

Gabriel knew from his experience as a trial lawyer that sometimes people claimed to have seen things that in fact, they hadn't. They said people had told them things, when they hadn't. Sometimes they were simply mistaken. Sometimes they were simply lying, for whatever reason. So, in his business, he always needed at least two pieces of unconnected evidence to verify a fact. But the translated words of Joseph Kazapov alone were enough in this regard, he decided.

No one had made the connection but him, he knew.

His mouth felt parched, his stomach ached. He remained seated at the wooden desk, with his palm to his bowed forehead. He didn't congratulate himself. He didn't even want to move. He sat there for five minutes or more, wondering what it all meant for Sangmu — if in fact Kazapov was alive.

In truth, he didn't doubt it now.

CHAPTER NINETY-THREE

Washington DC — Brussels, the same day.

Sitting exhausted at a low-slung table in a hotel lobby at the Ronald Reagan Washington National Airport, Gabriel looked down at the envelopes in front of him, which he had placed like a span of outsized playing cards on the glass table top. They looked like relics, from a time before email.

One was addressed to Abe Murray, the NYPD officer who'd told him about the DVD and had been involved in the initial unsuccessful investigation into Sangmu's disappearance. Another was for Sam Cartwright, the private investigator. Another five envelopes were addressed to lawyers and academics he knew well. These five envelopes were accompanied by an explanatory note asking the lawyers and academics to pass by hand the envelopes they had received from him onto someone they knew well enough to trust. The only other criteria for choosing whom the lawyers and academics would pass their envelopes onto was that they weren't also known to Gabriel. They had to be strangers to him. The explanatory note stated that this was essential. It also stated that the lawyers and academics should ensure that their chosen recipients of the envelope should be instructed not to open it under any circumstances.

They were simply custodians of it. The final instruction on the accompanying note was that if he, Gabriel, died or didn't contact them by telephone within one week, then they should retrieve the letters from their chosen recipients and read the contents themselves.

He took a gulp of red wine, wiped his mouth dry and wondered if the contents of the letters were in fact a harbinger of his own death. The conversation he'd had on the mobile phone with Robert Dubois unnerved him still. He couldn't say why exactly, except that he hadn't met the man and surely Carla would have tried to contact him personally, if she'd been able, despite what he'd said? Maybe it wasn't possible.

Carla had never shown him a photograph of Dubois. After Dubois told him that she'd gone to a safe house, he'd tried to find a picture of the Belgian online, without success. He'd guessed that was because Dubois was a federal police officer; it would've been foolish to have his face online, where anybody could find it easily.

Both the unanswered questions and what he'd discovered at the Holocaust museum had been sufficient motivation to write the letters. He had nothing to lose in doing so; if it was simply a matter of his imagination being overactive, the letters would never be opened.

He took another gulp of wine, the questions coming to him again, one after the other like radio waves. He forced his mind to where there was no sound, where no inner dialogue existed.

When he allowed his thoughts entry once more, they settled on his reason for doing all this.

He took out his smartphone and called a national courier service. The letters would be sent. He felt pangs of panic and self-doubt. Then, he felt a sense of cowardice encircle him like a shroud.

*

Robert Dubois was sitting on the polished wooden floor of his living room, with his back against a leather armchair. He was listening to vinyl on a record player he'd had since the early nineties. He was thinking about Carla, about how she must be feeling. About little Monize, too. He'd only met her once, when he'd gone to Washington ostensibly on official duty, but in fact just to see Carla. She'd seen through that and he'd had to promise not to do it again. He'd never wanted children of his own, but it didn't stop him worrying.

He was flung backwards, flipping in the air, the sound like a ten-wheel truck travelling at seventy miles per hour an inch from his face.

Lying on his front, his left arm dislocated beneath him, he struggled to breathe and sensed blood running down his face.

The controlled explosion had blown the cedar wood front door against the rear wall, where it had splintered for several inches at its centre, and shattered the protective glass of the single print that hung there. The room had erupted in violent shudders as the shockwave hurtled through it, the stench of cordite unmistakable.

Blearily, through wet eyes and a thin cloud of white smoke, he saw two black shapes loom over him like colossal ants. Having registered black fatigues, gas masks and shotgun muzzles, he passed out briefly.

CHAPTER NINETY-FOUR

Berlin, the next day.

Albert Müller, a heavy-boned Berliner in his early thirties with thinning blonde hair, liked to ski off-piste and swim alone in open water. Five yards from the bank of the isolated lake, executing a leisurely front crawl, his blue eyes covered with rubber goggles, he thought he saw something shimmering below. At first, he took it for a windscreen or shoal of silver fish. Curious, he trod water before diving down.

Then, at a depth of some fifteen feet, he was confronted by plastic bags affixed to boulders that lay among the algae-ridden weeds, an inquisitive perch nibbling at one of them. Resembling giant limpets, they were too heavy to lift. But then, he just about made out a human torso.

Near traumatized, he returned to the grassy bank and used his smartphone to call the Berliner Polizei, specifically Direktion 2, Spandau, rather than the local force. He told them that a dismembered corpse had been dumped in the lake.

*

The German police diver was a former Oberleutnant zur See in the Deutsche Marine, a man for whom water was as natural an enviroment now as it had been in the womb. Directed by Müller, he located four bags with his torch in less than a minute.

Two hours later, he severed the rope that linked the boulders to the bags with his diver's knife. The macabre contents were winched to the surface, whereupon they were transported in cold storage via a private ambulance to the local pathologist's office.

*

The pathologist was Pia Neumann, a fair-haired woman of rare beauty, who had represented her county in the 100m hurdles at the Beijing Olympics. During an initial autopsy, she deemed an examination of the stomach contents mandatory.

She used a scalpel on the torso as it lay on a stainless-steel gurney. If the stomach was empty, the victim had died more than six hours after a meal. The dissection of the stomach revealed traces of popcorn, and to her surprise, a small piece of latex that looked like the curled edge of a condom. She guessed the deceased was a drugs mule.

However, after easing it out with a pair of surgical tweezers, and upon closer examination, it became evident that it was in fact *not* a fragment of burst condom. It was a capsule, like those used for protein supplements, except this one was evidently not prone to dissolving. She used the scalpel to slice open the capsule.

It contained a tiny fragment. She made a cursory investigation of it with her microscope, which revealed the fragment to be a sliver of microfiche. To Pia Neumann, it was like finding buried Visigoth treasure.

*

Thirty minutes later, the microfiche had been read by a veteran officer in the Wasserschutzpolizei, the state water police. The minuscule writing stated the dead man's name, his social security number and his rank in GSG 9. If his body was found it meant that he'd been murdered, but he'd had time to swallow the capsule beforehand.

It also stated that his murderers were linked to a serial killer in Berlin, who was now a pensioner, but had no criminal record. He had a moniker: Snow Lion. It meant too that other men and women were in danger, among them, Raymond Dubois, a Belgian federal policer office. A pornographer known as the Chechen, who was known to be in the US, had sold a DVD belonging to the serial killer to an American, the deceased Jed Watson.

Flabbergasted by the discovery, the veteran called a commander in Spezialeinsatzkommandos, the specialized armed response units of the German state police forces, the equivalent of GSG 9 of the federal police. He told the commander that the dismembered corpse taken from the lake had been a federal police officer named Finkel.

*

When the special deployment commando rang the Brussels federal police, an officer there said that Robert Dubois had been abducted from his apartment in a military-style operation, and that a terrorist attack could not be ruled out.

CHAPTER NINETY-FIVE

Brussels, the same day.

Gabriel had agreed to meet Dubois at a named bar in the Grand Place. The Belgian had called him again on the disposable mobile phone given to him by Carla, this time a hundred yards or so from the hotel he was staying at. The hotel stood opposite a limestone Catholic church and an apartment building, with Juliet balconies. Dubois said he'd be wearing black jeans and a red polo shirt with matching trainers, and that he was clean-shaven.

It was 5.13 pm, the air still, the sun well-defined. A teenage string quintet played Mendelssohn at the entrance to the side street leading into the cobbled market square, and a small, appreciative crowd had gathered around them. The square was dominated by its edifices, the Gothic-style town hall, with its splendid bell tower, the elaborate colonnades of the king's house, and the baroque guildhalls, the sunlight reflecting off their golden embellishments.

Leaving the side street, Gabriel saw a long-limbed, wide-shouldered man, with black wavy hair sitting at a wooden table under an awning outside the bar proper. He wore black jeans and a red polo shirt, with trainers. Gabriel walked over to him and the Belgian stood up.

Gabriel stepped up onto the elevated decking, with its fixed tables and benches.

'Gabriel Hall?'

Gabriel nodded. He recognized the voice from the phone calls.

'It's good to meet you,' Dubois said.

'You too.'

They shook hands and sat down at the table that would've comfortably seated eight people. Gabriel caught a waft of Dubois's pungent aftershave. There was an elderly couple to their left and a Pekinese sniffed around the woman's shoes, irritatingly. A waiter of North African descent came over and placed a fresh dish of nuts on the table and they both ordered lager.

'Thank you for coming so far,' Dubois said. 'You should visit when the flower carpet is here. The cobbles are covered with a million multi-coloured begonias. It happens on the Feast of the Assumption.'

Gabriel shrugged. 'The flight was less than eight hours. What do you have for me?'

Dubois bent to his right and lifted a tanned-leather briefcase and placed it on its side on the table. He opened it and took out a smartphone.

'The German federal police have found Kalmyk girls at several addresses in Berlin. Remote houses and barns were raided on a tipoff. They were all alive.'

He thumbed in the passcode and handed the phone to Gabriel.

'Is one of them your niece?'

Gabriel hesitated at first, his neck muscles tightening. He flicked through the photographs of a dozen or more young women that all could have been from Kalmykia. As he did so, Dubois gave him what further information he said he could, which wasn't much, it had to be said.

Gabriel held out the phone to Dubois. 'She's not there.'

'It seems you've had a wasted journey. I'm sorry.'

'I realize you couldn't email them to me. I'm grateful to you.'

Dubois replaced the smartphone into the briefcase and put it under the bench. The waiter had arrived and placed the straight glasses bearing the alcohol brand on the table.

'Did the Germans arrest anyone?' Gabriel said.

Dubois shook his head.

'Nobody?'

'It appears the perpetrators had a tipoff, too,' Dubois said.

Gabriel observed Dubois with a serious expression. He said, 'I imagine the flower carpet is a glorious sight. But begonias symbolize a warning of future misfortunes, don't they? I'm not superstitious, Mr Dubois, but I am curious. Do you know who the old serial killer in Berlin is now?'

Dubois blinked twice. 'I don't,' he said.

For a split second, the Belgian's eyes betrayed a hint of fear. Something wasn't right. Something didn't gel.

'Well, I'll finish my drink and get a cab to the airport,' Gabriel said.

'As I said, I'm sorry.'

'Have you heard from Carla again?' Gabriel said.

'Not since she told me she'd gone into hiding and what I told you about the FSB.'

'Do you think the FSB are lying about Joseph Kazapov, or that their records are incorrect?'

Dubois's head tilted to the side. 'No, why would I?'

Gabriel took a drink.

'Were the begonias here when you first met her?' he said, after lowering the glass to the table.

'Met?'

'On official business. What else?'

Dubois cracked a half smile. 'That's an odd question.'

'Carla said she first met you here in the Grand Place.'

Dubois lifted the glass to his lips and drank.

'That's right,' he said. 'But it was June and there were no flowers.'

Gabriel leaned forward, with his elbows on the table. 'But you *didn't* meet her here, did you?'

The man looked at Gabriel, his teeth clenched.

'She said she first met you in Bruges. I guess Robert Dubois wouldn't forget that kind of detail. She leaves an impression. Who the hell are you?'

'I don't like your tone, Mr Hall.'

'I don't care. I've been around cops most of my adult life, and you're no cop.'

'I'm Belgian, not American.'

Gabriel nodded knowingly.

He said, 'I lied about Carla meeting Robert Dubois in Bruges. I don't know when or where she first met him. So, who are you?'

The man looked a little flustered. He got up, but Gabriel didn't feel threatened by him.

'Have a safe journey home, Mr Hall.'

CHAPTER NINTY-SIX

The secret prison, the same day.

Section Chief George Hester had had a call from a deputy director in the Criminal Justice Information Services Division of the FBI. The conversation had centred on intel from INTERPOL's National Central Bureau for the United States in Washington, which had instant access to databases known as the Criminal Information System, via the I-24/7 network. A notice, which was an alert of a suspected criminal, or a person linked to or of interest in an ongoing criminal investigation, had been issued by INTERPOL.

The notice in question had given a moniker, Snow Lion, together with a few sentences of explanation. The source of the information had been GSG 9 of the German Federal Police in Berlin. When the deputy director told Hester that the notice had described Carla Romero as being at high risk, he'd made a secure phone call, demanding action by those with real power. Carla and her daughter, Monize, had been missing for days.

After obtaining an official document, Hester had travelled back to the secret prison, masquerading as a military base, to speak with the Chechen, who was still there for his own protection and with his continuing consent.

*

Hester was sitting now at the same chair in the same facility. The Chechen sat across from him, as before, except this time Carla wasn't there. The Chechen wore military fatigues and had shaved off his goatee, his hair was cut short to his head. He looked younger, healthier. Hester put it down to the nutritious food he was no doubt eating, and the fact that there was a ban on alcohol and all drugs other than tobacco.

'They look to be treating you well,' Hester said.

The Chechen exposed the inside of his lower lip such that the corners of his mouth turned down, and he raised his eyebrows and shifted his head to the right: So-so.

'Where's the Amazon, the good-looking one?' he said.

Hester knew he was referring to Carla. 'She's busy.'

'She's in danger, isn't she?'

Hester forced himself not to clench his teeth.

He said, 'Do you know something?'

'I know you're here because you want more information on the serial killer and because you're prepared to give me something in return. That much I know.'

The Chechen grinned. He took a toothpick from behind his ear and snapped it between his fingers.

'If he has her, you'd better pray to your Christian God.'

'I didn't take you for a religious man,' Hester said.

'There are many Muslims in Chechnya. We have an old saying; it was only when they pulled at his ear that the donkey was reminded that he was a donkey.'

He grinned again.

Hester put his hand in his pocket, took out an official-looking piece of paper and pushed it across the table top.

'This is a promise of immunity from prosecution, signed by the

Deputy Attorney General. I want the location of the serial killer. All other details that you know. You'd better hope that we find him.'

The Chechen nodded. 'You're right. I don't want him free after this. But I don't know his name.'

'I didn't ask you his name. But you'll need to state yours for the paperwork. You will enter a witness protection programme. You will be given the sum of 45,000 dollars a year, US, and a house in Idaho. You will be under surveillance twenty-four-seven. There'll be restrictions on your movement. There isn't anything else. If we don't find him where you say he is, the deal is off.'

'It was eight years ago,' the Chechen said, his face betraying his unease.

'I don't care,' Hester said.

'It was a villa near Spandau. But he has a farm near Potsdam, too.'

Hester took out his smartphone.

'Show me,' he said.

CHAPTER NINTY-SEVEN

Brussels, the same day.

Gabriel was sure the man who'd just left hadn't been a Belgian police officer. He was sure he wasn't Robert Dubois, either. But in truth, he'd found the encounter with him unnerving, despite his bravado. He was used to dealing with criminals, but in the sanitized environment of his office, a police building, a prison, or courtroom. A place where he was safe and had the upper hand. Perhaps the man wasn't a criminal. What *was* he then?

He almost sniffed the clean air like a nervous animal as he checked the square. Shielded from the sunlight by the bar's awning, he had a fair view of the sightseers there, a diverse bunch. One stood out for no other reason than his physique was squat, and he was looking in the direction of the bar.

Gabriel stood up. The man pretending to be Dubois had tried to, what? Derail him? If he had, that meant that he was getting close to something significant. Or did they know that he had already discovered something significant? But how could they? The squat man was probably nobody anyhow, he decided.

He was duped into coming here, for sure, but what had just transpired wouldn't put him off the scent and they must have known that. Perhaps they didn't. But what now? If it was obvious he wasn't to be derailed, they may do something more permanent. The thought rattled him.

The squat man began to move towards the bar and Gabriel decided to move too. He put a twenty euro note under his glass and headed for the alleyway about ten yards to his left that he'd used to access the square. He would leave the Grand Place from there.

Then what? They'd already killed Hockey. Hadn't they?

The thought had seemingly come from nowhere, although he realized a second later that it had risen from his subconscious.

The alleyway was narrow and still busy. He convinced himself that no one would risk anything in the open and in daylight. He turned right at the end of the alley into a smaller square, and walked up the incline, past the bars and newsstands towards the underground railway station.

He didn't want to turn around. He didn't want to run. He couldn't be sure that the man was following him. He convinced himself he wasn't.

At the top of the square, the pink flagstones led to an arterial road. There was a pavement on the opposite side, bustling with inoffensive-looking people. It was as good a place as any to stand and hail a cab.

Then where? Home? What then?

He had to think. He had to decide.

Was Carla in a safe house? Was Joseph Kazapov really Snow Lion?

He turned. He couldn't help himself, his negative inner dialogue undeniable. The squat man was less than five yards away, shielding his eyes from the sunlight with a cupped hand, his face shadowed. He wore black trousers and a black button-down shirt.

Gabriel felt a spasm in his stomach. His mind was reeling.

'Gabriel Hall,' the squat man said.

Hearing the man call his name made Gabriel freeze, even though it wasn't odd that he knew his name. The man was one of them, wasn't he?

He heard a car skid to a halt behind him, the sound of horns blaring. Turning, he saw a red SUV with tinted windows at the side of the road. The car's back passenger door opened, and he squinted.

'Get in, Mr Hall.'

It was a man's voice.

Gabriel turned back around, feeling cornered. The squat man had reached the pavement. He looked to his left, and Gabriel followed his eyeline. Among the shoppers and businesspeople, a pair of police officers in blue fatigues and side caps, armed with submachine guns and holstered pistols, were walking towards them. The male officer was over six feet tall, the female officer broad at the hip.

'You can see her. Your call, Mr Hall.'

The voice, thickly accented, had come again from the car. The police officers turned down towards the small square Gabriel had just come from.

He hesitated for perhaps four seconds before he walked forward, sensing the squat man move behind him. He ducked down and manoeuvred himself onto the back seat. The squat man shut the door and walked to the front passenger door and got in. The doors were locked remotely.

The SUV drove out into the road and almost hit a black and gold delivery van. The bald van driver leaned out of the open window and snarled a tirade of curses. The SUV barrelled forward.

The squat man turned around, his eyes reminding Gabriel of a snake's. His heart was pounding and sweat broke out on his forehead. The squat man had a pistol in his hand, fixed with a bulbous suppressor. He didn't say anything. He put on a pair of aviator sunglasses with his free hand.

The SUV turned a sharp right down a backstreet, edged with natural stone warehouses and some derelict, three story buildings, with boarded-up mullion windows. The commercial bins that lined it were overflowing with black plastic bags, folded cardboard boxes and polythene sheets.

'You shouldn't have questioned him,' the driver said. 'He was wearing a wire.'

Gabriel knew he was referring to the man pretending to be Robert Dubois.

What did all this mean for him? For Sangmu? Would he see her again?

'Now when I stop the car, the gentlemen with the pistol is going to give you a pill. You're going to swallow it without a fuss. Got it?'

CHAPTER NINTY-EIGHT

The farm, the same day.

Gabriel's eyes were stinging, his face swollen and bloody. He was nauseous, his stomach churning. His body felt drained of fluid. His head was bowed, his neck flaccid.

He had a vague sense of dim light coming from behind him. He breathed with a disconcerting erraticism that sounded as if he'd contracted emphysema. He was naked apart from his long-sleeved shirt and boxer shorts.

'Yes, you're still alive, Mr Hall.'

The voice had a slight European accent, the tone low and a little frail. He couldn't see the man who'd spoken. But even in his depleted physical and mental state, he knew it was the old man, the serial killer. Snow Lion. He closed his eyes, a sense of desperation swamping him.

'Look at me. Mr Hall. Look at me.'

He heard faint footsteps behind him and a rough hand cupped his jaw and raised his head up. He blinked repeatedly. He wanted to puke, but he could not. With the hand still on his jaw, he felt a finger and thumb prise open his right eyelids and remain there.

In the faint yellow light an image formed, just in something like silhouette at first. Then the image was moving towards him, lowering to his eye level. He saw the bald head, the folds of skin at the neck. The all but non-existent lips. The slits for eyes. The man resembled an ancient tortoise. Gabriel didn't have the strength to grimace.

'I have something to show you, Mr Hall.'

The old man smiled.

'You will know that Da Vinci was more acquainted with anatomy than the anatomical universities of the Renaissance were. But do you know that the Florentine painter, Antonio Pollaiuolo, was the first person to skin corpses? Do you know that, Mr Hall?'

Gabriel did, but kept silent, his mind torturing him.

'This was no macabre fetish. He did it to gain knowledge of the connection between ligaments, tendon and muscles. Six hundred years ago, he felt compelled to perfect the nude. I know a man of your education and sensibility appreciates that degree of dedication to his art.'

How does he know about my love of art? Gabriel thought. He wondered if his house had been broken into and searched.

'And it worked. Pollaiuolo's engravings of the *Battle of Naked Men* is a lasting testament to that. Do you know the piece, Mr Hall? Do you?'

Gabriel knew the piece. The nude warriors appeared almost flayed, their musculature displayed in heroic and idealized poses. It was both beautiful and morbid. He didn't want to consider what that meant.

As if reading his mind, the old man said, 'I have recreated it, Mr Hall, for your critique and my amusement. César Vezzani will unveil it for us. But you must look, Mr Hall. You must. I insist that you look.'

Gabriel's jaw and eyelids were released, and he struggled to keep his head up and his eye open. The man behind him passed by and walked now to the left of the old man, a holstered pistol hanging down from under his right armpit. The man named César Vezzani was the squat man that had drugged him in the car. He switched on a bare lightbulb, revealing a white sheet that hung from a hook in the ceiling.

'An out of work actor met with you in the Grand Place. He believed he was going to spend the next few months in Bali. Now he is in another place,' the old man said.

The old man put on his glasses and eased himself up. He turned and nodded to Vezzani. Vezzani reached up, his hand grasping the sheet about midway. He pulled the sheet down with a jerk.

'Behold,' the old man said, with a flourish of his arms. 'The real Robert Dubois. What's left of him.'

Gabriel groaned.

The corpse hung from a web of chains attached to several karabiners. The chains were arranged such that the corpse looked puppet-like. An arm was up above the head, a thigh pivoted sideways at ninety degrees, the calf and foot dangling. It was a reddened monstrosity of a thing. The skin that hadn't been flayed fell loose and lacerated, exposing the muscle and other body tissues. Not one drop of blood dripped from the corpse. The head had not been skinned, but the visible tongue and lips were black, the eye sockets barren holes.

'Do you believe in predestination, Mr Hall?' the old man said.

Gabriel spat bile and strained to arch his back.

'No,' he said.

He realized that his ankles and wrists were tethered to a wooden, high-backed chair.

'But I believe that we all must pay for our sins,' he said.

'And what sins have you committed, Mr Hall?'

Gabriel could see now that the old man wore a loose-fitting, cream coloured shalwar kameez and a pair of tan slippers. He looked, what? Comfortable? At ease with himself?

'No sins, Mr Hall? At least none you are prepared to confess.'

He gestured towards the corpse with his hand.

'Who or what is this now? It is no longer human, is it? No, how could you call that human? What makes us human, Mr Hall? Compassion? Hate? Revenge? Philanthropy? War?'

He paused. 'Happiness, Aristotle said.'

He grinned.

'Love, perhaps. Does love make us human? Is it the driving force of our piffling existence? Did love bring you here, Mr Hall? Did it bring me here?'

He gestured to the corpse again, this time with his button chin.

'Did it bring that here?'

He interlinked his fingers, looked meditative.

'What about freedom? Does that make us human? Goethe said people fear freedom, that they seek out every means to rid themselves of it. I think he was right. They join political parties. They adopt religions. They sign up for clubs, for ideologies. They spend their time watching or reading what other people are doing or have created. They live by rules, customs, norms, conventions, traditions.'

He grimaced, and his hands went to his sides.

'No, Mr Hall, a perceived sense of freedom does not make us human. It is only the will to act that makes us human. The will to act that does not know any bounds. That is unrestrained. That is vigorous and bold. That is what makes us human or life is nothing at all. The will to act. The will to do what you desire. To do what must be done. I have learned that in my life or I have learned nothing. Nietzsche knew this. Stalin and Hitler, too. I think you understand this, Mr Hall. It brought you here. It brought us both here. And, so, we are more alike than you would have imagined. Aren't we?'

The room fell silent and, in that silence, nothing else on earth existed.

CHAPTER NINTY-NINE

The villa, the same day.

Carla and Monize were sitting on a stained mattress, with a small gas lamp in the corner of an otherwise empty cellar. It reeked of damp, of something resembling stale cabbage water. Carla had wrapped Monize in a musty duvet. She'd heard at least two distinct footfalls above her.

She'd named Finkel and Dubois to the old man, and had stated the motivation behind Gabriel's actions too. She knew that Finkel had a wife and two girls and she'd almost vomited after she'd betrayed him. Following an initial reticence, the old man had seemed content. There hadn't been a safe house. There hadn't been any action by the FBI, simply because she hadn't informed them of the attack by Jim Saunders, as he'd ordered.

Monize had been kidnapped the night she'd been Tasered, and she had come here to Berlin after being told what would happen to her daughter if she hadn't. She'd known that it hadn't been an outrageous threat.

She was questioning her judgment now, but decided morosely that she hadn't had a choice. If things turned bad, at least she would be with her daughter when the end came, although that thought made her feel faint.

The Russian woman guarding them had muscles that bulged against her light blue blouse and jeans. She stared hard at Carla, bunched her shoulders and moved uneasily from side to side, as if she was deep in thought.

'How long do we have to stay here? I've done all that was asked of me,' Carla said.

The Russian walked over to her and crouched down. She smoothed Monize's hair and Carla frowned. She saw the span of the woman's powerful thighs. Then she put her large hands on Carla's thighs, too high up to be comfortable. The woman's eyes were vivid green.

Carla shuddered.

'My face scarred,' the Russian said.

'Is it?'

Carla's body tensed. She felt tears form in her eyes, although she held them back for Monize's sake.

'Men are pigs. Yes?'

'Yes. If you say so,' Carla said.

'I do.'

Carla flinched, suspecting the Russian would slap her but without knowing why, except close-up her presence bordered on malevolent.

'My uncle did things to me when I was young girl.'

'What?'

'You know what things. And he burn me with hot iron.'

'That's awful,' Carla said.

'Awful, yes. I smash hot iron in face when he lie on floor. Again, and again. I lose count. His face stick to floor.'

'Why are you telling me this?'

Carla saw the woman put her hand in her back pocket and take out a pair of hairdresser's scissors. She tapped them on Monize's nose.

Carla started to weep freely and placed her hands over her daughter's ears, felt her shaking.

'Maybe I take something from little girl. Maybe not.'

Through her tears, Carla saw the woman scan her daughter's body.

'Maybe I take something, so you remember to leave it here. In room. It stays here. Yes?'

'Please don't hurt her. Please don't.'

'When it over, you forget me. Yes?'

'Yes. I swear,' Carla said, nodding involuntarily.

'You forget?'

'Yes.'

'Never speak of me.'

'No. Never,' Carla said, shaking herself now.

'They say I Fury. They think I not know. But I know. When I play, it not nice. People die screaming. It stays here. Yes?'

'I don't know you. I won't say anything. Just please don't hurt my little girl.'

'If it don't stay here, you and daughter die. Slow. I come when it dark, wherever you are. You die in your own shit like cattle.'

CHAPTER ONE HUNDRED

The farm.

Gabriel felt the tight nylon of the disposable restraints chaff his skin every time he shifted on the hard seat. He wanted to ask about Sangmu, but checked himself, unable in that moment to face the consequences of her death, if he'd been lied to by the man that had driven him here.

The old man looked a little whimsical.

He said, 'I should tell you that Special Agent Carla Romero is in Berlin. She is my guest. Her daughter is my guest here too. A mother's love, or should I say a *good* mother's love, is so powerful that betraying transient acquaintances to protect the child is as easy as shooing away a cat from the dinner table.'

Gabriel knew then that Carla had told the old man about his love of art. But what else had she told him? Everything?

The old man smiled eerily and motioned to Vezzani to cover up the macabre remains of Robert Dubois.

'Don't hurt them,' Gabriel said.

'I don't intend to. Not if the mother does as she's told. But you're pleading for yourself as well, aren't you, Mr Hall? I know everyone pleads when confronted with the inevitable. That's the great paradox.'

The old man wheezed and scratched his throat.

'You thought that your investigations would lead you to find your Kalmyk niece, Sangmu. Is that not so?'

Gabriel sensed his body start to recover from its dulled state, the nerves tingling, the muscles twitching, his head clearing. Carla had betrayed him. He knew why. He decided to go on the offensive.

'I know why you're doing this,' he said. 'I know more than you think I know.'

Vezzani walked towards him, his fists clenched.

'Let him speak,' the old man said.

'A man I met said his brother remembered you from the Battle of Berlin. The bunker. Remember the bunker? The brother's name was Icchak Stolarski.'

The old man looked deep in thought.

'Tell me what else he said.'

'That his brother saw things. A mummified hand and a butchered corpse. He dropped a crate and you told him not to worry about it. But you sent him to the Gulag. His brother told me your name.'

'Vezzani, leave us,' the old man said.

Vezzani's face was edged with concern.

'Leave us.'

Vezzani walked from the room, a look of puzzlement replacing the worry.

Gabriel knew that he'd gained the old man's attention.

'Why do you say these things?' the old man said.

'Carla and Monize. Tell me that not a hair has been touched.'

'Not a hair,' the old man said.

Gabriel knew he had to face his worst fears now.

'I want to know where my niece is.'

'She's almost eighteen. Is she not? Now tell me why you say these things. I will not ask you again,' the old man said.

Gabriel spat some green fluid onto the floor, raised his head and stared at the old man. 'I've sent letters to lawyers with instructions to send them to other lawyers. There are strict instructions that if I die or go missing for a week, the letters are to be opened. I found connections.'

'Letters. How quaint and anachronistic. Even if I believed you, as a lawyer you know you had no evidence against me when you wrote them. What use will they be?'

He walked towards Gabriel, his palms up.

'And so, what are the connections you think you've found?'

'You're not German, you're Russian,' Gabriel said. 'You kill Kalmyk girls out of revenge for what happened in Kalmykia in World War Two.'

Gabriel didn't know this for certain, but it wasn't much of a leap. He knew Kazapov's mother and sisters had gone missing there. What other logical explanation was there?

'You were driven insane by it, by all the horrors you no doubt experienced as an officer in the NKVD. You're Snow Lion. Your name is Joseph Kazapov. I came to find my niece, sure. But I came to stop you too, because no one else can. This has to stop,'

The old man didn't flinch.

'Go on,' he said.

'That's all I'm telling you for now. Tell me where my niece is.'

A faint grin passed over the old man's all but lipless mouth.

'She is here, Mr Hall.'

CHAPTER ONE HUNDRED AND ONE

Bonn, the same day.

The state police had agreed that the federal GSG 9 should be allowed to storm both the villa and the farm. One of their own had died, after all.

The airborne operations sub group of GSG 9 was based in Sankt Augustin-Hangelar, five miles north-east of Bonn, and 370 miles south-west of Berlin. Twenty-four assaulters had received a hasty briefing there, including satellite imagery of the insert points.

There'd been no time for the usual perusal of detailed situation maps and plans of the buildings. There hadn't been any information with which to do the usual analysis of the target's personality and threat assessment either; the special ops mission had been approved by the Federal Ministry of the Interior within minutes.

The GSG 9 airborne assaulters were sitting now on red canvas seats, secured with belts to minimize the effects of downdraft, resting their Adidas military boots on the metal decking with exposed rivets. They tested their radios.

They were travelling north-east in four black Bell UH-1 variant Iroquois military helicopters, known affectionately as the 'Huey'. The high-pitch whines of the twin turboshaft engines had been muted by light but effective cladding, the staccato *whop-whop-whop-whop* of the whirling two-bladed main and tail rotors subdued by specialist engineers. All but essential items had been stripped from both the cockpits and the cabins, to allow the helicopters to reach their maximum speed.

Dusk was morphing into night, the clouds high and wispy, the sky above Bonn awash with light pollution. The assaulters had a wide assortment of weaponry, including Swiss, Belgian and Austrian assault rifles, and bolt-action sniper rifles. They wore charcoal-grey combat fatigues and khaki body armour, dark balaclavas and camouflage Kevlar helmets and the German flag as a patch on their right breasts and left biceps, above their insignia. Their identities were top secret.

The four Hueys split formation four miles out from Potsdam. Two headed for the farm, the other pair for the villa. Video cameras had been mounted on the helicopters' fuselages and their individual helmets, relaying real-time images to flat screens at base.

The land around the target sites had been cordoned off by armed state police. They had searchlights and German Shepherd protection dogs at the ready. No one was getting in, or out, at ground level.

*

The pilot in the lead Huey heading for the villa, his head encased in a huge aviator helmet, informed the assaulters that the ETA to the insertion point was in five minutes. The amber LED lights were cut. The assaulters rechecked their equipment, pulling out the magazines from the wells, adjusting sights a fraction, rechecking their modes of communication. Some shuffled their feet. Others sat as still as pillars.

*

The Huey began to vibrate, due to an uplift of trapped air as it hovered about eight feet inside the wall and ten yards above the grass at the rear of the villa. An assaulter flipped off a lens cap and aligned the swivel cheek piece of his suppressed sniper rifle. He aimed out of the open cabin door, scanning the terrain, cast a muted green by the night vision.

The lead assaulter fast-roped adroitly in black leather mitts from the iron bar jutting out from the fuselage, landing in a cloud of swirling grit and loose topsoil. He was propelled forward by the rotor wash and took point about seven yards from the hovering Huey, adjusting his small headphones before speaking into his cheek microphone.

The villa was directly in front of him, a few outbuildings and vehicle ports left and right. He scanned around with his Heckler and Koch HK G36 assault carbine, fixed with a thermal imaging scope and a red dot laser. The night air was mild and there was no breeze.

The seven-man team moved up behind him, their bodies weighed down by equipment bags, extra magazines and sixty-pound ballistic plates. The second Huey hovered at the front of the villa, its on-board infrared checking for heat signatures as the assaulters slid down the rope. It would circle above, its remaining occupants ready to act as reinforcements, its cabin as an emergency air ambulance facility.

CHAPTER ONE HUNDRED
AND TWO

The farm, the same day.

Gabriel had done his best to control his emotions after the old man had said Sangmu was there. Was she still alive? He had to believe it, although part of him didn't. His breathing had become shallow and rapid, his hands had trembled. He'd felt as if his brain had swelled. He'd felt the rapid beats of his heart against his chest.

He knew now that to ensure no one else died, he had to convince the old man that he couldn't risk any more bloodletting, that he was on the cusp of spending the rest of his miserable life in prison.

Gabriel said, 'Some people thought you'd died in 1945. But there was an article in *Der Spiegel* about the murder of a young woman in her own apartment in West Berlin in 1954. Brigitte Bayer. The only witness was the daughter, Helma. She told the authorities who'd done it after a photograph of you was shown to her. It was Brigitte's photograph. One you'd given her, no doubt.

'But there was a lot going on back then to occupy them, as you know. Besides, you'd slipped back over to East Germany. They couldn't have reached you even if they'd had the time and inclination. No one could get to you. You had vanished. Except you hadn't, because all men have an Achilles heel, and yours is your daughter, especially after what you'd done to her mother. You rang her periodically. She said that she screamed at you at first. Then she would slam the phone down. Lately, she just listens to your pleas for forgiveness. Your vile snivelling. Her words, not mine.'

The old man's expression hadn't changed. There was no indication of what he was thinking.

'I tracked down your daughter to her home near Palm Springs. It wasn't difficult. She was adopted by a military attaché at the US Embassy. I went to see her. She told me what you had done, told me face-to-face. But you were a shadow. Even the FBI couldn't find you. She confirmed what the article had said was true, that her mother had signed an affidavit after the war that stated her child was a war child, the daughter of Joseph Kazapov, a Russian NKVD officer. A man with a scar that runs from his shoulder to his neck. I suspect it's still there. Your daughter is now named Barbara Murray. She gave me a translated copy of the affidavit.'

Now the old man's face had reddened, and he was nodding a fraction.

'Barbara Murray still had the photo. She gave that to me too. You're in an NKVD uniform. I think you killed Brigitte Bayer because she knew something. I don't know what. It doesn't matter. Your daughter asked me to find you and bring you to justice.'

'Because you told her what I have done?'

'What I suspected, yes. I did,' Gabriel said.

'I wish you hadn't done that.'

Gabriel forced himself to grin.

He said, 'Records were recently released to the US Holocaust Museum, detailing what happened in Kalmykia to Jews in World War Two. Other atrocities too. Four women went missing there, all with the name of Kazapova. Your mother and your sisters, given their ages and the fact that you yourself wrote the report. The Kalmyks killed them. You found that out too. But you didn't report that, because you knew someone could make a connection then. That's the reason for all this, isn't it? I know it like I know my own face. Everything is in the letters. Every detail.'

The old man seemed to teeter on his feet. He wiped a sheen of sweat from his brow with the back of his hand.

He said, 'The game is up?'

'It's up.'

'Except it's never up, is it, Mr Hall? It's like a perpetual game of cards and I have another card to play. The Queen of Hearts.'

Gabriel looked down at his chaffed wrists and up at Joseph Kazapov's aged and now half-grinning face.

'Carla Romero, the good mother, will remain silent to prevent her daughter from an unspeakable death at the hands of certain Russian acquaintances. I can guarantee that. She will resign from the FBI and live out her years with her daughter in the country of her ancestors, which is fitting. You will never speak of these things either. I will give you your niece and you will go home and Sangmu will recover, in time. With the right treatment, which both you and her parents can afford. You will do this because I don't have to tell you what the alternative will be.'

'You really have her?' Gabriel said, tears forming in his eyes, his breath quickening. 'She's alive?'

'Vezzani will fetch her for you and you will agree to the things I have said.'

'I will,' Gabriel said.

'No tears, Mr Hall. We all have what we want. Our paths part from here.'

'And the killing is over?'

'It's over,' the old man said.

He walked towards the door, opened it and called Vezzani in.

'Release Mr Hall, if you please. We have come to an understanding.'

Vezzani shook his head but walked over to Gabriel, removing a butterfly knife with mother-of-pearl handles from his back pocket. He flipped his wrist, releasing the blade. He sliced through the nearest flex-cuff before stepping over to release the other.

'Bring me the girl,' the old man said.

After Vezzani had left the room again, the old man said, 'When you return home, Mr Hall, tell my daughter that she will never hear from me again. I am returning home too, it appears.'

'Why did you continue killing for so long?'

'Why? You want to know why?' he said, as if Gabriel might not be able to bear it. 'You do not have Georgian blood in your veins. You would never understand.'

Gabriel said, 'I need to know.'

'You need to?' the old man said, mockingly.

'I do.'

'Very well.' The old man nodded. 'Your niece's great-grandfather was a man named Chon, which means wolf. He did things on the Kalmyk steppe that you are unable to imagine. He did things to my youngest sister, Oksana, that I will never speak of.'

Gabriel saw Kazapov's eyes harden, even now, even after all the years.

'I thought about tracking them all down and doing to them what I had seen done by the NKVD torturers. But then I decided that was too good for them. I didn't want them to die. I wanted them to *suffer*.'

He ran the back of his right hand across his mouth, removing something viscous from his lower lip.

'I made the men responsible suffer, day after endless day. They knew why their girls were being taken. Deep down they knew. Retribution for what they themselves had done. I killed their daughters, and the daughters of their daughters, and so forth. They are good breeders, like rats. I killed them on their eighteenth birthdays. Some that had given birth to girls already. Others that hadn't. They never knew who would be next. As for the one man that didn't have daughters, I disembowelled him while he was handcuffed to a gurney. Their very souls were filthy, Mr Hall. Their surviving relatives know this, now.'

Gabriel drew his open hand over his face, as if he was trying to cleanse his own soul in the process. After what he'd just heard, the thought of seeing Sangmu and what would've otherwise happened to her, were competing emotions that were threatening to overwhelm him.

CHAPTER ONE HUNDRED AND THREE

The villa.

Four assaulters at the rear of the villa ran to the flanks. Those that remained in their positions hunkered down. There was no sound from within the building, but their thermal imaging picked up three heat signatures in the room to the left on the ground floor.

The assaulter responsible for entry moved forward. He placed a ten-by-three-inch adhesive strip of breaching explosives over the lock of the heavy, oak-panelled door. He primed it with two blasting caps to guard against a single malfunction and reeled out the connecting wires. Now that they knew the occupants were aware of their arrival, due to the proximity of the helicopters, despite the soundproofing, they wanted to announce their entry with an explosion.

There was a four second delay. The door was flung outwards, sending a flurry of metal shards and splinters into the air with the smoke as the shockwave careered down the brick façade. The three assaulters closest to the front entrance activated their head torches and those affixed to their weapons. They moved at speed towards the smoky doorway.

Once inside, the man with the blast shield took point and the other two formed a short human chain behind him. Breaching charges were deemed too dangerous to be used here, especially given the possibility of the suspected recent kidnap victims being in situ. The assaulter carrying the Remington model 870 pump-action shotgun would use shells called Hatton rounds on the hinges of any locked doors. These dispersed into a harmless powder following impact. The assaulter behind him held a flash grenade and a Glock 17 semi-automatic pistol. They were joined now by another four assaulters, extending the human chain.

They shuffled towards the door of the room where the three heat signatures had been detected, once the pilot in the circling Huey had confirmed there had been no escapes from the sides and the rear, and that all the assaulters were in position if any were attempted.

The man with the Remington ran to the side of the door as another assaulter positioned himself on the other side, his hands grasping flash grenades. The door's hinges were blown off and the door thundered to the floor. The discharge of submachine guns from inside the room echoed, the multiple rounds shredding the doorframes and cutting chunks from the lintel. The side wall behind the assaulters was peppered with bullets, the plaster flying off in jagged chunks. The air filled with the acrid smell of the explosive powder. Unperturbed, the assaulters inserted earplugs.

Three seconds later, the stun grenades were lobbed into the room.

The two flashes were seen outside the door and looked as if lightening had struck the room, the loud blasts causing, the assaulters knew, both a temporary loss of hearing for those inside and a disruption to the fluid in their ears. They'd either been knocked off their feet or lost their balance. Depending on how close they'd been to the grenade as it had detonated, the blast may also have caused injury, the heat generated sufficient to ignite flammable material.

Five assaulters rushed through the doorway, their weapons raised. Amid the smoke, a man could be seen lying on the carpeted floor, blood oozing from his nose. A second man was stumbling backwards, his hands fumbling around to find a reference point, his eyes blinking. A third man had his head in his hands as he kneeled on the floor.

The flashes had activated all the photoreceptor cells in their eyes, making vision impossible for around five seconds until the eyes restored themselves to their unstimulated state. The assaulters knew too that an afterimage would be visible for a longer time, impairing the men's ability to aim with precision.

The man still standing was disabled easily, with a kick behind his knee followed by an assault rifle butt to his shoulder blade after he'd sunk down. He fell forwards now, like a plank of wood.

CHAPTER ONE HUNDRED AND FOUR

At the farm the door opened and Vezzani came in, pushing Sangmu in a wheelchair. Her head was bowed, her body limp. Her hair looked damp with sweat. She was dressed in a T-shirt and joggers. Drugged, Gabriel knew.

He wanted to run to her, to hold her and take her home. He felt something break deep within him and something simultaneously lift, this second round of competing emotions rendering him speechless and immobile.

Vezzani looked uncharacteristically nervous and his smartphone phone rang. He took the call.

'Security has been breached at the villa,' he said. 'The Russian woman has confirmed it. We must leave.'

The old man glanced at Gabriel accusingly. Gabriel shook his head. The old man raised his chin, pointing it at the ceiling, which was crisscrossed with lagged pipes and electrical cabling and wires, as if to communicate that he was above all that would transpire. He brought his hand down over his eyes, revealing a face that looked both unsurprised at the events that were unfolding, and unrepentant as to their cause.

Vezzani jabbed a finger in Gabriel's direction. 'He's to blame. You should let me kill him.'

The old man clasped his hands. 'Put him in the pit.'

'And the girl?' Vezzani said.

The old man shook his tortoise-like head.

'What do you mean the pit?' Gabriel said. 'What pit? We have a deal. I'm taking her home.'

Vezzani put his smartphone away and drew his pistol, pointing it at Gabriel's face.

'We *had* a deal,' the old man said.

'No,' Gabriel said. 'Sangmu, it's me. Can you hear me? It's me. I've come for you. We're going home. I swear it.'

Vezzani walked over the concrete floor to a mouldy throw rug. He bent down, aiming the pistol at Gabriel. He lifted a hinge and a trap door with his free hand.

'I keep them down there for a few weeks to subdue them,' the old man said.

The smell that rose from the disused well was loathsome.

'What about the letters?' Gabriel said, his voice betraying his desperation. 'What are you going to do to her? I'll fucking kill you.'

'Shall I gag him?' Vezzani said.

'No need. If he speaks again, shoot the girl. If he doesn't go down, shoot her.'

Vezzani used the pistol to motion towards the hole.

Gabriel got up, wobbling on his feet. He stepped slowly towards Vezzani, his mind a maelstrom of emotions.

'Hurry up, goddamn you,' Vezzani said.

Stumbling, Gabriel saw the edge of the hole, the stench clawing at his nostrils. There was a rusted metal ladder close to the lip. He knew he would have to climb down it. He knew that all was lost.

As he lifted his leg onto the first rung, he felt as though he was descending into a kind of hell. The walls were made of natural stone and damp. The darkness and the odour threatened to stifle his movement. But he went down forty feet or more and stood, looking up.

Vezzani's ugly head appeared and he pulled up the ladder.

*

The somewhat muffled sound of automatic gunfire, explosive charges and multiple footfalls had been heard in the villa's cellar. The woman who'd referred to herself as Fury had looked at first startled and perplexed, and then adamant that she wouldn't panic. She'd made a call, a fact that worried Carla, even though she still hoped she and Monize were in the middle of a recue situation. But she didn't have a clue how that may have come about.

She heard footsteps on a staircase and across the stone slabs outside now, followed by whispers behind the door to the cellar they were in.

'It's over,' Carla said.

Fury glanced at her, the eyes electric. She pulled a SIG SAUER 9mm pistol from under her blouse where it had been tucked into the back of her jeans. She held it skyward.

She said, 'Tell them not to use grenade or shoot. Tell them you FBI. That child here.'

Carla hesitated, although knew it was the right thing to do. What other option do I have? she thought.

She said, 'I'm FBI Special Agent Carla Romero. My four-year-old daughter is in here with me.'

She thought about telling them Fury was in the room, but the woman's eyes were on her now, the muzzle of the pistol aimed at Monize.

'Move away from the door. Do it now,' a voice said.

A few seconds later, what Carla took for two breaching rounds were discharged, and the door collapsed backwards out of the room. Monize screamed and Carla held her tight to her body.

When the dust and smoke had cleared, she couldn't see anyone outside the room. The short passageway and the stairwell were dark and silent.

After a prolonged pause the same voice said, 'Stand up. Put the child behind your back. Raise your hands and move forward. Slowly. When you get outside the door, kneel with your hands clasped behind your head. Do not hold onto the child. Do not make any sudden moves.'

Fury had her left side to the wall nearest the doorway. Carla looked at her and Fury shook her head and raised her free hand: Stop. Carla pushed Monize back onto the couch and covered her trembling little body with her own. Monize began to cry, her chest heaving. Carla smoothed her brow and held her head to her breasts.

Torch beams darted about. One lingered on Carla's torso. She saw a red dot there too, and others skittering about the walls and the floor, searching for potential targets. She knew the blast shields would be brought up and she guessed Fury also knew that. Then what? She didn't know.

'Don't shoot,' Carla said. 'Please don't shoot.'

'Listen to her,' Fury said. 'Now back off. Or I kill girl.'

Carla shuddered and struggled to keep her fear in check for Monize's sake. She heard the faint static of radio communication, then whispers just after it. The torches and lasers were killed a second later. Monize whimpered and Carla felt as if her heart was beating at twice its normal rate. Sweat beaded at her temples. She was, she knew, little more than a bystander to the events that were unfolding; they would spell life or death for her daughter, and the thought sickened her.

She turned her head to where Fury was still standing. 'Give it up,' she said.

'Quiet,' Fury said.

Now she heard the faintest *click* of metal, something like a fizzy drink can opening. She heard cylinders rolling across the flagstones.

Grenades, she thought.

She hugged Monize tight and turned her back to Fury. But the grenade detonations were two *phuts* close together. There was a hissing noise and the air began to fill with tear gas, a white smokescreen of the severe chemical irritant.

She covered Monize's eyes with her hands, knowing that the German police wouldn't allow a child to be subjected to its effects for long. In the worst cases, it could result in respiratory disease and blindness. But she'd been exposed to tear gas as part of her training and knew how to protect herself from it, for a while at least.

Her daughter began to retch and gripped Carla's forearms as her own eyes began to stream. She felt her face swell, her lungs burn. She heard the Russian woman's hacking cough. Amid the purposeful disorientation created by the gas's lachrymatory agents, she had one clear thought. The Russian woman nicknamed Fury would kill her daughter as casually as she herself would swat a bug. She'd threatened to kill her already. To mutilate her. She would come for her one day, because she could recognize her. The missing woman, Francesca Carpenter, had not been seen again, and neither had Charlene Rimes. She suspected the Russian had something to do with both of those disappearances.

She unfurled her daughter's little fingers from her arm, ignoring the distress and snivelling, her child's cries. She stood up, risking a negative reaction from the German police — a life-threatening reaction. She moved through the gas, holding her hand across her mouth and nose and resisting the urge to scratch at her skin and eyes. She moved towards the hacking cough. Slowly. Stealthily. Silently.

Vaguely, she saw the Russian bent double, fluid dribbling from her nose and mouth, the SIG 9mm hanging low in one of her veined hands. Carla rushed at Fury, snatching the pistol from her curled fingers before stepping back. The Russian twisted towards her, the beautiful features contorted in a visceral snarl.

The woman lunged forward, still bent at the waist, her movement both lumbering and erratic. Carla brought up her powerful leg, kneeing Fury in the face. She heard a satisfying *crack* and watched the Russian sink to her knees, her head slumping forward, blood falling from what was an obvious broken nose like glops of jelly.

She heard the scrambling of military boots over the felled door, the shouts of the police officers. Levelling the pistol to the crown of Fury's head, she squeezed the trigger.

Fury's head seemed to catapult backwards against the wall under the bullet's impact, her arms flailing briefly like a puppet's above her flat stomach. Carla flung the pistol behind her and raised her hands over her own head.

She watched as the woman slid sideways, her head oozing blood, her tongue hanging out of her twitching mouth. Like some great bull dying under the Spanish sun.

CHAPTER ONE HUNDRED AND FIVE

The farm.

Gabriel heard the *swish-swish* of fluid as it was slopped about in the room above him.

A few seconds later, he saw an uncapped jerrycan appear above the lip of the hole. Gas was tipped down, the smell, even when mixed with the reek, unmistakable, the liquid's consistency confirming it. The flammable liquid trickled down one side of the wall and with it the last semblance of hope drained from him.

They're going to burn us alive, he thought.

He trembled.

He heard the jerrycan clattering to the concrete floor and the footsteps of the old man and Vezzani exiting the room. The first flames roared then.

Within seconds, they flew over the lip and ignited a portion of the wall.

He braced himself for the ascent, forcing the horrendous consequences of failure to the back of his mind. But he had no nylon climbing rope to stretch to absorb the shock of a fall, no belayer to help arrest it, no bolts in the rock face to secure it to, even if he had. He couldn't top rope around a tree or a rock. There was no protection in the form of wedges or hexes. He had no fingerless gloves, harness, karabiners, chalk for the hands or rubber shoes, which meant less stickiness and more difficulty in directing his centre of gravity away from the stone as he attempted to put the strain on his feet.

He could not do what the well would naturally demand for an ascent, either: stemming. Then he would've pushed his right foot into the surface in front of him and his left into the surface behind him, as if he was climbing the inside of a chimney, his rubber shoes generating an upwards frictional force, opposing gravity and propelling him. His bare feet and the flames negated that option.

He'd traversed overhangs at a thousand feet, using thin fissures and outcrops, the wind howling about him, the sleet whipping at his face. He was used to climbing in the dark to take advantage of the cooler temperature, but with a headlight. The fire was something else.

He reckoned it was a 5.12 level climb at least, which only the top ten per cent of climbers could achieve. The current conditions made it a 5.13. He hadn't climbed at that level before, and his usual nimble body, with the strength and flexibility of woven bark, was depleted. But there was no other option left open to him.

He reached up to the nearest precarious fingerholds, pushed up with his bare feet, keeping his weight evenly balanced over them to remain stable. He pushed off with his feet again, using his arms and hands for extra balance and positioning only.

As the stone became smoother, it became harder to stay in this balanced position. Still he climbed, his wits and agility taken to their limits. The holds were little bigger than a matchstick, allowing access only to the tips of his fingers, where he held all his bodyweight, his skin beginning to shred. He searched out each lump, nub, rough edge, any irregularity.

He balanced on his feet now on the narrowest of jutting-out stone and reached up and held himself firm with his fingertips. He pushed up with his feet, grabbing the wall above him, finding a tiny gulley. The fire licked about him from the other side of the wall and was a foot-high furnace beneath him. Still he climbed.

The last of the fog that was the drug lifted, even as the smoke rose about him. His fingers bled and sweat filled his eyes, stinging them as chillies might. His forearms and calves ached, craving release. But the memory was there, the skills, the will.

He found a slippery cleft, a dryer fissure. He choked on the smoke as it entered his mouth and lungs. Still he climbed, finding the smallest nodule, the tiniest indent in the darkness.

Now his hands were slick with sweat, and he had almost no friction between his feet and the stone. The wall was not polished marble, but the cracks, lumps and rough edges were becoming increasingly hard to find. He stood on a tiny ledge, but without his tight-fitting, high-friction rubber shoes, he felt precarious, his heart rate going off the scale, his self-belief ebbing fast.

He lost his foothold and hung above the flames by three bleeding fingertips, the smoke all but asphyxiating him. His body was drenched in sweat from his exertions and he ached in every muscle, in each joint.

His hand began to shake. He knew that he was going to lose the perilously little hold in a matter of seconds. He felt his feet begin to blister and burn, the agony so great that he cried out. It threatened to make him faint. If he didn't do something now, he knew they would be both lost to the flames.

He shifted his hips away from the wall, executing the so-called rose move, his raised legs and body turning from left to right, the energy used all but his last, and he propelled himself to that portion of the wall further over.

Grabbing onto a larger nub a foot higher there, he winced, the surface rendered red-hot already by the flames. There was a jutting out stone and he wedged his knee and front thigh under it while causing sufficient tension with his foot, which was pressing against a nodule below. He thrust himself up, his eyes scrunched with pain, his right hand reaching over the lip.

He hung there for a few seconds, coughing, his neck beginning to burn, the skin to bubble.

He hauled himself up with enormous effort, his elbows exploding in agony as the flames ignited his shirt sleeves. He crouched and ripped the shirt from his body and clapped out the flames. He wrapped the shirt around his mouth and nose and launched himself forward into the darkness and the smoke and the flames, heading for the light outside the door, praying that they hadn't moved Sangmu further into the room.

His left knee impacted with one of the wheels of the chair, and he grabbed the armrests and heaved the chair back, his arms extended, using all the power in his legs to drive her from this room of death.

In the artificial light, Gabriel could just see that his feet and legs were badly burned, burned to the point that skin was sliding off them. He fought to stay conscious, hacking like a man from another time and place with consumption, half blinded by the smoke.

Sangmu had burns, he could tell, but the drug had saved her from the pain of it and the flames hadn't reached her upper body. He gulped for air, his head spinning, the pain coming in excruciating waves, and then he collapsed.

*

The old man and Vezzani had walked out into the night air, hearing the helicopters above, seeing the dark shapes of the assaulters moving towards them. Torch beams and red dot lasers had scanned their bodies and Vezzani had been shouted at to drop his weapon.

The old man had held up his hands, but Vezzani had raised his pistol, unable to face prison again, the old man had guessed, or just because he was still a soldier at heart and had decided his time had come and he wanted to go out in a blaze.

The first bullet hit Vezzani in the shoulder, spinning him to his left. The second tore off his jaw as he'd tumbled sideways. The third penetrated his right eye after he'd hit the stone pathway.

The old man had stood still throughout, without a smidgen of fear or regret. His mind had retreated to the time when countless men and women and children had died in precisely the manner Vezzani had.

That time had never ended for him.

CHAPTER ONE HUNDRED AND SIX

Berlin.

Gabriel touched Sangmu's little hand with his bandaged fingers. The lightest of touches, a mere brush. The back of her head was deep in a duck down pillow, her body lying on top of fresh bedsheets. Her legs were held at ninety degrees by a pulley, her arms impregnated by intravenous and saline drips, by tubes attached to monitors and machines that he could not name. The brightness of fluorescent light reflected off walls of white gloss paint. He bent forward, wincing at the pain that rippled through his body. He kissed her on the forehead and her eyelids fluttered.

They were recuperating at the Unfallkrankenhaus Berlin, the burns and plastic surgery centre that was state-of-the-art and catered for both children and adults. For him there was no memory of being stretchered from the farm, or of his first week here, but he'd insisted on seeing Sangmu every day since, and his insistence had been respected.

He was thinking now of what had happened after he'd regained consciousness. He had given a statement to the police, detailing the evidence against Joseph Kazapov, including the man's confession. But

Kazapov could not be identified as the man in the monk's robe and the death mask in the DVD found in Hockey's flat, or any found subsequently at the ghost house. There'd been no convincing evidence against him in respect of the murders of Johnny Hockey, Charlene Rimes and Billy Joe Anderson. Likewise, Finkel. The only DNA that had been found from any of the victims had been on the cadavers of Anna Belova, known as Fury, and two of her three Russians. Kazapov claimed that Vezzani had killed Robert Dubois and no one had been able to testify to the contrary.

There had been evidence against him in respect of the murder of Brigitte Bayer though, and no one had been able to change that. Barbara Murray had agreed to give evidence via a video link; she couldn't handle being in the same room as her biological father. He was toxic, she said.

But Joseph Kazapov had been judged unfit to stand trial. Competency was different to the insanity defence, Gabriel knew this only too well. The latter was decided by the mental state of the accused at the time the crimes were committed, the former at the time of the trial.

Gabriel had just managed to attend the first hour of the hearing, but Kazapov had benefited from the expert evidence of three physiatrists, all of whom agreed that he was incapable of understanding the nature and consequences of the criminal proceedings that would have otherwise begun, and that he'd be unable to assist in his own defence. This had also negated any extradition proceedings to the US, and Kazapov had been sent to a secure mental health facility, where he would be evaluated periodically. Gabriel had decried it as an elaborate hoax, but to no avail.

He'd consoled himself with the thought that he had achieved what he'd so recklessly and haphazardly set out to do: find Sangmu and stop the old man from killing. He'd been responsible for putting him behind bars of sorts, too.

Carla had escaped a separate federal trial, due to lack of evidence, in the sense that no one had seen her execute Fury, and the Germans had judged it to be self-defence. She'd told Gabriel this in the days after the chaos.

She was receiving counselling now, he'd heard. He forgave her for her betrayal; he knew Monize had been threatened and that there'd been no other choice. In a telephone conversation she told him she'd left the FBI and had thought about returning with Monize to São Paulo. But her daughter needed her father and she'd stayed in DC. As for the deaths of Finkel and Robert Dubois, it had been generally agreed that she'd given Kazapov their names under extreme duress and while her mind had been in a temporary state of disorientation.

Gabriel's sister, Sangmu's adoptive mother, was staying at a nearby hotel with her husband until Sangmu was well enough to fly back to the States. They didn't speak much. They never had.

He returned to his small room now and settled himself on his steel bed, shooing away a bright nurse who berated him for overdoing it. He took a cocktail of drugs daily and they made him woozy. There were skin grafts on thirty per cent of his body.

He poured himself a plastic cup of filtered water, from a jug on a swing-around table top that stood beside the bed. It had taken him almost ten seconds to complete this simple feat. Every night, he slept the sleep of a man who was adrift on a black ocean beneath a starless sky. Fretful and disorientated.

*

A week before Gabriel was due to be discharged, he raised the top section of the bed remotely and turned on the satellite TV: CNN International. He watched grim images of terrorist attacks, of famine and political upheaval.

Then there was a breaking news story. The shooting of a patient. The patient had been murdered in the grounds of a secure hospital, in a valley in north Rhine-Westphalia near Bonn. The victim was an old man whose name was Joseph Kazapov.

Gabriel didn't react. He didn't know *how* to react. He was too tired to react. He just watched, unblinking, as the story unfolded. An American was in police custody. A man's face appeared, the alleged perpetrator who'd given himself up to the police afterwards.

Gabriel blinked now, wondering if the drugs were distorting reality as in a dream, playing with his memories such that his brain was making a bizarre film out of them. He rubbed his face with his bandaged palms and pinched the skin on his right cheek, wincing at the pain it produced. But he knew that the moving images were relaying facts.

The man in custody was the old Jew, Bronislaw Stolarski.

CHAPTER ONE HUNDRED AND SEVEN

Bonn.

Bronislaw Stolarski was sitting, unfettered and unattended by prison guards, in a white cinder-block interview room. It was brightly lit and smelled of the fresh fruit juice that sat in the plastic bottle on the plastic table, and the scented tissues — placed there to mop his tears, he imagined. He guessed that his age and infirmity had prompted his sympathetic treatment.

He'd read of the liberalism of the Federal Republic of Germany. The people once obsessed with ethnic cleansing and then with genocide had become the ones that had welcomed the dispossessed, the disenfranchised, the war fleers and orphans. Those seeking a Western dream, just as he had. And, just as with those that had travelled west with him in his time, there'd be the criminals, the idle, the thieves and the corrupt. The world was not black and white, but rather various shades of grey, he knew. Where did good end and evil begin in such a world? No one knew that.

He wasn't taken in. He didn't trust the German authorities, even now. Their recent actions were, he believed, born of a lingering guilt that time would not assuage. Besides, they couldn't save everyone in need, even if their intentions were honest. They still chose who lived and died, he thought. He wanted nothing from them, least of all sympathy.

He picked up the plastic bottle and tipped its contents onto the floor. He worried then that they would think he'd urinated. But what difference did it make, given his predicament?

He was dressed in a disposable hazmat suit, his shoes fashioned from single pieces of canvas and edgeless. He glanced up at the fluorescent strip lighting, itself encaged in taut wire. There was not a single item in the room that was both moveable and with which he could self-harm. Even the plastic bottle was too thick.

The shmucks, he thought.

He thought now of how it had been for Joseph Kazapov in the secure hospital. Perhaps he should have left him to rot in his hell. There, the anti-psychotic drugs would've dulled the sharp brain, his only companions the poor souls that slow-danced to the monotonous background noise of absurd TV programmes.

But no, he'd deserved to die by his own hand and in the manner he'd executed. A high-calibre bullet in the upper body. A liver shot. A slow death shot. The male nurses had been kept at bay long enough for him to see his enemy bleed out, the blood thick and black and glorious to his eyes.

Stolarski had found his faith again in an American city, twenty years ago or more. It hadn't been the result of a miracle he'd witnessed. He'd simply sought guidance and had been given it, he'd believed. He'd read what his finger had randomly fallen upon: *A false witness should suffer the same punishment which he sought to have inflicted upon the person he accused. Nor could any law be more just.* Deuteronomy. The speeches of Moses on the plains of the Moab opposite Jericho. It had been fitting, he'd believed.

He'd waited these two decades for the God of Moses to bring this to fruition, for this had been guided by the hand of God, or he was not a man and the words worth less than a granule of rock salt.

The door opened and in walked a man of learning, he knew. A brave man, though perhaps not in the conventional sense as he saw it. But brave, no doubt about it. His name was Gabriel Hall, the secular lawyer. God used all manner of men, he believed. He knew Gabriel to be a modern man, one who had not killed, nor had he seen others killed with his eyes. A man whose mind was not contaminated by images of total war. A civilian.

His own mind was lost in the distant past still. He saw nothing but the havoc and desolation of war, even in his dreams and when his mind wandered in his everyday life in a futile attempt to avoid it. He'd tried to subdue it once, with learning of his own, with a profession of his own. With a kindly woman from Nebraska with a teenage daughter, too. It hadn't worked out. Nothing had worked out for him. But he'd found a semblance of peace with Ned, partly because the black veteran was a man more disturbed by war than himself. He sat on the porch on guard duty, waiting for the Viet Cong to come out of the forest, with their conical bamboo-leaf sunhats and blazing AK-47 assault rifles. The poor bastard.

Gabriel Hall sat down, his expression resigned, and said, 'I'm listening.'

He wore a beautiful suit of fine cloth, a white, open-necked shirt that showed a mottling to the skin about the upper regions of his chest, and Stolarski knew the source. The hands were bandaged still. He'd walked with an awkwardness that had spoken of discomfort.

He knew Gabriel Hall did not realize the real source of his own pain — pain that he'd carried within him for years after the war, which ran much deeper than the cancer, even. How could he? He'd lied to him.

Besides, who knew the pain that transcended the cells and was the pain of the lost soul? The lawyer had been spared that in the end, thank God. But not even his rekindled faith had eased the pain. Only the act of killing Joseph Kazapov had come close to doing that.

'Thank you for coming, Mr Hall. It's appreciated. I am guilty as charged, you should know that from the off. But I will not lie to you again.'

'What lies?'

'I will tell you. I promise you that. I will ask one more thing of you, if I may? I know you to be a serious man, and this was why I asked you to come here. Serious men are hard to find.'

He stopped speaking and held his neck, winced and went to pick up the bottle to drink… but realized he'd poured the juice away. He knew it wouldn't have quenched the sense of parched wood in his throat, in any event. It was deep-rooted and a symptom of his grave illness. The cancer was real enough.

'No brother of mine was ever in a uranium mine. But I was. No brother of mine had cancer. But I do. The mine caused it. Icchak Stolarski did not have a wife and children, but I did. A boy and girl. I knew Icchak in the mine. As he lay dying, I asked him if I could assume his identity. To live, I suppose. He consented, of course. After I got out of Europe I decided to become Bronislaw Stolarski and use Icchak as a backstory. He wouldn't have minded.'

Gabriel's eyes didn't move. He didn't move at all.

'By the beginning of 1953 there were almost two and a half million inmates of Soviet prison camps, a fifth of whom were political prisoners. There were special camps for children, for the disabled and mothers with babies. There were special camps for the wives of traitors of the Motherland. There were special camps for traitors of Motherland family members. But my family didn't even arrive at a special camp. SMERSH killed my family — because of what Joseph Kazapov had said. I killed Joseph Kazapov.'

He wanted to weep even now, but he did not. Could not.

'They broke my children's little bodies. They whipped my wife with barbed wire. They tossed their corpses down a well, like the Romanovs. They told me this in the mine. As if I wasn't suffering enough, I suppose. They didn't want us to die, you see. Not quickly, at least. There was not sufficient punishment in that. Joseph Kazapov orchestrated the death of my family because of the things I had seen. The things I told you about. He could trust his fellow NKVD, but I was a risk. I could have made connections. But you found him for me. You and God found him for me. You made the connections. I am Russian by birth, not Polish. A Christian. Not a Jew. I was a sergeant in the Red Army. The sergeant that decided to go into the bunker, even though everything was telling me not to. It started all this. One decision, that led to my family dying. Can you see that? My name is Pavel Romasko.'

Gabriel shook his head. He said, 'I'm sorry for your loss. For you suffering.'

'I feel a little better now.'

Gabriel rubbed his brow with the fingers of his right hand. Pavel could see the stress there, but he didn't comment upon it.

'Why did you lie about your identity?'

Pavel said, 'To get to the US, of course. A Polish Jew had a much better chance than a Red Army solider from a village near Rostov. I heard about perebezhahiki. It means defectors. But what did I have to offer? What secrets did I know? Nothing worth more than a packet of cigarettes. I was Bronislaw Stolarski to the outside world. But I was always Pavel Romasko inside. Soon, I can be Pavel Romasko on the outside too.'

Gabriel sighed. He said, 'You'll spend the rest of your life in prison.'

Pavel thought for a moment, squinting.

'There was a white heat inside me,' he said. 'There has always been a white heat inside me since then. Now it has eased. I never thought it would. I never thought anyone would find him. He said I was a spy, you see. Death to spies meant death to their families too. I only survived because Stalin died before I did. Lucky, I suppose. I want you to represent me, Mr Hall.'

Gabriel nodded, knowingly rather than in agreement, Pavel could see. But Pavel wasn't averse to evoking sympathy.

He said, 'I'm dying, Mr Hall. I'll be dead in three months or less, they say.'

'I have no jurisdiction here.'

'No, no, no. No legal niceties. I will plead guilty and that is it. You will be my advocate. I want you to tell my story. All of it. It's important for the story to be told, isn't it, Mr Hall? It is, despite the horror. The only thing we can do to prevent it happening again is to speak the truth.'

'But you didn't kill Kazapov. I don't doubt you are familiar with firearms and know how to use a bolt-action sniper rifle like the one you handed in. But it wasn't you.'

Pavel was silent.

'I figure it was Ned. You told me he was a sniper. Remember?'

'Ned brought me to Germany, although we travelled separately through the airports. He had no notion of my plan. I told him I wanted to pay my respects to my men that had perished here before I died, is all.'

Gabriel shook his head and bunched his mouth. He said, 'I don't buy it.'

'Even if you are correct, Mr Hall, you should know that my finger pulled the trigger. It wasn't Ned's. No, sir.'

'But he lined up the shot. He kept the male nurses at bay. Didn't he?'

'We came to this country separately as far as the German authorities are concerned. I'd like to keep it that way. I will stand before God and He knows the truth of it.'

Gabriel said, 'How did he get a sniper rifle?'

'Anyone can buy anything anywhere for the right price, Mr Hall. You know that to be true.'

'Where is Ned?' Gabriel said.

'We said our goodbyes before I gave myself up.'

Gabriel stood to leave. He walked halfway to the door. He turned back but didn't speak. Pavel guessed he wanted to speak, so he spoke for him and forced a half smile.

'The death of my wife and children kept me alive, Mr Hall. I found my Orthodox faith, too. It left me in the war. God left the world then, whatever the priests say. I know that to be true. He came back again. After you represent me, I have decided to die. Choosing when you can die is something that millions didn't have back then. Civilization is a veneer, Mr Hall. Is it not? The brutal and primitive nature of man lies waiting beneath. You will represent me, won't you?'

CHAPTER ONE HUNDRED AND EIGHT

New York State.

Gabriel and Sangmu had hiked for five miles in the Adirondack Mountains. They'd sweated and ached and pushed their rucksacks up their backs to relieve the strain on their shoulders and lower backs.

He'd rented a log cabin with good facilities to placate the worriers. His sister and brother-in-law, principally.

It was a cloudless afternoon. The light here was without equal, the air so clean it possessed a primal quality.

Pavel Romasko had been a remarkable man, he thought. His duplicity had staggered him. Gabriel had left the prison interview room that day, silent and without any clear idea of when the law should give way to the purely moral, or whether it should do so at all. That idea had bothered him at night.

But he'd told the man's story for him in the courtroom — after he'd pleaded guilty. Pavel had said that Gabriel spoke the words with the authority and conviction of a religious litany, and that he'd repeated each sentence in his head, as was befitting. He'd thanked Gabriel and had shaken his hand before he was led away. Gabriel hadn't mentioned what he knew about Ned.

A week later, Pavel had died. Just as he'd foretold. Gabriel had suspected suicide, although that was, in retrospect, too harsh a word for what had been the last defiant act of a dying man.

Gabriel left his position at Yale and sold his law practice. He couldn't have continued after what had happened, the things he'd done. He didn't know what he would do in the future, and today he didn't care. He didn't care about anything but the here and now.

'There,' he said, pointing.

A bald eagle had left its huge nest, built from twigs and sticks, high up in a tree bordering a lake. The brown wingspan was seven feet or more. It beat its wings before soaring on the thermal currents acrobatically. A figure of eight. A double circle. Its call was staccato, a little shrill, resembling a gull's.

It swooped low now over balsam fir and red spruce, down the slope of the valley to the lake, the sunlight playing there like so many silver fish. But the eagle was not fooled, he knew.

'His eyes are keen, and he will find himself a lunch,' Gabriel said, as if to himself.

He watched Sangmu, fascinated and almost overwhelmed by the sight of the raptor, he could tell, its tufted white head and hooked yellow beak, its undeniable grace and power in flight.

The eagle's great sand-coloured talons came down like an aircraft's landing gear, and it snagged a fish from just below the surface of the glistening water, causing a white splash. It beat its wings again and rose with its catch.

Sangmu was smiling. The whites of her eyes were moonstones, the irises black pearls.

There was hope and vitality there.

And Gabriel smiled too.